Kill Well

The Steep Climes Quartet: Book One

I0690202

The Steep Climes Quartet, Book One: *Kill Well*
The Steep Climes Quartet, Book Two: *Dear Josephine*
The Steep Climes Quartet, Book Three: *Over Brooklyn Hills*
The Steep Climes Quartet, Book Four: *Farm to Me*

Kill Well
[The Steep Climes Quartet, Book One]
© David R. Guenette, 2023
(Revised December 2024)

ISBN 979-8-9885055-0-1
LCC 2023911828

CMTI Publishing
21 Corashire Road
New Marlborough, MA 01230
www.cmtipublishing.com

What reviewers and readers are saying about *Kill Well*, The Steep Climes Quartet: Book One

Murder is another dire effect of climate change in Guenette's labyrinthine thriller. This first installment of the author's Steep Climes series envisions a near future in which catastrophic heat, droughts, and floods are fraying society, hobbling the economy, and nurturing deadly conspiracies.... Even global-warming deniers will enjoy the resulting page-turner. Despite overdone soapboxing, vivid characters and hardboiled writing make this an entertaining suspenser.
  —**Kirkus Reviews**

Set in a near future where the DSM 7 includes a diagnosis of "climate anxiety," Kill Well, *the first entry in The Steep Climes Quartet, Guenette's pointedly realistic thriller series, opens with a bang... A pointedly realistic thriller of murder, the fossil fuel industry, and climate activism.*
  —**BookLife Reviews**

Introspective and solemn, Kill Well *by David Guenette is a story of murder and danger, written by an author with a beautiful grasp of the English language, and an obviously deep, powerful, and intense passion for the harsh and shocking realities of climate change. There is everything to be said about an author who can turn that much knowledge into a thriller that often catches the reader off guard with its stunning realism.*
  —**Independent Book Review**

Kill Well *is a smart, taut thriller that grabs you on the first page and keeps you guessing all the way to the suspenseful conclusion. David Guenette knows a lot about hacking and corporate skullduggery, and he knows a lot about people too.*
  —**Tom Perrotta** is author of *Election* and *Little Children*, both of which were made into critically acclaimed, Academy Award-nominated films, and for *Little Children* he received an Academy Award nomination for Best Adapted Screenplay. His novels *The Leftovers* and *Mrs. Fletcher* have been adapted into TV series on HBO. His most recent novel is *Tracy Flick Can't Win.*

David Guenette manages to show that the climate crisis is already affecting our energy and food bills and intensifying the drama of local politics. Kill Well *is a fun ride but uncomfortable, too, as we get another way to think about where we're heading all too quickly.*
  —**Karen Christensen**, CEO and Publisher, Berkshire Publishing Company and author of *Eco Living*, *The Green Home*, and *Home Ecology* (book and Substack newsletter)

No drowned worlds or climate-ravaged zombies, but a solid story with compelling characters that leaves you thinking that you haven't been thinking nearly enough about climate change. I can't wait until the next book in this series hits.

—**Larry D. Gussin**, Gussin Climate Action Fund at The Sierra Club Foundation

Climate change is not something that is happening independent of people's lives, but rather is already part of each of our lives. Kill Well helps you see that, and, like a magic trick, gives a poignant, entertaining, and funny read along the way.

—**Winslow Eliot**, author of ten novels, including *Bright Face of Danger*, *Heaven Falls*, *The Happiness Cure*, and *A Perfect Gem*

Kill Well *is more than just a suspenseful murder thriller. It combines the reality of climate change and climate activism, the potential devious tactics that the fossil fuel industry has at its disposal, and how difficult it is to exist without surveillance tracking you.*

—**Amazon Review**

This is a terrific book and the first of its kind that I've read. It deftly combines a page-turning thriller with the dangers of climate change and the dark forces behind it, all the while giving us rich characters that you either care about greatly or strongly loathe…. One of the things I love is that there's plenty of climate change consequences, but experienced the way most of us experience these, which is in the background, lurking, and so easily put out of mind. This tension between real danger and our lack of recognition of it reflects the plot's progress that likewise moves unthinkingly through self-centered interactions, but all with the punch you want in an entertaining read.

—**Amazon Review**

The detective story is gripping and unfolds in the context of dark corporate forces working to maintain the corporate status quo. Guenette gets us inside the heads of his characters, even into the minds of evildoers. The balance between the ordinary Main Street concerns and the bigger picture takes surprising twists and turns.

—**Amazon Review**

It is amazing how David Guenette is able to blend emotions, anxieties of ordinary people who besides facing the challenges of everyday life, live at a time when drastic changes the environment will be very soon real and frightening. Yet, the language of the novel is so down to earth and friendly that makes the reading of this breathtakingly seductive.

—**Amazon Review**

Table of Contents

Hope is a waking dream.
Aristotle

Kill Well

The Steep Climes Quartet: Book One

David R. Guenette

CMTI Publishing, New Marlborough, MA

Chapter 1: Of Cops and Rocks

Cynthia Wainwright is loving the view.

She's looking out at a landscape foreign to her since she's not been in the Mojave before, although now that she thinks on this for a moment, she knows she's seen desert, but about a decade back, on one of those interminable driving vacations her mom and stepdad had shanghaied her and the

twins into, destination Grand Canyon.

This is a different landscape she's admiring, standing outside her rental car, parked right at Mile Marker 27, just as Joe, her boss, asked her to do in the text, a text that strikes her as odd, and odder still are the two others he sent this morning, which she just now reads, but they're weird

Maybe a joke?

She's not going to worry about it. She's just too excited. She loves her job, her first fully-grown-up job, and she can't think of a better place to help solve the climate crisis, and today's upcoming meeting is the biggest such deal, at least that she has something to do with.

Joe has gone on ahead, not wanting to give anyone any excuse, even, as he had told her before getting into his car and heading out an hour ago, if it means he'll end up drinking far too many cups of coffee with the Chairmen of the investment group. *This is big*, he's kept on saying.

She's excited.

She was disappointed she wasn't riding with him. She likes it when they have time alone.

But even if she hadn't needed to make the changes they and the team at Carbon's End discussed this morning, she still wouldn't have taken her own rental, because Joe was heading back to the airport in Bastow and she was heading for a few days of hiking about Joshua Tree. She did also run late, with all the final touches and changes and it wasn't a big business center, nor the printer all the fast. Faster enough, though, and she's on her way, the amended sheafs of contracts in hand, until she'd received the text.

It's strange to her that he would stop to text on his way to their meeting this morning.

Meet me at mile marker 27.

Had his car broken down? she'd wondered. But now, as she glances again at the two messages that arrived before this text, she wonders, just curious, if Joe might be role-playing.

Maybe a quick fuck? it occurs to her, but his excitement this morning was for the meeting and their shared expectation this would be a big win for them. And no time for sex either, anyway. He should be mostly there.

She looks at her phone, confirming her estimation.

And that isn't like him, anyway, she thinks. He's forty years of age, almost a decade-and-a-half her senior, and he's married with another kid on the way, and the relationship between them is a simple thing, just sexual, really, just fun and comforting company. Although the thought crosses her mind there's something else at play in her relationship, but she stops herself thinking anything about her old history with older men.

She simply wants to appreciate the vista before her.

She simply wants to let herself acknowledge that she's feeling good, excited, even proud of herself.

And besides, she enjoys his company, their work at Carbon's End putting them together all the time, including on trips like the one they're on now, pushing fossil fuel divestiture, but she's more interested in reveling in the view of the large rock formations scattered across the open land, the formations and scrub lit by the low rising sun that casts long shadows this early in the morning.

She can't entirely dismiss thinking about the meeting she's heading to, and how the meeting with the investor group this morning was scheduled for an early hour. The resort where she and Joe are staying is an hour away, and she hadn't pushed back against the early meeting time, seeing in this an opportunity for her and Joe to fly out the day before and spend some time together. That had been her thinking, and Joe, of course, had very much liked the thought.

She smiles, thinking of Joe, his grin, looking at her undress.

She takes pleasure in his wanting her, in his chatter about how he loves her look, her shoulder-length hair, her green-gray eyes, her modest breasts, her hips, her toes, her height, and the way their two bodies fit together.

For an older man, he's boyish in some ways, even a bit goofy, really.

But the relationship is simple, and Cyn likes simple. She knows she has a hunger, a drive, for being wanted, but she's never cared for the stress of a relationship and has never been drawn to the working of being one within a couple, to build a life together.

She just wants to be wanted, needs to have this type of attention, needs that deep comfort she can feel even if, maybe, there's something off, but she is practiced at ignoring that.

But if he's trying to role play, that seems like a bad sign to her, a troubling complication.

She's been driving her own rental to the meeting, so the text she got from Joe not more than ten minutes earlier is puzzling.

Her text notification had read *Meet me at mile marker 27*, and then her eyes went back to the road in time to catch the glimpse of Mile Marker 24 passing behind her.

Well, here she is, wondering about Joe not being here and about the stranger texts she's just read scrolling up from Joe's last text, texts she hadn't seen. She hadn't heard any notification alerts for these as she'd been driving.

She shrugs, unsettled a bit by these texts. Her best guess is these texts are some sort of joke, but still, these texts don't seem at all like Joe.

But mostly she's enjoying the early morning light and how the long rock formations across this flat landscape seem to her as schools of half-submerged serpents, the backs frozen mid- swim through the scrubland and sand. She's also thinking about how much she's looking forward to her time alone, taking a few days after business is concluded.

But then her peripheral vision catches ghost-pale strobing colors up toward the curve of the road a hundred feet or so, off the cut rock face on the opposite side of the road. The blinks of light are almost lost amid the low, bright morning sun, and it takes her a moment to resolve the washed-out reflecting light is a police or ambulance. Her heart spikes with concern, and she begins to fast-walk a short cut to where the road ahead curves and disappears behind the cut-through long rock formation. She fears there's been an accident and hurries from where she parked, moving toward the source of light.

She walks and then runs over the sand and pebbles and the colonizing scrub weeds. Her dress shoes serve poorly for moving over the sand and stone, but her building anxiety that Joe has been in an accident is overwhelming other thoughts, and this blooms as an aching certainty.

She rounds the rock face cut and sees two vehicles sixty or eighty feet farther up the road with Joe's rental closest to her, and she sees a cop or deputy who's leaning into Joe's car, she sees a shadowed flash and hears the sound of a gun firing, and the flash is blossoming red on the rear windshield.

Panic crashes and she's trying to place herself, trying to roll the tang of danger flooding her from past the rock face she's ducked behind. In her eyes' after-image she still sees the big white SUV with a harsh flashing light bar pulled in front of Joe's rental, each vehicle half off the shoulder of the county road, she sees the man jumping back, wiping at the blood splatter on his face and on the blouse of his uniform, and she at this moment knows Joe is dead.

Her mind is a roaring blank but for a single loudest voice within shouting, *Joe!*

That's the loudest voice, but another part of Cyn's mind

is now trying to understand there will now be no meeting, even as another part is trying to grasp that something has happened, but the world is slanting off axis, and she is falling into a pressing darkness of overwhelming dread and animal panic.

She tells herself she's gone unseen, that the man — *the policeman!* — hasn't seen her, she's pulled herself back unnoticed.

Joe is dead, a voice keeps telling her.

His blood scattered on the rear windscreen.

Joe is dead.

She hasn't screamed.

Cyn pushes her back against the solidity of the rock, and then she slumps down. She can hear the man in uniform cursing, the sound of the shot still echoing off the cut rock formation on the other side of the road, drifting into the empty flat desert.

Just moments ago, she'd relished the landscape as she waited for Joe at Mile Marker 27.

Joe would like that, she thinks. But Joe is dead up ahead around the rock face cut. With a hiccup of surprise, she won't get to tell him her sense of delight in the landscape.

And then she is again seeing the man lean in and with the echoing sound of a gun firing, and then she locks back to her eight-year-old self on that day the police came to the house.

Eight-year-old Cynthia sees her father slumped against the wall in the hall by the front door, her father looking at her, that strange half smile above the blooming blood starting to sag his t-shirt. Out here in this desert she is slumped against this wall, and eight-year-old Cynthia is seeing again that her dying father is embarrassed. And she is slumped against rock and her mind again rolls, and she's aware Joe is dead, that she's twenty-six years old.

She didn't scream then either, back in her childhood home.

Her mind went off and on then too.

Joe is dead.

She knows all this, and some part of her knows just a moment has passed, and the gun fired on the other side of the massive cut face of rock still echoes here and in the ghost of her past.

Chapter 2: He Never Meta-Joke He Didn't Like

Davin has long joked about the invitation to others—friends, family, even sometimes, nearly complete strangers, depending on his mood or stage of mania—to move into the rather-too-large house on the hill he and Gwen had bought in the Berkshires, in Housatonic.

Davin stands before the 2,000-square-foot vegetable garden in the back of his property, seeing the first sprouting of weeds in this spring light. He knows he'll somehow have to keep up or risk having the garden being overrun. So far Chaplin has been pitching in with the garden work, liking the rent-reduction-for- labor offer Davin made to him.

Well, the joke has become the master, Davin tells himself with a mix of feelings he decides not to look at too closely.

But the feelings are there, insistent.

I'm feeling pretty fucking bummed, Davin admits, and then he pushes this away.

The joke he had been thinking about was almost always unvaried, as unvaried as it was frequent back when Gwen was still around. "We're accepting applications for serfs...ur, associates," Davin would intone, pretty much to the same nonreaction.

He had been willing to entertain the notion that performing the same bit too often might seem an oddity to many, but he didn't see much point in trying to change something so inconsequential. This joke, and too many others, was more symptom than cause of the growing discomfort between him and Gwen, their conversations increasingly scripted, removed, desperate.

With his time spent in his studio, money was tight and he

had suggested they take in people, for rent, sharing the big house with them.

Whether a straightforward proposal or a repeating joke, Gwen was not amused.

It hadn't helped that the pandemic hit, and a big chunk of that year and more kept the two of them in the same house.

Just another Covid divorcee, he thinks, a punchline he doesn't find funny at all.

Just like Trump getting reelected, wasn't funny, not after that one Biden term, and the progress made then, and then all the shit of Trump's chaos.

Trump Redux, that's his shorthand for the ongoing clusterfuck.

At the start of Biden's term, the world had already seemed upside down, what with Gwen and he were doing. They were considerate of each other with the exceptions of occasional blowups until, of course, there were no more conversations at all, Gwen going off to claim a new life as soon as the pandemic was declared dead, or dead enough—a declaration that took surprisingly longer than expected. After that, the only discussions and communication between them were practical matters of the proceedings and property, and Davin still thinks he's never heard her reasons for the divorce, not any real ones.

Like depression, he tells himself. Davin has long struggled with depression, although he's done well in the fight, according to his several therapists over the years. He's certainly never far from thinking about it or feeling some tendril or twist of it snaking through his mind. For the most part he knows he does okay, and he sees this reflected in his general effectiveness and his ability to usually avoid the most crushing aspects of depression. He long ago came to accept that the antidepressants would take care of the darkest turns, staying the too-far-down drop to where self-annihilation seemed a reasonable option.

Better life through chemistry, he tells himself as he looks around the property. He suspects he's managed to remain good at his work over the years largely because the edges of the depression were blunted by the pills, and the rest, well, because he's a *stubborn son of a bitch.*

It certainly is a beautiful day today, although yet another odd one for the late-May date. Still, what passes for normal weather has been shifting rather wildly over the last decade or so as the consequences of climate change have begun to hit closer to home.

His son, Jimmy, lives in Chicago and the upper Midwest is socked in some super-inversion system, and it's actually hot there, August hot, worse than August hot.

Hotter than hot and something to do with the extended La Niña, he's read, although he is always getting La Niña and El Niño mixed up.

Climate change, Davin muses, *and yet there are still deniers.*

And this thought gets him thinking about something he's been trying to better understand, something Davin has come to call "magical thinking," an exercised belief in actions that are not, on further consideration and rational analysis, warranted. He has come to understand the error of magical thinking in his and Gwen's move out of the city and his expenditure of considerable time and too much currency to turn the old Greek Revival duplex into a reasonably weather-tight and energy- efficient country retreat. A country retreat that wasn't really a retreat, of course, but their primary residence with no secondary abode anywhere in view.

And this thought gets Davin back to his serf gibe, which he thinks is a funny joke, if a bit hyper-ironic. He knows this joke—like many of his other favorites—resides on the "whiteboard" side of the humor ledger where, in this instance, the only way the joke could be seen as humorous by anyone is to follow the line of thinking. His serf joke depends on an understanding that the current state of western culture is one of income inequality, the drop of the middle class, and political polarization pointing the way to feudalism, and thus the rejection of the *Myth of Progress* once so dear to him.

Now that's funny, right? he tells himself.

On some sort of molecular level Davin still believes in the Myth of Progress despite the resurgent power of moneyed interests with big corporations growing bigger, and he remains hard-pressed to reframe the world to account for banks and other financial institutions taking on a larger and larger part of the economy even while producing little more than paper and digital money mostly for themselves along with a bewildering number of bubbles and collapse cycles for everyone else. He knows that this belief is shared by so many others born after the World War and well before Reagan, *the Antichrist*, when the American Dream's overthrow seemed inexorable, and it proves harder and harder day by day to maintain the Myth of Progress. *Neo-liberalism at its finest*, he thinks. He had been increasingly finding himself thinking this even when he still lived in Cambridge.

Costs go up, wages go down. Options disappear.

There have been some positive steps lately, he considers, but still, the concept of *serf* seems evermore relevant. There is some part of him that still clings to this myth, even as he sees the danger in the ever-growing income inequality where the rich keep staving off taxes, despite the obvious and crushing needs of the country and the world. He sees the extreme rich playing with politics and paying for politics. He sees the ongoing fall in real wages despite the occasional efforts to address minimum wages, but he knows inflation and cost increases have such would-be corrective measures play the fool.

Davin is relieved his kids seem to be doing all right. His daughter is in Spain working on a PhD, and his son is only recently out of college but has found a paying gig in his field, or had, until the recession, or whatever the economic professors *de jour* call things these days, but whatever describes the economy, his son had told him he'd been laid off.

He doesn't appreciate the lastest election, which turned out just about as opposite it could, when he'd been hoping for an uptick in progressive voting trends. With the White House and Congress back in Trump's hands, the extreme rich remain largely untouched and in control. And the bought-and-paid-for Supreme Court makes it all worse.

Plus ça fucking change.

Davin is well aware he and Gwen, with their two-income work in high tech and medicine in the city, had brushed up against the ten percenters, at least in several of their best years of work, even though such unseemly income exuberance had been all too easily offset by the cost of living with which they struggled, including all they could do with college costs, socking away whatever possible in 529 plans. Jimmy couldn't escape some student loans even with all their planning.

He steps toward the garden fence to check on the three blueberry bushes inside, near the front gate. The signs of budding are there, he's relieved to see.

He turns back toward the house, knowing he needs to get to work on a report for his client at *South County Interactive*, but he lets himself dawdle, again looking around his backyard, enjoying the light and warmth of the morning.

He closes his eyes, letting the sun cresting over the rise of Monument Mountain warm his face, but his hoped-for moment of stillness washes away in his torrent of thoughts. These days, he's fixated on costs and how anxious he too often feels about his economic situation.

It had been in part the rising cost of living he had tried to remove himself not so long ago, along with Gwen and their youngest, Jimmy, who had been halfway through high school at the time. They had moved to Housatonic from their small Cambridge Greek Revival where they'd raised their two kids. A *Greek Revivallette* as Davin joked about this former worker's cottage he'd fully renovated. One or another Mideast oil conflict flare-ups and fuel cost spikes in the last two years they'd lived there had become a problem, even when he and Gwen had kept the average thermostat setting low. Energy price jumps were nothing new, but the credit line balance built up, and cost-cutting a top priority.

Just like today, Davin thinks.

And mulling this over has him thinking about how the current *political whores* have long been hard at work killing the sort of public budgets Davin and Gwen and most other middle- class liberal Cantabridgians had always reflexively supported— education, infrastructure, basic research, clean energy, and the other long-term investments that seemed so obviously merited, and increasingly so.

And what do I do about it? I cash out of Cambridge and move to the Berkshires to be an artist.

His thoughts return to the subject at hand.

Magical thinking.

He and Gwen had found out the hard way that living in the country wasn't really any cheaper, especially with the profits from the hot-market Cambridge house sale getting eaten by the country house rehab project, which turned out to be more expensive than he'd assumed it would be and made worse by buying a house sized to overcompensate for their first tiny place. And then too, for Gwen especially, there were the much lower salaries the hill country offered compared to what city jobs had paid. It hadn't helped, he knows, that he'd spent too much time on the homestead effort and then in the studio with only modest breaks for the income-generating work from which he had been trying to move away.

Literally, he reminds himself.

Changing his work was the other main reason for his wanting out of the city. He had worked in book publishing and then electronic publishing from its early days. He had been an editor and later an analyst and consultant to digital publishing vendors and their publishing customers.

Magical thinking.

Davin wants to think of himself as an artist these days, a sculptor. He's got three unfinished pieces in the studio, but the studio is still cluttered by the tools and materials he uses for working on the house and yard and garden. He cannot help but think of O. Henry's *Gift of the Magi*, and the money spent building his studio into the side of his sloping property, and how that had guaranteed his continuing to work as a content management consultant more than working in his studio, bills needing paying.

The divorce, now well over a year done, had made for one hell of a financial hit too, with the shift to two one-income households away from one two-incomes one. And Covid was still being felt economically, almost three years from its start.

Davin finds himself thinking about income and costs all the time, and he still tries to make sense of Gwen's decision that she simply didn't want to remain married to him. There had been no affairs, he wasn't a drunk or drug abuser, nor wife-beater, nor gambler, or the perpetrator of mental cruelty.

Well, as best I can figure, he tells himself.

It had seemed, from all angles, that Gwen was somehow, for some reason, just done.

Period. Full stop. That's all she wrote, he thinks, for the millionth time, just like it occurs to him that perhaps his own struggles simply exhausted her.

He is a good-enough-looking man, although he's always happy to find fault, and as he gets older he's well aware there are more faults to be found. Faults such as carrying around an extra fifteen to twenty pounds, which he thinks really doesn't look so bad, although clearly there's more than enough fat building up in belly and kidney pads.

Bend and stretch, reach for the stars, he half sings to himself, looking again at the neat rows of dark earth, trying to make out which tiny sprouts are good and which are weeds. He knows he'll be doing a lot of bending down, with close work. *Bend down and reach for the Tums,* he adds, remembering all too well his recent seed planting and the acid reflux his extra weight causes in that stooped-over posture.

Fuck me, he tells himself, brushing hair back over his forehead, the wisps wind mussed and annoying. His hair is receding, especially along the front and top, a common enough pattern among men his age. The hair at the top of his head has grown thin, but there's still more than enough up front to continue to comb his hair back, although he now has to instruct his barber to reduce the volume of hair that still grows thick on the sides and back to offset what he thinks of as the Larry-look, the Larry of The Three Stooges with hair sprouting from the sides, not unlike, too, the style of Bozo the Clown.

Vanity, vanity, he says to himself. *Sayeth the preacher.*

He shakes those thoughts away and turns back toward the house.

He knows his joke about accepting serf applications is at heart a reflection of his ever-growing anxiety about the ongoing rise in costs, apparently without limits, including for food, especially the sort of food—organic, fresh, whole— Gwen had long ago deemed the only acceptable type. He keeps finding higher and higher food costs, even now with Gwen no longer here, and with his daughter an ocean away, and Jimmy in his post-college life in the City of Broad Shoulders, only coming home mainly for Christmas. If that.

Food is just expensive. The ongoing droughts in the West don't help, nor do the high transport costs to get the food products to market.

He hasn't seen his daughter for almost four years, although her being in Spain might be a good excuse, airline tickets being high.

Energy prices are always in flux, but always, it seems, ending up ever higher after any momentary price dip. He has to pay a lot for the oil heating his big house through cold winter days and nights, and while the much- tightened house needs fewer gallons per year, the reduction in volume hasn't offset the ever-higher prices. And then there are automobile fuel costs, and while he drives as little as possible, it's impossible not to drive in the country, and though electric cars are becoming ubiquitous, replacing his old Kia is currently a cost beyond consideration.

And even then, electricity bills have jumped rather vigorously, despite his and Gwen's religious use of CFL and LED bulbs and their increasingly regular energy efficient behavior. Behavior, to his surprise, that had included Gwen's decision to turn off the hot tub they'd inherited when they bought the house.

Of course, you were on your way out, right? He once again wonders.

Don't be bitter, be better, he chides himself with an out loud snort that has him looking around to see if there are any witnesses.

He steps toward the apple and peach trees near the garden and looks closely. He lost the whole peach crop last year to a ground fungus that was a new arrival from the South. He'll have to get the antifungal supplies soon and spray the solution around the root area beneath the peach tree or face another lost crop.

The micro orchard is another task and another expense, and throw in high property taxes, surprisingly expensive telecommunication costs for cell phones and the Internet, and of course, the many thousands of dollars paid in for the health insurance policy he signed on with after the divorce decree was official, and the driving dream of reducing costs by moving to the country has been proven a fool's illusion. Not that it would have been cheaper to stay in town, he knows, but in Housatonic, his costs keep going up even while his income drops.

He's considered doing more of his professional work, although he's old enough to be suspect to the young CTOs and CEOs and COOs and directors and managers, most of whom now seem uncomfortable with older colleagues. But he suspects it isn't ageism that's the main problem, even though that's not to be dismissed, but rather it's his lack of motivation to beat the bushes for the kind of work upon which he'd built his career, now seemingly so long ago. And he again suspects his antipathy to the work could well be palpable to others.

The *South County Interactive* contract might prove the exception, but little money has yet been produced from those efforts. He likes working with Alicia Soares, the owner and publisher of the recently established local online newspaper, and while he isn't getting big billings, he's finding the work more satisfying. A step or two closer to offering actual societal value is his theory.

Still, the middle-class status he had so easily dismissed as *bourgeois* in his younger days is slipping, and badly, and not without concern and discomfort on his part.

And this is despite the Airbnb apartment they—now he—rents out, a small two-bedroom that takes up the north half of the first floor, its front entrance mirroring the one for the rest of the house at the other end of the sunny, many-windowed front porch. The short-term rental income adds up and is a big help, but he is still leaking debt. He had bought out Gwen's interest in the house during the process of the divorce.

And the apartment is currently offline because of an actual leak, some water damage from a very heavy rainstorm the past November that managed to have water seep into the apartment's below-grade back wall, the house built into the slope. Davin still has the to-do item of hiring out a carpenter to replace part of the lower wall in the smaller bedroom, but he hasn't yet sorted that out and is still considering doing the repair work himself. He is afraid that putting in a claim will raise his house insurance even higher.

I really do want some serfs to help out, Davin thinks, looking back at the 2,000-square-foot vegetable garden where good sun exposure and good compost made for good yields, assuming Mother Nature behaves.

He looks to the edge of the back property where lawn gives way to woods past a low stone wall, and farther on, hidden by branches just starting to leaf, are powerlines, and then beyond that the western slope of the small mountain named *Monument.* And then, standing there, looking back over the just-planted rows of kale and the rows prepped for tomatoes, corn, and other crops, through Davin's mind comes unbidden and almost unnoticed a nearly automatic mantra: *Will work for food.*

Chapter 3: Mile Marker 27

Cyn remains behind the rock of the massive cut-through, the rock that blocks her view of the road farther up and the vehicles off the shoulder.

She keeps getting lost in the echoes of what she's seen, and she's trying to fight against the ever-rising static in her mind.

She forces herself to understand she isn't eight years old, she isn't slumped against the far wall of that childhood living room, but she keeps finding herself thinking of the odd shape of her father bleeding, her father slipped down on the hall floor, and of the police lights and the ambulance lights strobing through the windows and the still-open front door — of the cops crowding the living room, stepping in and out of the front door, her mother keening.

She can't remember what came next. She has never had a memory of this, but someone had surely come and taken her away.

She's trying to stir herself. She thinks about creeping back to her car down the county highway beyond the curve, but the idea that the man — *policeman, or sheriff, or deputy* — might see her freezes that idea with panic.

The man who killed Joe.

She knows the occupant in the car isn't Joe anymore but something else now. The blood and other matter sprayed against the rear windshield makes that clear enough. Sweat creeps over her, and she's having trouble breathing.

She's wishing with a growing roar she never saw Joe's car, or the other one, the white one with flashing lights, or the uniformed man, stark images along with what seems a thousand other high-contrast concurrent impressions, including her sense of the man's surprise and anger at the blood.

Cyn sits up, her back now no longer pressed against the massive and looming rock, her eyes no longer shut against the morning sun. The rock behind her is already warming, the sun already hot, and in the next moment she closes her eyes again and almost surrenders to sleep, but she fights this feeling because she knows on the other side of the massive rock is the shoulder of Route 247, the small county highway in the middle of the desert where Joe is dead.

She's getting lost in furtive waves of half-thought notions and cascading grasps for explanations that pulse in and out of her feelings, and then she knows with a wave of certainty that if she hadn't taken her own rental and had instead gone with Joe, she would be dead too.

Her body feels cold, even against the growing hot face of the sun-bright rock.

She pulls in the dry air of the scrub desert in a long stuttering breath, and it's as if she's in an odd well of gravity, a mix of bright light and shadow of past and present, and she's trying to bring herself back.

She's trying to form an idea about what to do.

She's trying not to think of Joe alone in the car, or of the blood on the back glass, part bright and part dark in early morning sun and shadow. Her eyes are squeezed shut but she sees it all, the bright flashing cop lights ghost coloring the rock cut on the opposing side of the curve of the road, the cop lights coloring the man as he leaned into Joe's car, and the moment too that burst red against the car's rear glass.

But now she finds herself getting up, and with animal caution she peers back around toward the two vehicles, peeking past the huge cut rock, looking up at Joe's rental and the policeman standing, except the man isn't a policeman, the uniform is nothing like a city cop, but a sheriff, or a deputy, and the man is walking back to the white patrol SUV that has a circle of gold on the door and lettering and a central image she can't make out, but the lettering reads *San Bernardino County*. She slides back around, back down, sitting on the ground, certain of her danger and her need to remain unseen, quiet.

Her eyes shut.

She sees her father smile at her above his blooming blood.

Dad, she thinks.

Her eyes fly open and she looks around, sees the scrub extending forever, without end, the scruff of dusty brown plants and the dirt, sand, the curved-back giant rocks and every small pebble, a bird, tiny, high up, a lone cloud, a contrail even higher.

Get a fucking grip, she tells herself.

And she whispers, "Okay, okay, okay," over and over. She's fighting for control of her panicked and jumping thoughts.

In her linen jacket pocket is her phone. It's vibrating, muffled.

Fuck! she silently screams and even that feels out loud, and her heart leaps up into her throat. Even this seems too loud, her blood beating noisier than the vibrating phone she tries to bury with her body.

Her phone goes silent.

Her phone chirps of text notification.

She listens, new panic rising, but she hears nothing but the hint of the man speaking into his phone, those several dozens of feet up beyond the rock, and she rises shakily and chances another glance.

Deputy, sheriff? she wonders, seeing him back to his vehicle, his lower torso hidden behind that vehicle's front end, his phone up to his ear. He's half turned away from her.

Cyn slips back.

She pulls the phone out and sees she's just received a text from Joe.

Hey, where r u? Imwaiting

She wonders at it vacantly, and then she hears the man say something, but she can't make it out exactly, but she catches some of what he's saying, he seems to be talking loudly enough on his phone, but her hearing is off, her ears still overflowing with surging runs of pounding blood.

And then she knows with a moment of clarity those earlier texts this morning weren't from Joe but somehow from the man.

She knows what she must do.

She texts, thumbs moving with strange calm, *At meeting.*

She adds, *Thought you were going early. Where R U?*

She hears a distant ringtone play and peeks around the rock edge in time to see the man pulling out a different phone. The first phone is still held up to his ear, he's still talking, and then the man goes still as he looks at this second phone.

Cyn pulls back and sits against the hard rock, concentrating on what she can hear. Her eyes pop open when the man starts cursing, his fury carrying past the massive rock still between them. Then a car door slams shut and the vehicle starts off away, kicking up enough gravel for Cyn to hear it ping off Joe's car.

Cyn remains sitting, a brief staticky relief rushing over her.

And then she's back, brought back by her body needing something.

I need to shit, she tells herself, surprised.

She's up, she feels the pressure, but her whole body is also about as clamped up as possible. She's moving with quick clumsy steps, stumbling on the tiny rocks underfoot, her steps giddy with reprieve.

She's trying to quiet herself.

She's suddenly powerfully thirsty.

She realizes the sun is hot.

She can feel the sweat blossoming beneath her arms already going dry. She thinks about the bottles of water back in her car, back down the road a bit, around the curve, and this makes her think about Joe's car on the other side of the rock, half-leaning off the shoulder.

Joe is dead, she tells herself, one part of her, but this is met with a silence from a hot and fearful depth that's swallowing what she's just again admitted.

Her body, her abdomen seems to be twisting, a pulsing twist back and forth. Her body feels like it's loosening gravity, she's starting to float, a wail rising up inside her in preverbal sounds.

A quieter part of her tries to take stock.

She knows her car is parked, pulled over on the shoulder some way behind her, and still half-crouched she can see through some scrub just a glimpse of the car, back at the start of the slow long curve that's kept the car out of sight from the roadside ahead.

Weeds, but dry, crinkly — she thinks, fixating on the scrub and landscape she doesn't know. *Not in Kansas anymore*, she tells herself. *Fuck you*, she tells herself.

Her bowels cramp. She moves to hold herself against a midsized rock, clumsily pulls down her panties, her left hand now holding up her skirt, her right hand steadying against the slope of the rock she's squatting next to.

Her right hand, her left hand, arms trembling. Cyn is trembling.

Breathe, she tells herself, trying for a calm voice within, and then she tries this voice out loud.

"Breathe," she says, but this isn't a calm voice, it's shaky and hoarse and a whisper.

And then she's throwing herself forward, both arms out, her hands planting as widely as possible, but some drops of vomit splash on them. She can feel it even as she heaves, spitting, but when she looks, she sees only one or two drops on one sleeve of the dress jacket, the off-white one, the fashion brand she cares less than nothing about except that Joe bought it for her, a welcome gift when she'd started the new job.

Before we started fucking.

"Shit," she says. *So that I look right for the meetings*, she tells herself. She's standing up.

I guess I had to puke, she tells herself, some strange calmness in this thought.

She stands up, tugging at her underwear as her skirt flops down.

She glances down her front, smoothing the fabric.

Who wears a dress jacket to the desert? she finds herself asking, or maybe it's just another random thought, these seem to be coming and going—all sorts of things.

So that's what a continental breakfast looks like, she thinks, looking at the ground darkening brown with the wet vomit.

She's feeling calmer.

She stands up and concentrates on pulling the skirt straight.

She looks around, glances back down at her throw up, and she pictures the impressive breakfast spread put out by the out-of-the-way desert resort, coming in the afternoon before the meeting this morning.

This image makes her laugh, but it's a strangled sob that comes out.

She's having furious on-and-off conversations with herself for what seems like hours, days.

Her dress jacket's pockets are tight, and it's a struggle to get the phone back out. She feels like she can't do it, her arm an independent clumsy creature, and then the phone is in front of her, a surprise.

It hasn't been very long at all.

She sees she's been here only a few minutes.

I thought I had to shit but I really had to puke, she finds herself repeating as she moves away from her vomit and sets herself back down gingerly, settling down like an ancient woman, like a dying person might. She slowly leans back, but her eyes fly open.

She doesn't like what she sees when she shuts her eyes. The blood, the man with Joe, the pop that keeps repeating in her mind like a bad spot on a scratched-up CD, the clipped pinging sound of it all, a loud and running rip.

She's got to go.

She's trying to piece together everything, and the pieces are trying to fit. After a moment, she says out loud, "Number one, my phone." She picks it up from where she'd laid it on the dirt beside her.

She'd gotten those messages on her phone, those messages.

That's important, she thinks.

She reads the most recent message.

"Number two," Cyn says in a whisper. "Dead."

She knows this. She sure as hell isn't going to go out to the road, to Joe's car, to check.

Because he is dead, she thinks. *And dead men can't send texts.*

She picks up her phone again and scrolls through the texts.

Com on don't be mad, is the first one, supposedly from this morning, less than thirty minutes back.

My life is done U ruined it, she had replied, although she hadn't texted this, except this was now on her phone as *Sent*. But she had been too puzzled by the Mile 27 meet-up text, the only one she'd really seen while driving.

She hadn't replied to any of the texts.

She had not really read them until now, not really. She'd been in a rush, the new printouts done, and she was in her rental heading out to meet Joe and the investor executive.

She knows Joe was excited for the big meeting, had left earlier. *Up and at 'em*, he'd actually said through the door of her room, his knock knocking her awake.

He'd sounded excited through the adjoining door. He was already yelling through the door about some changes they'd have to make with the contracts.

She'd known he was excited, the meeting likely to be a big win for them, a first for getting this kind of investment group to pledge fossil fuel divestment, turning away a big pipeline project for one thing. The changes to the contracts she saw as she'd made the changes, were more specific language about the pipeline.

She'd been glad for the trip, a chance to be with Joe without the eyes that might be watching, without worry his wife might drop by the office with the kids, and she'd been giddy with the idea of relaxing away from the signs and hints she always had to watch. But she also had been excited about the trip because she was going to Joshua Tree after she was done at the meeting.

On her own. It had been too long since she'd done that sort of thing.

Cyn sees all her plans, the time with Joe, the camping, the time alone, the hiking, all emerging and fading, just parts of her distractions and drifting thoughts.

But she's trying to settle herself, gather herself.

Joe had texted about Mile Marker 27. He certainly wasn't likely to pull over and text her weird messages. Maybe an *On your way?* query, possibly. Maybe *Don't forget the new printouts*, although that too was unlike him. He knew she was competent.

It certainly wasn't like him to text to ask if she'd taken his pistol, which she sees as she scrolls the text thread upward.

Why did u take gun?

Which he doesn't even have one, she tells herself, but a wave of what's happened washes over her again, her underarms prickling a new wave of sweat, and she swallows hard against the hint of nausea.

Which he didn't have, she corrects herself.

Never had had, as far as she knows, not when he was alive, not when dead. She tries to push the new wave of panic back down.

She knows she hadn't written the next text either. *Need to tell you something*, a reply from her phone that she reads as part of the text thread, the time of the text recorded as two hours ago, but she'd had her phone with her as she finished up with the contracts.

And Joe's reply, coming much more recently, wasn't Joe, not like him, not the way he talked, or texted.

Meet me at mile marker 27. I'll wait hurry.

She had already been underway, had stopped as soon as she came to the mile marker, puzzled Joe wasn't yet there. She had pulled over and gotten out to stretch her legs and look at the view.

She looks at the phone's time and sees the message was sent less than twenty minutes ago. Not even.

Joe was alive, she realizes.

She holds her phone loose in her hand and a flushing panic rises up again, sweeping over her entire body. Despite her efforts not to, she wonders about Joe's last minutes. What had he thought, what had he been feeling?

She's got to go.

Cyn gets up and begins moving back toward her car. She stays off the road to keep behind the rock mass that had hidden her original approach. She starts retracing her shortcut that cuts the curve of the road.

She won't look back.

In her mind she fiercely keeps the mass of rock as the only thing behind her.

Chapter 4: Local Papers, Plural Rural

According to Alicia Soares, when Davin first talked to her about providing consulting services regarding an online newspaper, the unusual problem with getting local news in the Berkshires wasn't that there were no local papers, but rather, there were far too many.

Her argument, some three-plus years before, was that too many papers meant they not only cannibalized each other's potential ad revenue but also offered different target audiences, so there wasn't one place to go to for a full pitch and perspective on the local goings on. Davin has been an intermittent subscriber to the digital edition of the one "big" paper, *The Berkshire Eagle*, a daily that tried to handle all of Berkshire County, from North Adams and Williamstown on the northern border all the way to Great Barrington and Sheffield to the south, but which acted like only Pittsfield, the main metropolis and county seat stuck pretty much dead center of the county, generated news. The *Eagle* only rarely carried news of the far reaches of Berkshire County, which is one reason why he's currently a nonsubscriber. Another reason is because even the Pittsfield news is typically overwhelmed by the rash of AP stories that populate this daily, and he still reads *The New York Times* for national and international news. The *Eagle* is also chronically rumored to be on its way out, changing ownership several times in the past decade.

He's sitting at his desk, letting himself reminisce about *South County Interactive* and how he got himself involved. He's letting his mind wander mainly because there's a work order and project definition he's supposed to be putting together for his subcontractor who does the API and software coding tweaks on the *SCI* platform. The current requirement involves changes to the metrics engine, so there's likely to be fussy PHP backend integration with the SQL database he's argued needs updating.

Be careful what you wish for, he reproaches himself. He knows he has something of a knack for pushing for improvements on any project he gets involved with, just like he knows he also has the unfortunate knack for underestimating the time he'll be required to spend pursuing any such improvements.

He thinks of his present situation as a good case in point. At least *SCI* is a pretty good service, he feels, and his strategy of the self-erecting site means this online service delivers a comprehensive picture of what's happening in South County.

In his early years in Housatonic, if he wanted to know about Great Barrington or Lenox or Stockbridge, Lee, or Sheffield, or any of these towns' select board or planning board meetings, or traffic problems, or if he desired a thorough bead on obituaries, real estate transactions, district court cases, and school sports, the old south county weekly, *The Berkshire Record*, was his best bet but hardly all that helpful considering its light content listings. Even the news — except for the local school sports — was hit-or-miss, not that *SCI* itself doesn't have a long way to go in comprehensive news reporting.

And Alicia keeps hinting I should write a lot of it.

But before *SCI*, the publication that was the place to see what was going on around town for dining or entertainment or tag sales or cars for sale, was the free shopper, *Shoppers' Guide*, but it comes, of course, with a complete and intentional absence of any news reporting. There were also several periodicals focused on art and culture, ranging from the local to the wider region that included northwest Connecticut, upper Hudson Valley, and even southern Vermont. There were magazines covering health, yoga, and metaphysics, and one with a slant toward women's issues, and others yet that covered real estate or home interior design, and of course, the stream of glossy and pulp realty porn publications. There was even a commerce weekly covering Berkshire businesses, and he finds this publication to be okay, just not that widely read, including by him. And then there were a bunch of online efforts from both the print publications and some digital standalones, all rather different one from the other, and most now a matter of historical interest because they all pretty much shared the characteristic thinness endemic to such efforts, and thus little income generation potential and therefore little in the way of actual content staff or longevity.

He brings up the bookmarked tabs he's been referencing in his effort to more clearly understand the issues of using PHP with SQL, but it's another nice day, and he really wants to be in the garden or in the studio.

He sighs.

No such luck, he tells himself.

Davin had made his original pitch to Alicia when she'd been—for what proved a very brief tenure—the editorial side of *The Berkshire Record.* It hadn't amounted to anything, despite her interest and her telling him she had great hopes for the *Record,* including the online component she was trying to push the publisher to fund. She hadn't needed to be convinced of the opportunity in the marketplace for publishing something that carried online news more people would want to read and therefore generate more ad revenue. She'd been quite positive in her attitude and knew it would take time and investment to pull off the *Record* remake. Her optimism was largely based on the new publisher's oft-stated commitment to back her, and the publisher was putting up real money for building a bigger reporting staff.

He'd gotten excited about the prospect for *The Berkshire Record* online work back then, but he didn't get any go-ahead for writing any specifications, and then Covid hit, and his occasional email reminders to Alicia got replies that took more and more time and increasingly cryptic responses, and then none, and then he learned about the *Record* being sold.

He knows he'd been half-relieved, thinking he'd be able to finish a series of pieces in the studio and restart his conversations with two different area galleries about scheduling shows. Not that either were then open, but the Covid shutdown couldn't last all that long, he'd assumed.

Gwen had been kept on salary, but money was tight, and he doesn't like to think about his income during this period. There had been a report or white paper here or there, but he's sure that time of low billings hadn't helped the marriage.

But, hey, I'm working now, he tells himself, shuffling through his notes.

Davin looks at the sites he's pulled up on his monitor and groans. It seems like he needs to catch up on the details of any and all new developments in the technical process of what he's trying to update, and he knows he's never been all that adept at application program interfaces.

He's interested enough in the *SCI* work, and he remains impressed Alicia hadn't let a little thing like losing her editorial position put too much of a damper on her goals. They'd reconnected well over a year ago now, a date easy enough for him to keep track of, coming shortly after the legal end of his marriage and the stint of self-imposed isolation he had fallen into afterward.

Alicia had called him and restarted their discussions. She'd made it clear she felt she'd had to do something because the way her career was going was a problem. Not a problem financially though, she'd pointed out, talking about Walter, her husband, who worked as a trader and was good at it, even better than good. No, money hadn't ever been a problem, and there always seemed to be more than enough money, mostly from his family. The house in Sheffield had been bought outright and the renovations expensive, but fully paid off, and there was the life insurance payout too after her husband died.

He'd been on game and could see her interest in his expertise, but the conversation turned stranger yet, later, their having adjourned the meeting to one of the small restaurants in town. Sitting at the bar with her, he'd been surprised to learn the husband had died in a car crash, and Alicia talked about having to figure out the financial situation in detail. That had come with a few surprises too, including her discovery that her late husband had bought the girlfriend Alicia had had no idea he had a place of her own, except the Manhattan co-op was still in Walter's name. There wasn't any question of his girlfriend getting the co-op anyway, considering she died along with Walter in the crash, Alicia had noted, seemingly matter-of-fact.

The estate was worth almost five million, all told, she mentioned, which had surprised him, not because of the sum, but because of her openness about her financial resources. She did make it clear that much of it was in the real estate, but with liquid assets too, especially after selling off the co-op.

He had certainly paid attention.

She seemed intent on telling her story, which was that the move to the Berkshires had been her choice because of *The Berkshire Record* job offer and because her husband had gone independent, a day trader, and could live anywhere. The job offer had been compelling, but she had told him she wasn't entirely surprised that in the months of increasing ad revenues the publisher took a buyout offer, and the new owner looked at the editorial costs and decided to trim staff, starting with Alicia. She talked about how she had wanted to be a newspaper person going all the way back to high school, and she had never considered any other major than journalism and had spent the first few years post-college on the staff of a mid-market newspaper. After that, she had found work as a freelancer because she'd gotten married and they were moving a lot as Walter jumped from one opportunity to another as he worked his way through better and better investment companies.

It had been a strange afternoon, and Davin still wonders how much that may have been due to their finishing off a second round of martinis as she talked. He had considered going for a third round but found himself noticing she was quite attractive, in her forties, probably, but in good shape, and with the short, cropped brown-blond hair that seemed right for a successful and fit woman of the world.

He had abandoned the idea of another drink, half-amused and half-confused by his turn of attention. But he'd felt there was grief still for Alicia, but mixed with anger, and maybe some feelings of relief too. But she still doesn't strike him as dwelling on feelings all too much.

Instead, she dwells on the business as best he can tell.

The two of them have never again had any conversation like that.

The bet with her online newspaper seems likely to pay off, he thinks, although he's sure Alicia still keeps her fingers crossed. And the competition has been withering away, and the pandemic certainly hadn't helped those publications. Most of the print efforts have collapsed due to a combination of pulp price hikes, ever- increasing energy costs, and the die-off of those customers who still retain the habit of reading print, a demographic increasingly small and increasingly economically irrelevant.

Still, that could be one big challenge, and Davin fears the demographics of Berkshire County aren't particularly encouraging for an online newspaper. Out of all Massachusetts counties, Berkshire remains at the top of the list for average age, leading the state in older population, and it's been getting worse that way for a long time. Not that there's any mystery about this trend, he knows, considering the county also remains the most economically depressed, which means most of those young people who could seek work elsewhere did seek work elsewhere.

But then, there are the second-home owners and the tourists, and there's also the newly-resurrected passenger train services from New York and Boston. House sale prices are among the lowest in the state and more and more people taking notice of this for some time, even if mostly out-of-towners, as the house prices seem quite high enough to most long-time residents. Prices went even higher during Covid with city-folk buying up property in their escape from cities as work-at-home practices took hold across many businesses.

Many of these city-folk stayed.

Berkshire County is close to New York—but not too close—which means a lot of affluent city people seek vacation homes, or at least vacations, among the green and relatively cool hills of the county. It's beyond dispute that Berkshire County is beautiful with its rolling lands, small farms, river valleys, and worn, gentle mountains, and a good number of big state parks and forests help keep it that way. The Berkshires is also home to cultural institutions of surprising quality, the poster child being Tanglewood, summer home to the Boston Symphony Orchestra, and still going strong, but there's plenty of art, theatre, summer camps, luxury health spas, yoga retreats, and outdoor hiking, biking, and camping activities as other big draws. When such folk are here, they want to know what there is to do, where to eat, where to spend money.

He tells himself to get to work, and for the next few minutes actually makes a dent in the project definition, but he realizes that he needs to confirm the likely scale of API work. Before he goes back to his open tabs, he checks his email.

He still has at least one room to let, so he checks frequently to look at inquiries. There were two in his mailbox earlier this morning, both getting the form response of polite "No Thanks." There are now three new ones, and it takes him just a couple of minutes to reject two of them, but the third is well-written and answers the questions he's asked of the applicants, an action far rarer than he would ever have supposed.

The woman, probably young, he guesses, works a full-time job and is a part-time server at one of his favorite restaurants, Farm Table.

Deidre is an unusual name these days, he thinks.

He wonders if she's served him, but he knows the chances are slim since he eats out infrequently.

Employed, can pay rent, works at least some evenings, so less intrusive maybe, he wonders.

He replies with a request to speak on the phone,

providing several time windows.

He's been amazed at the number of responses, although he's not entirely surprised since housing is tight in the area. What does shock him is how poorly so many people present themselves in their queries. There have been a few exceptions, including Chaplin, his first house share, but he is worried if Chaplin will work out, especially since the safety deposit payment remains partly unpaid. But Chaplin likes the idea of substituting in-kind work, both with garden and carpentry labor, and he's already made up the shortfall. Davin's already growing concerned he'll end up paying Chaplin, considering all the projects there are to do.

And now a restaurant worker with a day job could work out, and the extra rent income will certainly help him. She seems more financially steady than Chaplin, and there should be plenty of additional restaurant shifts come high season.

In the high season, Davin knows, New Yorkers rent cars by the thousands to make the quite pleasant ride to the Berkshires — pleasant, at least, once that ride gets out of Metro New York. Increasingly, tourists and second homeowners are taking the reestablished passenger service that connects with the Metro North commuter rails out of Grand Central Station, then transferring at Southeast Junction, passing through upper northwest Connecticut to run into Massachusetts with stations through Sheffield, Great Barrington, and Lee, all the way to Pittsfield where other new connections will eventually head farther northward to North Adams and into Vermont. The Berkshires draw visitors from Metro Boston too via the straight shot west down the Mass Pike and the east/west rail that's been reestablished through Pittsfield. The Berkshires also sees its share of overseas travelers and west- coasters, and even with the economy down and energy prices back up, the Berkshires is a lovely and easy place to go for a lot of people, and people with money, at that. That had been Alicia's argument, at any rate, and nearly a year into the venture, the online publication is making money. Not all that much money yet but heading in the right direction, and this makes Davin happy because she's had to start paying out some of the revenue to him. He had contracted out as content management consultant, and he'd put together the RFP and vendor options for the *South County Interactive* platform, and he'd vetted the various proposals for her until they had a plan in place, but he'd deferred part of his payment until certain revenue marks were hit.

After last month's tally, the revenue has reached the first trigger amount.

Davin pulls a copy of the latest revenue report from a pile of papers on the surface of Gwen's old desktop, and he finds himself wondering if the day may come when Alicia finds herself a bit envious of the way Davin made his deal.

And then he looks out his window and sees the light will fade soon, and he groans.

Time to figure out the PHP SQL parameters.

Chapter 5: Whoa Nelly

Cyn walks back to her car, her steps and stride growing faster until she's almost running. She slows, focusing on the instances of her earlier shoe prints, where sufficient wind-sifted sand has collected to catch an impression. She fiercely concentrates on retracing her steps back toward her rental.

She remembers nothing else about returning to the car until she's surprised to find herself underway, and her quick glance at her phone thrown onto the passenger seat shows she's been driving only for a few minutes but enough to have her rearview glance see nothing of the curve or the cut-faced looming rock, just the road she's advancing along receding like a movie run backward. She feels nauseous again, but she keeps that in check with a sudden fury at backtracking the way she'd come, upset and angry she has to take the risk.

Everything's a danger, she feels. She's driving back toward the resort, thinking she'll go straight past and make the Interstate instead, but a white vehicle is driving east on 247, covering ground like a bullet toward her. She fights to stay in her lane, to keep heading west and north, fights not to give in to her impulse to drive the car away, off road, into the scrub, away, away.

The pickup passes.

The driver, seen in a glimpse, is an old lady with tight gray curls fluttering in the air of the truck's open window above a logo for *Lucerne Valley Pecans*. The woman lazily lifts a hand off the steering wheel as she passes, a greeting to another lonesome vehicle.

Shaking, she releases a breath as she watches the truck

recede in her side mirror. Then she sets her eyes and thoughts to where she should be heading.

It's not easy. She struggles to maintain her awareness of the road, still beset by cascades of tumbling thoughts and feelings of dread, and her flashing memories and formless old feelings and anxieties are a surprise. She had developed the belief, or habitually assumed, anyway, that her past and all the trouble that had followed on was long ago resolved. She hasn't thought of her father for years.

Dead father.

Driving, she figures she owes her life to her father.

"Probably," she says out loud in her rental car, trying to figure out where she needs to go, but still on the desert highway, trying not to press the accelerator to the floor, which is what her animal self seems intent on doing.

It occurs to her that the Chevy Bolt isn't exactly a speed demon.

She tries to remember Barstow, which is up ahead. There's the intersection of the county highway she's on where she thinks it meets Interstate 15, just south before she hits the town.

The miles pass in a mix of dread, panic, and elation, the mix like a buzzing cloud that envelops her.

If I hadn't stopped right at Mile Marker 27, I'd be dead.

If I had gone with Joe in one car, I'd be dead.

And some other part of her understands that if she hadn't had the childhood trauma, she might have reacted differently. She almost never thinks about it, what happened when she was young, the force of habit of years now, but she certainly knows that seeing her father get shot right in front of her when she was eight qualified as *childhood trauma.*

She sniffs. *No shit.*

Her father shot by the police responding to the domestic violence call, one of those things she would never really get over, despite the therapy, the childhood PTSD work, her own history of dysfunction, the dissociative problems, and all the efforts to sort her out.

The relapse in her mid-teens, the trouble at school.
Acting out.
She had always thought that phrase was funny.
Hilarious.
Nothing feels remotely amusing.
Cyn is trying to figure out what she should do.

Part of her understands she should go to the authorities, but she knows she can't, and part of her tells herself to just wait until she's far enough away, far enough from that sheriff or deputy or whatever he was, far enough away from his colleagues even. She can't know who to trust locally.

But what she really keeps telling herself is to go away, get away. She considers if Barstow is far enough away, but nowhere feels far enough away, not in any way. She only has the briefest flashes of such thoughts, though, because despite her effort, a darkness keeps coming over her, a cloudbank of blankness, a smothering static from which she only sporadically rouses herself before the absolute sense of annihilation propagates glimpses of her old living room, of the spike of bright that is her father's white t-shirt disappearing with dark blood eating the light.

Cyn starts, seeing that the car has slowed, her foot has receded from the accelerator at some point beyond her recollection, the car barely rolling, already at the gravel edge. The crunch of the tires on gravel is the first real sensation to come through. She shakes her head, looks backward in a glance, and pulls back onto the road, toward speed.

Jesus, she tells herself.

She knows she has to get a grip on what was, is, happening, and as she makes the effort, she finds herself wondering if her childhood trauma is why she's alive. Wouldn't normal people have shouted or stepped out?

I'd be dead.

Thanks, Dad, Cyn suddenly thinks, and she starts giggling even as she knows she's having another inappropriate reaction. She knows she has to settle herself and so is breathing deeply, slowly. She needs to go over what's happened.

She had pulled over right at Mile Marker 27, that little green and white sign, the sort that's everywhere but is almost always unnoticed. The text said mile marker 27, and she had pulled over, figuring he'd show up.

She'd been surprised Joe's car wasn't there, but somehow — *well, the weird text?* she tells herself now — knew that something was off, something had felt odd.

And then she had noticed the bounce of lights, the flashing subtle strange colors bouncing off the sun-lit rock on the other side of the road up at the far curve and she had known, somehow, had understood something was wrong, very wrong.

And then she had looked around the rock edge.

She sees it again in a flash that feels like she's there again, there, seeing the man leaning into Joe's car.

She tries to force her focus on the road she's driving down.

> *A policeman, the sheriff, whatever and whoever that person is,* had killed Joe.

The county highway has no other traffic, but she keeps drifting faster.

Whoa Nelly, she says to herself, and in this moment she is aware of the strangeness of it, she's in a cowboy movie, rocketing through the desert.

"Whoa Nelly, indeed," she says to the car, willing her foot back off the accelerator pedal.

She's still in a stretch of the highway that looks the same as all the rest, same shallow rises of scrub, but she's put dozens of miles between her and Joe and the sheriff, deputy.

Dead Joe.

She hadn't screamed when the gun fired, which was good, of course, but then, she'd never been much of a screamer. She hadn't run out, asking, *What the fuck!* but that's because she already knew what just happened, and even still processing, she had already been ducking down.

And then time behind the giant rock formation had

stretched, and she was in two places, flickering in and out of each.

It had finally occurred to her, moments or minutes later, that the man was sticking around. She heard him talking, muffled by distance and the mass of rock.

This had confused her, until it occurred to her he was sticking around for her to show up, she had suddenly been sure of it. Her body had gone still and cold with that knowledge.

And then she had received the text asking her where she was.

I*mwaiting*.

Her moment of brilliance had come, a moment of clarity among her bouts of confusion, panic, and flashes out of time.

She had taken up her phone and texted back.

Straining, she thought she could hear a text notification tone up the road, and he had muttered and sworn into the phone he was using, and she had chanced a peek and saw him pull out another phone.

"No," he shouted into the first phone. "A new text from her." "No shit, she sent it," he had said, and then, "She was supposed to be in the fucking car!"

"Fuck!" he had yelled before saying, "Okay, okay," and then he was gone, driving, flashing off to where she had hoped to send him.

And now here she is, speeding down the county highway in the other direction, past dust and dirt and rocks and scrub brown and black with the morning's shrinking shadows, everything stretching along her sight, a corridor, a strobing tunnel of light and shadows in the morning sun.

And now here she is, speeding down the highway, wondering where she needs to go.

Chapter 6: The Good Boss/Angry Boss Game

Larry Larsen sits in a hotel room that could easily be in one of any number of such hotels, and he takes a moment to double check which one he's in, happy it's indeed a Hampton Inn as he had thought.

He runs memory checks like this all the time.

Still, he likes that these rooms pretty much look all the same.

What he isn't liking is having to tell Rocky the assignment has gone sideways.

The boss is going to be furious, is the first thought that comes to mind after Larsen has finished talking to the freelancer on the arranged burner phone.

A complete and utter fuckup, is his second thought, furious with the freelancer who had fucked up badly.

Larsen decides he has to speak again with the freelancer out in Barstow—*Well, somewhere the fuck around there, out on Route 247 or parts thereof,* he corrects himself—and he's using the burner for this specific purpose. He's calling from Anaheim, there ostensibly and provenly at a conference, not that he'll get to any sessions today, but instead is scrambling like an idiot trying to run herd on his hired talent for this assignment. His so-called talent can't seem to get anything right.

Talent, he thinks, all but rolling his eyes. The guy is proving to be a big-ass problem. The situation may be fucked beyond repair, and that will not make the boss happy.

Larsen is operating out of Anaheim because this provides good coverage. He is close enough to act under emergency situations, but far enough not to be a possible involvement trigger if it ever comes to an investigation.

He knows a burner makes for some protection too, but he'll use the second burner when he's in Barstow trying to un-fuck the situation. It's perhaps paranoid, but cell tower pings can bite you on the ass, so he'll leave the current one here.

He knows it should never come to an investigation, not one that goes anywhere anyway, but meeting the objective of this operation looks less and less like a win. But perhaps not all is lost. He's got some contingencies he's mulling. It shouldn't have come to contingencies if his talent had half a brain, but it looks like this is too much to hope for despite the care and thought he'd taken vetting this guy and then mapping out the play.

He admits to himself he should have listened to that little nagging doubt in the back of his mind when he'd decided to go with a complicated play, but it had seemed a solid plan.

Set up as local law, pull over the targets before the meeting, shoot them, at least one close up, the phone texts telegraphing murder-suicide from a lovers' quarrel.

He had even taken the trouble to discuss abort points with the talent.

What talent? he mentally scoffs, but then, really, this is his own screwup since he hired the guy, judged him competent, or competent enough anyway, and from a talent agency that had previously proved reliable. The freelancer should have simply let the target go on his way the very instance he discovered the young woman wasn't with him. But instead, the target had gotten suspicious while made to wait, at least that's what he assumes from the freelancer saying that he'd only been trying to keep control of the situation while he waited for the other target. Control of the situation turning into shooting the man in the head.

By accident, of course, the freelancer tried to make clear repeatedly.

But there is his own judgment to second-guess too. He'd thought he'd taken the guy's measure during their one video call, all with the necessary precautions of using the VPN and the encryption, and the guy had struck him as smart, attentive.

That's why I get the big bucks, after all.

But what he's going to get this time around is a lot of shit for what happened, and he's not enthusiastic about what he's doing to try to fix things.

But sometimes you got to wing it.

Of course, winging it was exactly what the idiot had done. Larsen makes the call.

The guy's poor decision is why Larsen is now yelling at the man.

"So, if target one was not with target two, why didn't you just walk?" he asks the man on the other end of the call.

Why didn't you think that the plan was already off the rails, you fucking idiot, is what he's thinking.

He interrupts the man on the other end of the phone. " — no, I sent that slip text because you asked me to, not that I'm not sorry I did, considering." The other man is saying something more, but Larsen cuts him off.

"No, goddamnit! The whole idea was to wait to see if she showed up, and see if it was clear, and then proceed with the original action."

He shuts his eyes. He mightily regrets the follow-up texts he'd inserted in the hope the woman would show up. He's usually good with improvising, but his most recent example of improvisation is not so good.

Should have aborted, you asshole, he thinks, but holds off saying it, not entirely sure if his anger is directed only at the freelancer. He really wants a cigarette, but he's not going to have this conversation huddling outside with other smokers where he could be overheard. That would be poor operational hygiene.

God forbid I smoke in the room.

He finds it funny that he worries about violating the hotel rules, considering all he does, including the present operation to kill a couple of greenies inconveniencing his boss's clients. Probably billions of dollars' worth of inconvenience.

"Yeah, I heard you that she never showed up, and I'm

He is indeed sorry. His gut had screamed *Abort!* but he himself had overthought the situation, probably because he'd picked up from the boss a species of delight in the undertaking, back when the operation was assigned, although he might have simply read that wrong.

"Yeah, the gun just went off," he replies, but adds silently, *You fucking moron*, although he is now clearly directing this judgment as much to himself as to the idiot in the field. If this had been called off instead of waiting to see if the girl would show up, then the freelancer wouldn't have killed the man, *no harm, no foul.*

"Yeah, sure the target tried to grab the gun, uh huh," he replies tonelessly.

If you weren't in the guy's face, asshole, in the first fucking place! he keeps from screaming out loud.

Larsen can hear the wind over the phone. The freelancer is on the move, driving, but the guy's not thinking, and for some reason Larsen simply can't imagine, the guy is on his way toward the meeting location.

In a stolen law enforcement vehicle, he reminds himself. *Fuck.*

"Obviously," Larsen says, "you're not going to the meeting." He is speaking calmly, even if he's shouting in his thoughts, *Idiot!*

He tells the freelancer talent he needs him to ditch the vehicle and gives him the coordinates he had determined in his earlier planning would be a good place to do so.

"Let me see if we can pull a delicious donut out of this pile of shit," he tells the man on the phone, instructing him to keep the same extraction coordinates, about a two-hour hike from the vehicle ditch point.

Always a bad sign when I find myself using my father's old expressions, he thinks. He half remembers his old man telling him it was some translation from a Norwegian saying.

It will take Larsen a little more than two hours to get out to the extraction coordinates, but he's got no choice.

He tells the freelancer they can still find the girl after he picks him up. He tells the freelancer they can surveil the girl and see if they might wrap this up without further trouble. It doesn't matter, Larsen tells him, if her suicide is in the original car or not. The murder doesn't have to be followed immediately by the suicide, Larsen tells the man.

Larsen knows this is stupid longshot. She's at the meeting, according to the freelancer, and Larsen had immediately confirmed the text she'd sent claiming that, using his cell-server-installed shadow program. Craigson sure isn't there at the meeting, being dead, so she'll think something is wrong and the cops will be called, and so, *over and out.*

But he needs to get the freelancer thinking they can still pull this off. He texts the man with a confirmation of plan, telling him to lie low at the extraction point and wait for a rendezvous.

If law enforcement finds Craigson sooner rather than later, then even being out that way gets tricky.

Best not overthink any further, is what he's decided. He has the hotel room for another two days, a day past when the security conference ends. He can get to Barstow and back, two hours each way, plus whatever other time needed.

The operation, he thinks, is now only cleanup, so he'll have to buy a shovel.

Rocky is going to be unhappy.

Larsen's interactions with the boss are minimal, and on this side of his work for Rocky the interactions are always carried out through encrypted channels. The rare face-to-face meetings are only for the public side of the relationship when he sometimes serves as a digital security consultant for the boss's business management consultancy, but even then he almost always meets with others in the company.

Sometimes his two roles cross over. A recent job involved installing a backdoor on a server while doing a security audit as part of the process his boss undertakes for client corporations, something to do with business efficiency and management improvement. That job was at a law firm, and he can guess that firm handles many of his boss's big clients.

They've got a clerk there on board just in case, not that the clerk actually knows Larsen since he always works asymmetrically with such assets, and they've never met.

Thinking about this isn't getting anything done, he decides, trying not to scold himself.

He's not succeeding.

The boss won't be happy he'll head to the Barstow environs, but there's no other option at this point, he's sure. The operation has badly screwed the pooch, and cleaning up the occasional pile of shit is also part of his job.

Not causing shit for Rocky is the point of my job, he reminds himself. The freelancer had looked good, and had been vouched for, but no references, of course, by the nature of the work being unattributed, but then you don't go shopping for killers in the Sunday paper classifieds. And using the same freelancers too often carries its own risks, so he had decided to try again one of the other services because that was best practice, but he had ended up with this idiot.

He's willing to admit the plan may have been a bit too complicated with too many moving parts, although the targets taking separate vehicles to their meeting was unexpected.

Unexpected! he thinks.

Fuck, he thinks.

Has he perhaps loved the application of planted phone texts a bit too much, he is finding himself wondering. One of his newer tech tools he'd been too eager to try.

I do love my fucking tech, he admits to himself.

He knows he has to get out there for the rendezvous, but before he goes, he takes a minute to write up a job submission for some BOLO locate services just in case he needs them.

I sure as hell hope not, he tells himself, but he knows he'll need to find the young woman if there's any chance to come up with something he can figure to fix the fuckup.

He also puts together a job request that will go through a heavily encrypted TOR routine to access one of the kill services he's used before with never a problem. Now he wishes he'd started there.

    Fuck.

Chapter 7: I'm an Artist! I'm a Content Management Analyst! I'm an Idiot!

Davin sits at his desk in his office, the big room on the second floor he had made by opening up the common wall of two smaller rooms, and his desk fills an outside corner with Gwen's own desk running perpendicularly to his along the front face of the house, except that the desk isn't hers anymore. He has metastasized the space, and this veneered door blank sitting on top of two-drawer filing cabinets now holds his old monochrome laser printer and what seems like ever-growing piles of papers, periodicals, and folders. He likes the office, with its generous amount of work surface and the nice light from the south- and west-facing windows.

He really likes the office, except, of course, when his feeling about this space is less than positive, and, at the moment, matching his dour mood.

Gwen had mostly only used her laptop, and later, mostly just her phone, and was less and less at her desk. The office doesn't trigger her absence particularly, at least not nearly as much as their bed—his bed, now—and the empty side on which he still doesn't sleep.

He's in the middle of reviewing *South County Interactive* ad reports, cross-referencing the ad-to-sale ratios and checking subtotals to be sure his first real payout is what Alicia figures. He has learned the hard way over the years it's always best to double check, as much as he has to push himself to take the time to do it.

With age comes wisdom, he thinks, even while wondering if

it's especially true.

Part of him keeps thinking about swapping the old recliner in the back corner of the office for a smaller armchair in the living room, which would then make room for an extra side table, but he recognizes the delay tactic. He has come to know his frequent thoughts about changing, adding to, and otherwise manipulating the space and structure around him are a kind of daydreaming in which he engages, a kind of reverie, and there's comfort he draws from such thoughts, but he suspects there's something unseemly, unhealthy, in such thoughts too.

Mental masturbation through redecoration.

Christ, he tells himself at this thought. He's not feeling particularly depressed, but he knows he's not always the first to notice.

He glances out the window behind the left corner of his desk, then stands to better look out. It's a nice sunny day, a bit warm for the time of year, and unusually humid. The adolescent leaves of the second-growth northern cherry trees are bouncing in the breeze, and he thinks it's another good day for some garden work. But he's looking over the *South County Interactive* ad revenue reports for the last couple of months, checking them against the amount on the first check he'd just received from Alicia.

He has no real confidence he'll ever make much money with this work, especially relative to the long hours he's already put into the project, and especially considering he'll likely not leverage this work into other similar work. After all, he'd been intentionally winding down his professional efforts, when, before the *South County Interactive* assignment, he'd been working mostly as a freelance analyst, researching electronic publishing business processes and technologies for a boutique consulting firm. He had produced white papers, webinars, case studies, and reports, and on occasion, had been hired out for some hands-on project consulting.

More than I wanted to do, he thinks.

Less than I should have done, he considers.

He had worked for this small consulting company before his exodus from the city, and for a while he had mixed the Housatonic house renovation work with more such professional work, but that work had grown less frequent. All for the best, he had thought at the time. After all, he had made the move to Berkshire County to build a studio and concentrate on his art, and the disappointment he's felt in his last few professional projects seemed just another sign to stay the course, confirmation his interest in such professional work was over and done with.

And who could have possibly known it's hard to make money making art? he jokes for the hundredth or thousandth time.

And yet here he is, working with *South County Interactive.* Somehow though, this work feels different, and he would have to guess it has something to do with it being local and something that could contribute to the community whereas the bulk of his previous work involved large corporations and publishing segments that held little personal interest for him. He had long ago also noticed the better a job might pay seemed to correlate with his not liking the assignment, so he's pretty sure he'll be liking the *SCI* work for quite a while.

And Alicia has been talking to him about writing pieces for *SCI*, which, he admits, makes him feel good, at least if he ignores a species of dread when imagining he's back in the writing business.

He starts pacing around his office. When he draws near the window he can see the retaining wall structure that holds back the cut of the driveway and thinks yet again about the unexpected cost of making the back property accessible. The cost was largely caused by the steep slope the house was long ago built into, and the driveway problem turned out to be a $40,000 solution to get drivable access to the upper yard, but the parking area up top is an essential requirement for the first-floor apartment rentable to Airbnb guests, and now, for the two paying additions to the household.

Well, one, so far, he reminds himself, wondering, and the yet again wonders if Chaplin will work out in the long run. Chaplin, the first of the house sharers, is a young twenty-four years of age but seems an okay fellow, even though cash availability seems tight, which has Davin wondering if he should talk to him about some sort of regular property work schedule since the kid seems pretty competent, according to the construction work references he'd given.

But the main thing he notes as he looks at the retaining wall and the part of the driveway he can see from his office window is, *I'm a fucking idiot.* Considering how much had been spent on the property to date, this is not an infrequent refrain.

And then he's back at his desk and retakes his chair, getting back to the reports from *South County Interactive.* "Fuck you, I'm not an idiot," he says out loud as he brings up an Excel spreadsheet with the latest tracking of ad buys.

The numbers look stronger and stronger the more he looks at them.

Davin knows businesses that advertise with *SCI* like to see if the money they're spending on their ads has demonstrable and positive results. The design of the backend operation of the *SCI* content management system he'd spec'ed has expanded tracking routines, so he can easily illustrate ad spending successes. If all goes as planned, *South County Interactive* should be selling more ads to current and new clients alike, which will mean he'll get a bigger percentage for new or expanded business the online publication pulls in.

And with the Airbnb, once the season starts, there's more income, although he hasn't yet selected a contractor for the repair of water damage in the apartment, so the season won't start all that soon for him this year. But having finally agreed on another boarder—*Well, house share,* as he always corrects himself—then maybe, just maybe, the ends will meet.

He gets back to work, building a presentation of the data that will interpret the results of the report. This kind of presentation has its challenges, but the data looks good, especially if no one thinks to challenge one or two key assumptions.

Like the assumption that $10,000 should be plenty to improve access to this property, he hears himself think, before telling himself to focus.

He clicks on a PowerPoint template and pulls it over to the second monitor in front of him.

And somewhere behind his sudden sigh he wonders when he's ever going to get back to the studio.

Chapter 8: On the Roll and On the Run

Cyn is on Interstate 15, heading north, putting distance between her and what's happened, still not quite believing anything is real. That includes the night before, after getting to Ironwood, the nice resort hotel she'd found for her and Joe after they'd flown the small intercity turbo into Barstow-Daggett Airport, gotten the two rentals, and then driven up to Ironwood to get ready for the next day's meeting.

And each other, Cyn thinks, and for a moment the excitement of her affair with Joe stutters into her thoughts, but then the terror sweeps back. It's as if there are multiple worlds, one as unreal as another, one striking against the other, strobing back and forth.

Joe is dead, Cyn thinks, but doing so means she must fight the part of her that keeps such thoughts distant. She shakes her head, fighting to keep what has happened in mind. She understands that she needs to figure it out, so she can know what she should do.

That meeting had been set for the morning, was to be at the executive's house in Newport Springs, the one next to a golf course she had discovered was owned by the person with whom they would be meeting, as she had learned during a conversation with one of the man's assistants as she finalized the meeting details. She can remember that particular exchange with such detail, this recollection overlaying the image of Joe in his car, overlaying the sheriff cursing at the blood splatter on his face.

She shakes her head yet again, and this yet again fails to push the images from her mind.

She wonders what the sheriff, or deputy, or whoever it was, what he thought he would do once he caught up with her at the golf course clubhouse where she and Joe were to meet the investor group to sign the divestment deal.

She imagines the sheriff walking into the meeting covered with Joe's blood, what the reaction would be, and she feels herself on the verge of hysteria again, on the edge of crazy bursting, and she comes back just in time to step hard on the brakes, falling back from nearly rear-ending a Greyhound bus.

She tries to settle herself. She's trying to figure out what the murders could have been, and why. Where it happened seems more than a coincidence, of that she feels sure.

The divestiture deal is the only thing that makes any sense.

They had occasionally run into pushback with other deals, but would someone actually kill? By the time a company or institution was ready to make the change, it was seen as a good thing, good PR anyway.

She's convinced the two of them in the same car had been expected, and she wonders what the man had thought, and how long it had taken Joe to figure out something was screwy, wasn't right.

A sob escapes her, her hands pushing at sudden tears as she pictures Joe then. *Was he scared? Did he know?* she wonders, her heart feeling like it's tearing.

Why would anyone bother killing him?

Cyn tries to puzzle out an answer. But she can't think of anything that makes any sense, and she's puzzling over an explanation as another thundering wave of dread blossoms, and her sense of being pursued dominates once again, and then she thinks about the GPS, *or whatever the fuck it is!* that she now half-remembers rental cars might have, some sort of LoJack tracking, and she understands, clearly and entirely, she needs to not use the car, she needs to dump it and catch the bus, she needs to strip her phone. She's behind the bus, following it, her flush of panic growing, her armpits tingling with new sweat pinpricks, a single course of perspiration rolling down her left side beneath her blouse.

She cranks the air-conditioning. She keeps her eye on the bus. She concentrates on breathing and keeping a steady distance between her and the bus.

She reaches into her bag for her phone with her right hand, hauls it out, and fieldstrips it to pop the battery, both hands at work on top of the steering wheel, eyes back and forth from the phone to the road, up and down, until the battery fumbles out.

In her mind she sees the phone tossed out, the battery too, bouncing along the pavement behind her speeding car, but that's a clip from a movie, maybe from dozens of movies. *No,* she tells herself, placing the phone, disassembled, on the passenger seat.

She concentrates on the bus ahead.

This calms her, but then she's thinking about her affair with Joe and feels a rush of embarrassment and shame as it dawns on her everyone will know she'd been fucking him, a married man, her boss. She tries to convince herself this is hardly important, this is irrelevant in comparison to Joe being killed, but she's grown viciously angry with herself, falling into a discomforting cascade of mortification.

But there's a species of surprise too.

She knows that she sometimes had worked very hard in past moments to examine how she would end up doing this sort of thing, her history with older men, the pull this has had for her.

Dr. Becker, for example, she tells herself, feeling anew that incident's humiliation, the resignation of her advisor during her second year in college, and she repeats her old argument that it hadn't been her.

Not exactly, she thinks, but her carelessness, she knows, had helped bring their relationship to light.

Well, if sucking him off in his office, letting him eat me, is a relationship, she thinks, seeing again the cramped small office thick with paperbacks on shelves and stacks of papers and his laptop and that afghan-covered recliner that had the tendency to push back up as his weight settled on the footrest, his chest counter-tilting the lighter mass of her arching back, her arms squeezing the armrests. She remembers laughing when that would happen. She remembers his smell, how the recliner worked well upright when she went down on him. She remembers the sense of comfort she'd felt in his excitement toward her. She remembers her sense of control.

Billy, he had told her to call him, something that seemed more incongruous a thing than his penis in her mouth.

What had she been thinking, she wonders, but this is a question she hasn't been asking herself for too long, not since transferring to Ohio State after that semester. She had managed to get back into therapy there, a woman therapist who had helped her a lot.

Well, apparently not enough, Cyn thinks.

She's been sleeping with her boss.

Had been, she thinks with a shudder.

It wasn't a big deal, or so she had told herself when it started. She'd been horny, alone in a new city, and Joe was charming in his funny way, his excuses for dropping by, his inappropriate texts, the way he could bring his full attention to her or act strictly professionally, depending, and it had all seemed to her simple fun.

Cyn doesn't want to be thinking about this, but fun isn't it exactly, she knows, and she knows she let it all overwhelm her—the new job, and a big opportunity finally, and an all-new city, and her own expectations enormous, but tenuous too.

She had fallen into her old trap of looking for safety, comfort, and the sense of self as someone deserving attention.

Inappropriate, she now sees.

Demanding attention, she thinks.

She had been anxious, stressed, and vulnerable too, not to Joe's predation but to that thing with which she had long struggled, that need she had assumed had been dealt with years before. She was wrong, and it makes her angry and self-hating, but she knows she needs to stop these feelings.

"Fuck!" she screams in the car, wanting to tear the steering wheel off, both hands' knuckles popping white in her anguish.

She knows negativity is just another part of the trap, even as she can still feel how much she still wants the relief of his attention.

She tries to stay focused on the back of the bus.

Some people are going to blame Joe, she realizes, and she feels this will be wrong.

Of course, he could have resisted, she tells herself.

But if not Joe, there would be someone else, this is what she's thinking, and that Joe was hardly like that, not a predator, and the friendly attention, the playful flirting, and then the divestiture trips. The affair started on the second trip, and some part of her feels fondly of him, but the feelings are more complex, anchored in an emptiness that is existential, anchored in an old wound.

And then the guilt pours into her, shame exploding, and she wants to squeeze shut her eyes, but she needs to follow the bus, but she keeps picking away at these thoughts, now thinking back to high school, another of her troubled times when she had been caught fucking her neighbor, the adult son living with his mother, the man older by a decade. Cyn can't think of any reason why it should have happened, and there had been talk of charges against the man, and her mother and stepdad were furious, hearts broken, bewildered.

The shrink she'd been sent back to had talked about daddy issues, not that he ever used that term, but he had spoken of her hunger for protection or safety, and he had worked with her to come up with ways to think about these impulses. He had shown her a way of coping with her feelings and had offered her exercises that were flashbacks to those first sessions after she'd seen her own father shot dead.

She doesn't like to think about those days, about the way she could be, and the panic and the racing fear that would overwhelm her, and the guilt too, the same guilt that threatens to engulf her now, guilt that Joe is dead, guilt that she had slipped back to old and unhealthy choices for her life.

Fucking a married man, Cyn faults herself.

You are an asshole, she tells herself.

She squints through her tears, eyes still affixed on the back of the bus.

She tries to undertake those steps she'd learned to self-calm, to center, to breathe, even as she fights through tumbling images from this morning and from her past and the confusion of spiking impulses toward self-annihilation.

She breathes and begins to calm herself.

And after a mile or two more, she wonders if the bus will ever stop. She wonders if she'll be following it over some great distance, long enough for the car to be tracked, her getting pulled over, and some part of her realizes if she gets far enough, then she should go to the police, tell them what happened, but her bowels flair with an animal anxiety that keeps her thinking only of the bus, getting on the bus or getting caught—the only two choices.

She glances at the digital clock above her car's radio, and her rational self sees that less than an hour and a half has passed since the mile marker.

Mile marker, she thinks, anger flaring in her realization she's using this as code for Joe's death.

Joe's murder.

She is feeling more than halfway crazy.

She glances forward and sees signs for Mojave National Preserve, Hollow Hills Wilderness Area, and Highway 127, and a town or city called Baker. She sees the bus signaling and dropping into the off ramp, and she bursts into new sobs, pushing at the sudden tears with one hand while she turns the wheel to follow the bus that takes the sharp left at the end of the ramp onto the road under the Interstate. Cyn follows the bus onto Death Valley Highway/Route 127 and pulls into the 76 Gas Station and Country Store parking lot where the bus has stopped, and she is out of the car, big backpack in hand, wiping at her tears, her face drying into the hot desert sun.

Fifteen minutes later, from her seat on the nearly empty bus as it swings out of the parking lot, she sees across another parking lot a sign reading, "The World's Tallest Thermometer," and behind a big restaurant building, the top of the same said thermometer, tall, shining, and glaring red.

Chapter 9: Go Birddog, Go

It's almost evening before Larsen gets back to his Anaheim hotel room and positively evening by the time he finishes showering, letting the dirt and dust wash way.

He looks at his reddened palms and notes the start of two small blisters.

Getting soft, the thought comes to mind.

He steps into his business suit, adjusting his tie in front of the bedroom's big mirror, and he decides to shop for another set of casual clothes tomorrow. He's already packed his dirty clothes and the shoes he'd been wearing into the plastic bag supplied by the hotel for laundry. He'll throw these out, and he'll dump the field operations burner in the trash too, some place right, next time he goes out.

There's no reason to keep this field operations phone because the only person he calls on it won't be answering any phone ever again. He removes the SIM and twists it until it's torn, and then he cracks the phone by leaning it at an angle against a baseboard and hitting it with a fast kick of his foot.

He is wearing his dress shoes. He is wearing the suit he would have worn on the trade floor today, or for any other sessions he will say he attended, not that there's any chance anyone would ever ask, but good cover means thorough cover, so he'll head down to the bar where he'll likely find some other conference attendees and chat them up about what they thought of one or another of the afternoon sessions.

First, though, he's got other business to take care of, so he sits at his hotel room's small desk and opens up his laptop and signs onto a VPN redirect service. He accesses his email persona account and contacts his man at the law firm to ask for an update from his morning's request to get some private agencies on to Cynthia Wainwright's trail, a request that had included a backgrounder on Cynthia Wainwright he had been sure to run through a metadata stripper before he headed out past Barstow.

He keeps his email's tone calm, although he's annoyed there isn't an update already waiting for him in the email box of his untraceable persona.

He needs to exercise caution in his relationship with the clerk since the relationship is young, and he doesn't want to spook him.

Spook him, Larsen scoffs. *Or spoof him.*

Larsen is in fact spoofing him, in that the email persona is fictitious but by all appearances a real person's account, and as far as Larsen is concerned this serves his interest in this guy Madaki not knowing anything about him. Only a systems analyst could dig deep enough to find that his emails aren't actually going through the firm's email server.

The first email he sent this morning had contained a malware insertion that will alert him if a security review is done because any decent review will show the law firm's network is compromised. This insertion routine carries timestamps well past his previous consult work, and the insert routine is a new one beyond the protection he had recommended, not that the network admin likely has implemented all his recommendations yet. He wants to roll his eyes, but such sloppiness in the system administration works in his favor. No one will seek any connection between his recent security audit and the intrusion, and all and any efforts to find out who created his fictious email persona will be unsuccessful. Covering one's tracks takes redundancies, although he thinks that any of these routines ever being discovered remains a negligible probability. His false identity email asks Madaki for a locate update on Cynthia Wainwright.

This shouldn't have to be asked, but the law firm contact is one of the junior clerks, an immigrant who loves cloak-and-dagger bullshit.

He also loves the anonymous cash drops, Larsen considers, and as far as Larsen is concerned, that is a comforting state of affairs, although that cash has already ended, even if the guy is clueless the spigot is closed now. The persona who Madaki thinks he works for is itself just one step away from disappearing completely. Unfortunately, the clerk is not a natural at this sort of work, and the guy's earlier reply to a query from Larsen is as good an example as any of the guy's lack of experience, because what he now gets back from the clerk is almost unintelligible, and this annoys him, but at least he has learned there are three investigation services engaged.

He is going to flag another service for Madaki, and he'll tell the clerk it's another BOLO agency hire but will ask him to use the codename *Birddog.* He explains in his email that this other service the clerk could be hearing from will use the codename because it's from a guy he knows, a person doing him a favor, but the guy can't be named because of a noncompete situation, and the guy is a bit paranoid about doing this favor for him, worried it could end up biting him on the ass. Larsen adds that this person will get paid directly by him for services rendered.

Larsen needs to keep Madaki in the dark about the purpose of the contractor he intends to hire, but Madaki will need to share location information for the target, assuming one or another of the legitimate investigation services succeeds.

So don't mention him to the other services, please, Larsen adds, along with instructions to keep Birddog in the loop on any results from the other services. *Don't care how many agencies on board, but your email doesn't include progress. Anything on the locate yet? Anything on official sources?* Larsen finishes with in his reply to Madaki.

He looks at his watch. He's got to get down to the bar while the getting's good.

Update in real time, he ends up adding, but then erases that and writes out more clearly what he wants. *Keep me informed of every and any updates on the location effort, including monitoring of official sources, news items.*

Larsen knows his own access to law enforcement wires is minimal, but he's been hoping the legitimate agencies hired will have connections, maybe even to the national network used for interstate law enforcement requests. He's already set up a bot search on one of the California nets and a couple of others, but he doesn't know if or when there will be any public-facing information.

Of course, he already knows she never showed up for the meeting, his gaining this confirmation from a call he'd made to the investment group posing as a Carbon's End staffer.

Another reason to dump that burner.

He knows the Craigson target never showed, of course, *having got his face shot off by that idiot.*

He spends a few minutes checking his alerts but sees there is as yet not all that much in the news, despite his leaking ploys. He knows law enforcement is already looking into the shooting, but how fast and how effective these entities will be is an important consideration. He's second-guessing his leaking the phone texts angle, nervous about how well these might survive scrutiny, but he wants to keep the lovers' murder/suicide premise upfront of the developing new stories. He doesn't really expect anyone to check to see if the texts are external insertions, and he's already seeing some mention of the embezzlement angle he's engineered in the few news reports out already, which impresses him given he only put this into action this morning. Unfortunately, his crypto balance is now dangerously low, having forked over a good chunk to one of his subcontractors to another dark web service, but at least it is one that's been reliable in the past, and he can't complain about the fast turnaround. With any luck, the leaks being orchestrated will keep pressure on the target.

With any luck, Jesus, he scoffs. The possibility that the young woman still hasn't yet contacted the law has become the centerpiece of his Hail Mary hopes. His play now is to beat the law enforcement agencies to her because things will get very messy very quickly if he can't bring resolution, and Rocky won't like that. There's little or no chance of trace-back, but Rocky doesn't like fuckups. Larsen has to find out where the hell she is as soon as possible and get this mess taken care of.

The bar and the conference chatter will have to wait a bit more. He's still got to get online and secure a contractor for this extreme prejudice action.

That contractor needs to know where to find her, of course.

Go Birddog, go.

Chapter 10: The Wheels on the Bus Go Round

Cyn doesn't answer calls on her phone, doesn't make calls, because the phone, battery pulled, is somewhere at the bottom of the side pocket of her leather tote bag with its cross- body strap, serving as combination briefcase and purse. The draft agreement documents for this morning's meeting are still stuffed inside, but now the bag itself is crammed back into her backpack. She suspects holding on to the phone is a good idea, considering it has texts she never sent and received texts from Joe after she knew he was dead.

The last one, *Where R U?*

Fuck you, she says, thinking of the sheriff, or whoever shot Joe, and who would have killed her too if she'd ridden to the meeting in Joe's rental.

Or…if I had screamed, or made any noise, or had walked along the road, or…

But she's trying to stop these thoughts.

Or hadn't stopped right at the mile marker, she can't help thinking.

She is suddenly not sure if she's talking out loud. She looks around and the nearest passenger is several seats ahead, apparently oblivious to any sound she may be making, lost, apparently, in the small screen built in the back of the seat in front—CNN, she thinks, a clip she recognizes as the fires, either the Northwest, or Colorado, or Yellowstone.

She turns her face up toward her own fuzzy screen and sees the caption identify the clip from Yellowstone.

Or killed if I wasn't crazy, Cyn says to herself.

She thinks this, but not harshly, but softly. She is thinking about those days and months and years that followed the shooting of her father, right in front of her. Her two younger brothers were in their bedroom, their habit of retreat whenever their father grew in rage, their shutting the door on the ugliness always sure to result. She had called 911 that day, worried for them all, desperate for their mother who had plenty of scrapes and bruises and black eyes, the broken hand that one time, the other time when he wrenched her mother's arm back, putting her arm in a sling for weeks afterward. She had grown hyperalert to the grimaces that would flit and flash across her mother's face as she did simple things like laying down a casserole on the table or folding clothes.

She had been in therapy for almost five years after the shooting, although the last three were less frequent and mainly to check if she was disassociating again, retreating into the comfort of the separate self to abandon her day-to-day stresses that were normal enough ones for any kid, but not for her, not then.

With therapy across the remaining years of her childhood, she had come to realize she had done her best to help her mom, done her best to help and comfort, and she had learned, through practice, through the months and years of going to sessions, that she wasn't at fault.

She had been strong, she had been a help. That's what they all had told her.

Some help, she scoffs, a shadow of a snort that makes her again look up and around at the nearby seats — the bus mostly empty, *thank god*, which makes her snort again, a short burst of air pushed through her nostrils like a horse.

She works to quiet herself.

Who are you? Where are you? How do you feel?

The old habits of self-observation taught to her long ago, and here the habits are back, right on time, the deep breathing she tries, the self-forgiveness she has to re-practice, the recognition of her sense of guilt about Joe's death, and recognition, too, that she hadn't been at fault. These efforts mix with the horror of the shooting, the shock, her often tenuous hold on herself.

Cyn knows what makes sense, would make sense, and that is to go to the police when she's far enough away. Las Vegas, where she's heading, would be fine, but she's still too shaken, too shaky, and she needs to give herself more time. More time to rest, time to practice being in her own self, time to resist the still strong tug of dissociative escape that had shaped her time after her father's death.

And now, yay, reset, she tells herself, anger flaring.

Fuck me, she tells herself, but she attempts to tease out the tenderness too that she's trying to give herself and is glad for it.

She is heading to Las Vegas, and it occurs to her there may be fire regions the route will bring them through, and so she waits until the cable story comes back around, but she almost misses it, snapping her attention back just in time to get an impression of the graphic of the major fires in the west.

Clear skies, baby, she says to herself, a giddiness rising, then vanishing as quickly, and she wishes she had some Xanax or Ativan.

The fires at these scales have been an annual occurrence for the last five years, maybe more. There was the bad year before Covid, and the Covid years were even worse, the skies over Portland and Seattle and San Francisco dull orange sometimes, just images from news stories until she was living in San Francisco after joining Carbon's End. Even in her short time there she'd seen her share of smoke-choked air. The fire season this year had started ever earlier and was thought likely to run longer. If she remembers right, the count is already closing in on ten million acres.

You'd think we'd run out of trees, she tells herself, although she knows full well there's plenty more to burn in the sixth year of significant drought.

She has one of the new hoods, although this is back in San Francisco, in her bureau, one of those HEPA filter hoods, with a clear visor. The thing looks like something out of a science fiction movie, but a month earlier the winds moved the smoke toward the city from the Putnam Creek fire and the Atlas fire complex east of Napa. The smoke had plumed over the city for three days before the wind changed, and she had been plenty glad for the hood rig even if it all flashbacked to the coronavirus mask days.

She's been an activist in some shape or form since her high school days, a climate change person, a person committing herself to the change needed, a long-term foot soldier, a veteran, is how she thinks of it. The Carbon's End job was perfect, the divestiture effort exactly the sort of work she'd been aiming for, her years of volunteering and low wage work in the trenches finally paying off.

Well, not paying, at least all that well, she thinks, noting the pay was good only relative to the sort of hand-to-mouth existence she'd long gotten used to. The actual salary was a big deal, even if not all that big a salary, as she discovered when she couldn't afford an apartment in the city, at least one that didn't include passels of roommates. Not even the tiny studio she lives in, thanks to Roger, the executive director at Carbon's End, who had owned a bunch of rentals around town. He had used these properties mostly for short-term rentals, at least until the new ordinances went into effect against Airbnb and its kind, but he's kept one of the apartments, the one near the office. This studio apartment he included as part of Cyn's remuneration, although she'd had to share it at times when out-of-town staff or contractors came to the headquarters.

When this happened, she usually stayed at her colleague Ellen's place, and the two of them would BART in from Richmond together.

Joe had been by the studio apartment, after hours, a couple of times. He was charming, she was horny, lonely, but she had kept things frosty.

Until I didn't, she corrects herself.

And then Cyn again realizes with a start, *he's dead*, a surprise in the form of a periodic mantra.

She starts her exercises again, but after a few minutes she's back to thinking about the texts on her phone, the texts she'd never sent, with their story of an affair, and these make her again feel guilty and alone. She cannot help thinking about it, about Joe, images still come and go like flickering shadows, and she despairs, she wants to wail, to shout, to tear this bus apart, throw the pieces, kick down the hills they're passing through, pull the sky down and swallow it.

Of course, she had thought about sleeping with Joe, and Joe had talked about his wife, the new baby, the lack of sex, the exhaustion and routine that buried his days, and about everything he missed — the fun.

Of course, I would never sleep with my boss, she tells herself., and then out loud, "Never would," she hears herself say, low, a whisper, and the sound of it outside of herself shocks her.

On this bus, she knows that she had sleeping with Joe, and she wonders if they'd been followed, spied on, but the odd texts don't suggest this one way or another.

And they hadn't known she'd set off in her own rental.

Cyn is suddenly ravenous for news. She needs to know what's being said about him, the story must be breaking, but it's not going to be on CNN, for sure.

She scrolls through the channels, there are an even dozen, but neither of the other two news channels is Environmental Network News, which she figures is the only one likely to carry anything about Joe being dead, that, and maybe, local stations in San Bernardino, if there are still such things.

Or in San Fransico, she thinks, *it will be a local story, there.*

She won't put her phone back together to check, of that she's sure, and so she tries to decide whether to take a nap or watch reruns of *Friends* — the sort of old syndication programming one can expect on crap TV.

Crap TV, a great name, she thinks, but her effort at escape evaporates, and she's up in the aisle, swaying gently as she pulls herself up to her neighbor several seat rows forward.

"Um," she says, and the man, probably near fifty, slowly turns his face away from, yes, *Friends*, as if it has a precious pull on him.

He just looks at her, his eyebrows raised high, doing his

talking for him.

He looks like a goddamn cowboy, she realizes, and then she sees a Stetson on the seat next to him.

He pulls one earbud free.

"Um," she repeats. "Do you have a phone or tablet I could borrow, mine's broken and I need to look something up," she tells him.

He looks at her, his eyes surrounded by deep tan and wrinkles. She can smell his hair lotion, or maybe cologne.

He turns away and Cyn thinks she's been dismissed, but he's reaching for a small duffle bag stuffed into the footwell of the Stetson's seat.

"Here you go, little missy," he says, handing her a mini-tablet, and his grin reveals three missing teeth from his left upper canine back to a gold-capped molar.

Chapter 11: Ink-A-Dink-A-Doo

D avin likes going downtown to *South County Interactive*'s office in Great Barrington, even though he still more or less hears the quotation marks he puts around *downtown*. Boston has a downtown, Cambridge and other sizable towns and cities have downtowns, but the term *downtown* doesn't feel like the right fit for Great Barrington.

He steps out of his old Kia, or really it's more like he pulls himself up and out with grunts since the car's not roomy and it's low to the ground, and he's less spry than he'd like. And the door handles have a tendency to pull right off, the exterior ones. He's had to replace handles four times already. He hates the car, hates driving, hates the whole stupid idea of it, but then he's not in Cambridge anymore.

What was I thinking? he asks himself, and not for the first time, but still, it's a beautiful day, and the morning rain is gone and the day now hot enough, if perhaps too hot, but clear and sunny. He's found a parking spot right on Main Street, not three doors down from the building entrance of the *SCI* office. Parking can sometimes be a problem during high season when the town is crowded with visitors, but it isn't high season, even if the temperature and humidity feel that way.

He growls a *howyadoin'* at a passerby, one of the many regulars he sees around and maybe has met, but he's not sure. He then spots Deidre, the new house sharer-to-be, coming up the sidewalk, and he offers a half wave. The young woman has a nice smile.

He's offered to help her move some of her belongings in early, after she told him her car is in the repair shop. He was coming downtown anyway, he'd told her, and she lived nearby, and was off work at the right time to meet up at the *SCI* office.

He knows Deidre works full-time at the crystal and tarot shop downtown and part-time at a restaurant as a server. He also knows from what she told him previously, that she thinks of herself as a writer—albeit, unpublished, she'd readily confessed. She'd told him she writes poems, or something akin to that anyway, as she had put it.

He hadn't any response to that declaration. Deidre is young and may or may not yet know things take time, but it isn't his role to tell her. She'll figure things out.

As she steps close, Davin says, "Hey roomie," and immediately feels stupid, so he adds, "Sorry. That was weird."

Deirdre says, "Well, we are, right?" but Davin can see she feels a bit embarrassed, or maybe just shy.

Davin grabs the door and points upward. "Second floor. Shouldn't take me long."

Deidre steps through and starts up the stairs.

SCI is up the stairway, which is cool and dim with the sun already around the building, leaving the east-facing street entrance door in shadow. The *SCI* office door is open, and he steps in, but Deidre doesn't follow. Instead, she takes a seat on a chair in the hall near the office door. He hears Alicia on the phone in her back office, so he goes to the banquet folding table that's been set up in the front room as a work surface.

He sets his laptop down and logs into his Google account to look at the news. His Google News AI feed is well shaped and has some balance in sources so he can at least argue he's avoiding *bubblizing*. Of late he's been fine-tuning to see how good the local filters can get, although he more and more finds he's in something of a feedback loop with a lot of *SCI* hits showing up.

He seems to always be upgrading his ad block extension. He's noticed searches still increasingly slant toward results that clearly have some commercial benefit for Google, including the ever- plentiful *Ads* and *Sponsored* results that crowd out the actual search hits he's pursuing. And despite his use of ad blocking, it seems like half of the links he clicks on go to pages that must be whitelisted to see the content he wants. So far, he's managed to keep Alicia from making *SCI* demand whitelisting, and the analytics back up his argument that people mostly like to see local ads.

Or at least don't hate them, he considers, thinking of his constant frustration with the state of the Web these days where everything is about *monetizing* and barely any attention paid to the initial promise of the Internet to make information discoverable and available to all. He mostly doesn't like to think about the ever-expanding commercialization of digital content. The potential of more positive cultural benefits from developments like hypertext and wide accessibility to content had been a driving force early in his career, and he had moved away from book publishing to explore the emerging world of electronic publishing.

He'd finally canceled his several Facebook pages right after Harris and the Democrats had failed to keep Don the Absurd from regaining the White House.

He puts such an unpleasant thought away and starts reviewing the news.

The fires out west are at the top of his Google News, the sort of news items that are present nearly year-round these days with the enduring drought supplying fire conditions across much of the West. But parts of the Amazon are on fire too, and vast areas of Siberia are once again ablaze, already surpassing that region's previous high mark of more than 50 million square miles burnt back in 2020, the now second-worst recorded.

Ah, 2020, the year that keeps on giving, he says to himself when he sees the year referenced in the story he's skimming through. Neither Gwen nor Davin had anyone close to them die from Covid, but that year had been difficult in many ways, and he knows he's still recovering economically.

Never mind recovering mentally, he notes silently, but he knows better than to dwell too much on that *annus horribilis*.

That year Siberia had burned an area bigger than the size

of Greece.

And 2021 wasn't really any better and the floods in Pakistan in 2022 had covered a third of that country's land and a dozen monster storms had wreaked havoc in many places. He had been fascinated by the satellite images.

These days the smoke particulates from the fires out west sometimes make their way to the east to provide haze and spectacularly reddened sunsets, but the smoke also has become a significant public health issue, and he well remembers last year's warnings and advisories when a western weather system helped the smoke travel far. Those few days of mask wearing had produced a Covid memory for many people. So far though, this year the air quality this far east has not been compromised.

The year is young, he reminds himself.

He calls out to Deidre through the office entrance door. "Come on in. Make yourself comfortable." But then he realizes she's sitting on the same kind of chair he has to offer within, and then he realizes the chair near the door is the same type of chair because it comes from the office, it being the exact chair he had taken from the front office space and placed near the door the last time he was here when he'd gone out into the corridor to give Alicia some privacy as she talked. As best he'd been able to make out, she was talking with some financial advisor or another.

It's not a fancy office, but he approves because it means Alicia is putting her resources back into *SCI* and not fancy furnishings or palatial suites.

Deidre comes in carrying the chair. He nods to a small pressed-wood table where two more matched folding chairs are nestled, and Deidre sets her chair close by the others and sits back down.

"Fancy office, huh?" Davin quips and Deidre is polite enough to smile.

He points toward Alicia's office door, which is half open.

"She'll finish up and I won't be long."

"No problem," Deidre says.

"Which restaurant do you work at?" he asks her.

"Farm Table," she answers. "The one toward the north end of Main Street."

Davin knows it, likes the place, and is sure he must have eaten there more than once or twice, but he's not one for dining out, especially if he's alone.

Deidre tells him her evening shift is a Monday and everybody knows that to be the slowest night of any week, but she'll do better during the high season when a Monday night can be busy and the tips not bad, and she may get more shifts too.

High season, Davin thinks, keeping his sarcastic reaction to himself, but then he realizes these days he often unironically uses this exact phrase.

She's a good-looking young gal, Davin can see, with a nice head of black hair that curls to frame a symmetrical face, frank dark eyes and full dark lips, and skin that carries a hint of hard-to-determine ethnicity, but her age makes him feel like she is alien. She is younger than his youngest.

But she seems levelheaded. She'll be living on the second floor, at the opposite end of the house, in a room with its own deck and outside entrance and about as far away from his second-floor office as is possible, the big library room separating the two spaces. Levelheaded, responsible, quiet, that's what he thinks she will be.

Hopefully.

He's got a security deposit from her, plus first and last month's rents, already, something of a victory in comparison to Chaplin's status. Maybe he's getting better at this boarding thing.

Who the hell knows, he tells himself. *Luck, more than anything.*

He wants to ask her if she has a boyfriend but can't figure out how to do so without it seeming weird, and besides, the rental agreement limits overnight guests, so he'll just have to wait and deal with that problem should it arise.

"It doesn't matter," he asks, "but why are you leaving your apartment?" She hadn't talked about her current rental, but then they'd talked about a lot of things when she'd been by the house to see the room, and there was his rambling on about the house and the lease, so it wasn't like she hadn't been forthcoming.

"Well, my landlord informed me and my roommate we had to be out by the end of the month," she tells him.

It's only a few days from the end of the month, he notes.

"Wow," he says.

Deidre nods. "Yeah," she says, "we got word nearly halfway to the end of the month, that's when we were given this notice."

That seems to be everything he'll learn about it because she has stopped.

But after a moment, as Davin is about to get back to his news, she tells him she and her roommate were plenty annoyed by the notice, but in a way, it hadn't really surprised her because it was just another instance of what has been happening to a lot of people she knows.

"Just one more homeowner changing the use of apartment for short-term rentals. He wanted us out early so he could fix up the place, which I'll tell you, seems kind of like a Herculean task, the poor shape of the house outside and in," she says, shrugging, and then she looks up at Davin, blushing. "I mean, I don't have anything against Airbnb, and I love your house, I love that there's a lot of space, a lot of yard...."

Davin smiles and waves away any concern she might have. "No problem," he tells her. "Anyone who uses the term *Herculean* is good in my book."

She smiles.

"The short-term rental situation is a problem," he then adds. "I hear you. It's just that these days with costs all up sometimes it's an important piece of, the, uh, Berkshire Shuffle, right? That term still used?" *Berkshire Shuffle* was a colloquial phrase for the amalgam of part-time and second or third jobs a lot of people in the Berkshires were forced to pursue in order to make ends meet.

She smiles, then grins. "Oh yeah," she says.

"The house is big," Davin continues, "and it makes sense that more people use it, so house shares helps cover costs too, not" — and he is for a moment flustered—not that there's any danger of losing the house or anything, but there is still some work I'd like to do with the property."

Deidre nods.

Davin turns back to his laptop. Climate change is one of his alert filters, and greenhouse gases a selected subtopic, so he's looking at a story in *The Washington Post* that has been following various NGOs' efforts on the carbon tax bill that's been mutating in the halls of Congress, although *stillborn* might be the better description, considering the state of Congress. Still, the mid-terms are coming up and there's a lot of speculation about one or the other side of Congress slipping back under Democratic control.

Davin's not a Democratic, but he sure hopes this happens. Trump's first two years this second time around have been even more chaotic than before, with his loyalist appointees commuting by clown car.

All news, including climate change news, has been hard for him to follow since the 2024 elections.

As if to prove his point, there's a story in his feed that seems atypically sensational—a murder of a fossil fuel divestiture activist, a VP at Carbon's End, a spin-off or new division of ClimateProgress.Org, or at least he's pretty sure ClimateProgress.Org spawned it. He has an old colleague who switched over to climate technology and who may have had some connection to ClimateProgress.Org, although Davin knows that sometimes he doesn't listen too closely when his friend gets going on the subject of his work.

He more certainly knows he's got to do more work on the news filters because too many off-focus climate change–related news items are getting into the hit results, and he's been spending too much time reviewing all of them, even if it's just a fast skimming. The new AI feature is supposed to help by learning from the items he reads and rejects, and by judging duration of the read too, and by noting click-throughs, among many other factors, but as with a lot of other software and apps, he resents all the time it takes to purportedly save himself time and become more efficient.

Artificial, yes, he tells himself, *intelligent, not so much.*

The feed filter is natural language processing based, which Davin thinks he understands.

This AI needs a talking to, a joke he makes on a regular basis.

He clicks on the Response button for this murder story, and chooses *Ignore,* so the AI doesn't get the wrong idea. He goes back to the results list, and a few topic headings down in the feed there's a story about agricultural markets affected by the ongoing western droughts, and he thinks to suggest to Alicia that she be on the lookout for someone who can report on local agriculture since there's been an increase in active farms in the region, but then again, it's not his ambition to take the farm beat, which just might happen if he starts suggesting this sort of coverage.

He checks his email and notices he has new ones, and since he's been actively advertising the second house share and is still thinking of taking in a third house share, he's curious to see the newest responses. He'll hold off on the third house share for a while though, because his son Jimmy is getting out of Chicago mainly because the city is in what looks to be a prolonged heat wave, one of those crazy one- thousand-year weather patterns that happen more and more. He assumes Jimmy won't likely stay long, liking being on his own, but his son may be running out of money after getting laid off.

Davin will play it by ear on the third house share, considering the odd economic times, and Jimmy could well be around for some time. *Family first,* he thinks, even if the divorce has confused that guiding principle. Gwen's new place in Lenox is small, so there's no real option other than to have Jimmy stay with him.

Davin is glad about that.

He sees there are two new responses about the house

share, but the first, from some guy named Willy, has little to offer, including the lack of a last name or any answer to either of the two questions Davin posted in the listing, which has him wondering, yet again, if people even read these days. On the other hand, the second inquiry is more interesting, with the email in good form and the content on target. He'll reply to this one, letting the person know the offer's been filled but that he's happy to keep her on file if something comes up.

Davin sighs, and then stretches in the chair, his arms thrown widely, and slowly.

Alicia is still on the phone, trying to sell more ads to an event venue, if Davin's eavesdropping skills are on point. All he is really listening for, however, is for Alicia to end the call, so they can get on with the business at hand, which is the attempt by Alicia to talk Davin into taking on an editorial role.

He's tempted for the income, considering the consulting he's doing for *SCI* these days is mainly tweaks of feed structures for the platform, mainly because the platform has matured. There's the ad sales–related bonus payout, which, while growing, is still modest and his share will only likely grow modestly, accordingly.

And the Airbnb, he reminds himself, annoyed this is not now an active listing, waiting on repairs. He hadn't and won't make an insurance claim on the damage, as much as he can use the money for the renovation, but he doesn't want to flag flood damage with the home insurance. A big increase in home insurance for some policy holders, mainly concentrated on Florida and California, has made national news any number of times, but the insurance companies are more and more on the lookout for flood danger everywhere, and he knows of several people right here in Housatonic who have houses close to the river now paying in big bucks these days.

The last time he looked at the water damage, he had seen some of the damage had gone into the apartment's small bedroom's back wall where it shared a common wall with the bathroom. The contractor Davin hopes to settle on keeps getting delayed in his start, and this could very well become a bigger project with some mold remediation. It's this sort of thing, the unexpected cost, that can make him wonder just why exactly he bought out Gwen's share of the house instead of them just selling the damn thing.

Money does seem always short, and thus *Davin Caine, Cub Reporter*, he muses, knowing he'll let Alicia talk him into taking an editorial role, although he remains concerned there won't be much of any income from it.

He turns back to his Google News feed, looking to see how the Red Sox's early season struggles are going, but then Alicia steps out of her office, so he swivels in his office chair and points at her. "Alicia Soares, *SCI* Publisher"—he points to Deidre— "Deidre." And then he stops still. "Uh," he says, feeling embarrassed.

"Deidre Gustavson," Deidre says as she stands up, her hand out. "I'm the new roommate." She nods toward Davin.

"*House sharer*, he likes that term," Alicia says, but she still has Deidre's hand in hers and is looking at her, and for a weirdly long time, Davin can't help thinking.

Chapter 12: Cyn City

Cyn had thought the desert was hot, but Las Vegas seemed to be winning that particular bet hands down. She's been off the bus, walking around, popping into various casino restaurants and hotel lobbies for the last four hours, keeping cool and burning through her cash on hand to do so.

The sky is bizarre, although she knows it's due to the wildfires to the northwest, probably that major burn in southern Idaho that's been in the news for weeks, although she can't keep track of the name given to this one, and anyway, she knows the names can change because of the spread. *Payout?* A National Park or Forest, she's pretty sure. All she can recall with any confidence is the area on fire is not that far north of Boise.

The smoke pall northwest of Vegas is heavy, but the sunset, she'll admit, sitting on her streetside perch, is rather spectacular.

See the sunset, see the world, she tells herself, but there's little cheer in her thought. She's not in a good mood, that is for sure, and now back on the streets downtown, she recognizes she may have really messed up in not going to the police here. But the stories of Joe's murder that started showing up some hours ago are freaking her out. She had grown too antsy, too disturbed, to stay longer in the Internet café where she'd gone online to check what news there might be.

Especially disturbing is the news about the gun said to have been used to kill Joe. It hadn't been found in his rental car with the speculation in some stories that she might still have it, which is nothing anybody would want to read, especially because there was her photo, too, right on the screen of the desktop she'd rented for an hour. The picture's source is not cited, but she remembers all too well that particular self-portrait, the image she had used for her Bumble profile before that dating site collapsed.

And then, there in the middle of all those desktop stations — fortunately not crowded, a minor blessing — her thoughts had gone to all those awful puns among various headlines in reference to Bumble's bankruptcy, mostly along the lines of colony collapse. She's been trying to track all the different things she's thinking about and found it of some interest she'd been flooded by these old headline jokes.

Sitting in a pocket of shade in the long light of the late afternoon, she's still trying to chase all the stuff that pops in and out of her head, distracting with a vague curiosity, and then she finds herself thinking, *Jesus, only Vegas would still have an Internet café*, and then she tells herself, yet again, *There's no fucking gun*, and she tells herself this yet another time, and then again, as if she herself needs convincing.

She knows there was no gun, of course, and neither Joe nor she had ever owned one.

Well, she tells herself, there was clearly a gun. She saw it go off, killing Joe. But she tells herself yet again, *I've never had a gun*.

And then there's the suggestion in some of the news, some implication t h a t the killing could be related to a relationship gone bad and the references in the news stories that phone texts may help explain what happened. So far though, she's found no story with quotes of the so-called texts showing up, but she expects such coverage will emerge. She also expects her mental health history, all those times in therapy, will show up, but so far, nothing.

HIPA hip hooray, fingers crossed, she thinks.

In point of fact, she's usually proud of the work she'd done in therapy over time, although she's not so proud about a few recent failings.

Like sleeping with my boss, she thinks, for what seems a

million times already today.

This was one of the thoughts poking at her sitting there in the Internet cafe, her hour rental winding down, but that repeating shame had been replaced by the sudden dawning that the stories she'd been coming across, in some of the news articles anyway, seemed both too advanced and rather too specific, considering Joe was killed early this morning, only this morning, and here she is, sitting on a concrete ledge, early sunset, *a hop, skip, and buzzy bumble away*. She tries to think this through, but she keeps going in and out of focus, and now back outside in the heat of the waning day, she's noticing again that she seems to have lost chunks of time someplace.

She feels exhausted.

She keeps trying to focus on her situation.

There's no fucking text, she tells herself, still very confused about the phantom texts she—and she has no doubt, Joe— never sent this morning. *Except that I did send that text*, she says to herself, thinking about her last one, *Where R U?* with the declaration that she was already at the meeting, but the only thing she's sure about at this point is how goddamn confused and tired and completely lost she feels. And then she is considering the actual texts she'd sent Joe in the last month, and earlier, and those received from him, and she's convinced she'd been less than discreet, nor had Joe been careful.

The dick pic he'd sent her a couple of weeks back she had kept, still not deleted.

She had cracked up about it then, thinking it was a bit pathetic, but funny too. She had asked him if he thought it was sexy, but he had claimed it as just a joke.

There's a picture of Joe's penis on my phone, Cyn admits to herself. *In the cloud.*

She wonders who at the office is being interviewed and what they know.

And what they will find out, she wonders, too.

She settles down on the low wall, part of a bank's street-facing area where the bench-high concrete circle encloses a big planting of tall tropical foliage, and this spot provides some cover from the heat and prying eyes, and she leans back and closes her eyes, trying to empty her mind.

Shit shit shit, in a seemingly endless string, is what she thinks instead, her effort to calm her thoughts collapsing as another wave of shame and embarrassment and fear crests. She just wants to hide, disappear, become someone else, become gone.

She opens her eyes, leans forward.

She does the math and is shocked to see it hasn't even been twelve hours.

There are moments when she thinks she's thinking clearly, including that even half a day is enough to get on her trail, although she'd figured out she needs to use cash, and that this might be helping her stay under the radar. She is pretty sure that they — *Jesus! They? Who? FBI?* — might know she's in Las Vegas, or at least might be, and then she begins again to worry about cameras and CCTV, and she's up and moving in the now dimming light, the neon and incandescent signs and marquees starting to reclaim their rightful attention as the sun drops low. She loses herself in her fierce concentration to walk without twisting all around to see where cameras might be, and then she's surprised to see she's now in a coffee shop with what looks like a milkshake in front of her, but then she remembers the concoction she had ordered is a *macchiato,* and she's even more surprised she's looking across the street at the bus station, the light failing, and she's singing, inside her head, that stupid kid's song fragment, and then she's back again, remembering to go over her plan again.

Check schedule, use ATM, buy cash bus ticket. Get gone.

She sees a police car, and then another, pull up across the street, lights flashing, and pairs of cops getting out of each car, and for a moment one seems to be looking right at her where she sits near the coffee shop's plate window, and the others join him, and she knows it's done and over and out and she's about to be arrested, and she starts to collect her things, but when she glances back at the police they are disappearing in a rush into the bus station. She sits fully back down and doesn't even taste the drink in front of her that she's started mindlessly sucking at through a drinking straw.

She wonders if the police are waiting for her or maybe searching for her.

She stares out the window but starts at the sudden flurry of motion, two police manhandling a black man, the man handcuffed, and right behind them emerge the two other cops, one following the first pair on to the sidewalk with the other cop stopping a step or two from the entrance doors. That cop, she notices now, is talking with a man holding something to his head.

Not me, she thinks. *They aren't here for me*, she tells herself, but the feeling accompanying the thought is flat.

She decides she'll call the office when she gets to Chicago and ask for help.

All she has to do now, she thinks, is not keep going back to wherever she goes in all those empty missing minutes.

Chapter 13: Dark Web, Spider and Fly

It takes a moment for Dennis Jymsom to calm himself down since the ringtones of his two phones are similar, and he first considered it must be Jean Paul calling since Dennis has been expecting it, and it feels like his expectation has somehow made the phone ringtone sound, but he's glad to see that instead it's his other, newest phone ringing.

Dennis had just gotten the new phone two days before, right on the tenth day of every month, just like clockwork. His handler always punctual, always reliable, and if he's calling there must be a job in the offing.

In the offing, Dennis repeats to himself, his laugh a shambling breath escaping through his lips, the very same lips that whore had asked him about, laughing, laughing at him, and he's annoyed he can't use any of Jean Paul's girls anymore, or at least he's pretty sure since he's pretty sure Jean Paul really doesn't appreciate the damage done.

But then she shouldna laughed, but Dennis figures there wouldn't be much point trying to explain what happened to Jean Paul, *that asshole*, and Dennis doesn't really care. *Fuck him*, except Jean Paul will probably want to do something about it, having to be seen by his whores to care, to protect them.

A day late and a dollar short on that, Dennis thinks, but he's swiping the burner to talk and sure enough it's Carl, but that's a stupid thing to think, Dennis realizes, because like, *who would it be?*

"Yeah," Dennis says into the phone. He hates these phones with their flat screens, thin, hard to hold, and he's always accidentally touching some stupid thing on the screen that kills the call or mutes it, and he's always having trouble getting the phone just right, so he can hear and the person calling can hear him, and it's like the assholes who designed these things insist on hiding where the hell you're supposed to speak into, and he prefers speaker calls for that reason, but he never uses the speaker thing with Carl's phones, another rule from Carl.

Mostly these phones get used for the text, getting addresses and updates from Carl, or *fucking shit*, his having to thumb some goddamn code or message back, not even in real English, mostly, but that's another one of those rules of Carl's.

One-Name Carl, Dennis thinks, only half-listening. He had asked Carl about this, the guy's last name, that one time meeting him, but the look from Carl that went along with him ignoring the question made Dennis asking that particular question *a one and done*.

"A job came up, a good one for you," is what Carl is saying on the phone, although Dennis misses some of it, trying to get the phone so it's placed right so he can hear clearly.

"Yeah," is what Dennis says.

"A little different procedure on this one," Carl now says, and that gets Dennis's attention because Carl is very big on procedure and very big on procedure not changing.

The whole procedure thing, that one time only of face-to-face with Carl, who had turned out to be a big fat fuck of a black guy and who had spent half the afternoon going over how everything worked, how everything was going to work with him taking Dennis on.

That was the afternoon he had learned about the Dark Web from Carl, and how Carl had some sort of thing on it where jobs would come in, get arranged, terms, times, that sort of thing. Dennis had wanted to make a joke about *The Darky Web,* but he figured he had better not with Carl being so serious.

Dennis doesn't really care about that, the race thing, it's just kind of how he was brought up. His father had been wild about that sort of thing and for a long time Dennis had been afraid of his father, *the asshole*, although that had worked itself out.

Fucking A, it did.

He knows plenty of black people, *Afro-Americans*, which of course, doesn't make a difference to him. He likes black whores as much as the white ones, although he does have a thing for Asians, and probably because the Asian ones tend to be small and Dennis is bothered by his being small and slight, but he's not one to think closely about such things if he can help it.

That fucking whore, what, Jazzy, Jasmine, some shit name like that, shouldn't have said anything about my fucking lips, is what Dennis is thinking even though Carl is saying more.

"Yeah, sorry, missed what you said, these fucking phones," Dennis says to Carl.

Dennis can almost hear Carl's expression, the staring bulging eyes, face all gone quiet like Dennis is the biggest fucking disappointment in the world.

Or maybe not because Carl just repeats what he'd just been saying, Dennis is pretty sure. What he is saying would need repeating anyway because Dennis is surprised about the procedure change.

And it's good money, even if Dennis suspects Carl takes more than his agreed-upon percentage, and that he could cite one price to Dennis but charge a higher one. Dennis has no way of knowing because payment comes through Carl from the customer, some other thing about the Dark Web, something about bit coins, *whatever the fuck that is*, but Dennis doesn't care. He gets paid in cash, usually dropped off, handed off, by that guy who works for Carl, the guy who sometimes brings over packages for the jobs, the guy who drops off the new monthly phone.

"It's a premium," Carl tells Dennis, and Dennis is surprised by the high pay offer, and he's thinking about the money, what he can do with it, including using some of it to pay off Jean Paul for pulping up his whore. *Not that she was all that pretty to begin with. Definitely not pretty after anyway.*

But guys like Jean Paul can get pissy about that sort of

thing, and Dennis likes hanging out in New Orleans, and he'd just as soon not have to worry about Jean Paul sending some sort of lesson his way.

"What?" Dennis says into the phone.

"I said you'll be reporting direct to the client, using your current phone, email only, same language protocol."

Jesus, thinks Dennis, *protocol*. But Dennis knows what Carl is saying, which is that even when Dennis is reporting to or calling Carl, the usual thing is that you never use names, or talk about the real thing, but instead use other words that will be clear enough if you know what's what. It's an evidence thing, that's what Carl has stressed, how records of calls, or texts or emails, nothing is absolutely safe, nothing ever really disappears, so just in case.

Dennis has had a few close calls doing what he does, or did anyway on his own, before Carl, and that's one reason he puts up with Carl's odd ways.

Dennis isn't interested in going back to prison. The hard juvie stint for assaulting his father with a baseball bat was enough for him to know that.

Plus, the work is better, and so what if *Carl the Big Black Frog* may be taking a bigger cut than he says. The targets are better researched, unlike how he used to do it when he sometimes just got a name, maybe a photo, maybe an address. He'd found out hard that some of those assholes had their own people for protection, and he was an up-close sort of guy with maybe sometimes rifles too, but using explosives, that was a great way to get caught because where do you get explosives?

From fucking feds or other dicks out to trap. No thank you.

And then with Carl there's real advance money, so he's never shelling out his own for expenses—his previous way of working having gone south on him twice. The first time this happened was because the fucking target had died before he had any helping it along, and one other time after all the cost and bother he'd gone through already, the client was, like, *teasing, never mind*, and that fucking client himself was plenty protected and had just laughed at him when he complained about his costs and getting zip.

He'd sworn he'd never let that happen again.

To go through all that trouble and end up with *fucking zilch*.

And with Carl, the pay is definitely better, which is decidedly a good thing.

"I'll send the package over shortly, if you want the job," Carl says.

Dennis is surprised, thinking he must have already said yes, but he's having some trouble concentrating. The whore's face keeps swimming into his thoughts.

Do you wear lipstick?

What a thing for her to say to him, was the first thing he had thought, and then that had exploded into that rage he gets sometimes.

But Dennis needs to put this out of mind and tell Carl he's happy to take the job and could he get another set of his favorite foods and some pantry supplies, meaning the Smith & Wesson model he likes and ammunition.

Carl tells him he's got a train to catch, and there will be a driver, and he's to go to the private airfield they've used before and he'll be dropped in time to get on the train, and all the details will be in the package the driver is bringing.

"No problem dating a woman, correct?" asks Carl. "Even if you have to wine and dine in that special way."

So, it's definitely a kill job, Dennis is happy to learn, although there are apparently special instructions in the package about the how, maybe the when too, he's supposed to take care of the woman.

Killing a chick, a dude, doesn't matter to him, both have their benefits.

After he tells Carl he can date any number of women, Dennis adds, adding an exaggerated emphasis on the stupid code word, "I gotta take care of my *pantry*," but that only seems to annoy Carl, who sighs, like he's dealing with a moron.

"Things are all there with the driver, when he gets there

in"—and there's a pause—"about twenty minutes, so scramble, it's a hot date."

Fuck you asshole, is what Dennis says silently, his thin bright lips slightly moving.

And that's the call.

Euphemism. That's the word, Dennis remembers later.

Chapter 14: Broke as a Joke

The so-called Heat Wave Riots, now plural as Detroit and a couple of other Rust Belt cities flare along with what's going on in Chicago, has made it hard for Jimmy Caine, proud college graduate, to keep in touch with the folks. Although the coal trains are apparently again on the move, the news says it may be another day or two before the coal will feed the hungry old power plants that have been in stand-by mode for the past few years, which means there's most likely another day or two or three of spotty water and power and unreliable telephone and Internet.

Or it may be even longer, as he's read one news report saying the coal may be further delayed because the power utility company or maybe more than one, needs clarification from the Feds. Jimmy can't name the agency but would guess it could be the EPA or maybe DOE. He is unsure of the agency, because another brownout had caused a reboot, and by the time he was back online, he didn't bother trying to re-find the news article. For the life of him, he can't name with confidence even the name of the company claiming the delay is beyond its control.

His dad had seemed to know more about this when they talked in their most recent telephone conversation, but that's the sort of topic his dad tends to fixate on. Or used to, anyway, before the last election, but he suspects that his dad's news reading is back up to standard, or even more so with the current administration's multitudinous escapades.

All Jimmy clearly understands is that it could too easily be far much more than two days until there's enough power to make life in Chicago bearable, and he reminds himself to check this out online, nail down the details, the names, the agencies, but he suspects he won't bother since he's already made up his mind. He has to prioritize important information since if he catches the right cell tower in between brownouts, he can get through, but trying to predict any pattern is less useful than simply repeatedly trying the cellphone. Phone and Internet is all rather catch-as-catch-can. He scans the news when he's able, and his sense is that things are likely to be a mess for a while still.

For one thing, people—including himself—are very reluctant to do without air-conditioning when the high reaches, as it does today, just under 110 degrees Fahrenheit, and as everyone knows, it isn't the heat, it's the humidity. He also thinks this joke is a lot less funny than he would like. Having lived in Chicago four undergraduate years and then a plus-one, he knows all about the Midwest humidity in summertime. Not that it's all that close to being officially summer yet, but it sure as hell feels like it, and then some.

He's sitting in his underwear in front of the window AC, and he tries to convince himself he's doing great with it being only ninety-four degrees, plus or minus, inside his apartment. It's his AC unit, together with the many hundreds of thousands of other ones, that has put the grid into the periodic stress that results in the rolling brownouts.

Of course, what had shut everything down for quite a while was when the utilities tried to bring in more Canadian hydropower, but that had only managed to trip some relays, bringing the city's grid down for thirteen hours the day before.

Yesterday's blackout is one reason he's sitting in a ninety-four-degree swamp of an apartment, the current temperature now lower than the ninety-eight degrees it got to inside as the sun beat against the bed sheet shades covering the large windows and behind the makeshift curtain that for hours had hung unmoving in the silence of the powerless AC in the one window that had a workable sash.

His frequent glasses of watered-down lemonade seem to shed as much fluid from condensation as they deliver into his sweating body. He's taken to wiping up the pools of water rings on the crappy desk he has his laptop and second monitor sitting on. He's using the dishcloth as a mop rag, and then he drapes the damp towel over his neck. Too bad the towel has not been washed of late, and he notices yet again its unpleasant tang. Hardly the only bad smell, he knows. He would love to take another shower, but the mayor has asked that people keep these to once a day, so okay.

He's looked up train schedules, figuring he's a big strong fellow and can walk to the El and ride to the train station and catch a ride out of this crazy weather system and into the cool safe arms of Daddo and get to see Mom too at her place in Stockbridge. He'll take his important stuff, which, because he's always traveled light, will be manageable. The futon and small stock of furniture he and his roommates collected over the better part of this year will be abandoned, and he's sorry the monitor will be left behind, but then again it's getting wonky, and he suspects its internal power supply subsystem has gotten damaged by all the power fluctuation over the past days.

Jimmy has less regret and guilt about leaving things behind than about abandoning his lease obligation. He just doesn't have money for his bills, and he'd been feeling bad about the position this would put his roommates in, but then the two had precipitously decamped to their own families' homes in the Chicago suburbs, and he's left wondering if they're permanently gone from here too.

It had been a fun apartment, near enough his former campus to let him enjoy pretending to still be a student when it suited him, but also well-located for CTA, which was great for his commute to the first post-college job he had landed, doing code QA, tedious work, but it would look good on the résumé, and he thought it paid well, which never hurt. What did hurt, as it turned out, was his getting laid off, along with more than half his group—the company-wide layoff close to forty percent of all employees. The word was pretty much the same across the town, although he had undertaken some half-hearted résumé submissions for a while.

And it was too bad that unemployment benefits were modest, but even that assistance was pointless to complain about now, at least until Congress got off its collective ass and passed the unemployment reauthorization bill that would put more money into the kitty. Nobody gets anything when there's nothing there to give.

Still, it had been a fun couple of months since the layoff, although the rate of drop in his bank balance had grown alarming, and then this heat wave hit.

"Goddamnit!" Jimmy shouts as a new brownout occurs, always just like that, causing the big monitor that is connected to his laptop to blink and then shut off. "Enough of this shit," he says, taking the towel and mopping up the rings.

He sees that the glass is empty.

Just like this former optimist would think.

Chapter 15: Cyn's Train of Thought

She's managed to get to Union Station from her old camp friend's place off Jackson Street, an old office building right in downtown Chicago that had been redeveloped as co-ops. Fortunately, Union Station had been close. Her cash, even supplemented by Sandra, is tight almost to the point of nonexistent, and that meant walking instead of hailing a cab. She can't risk using her credit card with Uber or one of those electric scooter things, and she sure as hell isn't going to use her credit card to buy the train ticket.

She's grateful she got to sleep at Sandra's apartment, not that staying asleep was what happened, even in the comfort of the gray couch. Still, she's feeling better.

Jesus, it's hot, she thinks, and she shifts her right thigh, half expecting her leg to stick to the gummy finish of the wooden bench in the train station's huge central waiting room.

She had changed into her hiking clothes. Her office outfit, courtesy of Sandra's laundry, is clean and fresh, rolled and tucked into her backpack.

There's morning sun streaming through the station's high windows, but already the surrounding buildings are moving the station into shade, the morning sun easing behind them.

Her camping outfit is better for the heat and better for the look, but just a half an hour's time away from Sandra's air-conditioned co-op, and she already counts as another one of very many who look bedraggled, who haul backpacks and suitcases and stuffed-full black garbage bags that pull and stretch the plastic, soft bundles that could be anything. These black bags sag long downward in the heat.

Old men's scrotums, she finds herself thinking when she

sees a woman of indiscriminate age carry one such garbage bag across the street, her arm out almost straight, the bag suspended as far away from the woman as strength allows, for whatever reason. *Full diapers?* Cyn wonders but thinks nothing further of it once the woman passes out of view.

Las Vegas had seemed full of the homeless, maybe even as many homeless as San Francisco, but here in Chicago, while there are signs of homelessness, the heat that's been bearing down on the city is probably keeping most in the shadows.

Welcome to the club, she tells herself.

Cyn feels bad about Sandra, her just showing up like that, and Sandra giving her cash too. Sandra, she had known for almost fifteen years, meeting at horse camp starting at age ten, although maybe it had been the second summer when Sandra had first shown up, and they became camp friends forever. If, she figures, not having had contact for three or almost four years still qualifies as *friends forever*.

But it does as it turned out. The last time she and Sandra had emailed was just after college when they both excitedly shared with each other the plans they had, with Sandra winning in the grown-up department by taking a real job. Cyn remembers the twinge of envy at the news of Sandra having landed back in her hometown of Chicago and buying an apartment. Cyn, when receiving the news, of course, had assumed Sandra received help from her folks, and seeing Sandra's place for the first time yesterday, she now assumes this must have represented a whole lot of help. Buying one of the new co-op apartments that had started filling up the once desolate State Street stretch below Jackson couldn't be cheap, and this does seem like a great location as claimed the last missive she had received from Sandra some years ago.

She still feels guilty for not emailing back, or texting at least.

She can't think of why she hadn't, and that had to have been four years ago, she realizes. A bit more, she concludes, after doing the math.

But yesterday the two of them had fallen right back into

it, Sandra excited to see Cyn waiting in the co-op lobby, a huge surprise, judging by her reaction, but a welcomed one.

Of course, the timing could not have been any worse, at least for being in Chicago, the heat still crushing the city, sirens heard far and wide, and another of the riot sort of thing, albeit the news reporting it was a small one, again down South Side.

Thank god the lobby was air-conditioned. Thank god the security desk had decided to believe her story about being an old friend of Sandra's, despite her rather grubby, much-traveled look, and there had been some eyeballing of the backpack. But then again, a lot of people looked withered in this weather.

Thank god the security desk was manned by a guy who was happy to flirt with her, and who had been, quite honestly, quite solicitous, even calling her over to watch the special report on that day's riot. That update had been followed by two other news features she'd found notable. The first had "Heat Watch: Chicago" up on the greenscreen backdrop, complete with a glaring sun and thermostat and what was basically a death counter, now up to 462. Lingering, she had then watched "The Grid Report," which featured a stylized map of the Chicago metro area with colored overlays denoting the health or lack thereof of electrical service. Upon viewing, both news segments had struck her as being long part of the local news routine as unlikely as that must have been.

Thank god Sandra had showed up right about when the security guy, his shift ending, had suggested she could go hang with him.

Sandra looked great, especially if you happened to like the junior executive look, which Cyn had no problem with since there were plenty of times she had donned the look herself at Carbon's End, like when they were out meeting with companies when pitching the divestment campaign. Like the very clothes she had been wearing, although all the past day or so had significantly countered the put-together look.

Sandra was looking great, if perhaps a little plump, and had stepped out of a big black SUV that turned out to be part of her company's hire fleet but now being used to get people to work and back without their keeling over as Sandra joked later when explaining the specifics of her arrival. Sandra had then added that maybe it was all simply to keep body odor down to a minimum at the office. It was usually a ten-minute walk, she'd explained, but she had confessed the ride was really a necessity. Cyn couldn't dispute Sandra's point, herself having walked the fourteen blocks or so from the Greyhound station. By the time the Las Vegas bus had rolled into the terminal, the morning was half gone, and the temperature had slid upward past 100 degrees. She had had to stop twice on her trek to Sandra's place, once in the dark shade of a building just to catch her breath and rest and once going into a Starbucks to spend money she would have rather held on to for a water bottle and an iced coffee concoction and a seat in the interior that had proved barely cooler than the outside temperature.

It had taken her three hours to make the hike to Sandra's place with the two breaks and otherwise slow-walking the sidewalks and repeatedly crossing the streets as needed to keep to the shadow sides. It was early afternoon by the time she'd come to the right address and the blessed lobby air-conditioning.

After the nearly four-hour wait, Sandra's arrival had been without doubt a most miraculous sight for her, and very much high drama with the big car pulling up to the lobby entrance and Sandra stepping out of the air-conditioned vehicle, and with the accumulation of only a hint of moisture on her forehead as she stepped through the revolving doors into the building's air- conditioning.

And then a cop car had gone screaming past the building, cutting off the SUV pulling back out on to State Street, and unbidden, everyone's heads turned to look at the strobing blur, and Sandra was screaming and throwing her arms out when she spotted Cyn rising from one of the lobby's armchairs.

The apartment was nice, smaller than Cyn had imagined, but nicely and comfortably furnished, and most importantly, a cool eighty degrees and free from brownouts due to the big solar spread across much of the building's roof and some sort of backup system Sandra didn't know anything else about. Cyn assumed there must be a PV-fed battery storage or independent generator, but she didn't need any further explanation, could wait until after she, at Sandra's welcomed suggestion, had changed out of her grimed and stinky garment and underthings to be spun and tossed in Sandra's compact laundry closet.

She had taken a long shower after the laundry was put in.

Cold and delicate cycle, of course, Cyn had insisted, which had made her laugh hysterically once she was in the safe cool wash of the shower.

Cyn felt clean and comfortable sitting on Sandra's sofa, a state of existence that felt long absent, and this helped her enormously. Although, sitting there, she had found herself again thinking about where she would go, and this revived her anxiety, but she stuck with the story about visiting friends in Boston. She thinks she had convinced Sandra of the misdirection.

But then, she herself is still working on figuring out where she can go, sitting here in the train station, knowing she needs some place where she can control herself, take stock, and make the contact she knows she must. Probably to the office, yes, although she gets flushed by such strong surges of panic.

The one phone call she'd made hadn't helped.

She figures Great Barrington is where she'll head, hopefully back to the house where she'd stayed for those two weeks organizing for the march back in her Sierra Club days. She's hoping she can just show up at Patel's place. He had been, after all, so nice and so welcoming and had plenty of room, and he had become something of a friend during the short time he'd hosted her.

That time in Great Barrington now seems an entirely separate lifetime ago.

A quiet simplicity. This phrase keeps coming into Cyn's thoughts. This is what she longs for.

Her plan, as far as she can think it through at least, is to go to ground there, and then she can figure out the next thing. She's confident her Great Barrington connections and all the contacts she'd made remained too ephemeral with little if any trace that could be flagged across social media.

She had never so much as emailed Patel afterward.

She smiles thinking of Patel's home, his laid-back manner, his best assumptions he had always seemed to have about her. Patel is the best plan she can come up with, although the plan feels far too tenuous.

She tries to relax, but it's stifling in the huge train station waiting area. It's crowded, and her efforts to rest are interrupted by her worry she hadn't successfully hidden her distraction from Sandra the evening before. She had kept thinking about what to do and obsessing about what had happened even while she made an effort to present a reasonable facsimile of catching up with Sandra, or trying anyway.

It hadn't been easy. At one point while she was sitting on the soft gray couch facing Sandra across an oddly worn coffee table with some unopened mail scattered on the surface, she had fixated on an issue of *Vogue* lying there. A *big slab*, that was how she had thought of the magazine at that moment. She had been sitting there and Sandra was saying something, and she had had to tear herself away from thinking the magazine *is a slab*.

She had then said, "Yeah," apropos nothing.

"I know, right?" Sandra had replied. "I mean Daniel and I dated since high school, me a sophomore and him Mr. Senior, but you know, not so weird out in the suburbs, right?"

"Yeah," she had said again, which was all it took for Sandra to go on explaining the demise of her long-term relationship with the boyfriend.

"Everyone thought we were going to get married, I mean, not early on, like my parents were so, such hawks around Daniel, always thinking like we are going to be having sex. It was pretty funny, really, like they acted so Sex Patrol."

"Yeah," Cyn had said again, but she'd found herself now

mostly thinking about the coffee table. Its worn corners and scratched surface seemed so out of place with the rest of the furnishings, which were all new.

"We kept going out, mostly uninterrupted, all through college, everyone expecting we would get married when I graduated."

"Yeah, so," she said.

"I know," Sandra responded before trudging on. "It was like I'm going to take the HR job at Dad's company, well, he's a partner, and then marry Daniel, and all nice and neat."

She had then looked up from the coffee table and saw Sandra was shaking her head. *Going to cry*, she had thought with alarm.

But Sandra barked out a sharp laugh, and she saw Sandra looking at her.

"Yeah," said Cyn.

"He was *so* boring," Sandra continued, and then with a grin, "but of course, there are a few things I miss."

She had become worried she was coming across as one big blank. She felt blank, and it felt like Sandra was chattering in a different language. She had felt a surge of panic when she realized Sandra was giggling.

"Uh," she had said, concentrating on what she'd just been hearing. "So, he, um Daniel, you say you miss him?"

"No, but sex, like it's been a while, the new job position, so busy, although to tell you the truth he was kind of boring that way too." Sandra had giggled again and made a face.

Somehow this had given Cyn something to focus on, and she was asking Sandra about dating life in Chicago, but she was still having trouble really listening, the turn of her anxiety deep down below feeling like lead weight, and she had found herself thinking *What the fuck am I doing?* and the many variants of self- doubt and confusion were fighting for her attention with scrambling thoughts popping her up from the couch, and she had started to pace, trying to at least look as if she were listening to Sandra, who seemed quite content to talk, but then there was a change, a shift to interrogative.

"Um, sorry?" Cyn had said, stopping her pacing.

"Well, no, just, what about you, you seeing anyone?" Sandra then asked.

"Um, no," she had answered, stopping her pacing, but looking away. "Um, no, a breakup, but I'm over it, going to see an old boyfriend, in Boston." She was back scrambling, her thoughts racing, and she could hear herself say, *I've been fucking my boss but he got killed yesterday*, but she was actually making up a story about this old boyfriend, that they still liked each other, and as she was finishing up her second lap across the living room, Sandra had asked her another question.

"This Boston guy, is he married?"

It had taken Cyn a moment to process the question.

"No, no," she replied.

She and Sandra had been friends for a long time, but Cyn was surprised Sandra knows something, anything, about Cyn's relationships. Cyn hadn't ever talked much about it, as far as she can remember, but then she remembers that their last summer together she had come close to going off with the assistant head of camp, a twenty-nine-year-old newlywed.

Sam, she suddenly recalls.

Sandra had been an excited witness of it all until something serious seemed about to happen, and then Sandra had grown angry and had threatened to tell people if she was going to go through with it.

Sam had just laughed all of it off, and the next week camp had ended, and by then, for her and Sandra, it was all as if her flirtation with Sam had never happened.

She'd still been in contact with Sandra three years later while the Ohio State transfer had taken place, but she's pretty sure the thing with her professor hadn't ever been mentioned, but she might have, and she'd looked at Sandra, who was asking her if she was hungry.

It had taken Cyn a moment to process that question too, and to realize she was, in fact, starving.

"Yeah," Cyn answered, quite loudly, surprising herself. She realized as she did so, she had eaten the last of her granola bar earlier, down in the lobby, and that the bag with some baby carrots she'd been carrying had been beyond eating—too slimy. "Well," said Sandra, "you just relax. It will take about fifteen minutes. Glass of wine?"

Cyn had felt absurdly grateful for the ice-cold white wine Sandra opened and grateful for the break from having to pay attention or deflect questions. She took herself and the wine back across the living room, pulling the light curtains back from the glass balcony door to look out. The sun was way down on the horizon, darkness falling.

And then she remembered why she had never replied to Sandra. They had been keeping each other in the loop about post-college romances, and Cyn had asked after Daniel. More specifically, she recalled, she had asked after whether Sandra was happy with Danial and with the idea of getting married, and Sandra had snapped back a quick comment on Cyn's married men fixation, or something to that effect.

That was the last contact she'd had with Sandra, she at that very moment realized with certainty, standing close the co-op's large windows.

She could feel the heat on the other side of the balcony glass sliding door as she stood there sipping her wine, but it was just a reminder of heat, not a threat. For a minute or two she had tried to distract herself by looking for any sections of the El, knowing she was looking in the right direction, more or less southwest, but even the old low buildings closer to the El were high enough to hide the elevated tracks from the co-op's vantage.

There were, however, no buildings high enough to block an impressive number of columns of smoke maybe a hundred blocks down toward the southeast, the South Side, she was pretty sure. Then Cyn noticed, well over to the right and much closer, more smoke and sirens only barely audible through the glass of Sandra's co-op up on the twelfth floor, and then Cyn had noticed that most buildings around them were dark, including most of the big office towers. These looming buildings became harder and harder to see in the growing dusk with the air not just hazy but smoky too.

A nice time to be inside, she had been able to admit to herself. She kept looking back toward the South Side, and she could see as it got darker that flames were reflecting off the clouds of smoke or maybe just off lowering clouds.

And then dinner was served.

Chapter 16: Hot Under the Collar

Davin has no problem understanding the reality of the recently anointed DSM 7 diagnosis of *climate anxiety*, especially considering the disruptive amount of time he finds himself obsessed with climate news. Since the dismal 2024 election, he'd tried to curtail his news habit, but most recently, he's been worried for Jimmy out in Chicago, and his efforts to keep calm and moderate his news consumption have been failing. This has made him desperate for a shift in his attention, which is why his friends from Alford are over for dinner.

At the moment Tim and Wanda, husband and wife, are enjoying drinks on the front porch, Tim occasionally shouting a question or wisecrack back through the open front door into the kitchen where Davin is concentrating on cooking and getting dinner on the dining table.

He needs to concentrate when it comes to cooking, and he has sent Tim and Wanda off with their drinks so he can focus, but he takes a moment to ask Tim to go out to the back and let Chaplin know the meal will be on the table in a few minutes. Davin figures Chaplin will need the time to wash up from the garden work.

Davin is glad Jimmy's on his way back. He knows Jimmy would rather get another job, be on his own, stay out there in Chi Town, but unemployment is at a new high, Republicans and Democrats blaming each other for the economic woes. The Republicans — the fucking Trumpers, he can't help thinking, an almost automatic thought — on point to the trash the host of climate change legislation and a rash of social programs of the Biden administration, while Democrats blame the Republican tax cuts from a few years back that had shifted yet more money to the richest and biggest corporations and the ultra-wealthy, and the extension of such and new expansions that followed Trump's election. With their current minority status, the Democrats have failed any and every counteroffensive to keep new tax cuts minimal. There's growing talk about the tax cuts, though, as Democrats begin their efforts for the mid-terms.

The economy has been flickering between bursts of bull market and what some still call recession, although there is a new term he can't think of at the moment for the economic period the country has been in post-Covid and post-Ukraine. The interest rates are still high, although down from the peak in 2023.

His mutual fund retirement accounts have finally regained some small part of the big losses that had hit Wall Street, and he can only hope by the time he really needs the funds, they'll have fully recovered.

Yeah, right, he tells himself, before shutting down that bothersome line of thought. He knows he can get himself worked up thinking about such matters, and he'd been chronically disappointed in the lack of progress with the Democrats in power and outright frightened by the efforts of Trump to minimize the Infrastructure Act and IRA, and with lackluster support from his Congress, these smaller budgets mean than there's too little spending on what is needed. The problem, he thinks, is that those very same corporations and the extremely wealthy benefitting from the tax legislation passed in the first year of Trump's first administration and continued and expanded in Trump's second term continue to put that money to work making more money in the financial and corporate markets, mostly in the form of stock buybacks, with almost no discernable reinvestment toward jobs.

Or building actual shit, is what he thinks.

"Shit!" Davin shouts, pushing the lid off the saucepan as the rice starts boiling over. Wanda says something from the porch, but he lets her know all's well as he turns the heat down and stirs the pot. He takes a look at the chicken broiling in the oven and pulls the pan out to rest on some potholders next to the stove. He checks the rice again and puts the lid back on now that the rice is back down to a slow simmer.

He's already put four settings around the dining table in the adjacent room open to the kitchen. When he eats alone, or more recently, sometimes with Chaplin, he eats at the large kitchen island he had designed during the kitchen renovation. The island is certainly big enough to serve as a place to eat with five swiveled backed stools that make it a comfortable setup, but with guests he likes to use the dining table in the dining room, and this can be especially nice on days like this when that room's several windows let the late afternoon light in, along with the fifteen-light entry door to the side deck that brings in yet more light.

The dining table is still needed for large dinners and holiday meals. Having Wanda and Tim over doesn't make the dining room necessary, but these days, post-divorce, the dining table goes largely unused, now mostly assigned as a drop table collecting things, but he's trying to remind himself that big dinner parties remain possible.

Unfortunately, getting a nice dinner ready does nothing to stop his picking at his frustration with the political situation. He's been bugged by this all day. He keeps telling himself to stop checking the news so often, but he knows this is advice he's unlikely to heed.

Davin has been fixated on what he sees as the slow pace of the various and too modest green infrastructure initiatives, and now some are under assault. He still finds it hard to believe there can be the many millions of his fellow citizens who still think having a climate denier-in-chief is just dandy, but he also thinks the Climate Movement does a lousy job getting the right message across, mainly because they counterattack poorly, and they tend to be so doomsday in the climate effects projections even while too pollyannish about costs and solutions.

Well, no climate deniers, not in Chicago, not these days, he assumes. That whole region is experiencing an early season heat wave, and an unprecedented one that has been in the news the past two weeks. In the last two years, he has more often thought of the old movie *Idiocracy*, and reading about Chicago and the blame game on power failures proves no counter to this now regular attribution. The movie hadn't been particularly well made, he knows, but its prophetic quality has grown increasingly unnerving to him. It feels the country has been suffering from a long spell of stupidity, including that whole antivaxxer bullshit, not to mention Covid with the economy shutting down the Northeast early, and then by fall another stuttering stop just about everywhere, even while the Northeast took another hit as spring approached, and then there was the new variant.

He looks behind him to appraise the dinner settings and then steps to the table to adjust a wine glass and reposition the silverware to correct the placement of the salad and dinner forks.

Relax, pal, he tells himself and pours himself a bit of wine.

He really should not check on the state of the world, but the rice has a minute or two more, so he pulls out his phone and does just that. One of his recent obsessions is with a climate site that keeps an index of how well the range of market segments are coming into compliance with the Paris Agreement's CO_2 reductions goals defined by the International Energy Association. He figures this index is the one to track as it does a credible job defining necessary components for reaching net-zero by 2050.

Just six out of the fifty-five components of the global energy system are changing enough to contribute to net-zero global greenhouse gas emissions goals.

And here I am, worrying about whether I'll ever finish the three pieces sitting in my studio, he scolds himself.

He also knows moronic behavior isn't just on the national stage but is often writ small. Some of the more local challenges have become especially clear as he's been coming up to speed on a town warrant to be voted on at the next Town Meeting.

It's hard for him to fathom, but sure enough the NIMBYs and too many others are pushing back against the new solar farm proposal on grounds that include complaints the solar farm might spoil the pastoral view for some second-home owners.

Even here in the Berkshires, he thinks with a sigh.

On his way back to the stove he tells Wanda to come on in and that dinner is just about ready.

Stop and relax, he tells himself, but it all, everything feels nonstop. He's trying to shake his mood, and he does prefer to relax with friends rather than go down any number of rabbit holes the news—world, national, and local—provides on a constant basis.

He's back at the stove when Wanda comes in and asks if he's been getting into the studio at all, but his only answer is to close his eyes and groan.

She laughs.

"How's work?" she asks, but this question elicits another groan. Her husband is a social media consultant who's been extremely busy, and that makes Davin feel envious, even if he can't see ever wanting to do that kind of work.

Davin tells her he's mostly just doing work for *South County Interactive* and reminds her of the contract work he had gotten from an old colleague who'd had too much work, and how the work had proved something of a lifeline during the Covid shutdown and even beyond, during the divorce. She knows the story, but he can't help talking about the year of divorce with all the details and *i*'s to dot and *t*'s to cross, including having to take out a mortgage to buy Gwen's half-ownership. "Otherwise," he says, "work is pretty light. There were some white papers a couple of months ago," he adds with a shrug.

Wanda just smiles.

He tells her that of late, fortunately, there's more work for him with *South County Interactive*, and he feels like he has plenty to do and always has for that matter, for what feels like forever. "Especially with the various house projects that remain stubbornly numerous," he adds, forgoing the swear words he considers using.

She looks at him and takes a sip of her wine.

What he'd like to confess is that far too little of his time has involved enjoying using the studio, and what could have been a productive time in the studio for making art has somehow been overwhelmed by circumstances. He knows the last few years have been an unprecedented time, or so he keeps telling himself, but he's pretty sure he had been thinking that way even before those two years-plus of the pandemic.

Well, still going, he supposes, given the regular issue of vaccines and boosters for new variants he keeps track of.

At least the death rates had plummeted, he reminds himself.

Everyone had said the time of Covid was something to tell the grandchildren about, at least before that became something no one any longer said. His daughter has been in Europe seeking a postgraduate degree and married just before Covid, and so he's hardly seen her.

And no grandkids in the picture.

Davin sighs and spoons the rice into a serving bowl, and then he scrapes the steamed broccoli into another bowl and throws in a chunk from a stick of butter, tossing the broccoli half-heartedly before placing the bowl on the island. He's in the middle of plating the chicken when Tim comes through the porch from outside, stepping into the kitchen door to tell Davin that Chapin is heading in.

Tim checks out the food on the counter, and Davin feels like the dinner tonight is exactly what he needs, and he tries to make the effort to be in the moment. He pours himself a full glass, and then he's telling them about Jimmy.

"James is on his way," Davin says as Tim and Wanda settle into their seats, then he steals a glance at his watch, wondering if this is exactly true about Jimmy being underway. He'd gotten a text from his son with the time the train departs, but for the life of him he can't recall the departure time, but he resists the impulse to pull his phone out to check the text. The train ride is a long one, that much he knows for certain.

Jimmy-Jo, Davin thinks, shocked by the sense of relief in

knowing his son is homeward bound. Part of the feeling of relief, of course, is that Jimmy will be exiting the mid-country heat wave, but in the main he's looking forward to having him around.

He serves up the plates as Chaplin comes down the stairs and slips into his chair.

Unfortunately, thinking about Jimmy gets Davin back to obsessing about the news coming out of Chicago. "The rioting, uh, sure is unsettling," he says, and he mentions how the heat wave's consequences are wrecking Chicago's economy, which doesn't need any more hits, the Midwest already one of the hardest pressed regions these days.

"A lot of corn, or whatever they grow out there." Wanda adds, "The drought and heat is just destroying the crops." She frowns. "It's just so early in the season. I was just hearing something, had to be NPR, that this winter's low snowfall in the upper Midwest is a big problem, and this long-running heat just makes things that much worse."

Tim puts down his fork. "This past winter's snow or the coming winter's snow?"

Wanda shakes her head. "Oh Tim," she responds, but with a smile. She's had long practice with Tim always trying to joke about things.

"The rate of bankruptcies among the smaller farms is way up," Davin adds, having just read about this in an article about agricultural businesses, although the article had mainly focused on droughts out in the American West, in the huge agricultural sector of California and across large parts of many other states, including much of the Southwest. That long-running drought, despite being punctuated by occasional atmospheric rivers and record- breaking volumes of water dropped, has been relentless and many farming operations have scaled back or shut down entirely, and even some manufacturing that relies on a lot of water have shuttered.

But there's always water to divert for fracking, he can't help thinking. The market for exporting LNG has hardly eased — still high despite the normalizing relationship with Russia.

"Farms around here have been doing well," Wanda says. She talks about the consumer-supported farm she and Tim take part in, which makes Davin laugh.

"Zucchinis!" he shouts, which startles Chaplin, who sits across from Davin at the other end of the long table, but Wanda and Tim laugh. Trying to get him to take the squash from the CSA at the height of the season had become a running joke since the first year they had joined up.

"Zucchinis, coming right up," says Tim.

It's still far too early in the season with the summer squashes just starting to vine, much less blossom, but it feels good to think about the summer.

He tells them he's got some zucchinis of his own in the ground, and that he'll be happy to trade them squash for squash.

Davin notices Chaplin seems amused, something of a surprise given his read of him as shy. Chaplin originally tried to beg off dinner when Davin had told him about Tim and Wanda coming, and he had told Davin he didn't want to intrude. But he'd argued that a meal is part of the house share deal. Chaplin's been doing a lot in the garden, which Davin thinks is great, but he can't stop the thought from surfacing that Jimmy has never been keen on helping him around the place.

He notices Tim's plate is looking scant, and he pushes the big shallow bowl of cut-up chicken toward him.

Wanda asks Chaplin about his view of the garden this year and how the season looks to play, but Chaplin just shrugs.

"We can only hope we get the rain, but not too heavy," Davin answers. Last summer had two very heavy rainstorms, although these had come, fortunately, after most of the garden vegetables had established themselves. The only real consequence of that stretch of heavy rain had been the tomatoes did poorly with the extra period of wet.

"What's happening with the Airbnb?" asks Tim. The heavy rain that had really hurt was the November storm, the one that had caused the damage in the Airbnb apartment.

Davin shakes his head. "Still waiting on the contractor. I'm already missing the earliest part of the season."

Davin knows the November storm, as impressive as it was, still hadn't been anything like the West's series of giant rain events two years earlier. Although that rain should have been welcome as a respite from the long drought, the so-called atmospheric rivers had proved extremely destructive, and despite temporarily offsetting that region's drought, those storms had done a lot of damage, including a high death toll, although he can't recall any specific numbers. There had been plenty of images of washed-out gullies and wrecked roads and compromised structures throughout the affected region, and although Lake Mead's level had risen briefly, half that volume had been silt. *Mud Bowl* was the term of common use following those mega-storms, but he had later come up with *Earthenware Bowl* after the long drought had reinserted itself, baking the mudslides back into hardpack.

"Still, can't complain," Davin adds.

"Good chicken, bro," says Tim, or at least that's what Davin thinks is being said around the better part of a chicken thigh. Davin gestures with his wine glass toward Tim, and then drains his wine and pours himself a refill, asking Chaplin, down at the other end, if he's sure he doesn't want any.

Chaplin doesn't, but Wanda does, and the bottle now has only a bit left. There's another in the fridge, but he hopes he won't have to open that bottle.

Davin goes back to talking about Jimmy being homeward bound, and he then is talking of the pending move of the second house sharer, who is due to start living here full-time the day after Jimmy gets back. "Full house, bro," Tim says around another mouthful of chicken.

"You know Deidre, right?" says Davin to Chaplin, who is busy vacuuming up the food, but after he swallows, he answers in the affirmative.

"Yeah, she's a Monument Mounter," Chaplin replies. "A couple or three years younger." He then spears a piece of broccoli and eats it.

Davin gets back to telling Tim and Wanda that Jimmy's coming home will include a pickup time at Pittsfield's train station somewhere between two o'clock and three o'clock in the morning.

"The never-ending joys of parenthood," Tim says. He seems done with the food, but he's taken the wine bottle and drains it into his glass.

"Well, at least he'll be out of there," Davin says.

The table is quiet for a moment, as if reflecting on this development.

"The whole coverage of the Chicago grid crisis is bullshit," Davin goes on, after the pause. "Far too much airtime and ink and pixels spent parroting the utilities positions line, and there is this whole bullshit about the mandates making grid upgrades too unstable a business, and somehow the government is to blame for triggering brownouts and blackouts around Chicago and other areas."

"Yeah, but Trump's not part of the government, right?" Tim wise-cracks.

The talk about Jimmy and Chiago gets Davin talking about the morning's news reports of progressives in Congress calling for investigations into the Chicago troubles and the deaths mounting up. He mentions this and then explains, "I hope they do because, in effect, the utilities are playing games with existing supplies."

Both senators from Massachusetts are among those calling for hearings, he doesn't bother to mention. Neither senator, he has to wonder, might be confidently named by Chaplin. He doesn't bother mentioning that nothing will come from the call for investigation, not unless the mid-terms turn things around.

His pique starts to get away from him, his voice growing louder as he goes back to complaining about the media, and except for those assholes at Fox or Newsmax, the news still thinks they have to cover each side of an issue, as if there was anything, really, to debate. What is obvious, he continues, is that fossil fuel interests have far too long been pushing for the needlessly slow progress of some of the biggest renewable energy projects. He mentions delays in FERC smart grid rollouts, and with his voice's volume growing, is arguing the delays are because the implementations could very well move more energy to renewables and batteries, and that it's obvious the lobbyists are using Chicago as a power play, which is bullshit. Then he tries to catch his breath, musing on the accidental puns he's just uttered, but at this point Wanda asks Davin to use his *inside-your-head-voice*, which makes both the two Alford friends and Davin laugh.

Chaplin, he notices, looks confused.

It's one of Davin's favorite jokes. *Use your inside-your-head voice.*

Chapter 17: Red Ryder Radio

Larsen is in first class somewhere over Kansas when he pulls his encrypted laptop out of his carry-on.

There's no point in waiting, he admits to himself. He has his after-action report to prep, although unfortunately any such report will need be an in-the-middle-of-action update.

He'd overnighted in Anaheim, partly because he had a lot of setup to do to try to keep in control of the ongoing *clusterfuck*, and these efforts had included getting the right services lined up, but he also had arranged an early appointment this morning to meet with an exhibiting vendor to purchase a site license for new software he's had his eye on, and the purchase further reinforces his cover.

Which isn't a cover but the goddamn truth, which he thinks of as a fact, although hardly the whole truth.

So help me god, he then can't help but add.

He was busy much of the night, including working to shore up his counter-security intrusions on the several law enforcement networks he has whisper access to, but such access takes finesse and near-constant tending, but all the fuss is worth it. There are reports on the inter-state share nets that Cynthia Wainwright had been on a bus to Las Vegas, and speculation that she still might be there.

His big worry now is that she'll turn herself in, and why she hasn't already seems nothing short of a miracle. As long as she remains dark, there's still an opportunity to resolve everything clean.

So, I believe in miracles now. Jesus, he scolds himself.

There are several private investigators in play through his

indirect efforts by way of the law firm, plus there's his own man, although he is once again forced to trust a service selection. Considering his experience with yesterday's moron of a freelancer, this doesn't make him happy, but there are a lot of balls in the air, and he has to trust the reputation of the hit service, even if doing so makes him uncomfortable.

I'm in the fucking air, he can't help but tell himself, though he feels nothing funny about this.

He feels suspended between the possibility of pulling off the Hail Mary and his sense the better thing to do is call time. He is caught in his ambivalence about carrying on with the operation. But there's still a chance it can be adequately resolved despite the fuckup in San Bernardino, and he would rather not take a loss.

Rocky doesn't like to lose, he reminds himself.

Rocky is not a fan of fuckups either, he tells himself.

His thing with Rocky is a rare thing, and he's done well by it. The double role he plays is a solid way to conduct business— the provably legitimate digital security contracts make good cover for his other work. He understands his position is by nature precarious because people like Rocky are downright inspired when it comes to covering their asses and more than adequately motivated to do so. He too has self-preservation concerns, but his own resources don't compare— power is power and working for power is not, he well knows, and even Rocky works for other powers. But the higher you go, he also knows, the more remote you are from the danger of blowback, the better insulated from suspicion and prosecution.

If the operation goes south, he will likely be okay, as long as there's nothing leading back to him.

Leading back to Rocky, really, he clarifies, and this gets him thinking about the freelancer resting in peace under carefully groomed dirt somewhere in Rodman Mountains Wilderness Area that even he is unlikely to find again. Larsen spends a lot of effort on isolating his own exposure, but he knows the real danger always comes from above. Yesterday's desert burial is a stark proof-of-concept of that.

He looks out his window again, but the cloud cover below the passenger jet provides only the occasional glimpse of the ground surface, and most everything of what little he can see on the distant ground below looks brown, only broken up by occasional patterns of green circle dots.

He checks on his network taps, something he would rather not do using the airline Wi-Fi, but he has to be ready to move fast and needs real-time intelligence on the situation.

He works for a half hour, checking every resource he has access to, but he finds nothing new.

Intelligence seems to be lacking in all manner of ways, he muses.

Starting with myself, he adds.

He closes his laptop without starting his action report.

Middle-of-Action Report, he tells himself, settling in for a brief nap.

Chapter 18: Strangers on the Train

Cyn settles in her seat on the eastbound Lake Shore Limited, which terminates in Boston. Despite the uptick of expansions and improvements in passenger rail that had revived under Biden, this line remains true to its nickname, *Late For Sure Limited*, with scant improvement in its performance from the dog days of Amtrak, and Cyn knows this route will take many more hours to span the distance that could be covered by driving in something like twelve or thirteen hours. But she doesn't have a car, and she can't take airplanes either if she doesn't want to raise a flag about where she is and is going. She is toward the back of the rail car, in one of the seating setups with two benches that face each other. Her backpack is slung up beside her. She has her feet up on the opposing bench, hoping people take the hint.

The train is crowded, but not too badly so. She's glad she got the chance to clean herself up and wash her clothes at Sandra's, although she can hardly miss that a lot of the people climbing aboard apparently have not had that same chance. She digs a book out from her pack — why she had ever thrown it in was still a mystery, but she can admit that having the book had already proved helpful on the two bus rides. Even though she hasn't read a word, she believes the book has warded off unwanted conversations.

She places the book on the opposite bench on the aisle-side, hoping any fellow passenger thinking of sitting there will assume the seat is already taken. As the train starts and stops its way out of the station, it seems like she will continue to rule her kingdom of opposing benches at least until the next station.

She is on the bench facing forward, shoulder pressing against the window glass where the air- conditioning, or at least some effort toward air-conditioning, is huffing in a steady and noisy manner. She slides a bit toward the aisle and then lays her head down on her backpack, and she closes her eyes to see if this might work for catching some sleep. Her legs, now turned to the side, are still up on the opposing seat next to the window and the huffing vents.

She sits back up.

The phone call to her friend at Carbon's End, made using Sandra's phone, had been awful, devastating. Afterwards, she hadn't slept well on Sandra's couch.

She sits mostly in the middle of her bench, even though the midpoint feels a bit weird because her bottom is on the hump that divides the bench into two seats, but this is just another way she tries to keep people from sitting with her. This uncomfortable middle position also keeps her away from the direct assault of the vents at the bottom edge of the window where the air emerging seems to be growing both warmer and dusty, although she's pretty sure the latter is just the smell of the forcing air. The train is already out of downtown and into an industrial zone, but as she keeps watch, she sees this is really a series of industrial zones, and then she hears the rear train connector door open with a sigh and a clang and she feels hotter air pushing in.

It's the conductor. By the time the very large, sweat-drenched African-American woman gets to her, Cyn's feet are on the floor and she's tucked in on the aisle spot, her bag pushed to the other side of her. She has her ticket out and up, so the lady doesn't even ask, just takes it and punches it and places the paper stub on her seat back.

"Is someone sitting here?" the lady conductor asks, nodding to the book on the seat opposite Cyn.

"That's my book," she answers, and with the smallest of nods, the conductor turns her bulk to the other side, calling for tickets.

The hot air that came in with the conductor seems to be

disappearing into the somewhat cooler car air, for which Cyn is grateful, and she's sure all the other car riders are too. At least one of the passengers near her has especially strong body odor, but she can't tell which one or ones, and besides, she's been there and done that, so fair is fair.

She stays sitting up, but closes her eyes again, hoping she'll stay asleep for the whole nineteen or twenty hours the train takes to get to Boston, which is what her stub says is her destination. Cyn is not planning to go all the way but get out at Pittsfield and call Patel and ask him for a ride.

She's worried he won't be there. Or he won't pick up. Or that he says *no*, or even, *fuck off*. She's counting a lot on what had been a brief friendship, and while she's pretty sure Patel will want to see her and help her, she can't help wondering if she's thinking straight. He might have already heard about Joe's murder, and she's sure Patel knows Carbon's End is where she works, although she thinks — or hopes — the story isn't that widely reported. Her assumptions about coverage don't keep her from worrying the cops or FBI or whoever does that sort of thing might be there to greet her.

She should have gone to the police in Las Vegas, or in Chicago. This is what she repeatedly tells herself, but there's a deep cored-out feeling that overwhelms her when she thinks like that, a feeling that is a breath-stopping blackness.

She had checked out the online stories as best she could in Las Vegas, and there are moments when she wonders if her name and image are plastered all over.

The fugitive, she tells herself.

But she also tells herself, for what seems like the hundredth time, this won't be the case, and maybe some law enforcement might have a bulletin, *whatever*, but this isn't a manhunt, the story just isn't that big, not with everything else going on. She knows she may not be making sense, but she can see she now at least knows this more clearly, as if the distance is bringing clarity, but then she realizes there's something bullshit in this. What she really knows, and is only just letting herself think about, is this dark hard lump of fear and insecurity and terror. And something else too.

Guilt, she realizes. And *self-hatred*, too.

She knows this with a sudden lucidity, now recognizing this feeling from across the years of her life after her father was killed. It's this same old sense that's been busy reconstructing itself, and this mixes with a rising wave of deep hatred for Dr. Williams, the therapist she'd gone to after coming back home from foster care, and she needs to remember what she'd learned about *transference*, and that she doesn't hate him, didn't, and that she doesn't hate herself still, and that she was just a child then, had called the police just as much to help her father as her mother, just wanting it all to stop, for things to be better.

"Fuck me," she says quietly. She realizes there are some of those old feelings that still lurk in secret, especially the guilt she's been feeling about Joe.

And it isn't survivor's guilt, *fuck that*, but she has fallen into the old framework, what Dr. Williams called a complex across those sessions after she was sent back to him after she'd been found out, barely fifteen years old, with the man who lived next door. Dr. Williams had told her it had been a false comfort in getting the man to want her, and that she was trying to fill an emptiness so she could gain a sense of safety, a sense of being okay.

Fuck, she tells herself.

She had dealt with all of this, then, those new rounds of sessions with Dr. Williams when she was fifteen, but also a few years later too, in college, after that thing with her professor, and she can't even recall the name of that therapist, although she pictures the woman's living room where she went for sessions.

All those ceramic cats, she tells herself. Her memory sense of that room is clear, the late-afternoon sun sneaking through the mostly closed venetian blinds, the light striping the wide but crammed sill's cache of ceramic cats lining the long surface of the triple set of windows that put the therapist into back-lit silhouette.

Cyn is puzzled that she can't remember the woman's name.

Four years back, she figures, the last sessions.

Clearly, she can now admit, she hasn't been keeping in mind all she was supposed to have learned in those sessions.

Not *daddy issues,* no, that was called something else, something better understood now, the therapist had explained, and there was all that work on the *Five Factors* and the cognitive behavioral therapies that were part of her practice.

Six years ago, Cyn realizes. *Almost seven years.*

She can picture the therapist's face, even her posture, even the always lingering scent of the incense the woman burned, but the name remains a blank. They had talked a lot about replacement transference, and what her experience had been with Dr. Williams, and about transference resistance, and the two of them had drilled on mental exercises and techniques, but it is now obvious to her that at some point she had gotten lazy, careless, and had presumed this all was in the past.

She wants to scream in frustration.

Yeah, no, she tells herself. *Sort of let that drop.*

She closes her eyes and sits back, trying to calm herself. She thinks about all those sessions and what she'd learned.

Good good good, she tells herself after spending some time thinking about those sessions, and she starts feeling more in control, but she's still anxious about her current situation as a *person of interest,* as some of the news pieces she'd scanned in Las Vegas called her. She's worried she'll have an anxiety attack every time the train stops at a station. She has trouble ignoring the persistent images of wanted posters with her face on them, and anytime anyone just glances at her, her heart stops.

She pulls out the crinkled *Chicago Tribune* newspaper she'd retrieved from the recycle bin at the train station and gives the cover story another look.

There's no photo of her there, of course, and no story, but that relief, as absurd as it is, still feels tentative even this fourth time she's rustled through the paper and not found anything about herself. The front- p a g e story above the fold is about methane increasingly out-gassing from permafrost, and the early reports from Siberian Russia are supported by American and Canadian scientists in Alaska and the Arctic, although after more widely cast studies are cited in the news piece, the actual volume seems to be significantly less than the headline intimates, and by good measure. The story runs the headline "Climate Tipping Point?" with a deck line that reads "Russia's Scientists Warn that Permafrost Methane Release Will Speed Global Warming." Cyn has read through the story several times already and found some escape in analyzing the story and scrutinizing the facts and details in it, and each time she reconfirms the headline doesn't warrant the sense of the immediacy of the danger, although any uptick in methane is bad news, of course.

She also concludes through this repeated exercise that there's nothing like news of the apocalypse to take one's mind off personal disaster.

The train is starting to find its rhythm, and out the window some brown brush-clogged stretches of flat land show up more and more often as the building density dwindles, and she sometimes glimpses some clumps of dry-green trees in the distance. There are still groupings of short low buildings alongside the tracks, buildings of mostly hard-to-determine ages that flash by, interrupting the longer sight lines. Sometimes there's a sign facing the track. She sees that a sooty building the train is passing is, or was, a machine shop, *Calumet Precision Machining*, as she's able to read before it disappears past.

She lets herself drift into the passing landscape.

The woman therapist's name comes back to her. *Melanie.*

Cyn lets out a long sigh, and then takes a long breath, and she realizes she needs to hit the restroom. She's been making it a habit to act ASAP on such urges. Traveling, the heat, and being scared out of her mind have made her somewhat constipated, and she thinks, *I literally really don't need this shit.*

Okay, so she has to defecate, and she's standing up and she turns in the aisle toward the rear of the car, and from somewhere in her mind she's now half thinking of that pooping song that had been refined and rehearsed by her and her younger twin brothers over those long car camping trips her mom and her new stepdad—school teachers, both—had put them through summer after summer until they were old enough to revolt.

The song, she realizes, first learned during that time in foster care, and sometimes this seems about the only memory she'd taken away from that time. It hadn't been a good time, and she remains somewhat unclear about how this had happened and why she hadn't simply stayed with her mother's sister, their Aunt Fione, like the twins had. Cyn simply doesn't have much in the way of memories from this time, a time that had lasted only three or four months, she believes. She barely recalls those few months and can't even picture the foster parents who had to have been there, when she had started going to Dr. Williams.

She retains some vague sense there were other kids— *Little Johnny* and *Auguste*—these names pop into her mind, accompanied by an image of a young boy about the twins' age and of the slightly older Auguste. She suddenly has a clear image of the three of them singing the poop song with Auguste conducting, and this makes her smile.

What were the words? This is what she finds herself musing as she steps into the rear area of the train car. She knows when she got back to her home the twins had taken to the song enthusiastically and had greatly expanded it, coming up with many more verses and crude or funny euphemisms that she guesses she could recall probably only under hypnotism. But she has barely locked the restroom door, or closet, or whatever this stainless-steel space is called, when she comes up with more of that stupid song, and this gets her thinking about her brothers and that makes her sigh long and hard, her heart swelling with the thought of them.

Rocking sideways back and forth on the stainless-steel toilet with the sounds of the metal tracks clicking beneath her, she moves her bowels.

Praise the Lord, she thinks, and then she feels a bit guilty by what some would call sacrilege, although she has not gone to church services for a long time now. On the other hand, she's thinks, *Jesus had to poop, so what the hell.*

The train rocks harder now that she's standing and trying to wash her hands under a slight trickle of lukewarm water, and moments after she pulls out the forest of unabsorbant paper towels to dry her hands, she's out and with that drunk train motion is walking back to her place.

Looking forward, she realizes with a start that someone is sitting where she is, and when she step-stumbles up, she sees he's actually sitting in her very seat, reading her very book.

"That's my seat, that's my book," she says when she's standing by her seat, hanging back a little.

"Yup," the guy says, twisting to look up at her.

The first thing Cyn thinks is that he's not nice-looking, not in any way, and what leaps into her thoughts is that he has a face of a rodent, a rat. The bridge of his nose is flat, like maybe it was broken once and never fixed, but she notes this exaggerates the pointiness of the tip of his nose. His hair is dark, maybe black, or maybe just kind of greasy. His eyes are small and close together, and he doesn't seem to have much in the lips department, but what lips he has are very thin and very red. Not lipstick red, but red, enough so you notice.

He's wearing a windbreaker that's zipped up, weirdly, considering they're in a warm train car. The windbreaker seems about four sizes bigger than it should be, and even sitting he seems small with the windbreaker almost like drapery.

The guy is not getting up.

"You are in my seat, please," she says, nodding her head slightly to indicate other seats to be had farther down into the car.

"I just wanna talk," the guy says, staring up at her, and he suddenly starts blinking, which confuses her, and then she's back on track, pushing the whole of her previous observations into the familiar category of a guy-who-wants-to-chat-up-a-gal, and she feels a little bit unkind thinking this rat-faced guy is batting way out of his league.

"No thanks," she says. "I'm hoping to nap, so the space is mine, if you don't mind." She now actually gestures at some empty seats in the middle of the car, mostly single benches facing forward except those few sets of opposing benches like the one she has set herself up in. "There are some open seats over there," she says, and the back-car door hisses and bangs open. The large conductor is checking the stubs and stops behind Cyn, planning to patiently wait, apparently, for however long for Cyn to move so she can get past.

Cyn looks at the conductor and then back at Rat Face. "Excuse me, sir," she says, "that's my seat."

She looks back to the conductor.

Rat Face says nothing, and is just looking forward, evidently at nothing.

The woman conductor asks him where his seat is.

"Back there, has a stub," he says curtly, now looking at the conductor, and then to Cyn, and then back to the conductor.

"Please take your seat, sir," the conductor says. Cyn is amazed by the absolute neutrality in the conductor's voice. She steps forward to let the conductor step past Rat Face so he can get out, which, after a moment of suspense, he does. He steps toward the back and vanishes into the restroom without a sound or word.

The lady conductor steps back and Cyn climbs into her seat, feeling, creepily, the man's body heat still sunk into it.

"You're Boston," the conductor says, again without any inflection.

The conductor turns forward and makes her way down the car's aisle and then finally out to the next car through the rumble of that carriage door.

It's a surprise to Cyn that the moment, it seems, the

conductor has left the car, Rat Face is back standing next to her. *I really hope this guy's not going to be a dick*, she thinks, but he's holding out her book, which she takes.

"Ok," she says, opening the book, trying to pretend she's reading.

He's still standing there.

She looks up at him, a frown on her face.

"So where you heading?" he asks.

Cyn manages not to roll her eyes. *Please, dear god*, she thinks, but then she looks at her stub, but it has been moved from where it had been before she'd gone to the restroom.

Creep, she thinks.

She tries to get angry, but disquiet steals in instead.

"I'm not interested in a conversation," she says. What she is thinking is that there must be something wrong with this guy, otherwise he would have already taken the hint.

"Hey, least tell me your name," the small guy with the thin red lips says, but Cyn can hardly do more than a quick glance up.

"Hey, c'mon," the guy says.

There's something a bit southern in the way he speaks, but there's more of another accent too. Her discomfort is growing, the anger she wants to feel is getting displaced by anxiety.

"C'mon, like, I'm guessing Georgina, am I right?"

She tries to ignore him, but his presence feels like heat next to her.

Just go away, go away, she says to herself.

"Naw, you look like a Carol, no!" the rat-faced man snaps his finger, and she looks up and his expression seems a bit fevered with a grimace smile that doesn't improve his looks, but then he says, "No!" and then, "No, that's not it," and she can't look away from that grimace stretching his ugly thin lips into something like a grin.

"A Cynthia, am I right? Cynthia, right?" he says, and his eyes lock on hers. She tries to look away, afraid he sees she's flushing with panic, and her world is dropping away, her surge of fear pushing her into a darkening tunnel, and she knows in that instance this guy is connected with Joe, with what happened to Joe. She knows it, and then she thinks, *Joe's dead*, and she feels the panic washing through her even while she tries to tell herself there's no connection. She wishes the guy is just an asshole, just one of those guys.

But she knows.

"Get away from me," she says louder. A few heads turn around and then turn back.

"Don't be like that," he says, low. "You look like a Cynthia, all I'm saying. Just chatting, right? Like, you visiting a boyfriend, maybe, right? Used to live there? What town?"

She closes her eyes, and then looking up at the guy, she says, "No."

The guy just stands there with his ugly grin. The word *rictus* pops into her mind.

"No," she says again, trying to calm herself, trying to tell herself it's just some asshole guy. "As in, *no*, leave me alone."

Cyn is trying to play *young independent woman*, but she feels herself slip. Her efforts at projecting confidence keep sliding into more fear and panic. She starts to shake, or at least that's what she feels, and she turns to face forward to ignore the guy. She stares straight ahead, trying to tell herself she's making this all up, but the image of Joe, the back windscreen, the echoing shot break her thoughts, and she sees a young man, but very big, maybe six foot five or six, walking toward them.

Cyn had noticed him earlier, noticed he was sometimes looking at her from his backward-facing seat in the one middle set of opposing benches halfway toward the other end of the car.

It now occurs to her he's with Rat Face. She feels clammy and cold and tries to hide her shaking.

Chapter 19: Gun Flub-A-Dub

L eave me alone!" Cyn says, loudly, involuntarily. She hears herself and thinks she sounds like a little kid, and she has some sense of embarrassment adding to her flurry of other feelings.

She is looking up at the young tall guy who looks right at Rat Face, and when she shifts her gaze, the creep is looking back up at the tall guy, and she sees now, picking up on Rat Face's reactions, there's no connection of him with the young guy. There is a marked change in his posture, his stance, which only grows more pronounced as the young guy stands surprisingly close to Rat Face, whose chin, even tilted up, comes only to the young guy's breastbone.

Looming, strikes Cyn as the more accurate description of the young guy taking up physical space, but now he's not looking at the small man but is looking at her.

"You okay?" he asks.

"Mind your own fucking business," Rat Face hisses, which shifts her attention back to him for a moment, but she sees he's keeping his eye on the guy, cricking his neck back to do so.

The guy ignores Rat Face, not even looking at him when Rat Face hisses again, but keeps his eyes on her.

"May I sit?" the young guy asks, pointing to the seat in front of her that faces her. Cyn realizes he's close to her age, at least she thinks he's in his twenties, probably a couple years younger, maybe. He's wearing green cargo shorts, long and a bit low, his black or dark blue XXL-T t-shirt is pulled out over the waistband, and there are dark sweat spots under his arms and some sweat spots on his front.

She nods and scoots over to the window seat. The guy flop-crashes down, his knees spanning the space between the opposing seat benches, shins pressing into the forward-facing bench's front edge, a wall of thighs that feels like a protective barrier.

Rat Face has been watching all this with some surprise, but he rallies with a mid-level, "Fuck you," directed slightly downward now that the big guy is seated.

The big guy ignores him, turning back to Cyn. "You okay?" he asks again. She nods but stays quiet, still pretty freaked out, but that's ebbing, at least a bit.

Rat Face's expression has shifted into something uglier, when she again glances at him.

He's still glaring at the young guy sitting across from her, but his face is starting to redden, his eyes are jumping, vibrating.

"You think you're a tough shit?" Rat Face addresses the young man, shifting to stand a bit closer to him, putting his back to the car's other occupants, his face is still darkening with rage. He repeats himself through clenched jaws, his voice hissing through.

The young man holds up a hand, taking a quiet tone, barely looking toward the seething man. "Hey, peace brother."

The rat-faced man leans toward the younger man, his eyes squinting, voice, a harsh hissing whisper. "You fucking think you're a tough guy, a big tough guy?" He pulls the zipper of his draping windbreaker, leaning forward farther and Cyn is looking at the younger man's face and sees him blanch, his eyes widening, which makes the rat-faced man laugh unpleasantly. He then stands back up, and the zipper rips up to close all the way to the top.

He has a gun. Cyn is pretty sure she's glanced this, but her mind is not a cooperating witness, but hissing static, and she feels like there's a wave of white-hot heat radiating outward from her.

The rat-faced man is still looking at the younger man

seated diagonally across from her, and Cyn's eyes go back and forth between them. She sees the rat-faced man raise two fingers toward his own eyes and point the same fingers toward the young man, and then he steps back but pauses again to repeat the gesture.

"Yeah, what I thought," the small rat-faced man says, or at least that's what Cyn is pretty sure he's said, but before she can fully process this, Rat Face turns toward the rear of the car and straight-arms the panel on the connecting door. He slips through even before the door finishes clunking all the way open.

The big guy looks at Cyn. His color is returning. Her shaking rolls through her again.

The big guy leans forward, not smiling exactly, but with some breaking relief in his face, and he holds out his right hand. "I'm Jimmy," which for some reason makes Cyn start laughing, to be joined, after a moment, by Jimmy.

They are sharing something of a hysterical reaction, Cyn can't help think.

After they quiet a bit, Jimmy says, "Well, that was intense," and Cyn is off again, either laughing or crying, and the loudspeaker announces the next station coming up, and the conductor makes her way through, repeating the announcement.

Jimmy stops her and with some nods and some words from Cyn, Jimmy tells the conductor about the guy and the gun tucked into a waist holster. He takes great care, Cyn thinks, describing the windbreaker in detail.

Chapter 20: Train Talk, Rickety Rackity

The train slows into another of the interminable stations, and Jimmy goes and gets his backpack and a duffel bag. He has his stub with him when he settles himself in the double-bench seats with the upset young woman, who nods at him, her failing attempt at a smile fading fast.

Huh, he thinks, *upset, pretty, pretty upset*. He has no idea why he thinks that only about her, considering how freaked out he still feels about that guy.

In fact, he is having a bit of trouble looking directly at her, a sudden shyness coming on as he fusses about with his things, trying to square away his belongings.

The train gains more passengers from this station than it delivers, so the car is getting more crowded, but still there are other seating options more attractive for the new passengers than trying to squeeze in with a big, scruffily bearded, brown-haired, and somewhat sweaty young man, along with his big backpack and duffle bag, along with another bag, and a smaller backpack, a book, and a water bottle scattered about the seat benches. Not to mention a red-eyed young woman who looks like she's recently been crying.

Jimmy looks out the window, but a quick glance back is enough to see the young woman has turned to look at what has his attention. It's two police walking with Rat Face between them, disappearing past the dwindling number of people still boarding.

"Cheerio, asshole," Jimmy says, quietly. He turns back again, looking at the young woman, but he sees she is back to looking down at her lap.

But then her head comes up and she looks right at Jimmy.

"Cynthia," she says, and then, "Cyn. Interchangeable for me."

"Hello, Cynthia," Jimmy responds solemnly. "Jimmy Caine, nice to meet you." He pauses, then continues, "Jimmy to my friends, James to my folks, Jim, well..." He shrugs, which makes Cyn smile. "I'm heading back to the land that calls me James, as it happens," and he mentions he's going most of the way, but short of Boston, getting off at Pittsfield to get picked up by his dad.

The mention of his home in Housatonic seems to startle her.

"You're getting off at Pittsfield," she says.

He nods.

"You live in Great Barrington," she says, although Jimmy had said his parents, well, now just his dad, still, he had added, lives in Housatonic.

"Are you from the area?" he asks. He would be surprised since he can't place Cyn's accent, but it isn't Massachusetts, neither Boston nor below the line that divides the state in two linguistically, the other part carrying traces of New York in it. Her look does not say Great Barrington, although he doesn't exactly know why he thinks that.

He knows that he likes her looks. She's in some sort of hiking outfit, but it all looks new. The shorts are short, the top she's wearing has its sleeves rolled up and buttoned up by tabs, but Jimmy is drawing a blank on what the style is called. She's not particularly tall, maybe five foot, six or seven inches or so, he guesses, and her haircut is something he thinks of as free-spirit professional. The cut looks new and shorter than he usually sees, but still great hair, almost to the shoulders, dark blond or light brown, maybe, depending on the light, he finds himself thinking.

He's looking right at her, she's looking at him, and then unbidden his eyes sweep over her breasts, which makes him look back up and hope he's not blushing.

Jesus, he says to himself.

"Safari shirt," Jimmy blurts out, but she has little reaction other than a brief quizzical look.

"Housatonic is a part of Great Barrington, right?" she asks, and he thinks he's probably gotten away with the unconscious breast scoping, although it takes some effort to stay focused on her face, even though, he notices once again, it's a very fine face indeed. Great eyes, he says to himself, although he's puzzling a bit about their exact color, which he then concludes is a grayish green, but...*luminous* is the word he comes up with.

Despite their redness.

Her shirt is green, and he finds himself wondering if that affects the color of her eyes.

"Yeah," he says, rather slowly, realizing he'll have to keep fighting his urges to look at other parts of her. "'A Village of Great Barrington,' as they say," he says. "Although my father always adds, 'Trademark.'" A pause for a laugh or smile, but like many of his dad's jokes, this one doesn't do it.

"Have you been there?" he asks, thinking maybe she'd gone to Simon's Rock, the early age admittance college where his mom ran the health center, at least until the small campus closed, consolidated with Bard College in the Hudson Valley.

"A little while ago," Cyn answers. "I was there doing coordination for the Sierra Club Climate March. I had the Berkshires."

Jimmy nods. "Cool. That was an awesome turnout in New York, what, they say about a million, double the last big one in, was it '14?"

"Right," Cyn answers. "We—well, I'm not with Sierra anymore, so they, I guess, think the real count was way over the news counts, probably closer to three million nationwide."

"Yeah, the whole count thing is odd," Jimmy says. "The Chicago one was pretty much not great, from what I saw."

"You marched?"

"Of course," he replies, smiling. "I have to keep my options open about coming back to the Berkshires, right? Have they instituted PC border checks yet?" Unfortunately, there's no rim shot for this joke either. But then Jimmy is off and running, finding himself talking about the climate situation, and then the political situation, and the fights in a still-divided Congress, and then somehow he's on to the battle on income inequality, and gender identity, and a few other topics that hit all the politically correct highpoints, all mostly in a rush, and when he stops for a breath, he thinks, *Jesus.* He feels a bit embarrassed.

It dawns on him he's talking like his dad.

He now feels self-conscious, but he also observes she seems a bit agitated, and he wonders if it's about what he's saying. He decides to stop talking and let the clacking rhythm of the train take them forward.

Chapter 21: Miny Moe Memories

Cyn catches some of what Jimmy is saying, even though it seems all run together. Nothing he's talking about is new to her, really, except he seems to be joking about some of it in some way, i n c l u d i n g something about PC border checks. She can use the distraction, but she's having trouble paying close attention, because despite the effort she's making, she's still fighting ever-renewing flares of panic. She's trying to not think about that rat-faced guy, but it isn't easy even though he's gone. She can't shake her certainty that somehow the man knows who she is and what had happened in San Bernardino County.

She's angry at this new flush of panic and spiking fear.

Cyn tries again to pay attention to Jimmy, but w h e n s h e d o e s, she doesn't quite know what to make of his sudden silence.

She finds herself stealing looks at Jimmy and then she closes her eyes, but that doesn't last long. She sits straight up looking around, feeling distressed by all that's bouncing around in her thoughts. She works on calming herself, and the noise of the train and the murmurs of their fellow car passengers finally start having some soothing effect on her.

And then Jimmy starts speaking again, breaking her emerging calm.

She feels annoyed.

"So, uh, what was up with that guy, you think?" Jimmy asks.

Cyn sees that Jimmy has his phone resting face up on one of his thighs, and it looks like a Kindle app is open.

She doesn't want to talk about the rat-faced guy, having

just calmed herself down a bit. She nods toward Jimmy's phone.

"What are you reading?"

Jimmy shrugs and picks up his phone. He thumbs the screen dark and tosses the phone on the seat beside him. "Trying to read. Just some ninety-nine-cent sci-fi, but I'm too jazzed-up to really stick with it."

He's kind of cute, Cyn thinks, good-looking in some sort of mix of giant teddy bear and earnest warrior way, but he strikes her as young, even though she guesses now there's only three years difference between them, and she can't escape her sense though, that there's a large gulf. For one thing, she'll guess he isn't someone who's just seen her boss killed.

Boss and lover, she tells herself.

And she has the history of frenzied choices and pathologies loosed upon her life, and each and every variant path seems to offer only disappointing options and a crushing sense of being stuck.

There's my preference for older men, right? she tells herself, accompanied by a flare of self-censure and confusion about her feelings at the moment.

She looks at Jimmy.

And married men, she reminds herself with another spike of negative self-regard, but she's also experiencing countervailing feelings too, including an intense outwardly directed anger at her work friend that she keeps coming back to, repeatedly thinking of the phone call she had made the day before to her colleague at Carbon's End, the one other young woman on the staff.

Cyn believes she had covered her existential disappointment, her crestfallenness, from Sandra as she'd handed her back her phone. The response by this friend, Ell, had been an attack, the opposite of what Cyn had wanted, had hoped for, had needed, to get some help and some clarity on her circumstances.

She's still thinking too much about that awful conversation, and she can't push away the trouble she's feeling.

And married men, Cyn thinks again. Ell had been furious about her and Joe, and she had been stunned by Ell's reaction. Even now, Cyn can't escape her sense that her cheating with Joe was the bigger transgression, never mind that Joe had been killed.

Fuck her, she says to herself yet again, but she's still shocked by the conversation.

Not really a conversation, she tells herself, remembering how she had said very little to Ell. She had never had the chance, it seemed to her. As she goes over the call yet again, it seems like the way the call played out had made her feel more crazy and more desperate, not less.

She's been thinking on and off about the call ever since, and remains upset by it, but she knows part of what bothers her is the call has her thinking about her history and her tendency with married men. The convenient explanation she'd grown comfortable with was that her attraction to married men was simply because such men were otherwise less likely to put demands on her or to expect her to be girlfriend material. Girlfriend status was something that has never held much interest for her.

My thing with Joe, she thinks, another example.

She likes sex, just not the whole dating thing, the relationship thing. That's what she had told herself these past few years, and that she values her independence too much, at least that's what she'd come to conclude, but that phone call with Ell has Cyn wondering about calling bullshit on this conclusion.

Her tentative forays in coupledom in high school and as a freshman in college had ranged from the ridiculous to the regrettable. Boys her own age had consistently struck her as retarded in some fundamental way when it came to relating to a woman.

Except that hadn't been the problem, really. She had a sense of this even in high school, knowing she couldn't get what she wanted from her peers, not that this knowledge had come to her smoothly or easily. There had been a raft of relationship demands and such social expectations had hardly been offset by the clumsy fumbling and embarrassment and awkwardness that had been her first sexual experiences, but somehow she had discovered what she wanted, what she needed, just weeks before her fifteenth birthday. From that point on, except for the two mercifully brief boyfriend efforts in her first year in college, she had not looked back.

Older men. Fuck me, she says to herself.

It isn't that she doesn't know the pathology. She has had her share of therapy over the years and the connection between her father's abuse of violence and what had happened to her father had been pointed out any number of times before she quit therapy for good toward the end of her undergraduate years, all made irrelevant in her consistent denial of *daddy issues*. She had also flirted with the *gold digger* arguments of financial security or career advancement, but these explanations have always rankled her and struck her as stupid and irrelevant, and she remains confident such considerations have never been a factor for her.

She sighs, a quiet exhalation that brings her to open her eyes, but she sees Jimmy look to her expectedly, and she just shakes her head and closes her eyes again.

She's surprised when she realizes she's feeling horny, and she wants to laugh, or maybe scream, at the absurdity of her thoughts and feelings.

And then her feeling horny doesn't surprise her. *Comfort*, she thinks. Control too, she has to wonder. Escape, something to distract her from everything else. An old habit.

Cyn has a wave of want wash over her, and the form it is taking is wanting Jimmy, except she has some sense it isn't Jimmy in particular but the hunger she's so often felt before, to be touched, to be wanted, to be comforted by someone's attention, to have control.

Get laid, you mean, she scolds herself, scoffing silently, her eyes still closed, but even as she wonders, she senses this is a warning, this reaction is something too familiar, a sign of something wrong, such thoughts and impulses trying to tell her something. She makes an effort to sit with these feelings, but what shows up are the tumbling images of Joe's murder, the low slant of morning light, the echoing shot, and all the tension of the last two days, the incessant fear, her wild shifts of mind, and it's her sense of fragility, her own tenuous hold on herself that washes over her.

Jesus good god, she thinks.

The colleague of hers, Ell, had not even asked about how she felt about Joe's death, or if she was okay, or that she was sorry for her loss.

Cyn swallows hard, pulling in a gulp of air, and she's no longer feeling horny. She feels caught between laughing and crying, and she feels the nagging pull toward oblivion.

She starts her breathing exercises again, trying to calm.

She looks toward Jimmy.

She shuts her eyes, concentrating on her breathing.

Jimmy is saying something, and she looks toward him, but it's as if she's in another room, still in her own thoughts, not hearing him. The train picks up speed and she closes her eyes again. The movement rocks her back and forth into another place, other places, and she sees Joe that first time at her apartment, his wonder and gentleness as he stroked her, and then in her memories she's with Dr. Becker in his office back in college, his efforts to kiss her had been clumsy but his touch had been a comfort, and then she's thinking of her old neighbor, his name not remembered, and why would she? He'd been in his late twenties or maybe thirty but still living with his mother. Cyn's images are clear, however—his bedroom, second floor, and the shades drawn down but backlit with a sunlit glow — and she, almost fifteen, had pulled his hand under her sundress she had chosen specifically that summer afternoon, waiting until after her mom and stepfather had gone out shopping and the twins off with other neighborhood kids playing pickup baseball. She had closed her eyes and said, *Just touch me*, and he had.

Cynthia opens her eyes and sees Jimmy looking at her and

asking if she's okay. She thinks about how strange it is, her mix of memories and her efforts to calm herself, and a pressure in her groin, and her drive to be touched, her need to be elsewhere, to be soothed, and she fights not to be lost in the raw mix of it all.

She quiets herself by trying to think of nothing at all, eyes pressing shut.

After a long silence, after she has breathed herself into quietness, she opens her eyes and looks to Jimmy. "Thanks, by the way."

"What?" Jimmy asks, and she can see she's confused him, and then she sees him understand what she means only when she asks, "Do you go around rescuing damsels in distress all the time?" She tries to keep an ironic tone but finds it difficult because this guy seems so nice and because she feels a sob trying to bubble up. This incongruity is absurd, and she feels the hysteria rising, her short-won calm is again being supplanted by a renewing panic, her fears reasserting.

Cyn closes her eyes once again and tries to stay still.

Calm down, please, she pleads.

Chapter 22: The Tale of Righteous Fist and the Squishy Face

Jimmy notices these swings in her, these waves of stiffness, with a tension waxing and waning, some moments seem as bad as when that crazy guy with the gun was bothering her, the one, as she explained after she had come to call Rat Face, a name Jimmy thought was pretty good. *Perfect description*, had been Jimmy's exact conclusion. The guy did look like that, like a mad rat, the pointy long nose, those weird lips, something of a shrimp.

A rabid rat, he thinks now, and it's like an infection he's picked up from her, it all coming back, feeling the ghost of the sweat and fear he'd had when he glimpsed the gun.

Goodbye asshole, indeed, he tells himself.

The train thumps and screeches forward, taking a curve with a clang, and then moving forward more smoothly, picking up speed.

He can see Cyn hold herself still.

Strangeness on a train, he thinks, and then he realizes his dad would find that funny, which takes some of the fun out of the thought.

But mostly Jimmy finds himself looking at Cyn, who's now gazing out the window.

She looks more relaxed. Again.

He's worried she's noting his scrutiny, which could be embarrassing, but he feels he can't not look at her, but the next moment Jimmy's pleasure is offset by some sense something is off again with her.

Going in and out, he finds himself wondering, again.

He tries to let the silence continue, but he can't help himself, and he asks if she'd like to talk about what happened, or why, or whatever, talk about the something that's clearly bothering her.

She stays silent for a while more, and then she looks at him, saying, neither quite a statement nor a question, "You do a lot of rescuing?"

This makes Jimmy feel embarrassed and being embarrassed always makes him a little angry.

"Look," he says, "my parents raised me right, and I have an older sister who also tried to make sure I try not to be an asshole." He stops, suffering some further embarrassment when he sees her looking at him, and his face grows warm again. But then he relaxes away from his defensiveness, seeing that she seems more relaxed than before.

He's glad to see this, but now he's at a loss with what to say, and then he starts talking.

"In high school, I was the biggest guy," he starts in, "which was totally bizarre in that somehow that made some people want to fight me, and I just wouldn't do it, I'd just talk to them, and kind of kid them out of it."

Jimmy continues. "It was really in college, where I went was a pretty big drinking school, and I started seeing these guys, nice enough mostly, but they'd be drinking and girls would be drinking, and I saw this girl from my dorm sort of getting pulled toward this room, it was someone's place and a party, but kind of I don't know what her expression, how to describe it, but something made me go up and ask her if she wanted to go to that room with that guy and she said no."

Jimmy pauses.

"And unfortunately," he continues, "the guy was drunk enough to want to fight, and fortunately for me he was drunk enough not to really be able to fight. He tells me to mind my own business, well, screaming and cursing, right? And then he's rushing me to push me, which inertia-wise didn't really work out for him. He takes a swing at me, and I punched the side of his face and he goes flying."

As he talks about this his eyes close, and then they open again when he stops, and he looks over at Cyn, whose expression he finds hard to read. He doesn't want to freak her out, to push her, have her slip back away, so he keeps talking.

"It's not a hero thing, it's an awful thing," he tells her. "I still feel how the bones of his face were moving around when I connected, at least it felt that way, and that's not a fun memory. I still don't like that feeling."

He continues to look directly at her.

"The guy was basically all right, not hurt," he tells her. "I guess being drunk helps you roll with the punches."

He attempts a grin but quickly abandons it.

"It wasn't that I wanted to fight, it was just that if I don't speak up, that's wrong," he then says, but he flushes with another bout of embarrassment. The silence of his embarrassment is loud in his ears, the train and crowded car noise faded out.

"Hell, I'd like to meet your parents," says Cyn after another moment passes. She smiles at him.

"It may be more my sister," he jokes, which makes her laugh. "I don't know how long you're planning to be around," he then says to her. "My dad has a lot of room, if you need a place to stay, he likes having people over for dinner."

Cyn nods her head.

"My dad makes great cocktails," Jimmy adds.

Cyn smiles, then grins, showing two thumbs up and a big smile and then laughs, which makes Jimmy laugh too.

And then they talk a bit. She tells him she's been living in San Francisco, but she deflects enough questions, and they fall into silence every once in a while. But the silence doesn't seem so charged. The silence feels relaxed.

Chapter 23: Holy Toledo!

The train is coming to the Toledo stop. The day is falling past the afternoon, the lowering light of the sun spotlights its warm orange light into the train car when the track takes certain curves.

Cyn is quiet. Part of her wants to talk to Jimmy, but part of her does not.

She doesn't tell Jimmy her boss was running the fossil fuel divestment campaign, and with most of the colleges and universities already on board, they were mostly focusing on corporations and especially investment groups that weren't out and out oil businesses. All these companies chasing a lot of investments, often including fossil fuels as part of the portfolios and funds they ran.

The whole program had turned out to be a good model.

She usually cannot help talking about it.

She doesn't tell Jimmy she had been sleeping with her boss. She doesn't tell Jimmy Joe is dead, his head blown to pieces, that she had seen it and probably was a target too, that it looked like some kind of cop who had done it, and that she fled, was on the run.

Jesus. On the run. She wants to roll her eyes at this thought.

That Rat Face might be part of it.

This last thought in particular distresses her.

She does not tell Jimmy she knows she should have gone to the police, or a lawyer, or something at least.

But I'm too fucked up, she finds herself thinking.

Yet again, she adds.

But she's mildly surprised the thought isn't harsh, but gentle.

She looks at Jimmy, the hint of a smile and shaking her head just slightly, but Jimmy picks it up, smiles too.

I'm fucked up, on the run, so you want to go out sometime? she says to herself, appreciating the absurdity, and the absurdity of the thought almost makes her laugh, but then she's filling up with a freezing anger again in the sudden mix of feelings. *This guy that is being so nice* is one fragment, and then there's the persistent sense of fear she feels, and dread, and elation that she's here and not dead, and a shuddering worry about what that rat-faced guy might mean for her, for her safety, and suddenly she wants to cry, to scream, and one part of her knows what she should be doing and another part of her shuts that down.

Freaking the fuck out, is what she tells herself.

She knows too she's been having these episodes, these flashbacks, and then that thought freezes as she thinks where she is, that here she is, looking at this nice guy, Jimmy, as if everything is fine, the urge to flirt rising like a drug in her veins.

Fucking relapse, is what she now thinks.

Come on, it's just another person in my life getting shot, she tells herself, trying to joke her way into a better perspective, but this thought does nothing to make her feel any better.

And then she finds herself back to thinking about how she could ever get involved with her boss, a married man, at that. She had been done with all that, hadn't she? All the therapy, the work, but now she's back in the old place when she was an eight-year-old, or a twelve-year-old, or the time in high school, feeling alone, afraid, cut off from herself, in trouble. She keeps telling herself she'll handle it, she'll figure it out, it's only been a day — *well, two* — but then she's seeing the moment again, the cop guy leaning in, the shot, the blossom of Joe's blood.

And then she almost laughs.

She takes a couple of deep breaths, calming herself again. Jimmy is looking at her, a question in his expression.

"It's been quite the couple of days," she says to him. She wants to tell Jimmy, this nice guy sitting across from her, she wants to tell him everything. She feels like she has to, but she can't do it here, somewhere east of the Ohio line.

On a fucking train.

She can't tell him about the telephone call, the one she'd made in Chicago from Sandra's phone, to Ell, her friend at Carbon's End, her supposed friend, trying to reach out, trying to get a handle on what was going on, hoping, some part of her, at least, that she could get help, maybe just help figuring out what to do. It had taken all her strength to dial Ell's cell, convincing herself Ell's phone being tapped was too absurd a possibility, her fingers trembling on the keypad of Sandra's phone, her back to Sandra to hide her struggle, her pounding heart.

And all Ell could talk about was how disappointed and shocked she was to hear Cynthia had been involved with Joe, how fucked up that was. *Some fucking sister you are*, and other flooding recriminations, and talk of betrayal and turn yourself in, face the music.

Face the music, Cyn can still hear this, a repeating mantra since the phone conversation.

Ell's words had stunned her, and she's only processing the conversation now, really, on this train, still in flight.

What a fucking bitch, is what she now thinks, thinking about the call.

But she had been silent under Ell's barrage, barely saying anything, stopped by the surging disappointment with herself and by her panic, by the tolling absence of help she had hoped for, and by her sense of desolation, of isolation.

And that had so easily turned into terror.

She had hung up the phone, gone into Sandra's bathroom, and thrown up.

It had taken her enough time to pull together some semblance of calm that Sandra had knocked gently on the door to ask if she was okay.

Ya, ya sure, she had replied, nice to use a real bathroom was all.

his is what Cyn is thinking while she considers the

possibilities of her response to Jimmy's inquiries, but she mostly doesn't want to think about it, she doesn't want to talk about it because when she does, she sees the back window of that rental car bloomed with blood, and she herself as fucked up, no progress ever really made, and there's that part of her that just wants to die. But mainly, she keeps coming back to what had happened in the desert. What had happened with Joe.

Joe.

Why did I… she now finds herself thinking, but she shuts down that desert scene, and she's shutting out those thoughts, but her thoughts keep pulling back to Joe and to random stupid things, funny things.

His smile. He was like a boy, a kid, in his enthusiasm.

It was like selling ice to the Eskimos, he had joked several times about what they did, about the program, but she never had the heart to tell him he was using that expression exactly wrong.

They had been doing good work, important work, doing good, even if their divestment proposals were often simply a convenient reason for the investment companies doing what they were planning on doing anyway but waiting until Carbon's End came by with that little bit of extra PR and good will with everyone winning. The balance was shifting against fossil fuel investments as more and more banks and hedge funds were seeing fossil fuels as investments that were too risky.

Keep it in the ground was one of those slogans.

Of course, there were still some companies who told them to bugger off but usually in very polite code delivered from the lips of a chief social responsibility officer. There were still the *drill baby drill* assholes, with an Asshole-in-Chief in the Whitehouse.

Cyn is the administrative assistant, does the logistics of the *to-ing* and *fro-ing* to these C-level meetings, which means she oversees car reservations, plane tickets, and hotel bookings, along with being the reminder-in-chief for Joe and the porter of important papers.

And the gal Joe loved to eat, she thinks. An image of him down on her turns into composite images., the spot at the top of his crown was thinning, the way he loved to look up, *his stupid wink,* and she almost laughs, her heart tumbling with her thoughts about Joe, but her heart has barely beat before the panic, the grief, the static, all rushes back, and a spike of hatred competes with her fear, the thoughts about what has happened contending with her efforts to damp down and push these images, any and all of these images, and feelings, away. She doesn't want to think about any of this, but no matter how hard she tries, the vision of the blood-clumped glass can push up the moment she thinks about any of the San Francisco time, or Joe. The images and terror keep coming up or threaten to at any instance when she struggles to make any sense of what has happened.

It has to be the work, she thinks. Something was behind what had happened, but she can't make any sense of it.

And then she realizes Jimmy is saying something. Jimmy is trying to get her to talk to him. Jimmy is asking about what she had been doing in San Francisco, how she likes the city, where she's from, simple stuff, the kind of conversation that should be normal, she knows. But she just keeps saying she can't talk about it, and she knows Jimmy can see his questions are only making her upset.

There's no way he wants to upset her, that's what she realizes when Jimmy suggests he sit apart for a while, just so they can rest, "Or whatever," as he puts it, but she can't see the disappointment in his face, nor his concern, because she's gone back to trying the breathing method to keep herself from screaming.

Chapter 24: Meeting Mr. Coif

The train ride is long and slow with frequent stops on track sidings to let freight lines pass, and with a surprising number of station stops, each of which, Jimmy can see from his mid-car vantage, makes Cyn nervous anew.

Jimmy, now sitting in his old seat halfway toward the other end of the car, keeps turning to keep an eye on her. He figures there's no way another guy will hassle her like the rat-faced guy, but he's picked up a bit of her anxiety.

He's thinking about going to the dining car and wonders if Cyn might like something. They'd shared their snacks earlier, his were Doritos, and he can still smell the flavor on his hands, no matter the number of paper towels he's used.

Or I could wash my hands, he admits to himself.

He had gone off to the tiny toilet compartment to take a piss, and that was the last time he'd washed up, and the Doritos had followed on that.

She had shared a pack of cut vegetables and dip. Not one of those supermarket tray-sized ones, but the kind you could pick up at an airport or train station concession, and he had had to watch out that he didn't swallow the whole tiny pack. It had done next to nothing about his feeling hungry, and so after a while of sitting apart, he'd gone through the better part of a bag of Pepperidge Farm Nantucket cookies, but he has managed to keep two for her.

He knows he wants to check in with her, and he hopes she's feeling better. But he also knows he doesn't know her, that she's as capable as anyone else of being a strange weirdo, although he hopes not. But even as he's thinking this, sure enough, another guy comes walking into the car, right to her, and sits right beside her.

Jimmy is already walking back over.

"Who the hell are you," the man says, a slight grin, staring at Jimmy when he stops by her seats, and the contrast between the man's rude phrasing and his smile, his expensive haircut and manicure and a rather nice suit strikes Jimmy as incongruous. And then Jimmy notices the guy is wearing a really nice cologne. Jimmy is starting to feel like he's stoned, buzzed in some way, somehow, but then he says, "Excuse me," to the guy, pushing past the man's knees and sits down on the facing seat, diagonally across from the man's aisle seat, all the way farther in against the window.

Jimmy notes his heart seems to be beating faster than usual.

"That's kind of a rude way to address someone," he adds, after glancing at Cyn.

"Right-o," the man says, turning toward Cyn, ignoring Jimmy.

Jimmy glances at her, and she looks upset, but he thinks maybe a little less so with him there across from her, his long thighs bisected by her knees.

At least he hopes she's less upset.

"Don't let me interrupt," Jimmy says.

He's trying to take long breaths and hopes the man doesn't notice.

The man continues to ignore him. He asks Cyn where she's heading, and Jimmy says, "This isn't the train to Albuquerque?" eyebrows up, a feint of sincerity.

"What are you, her clown?" the man asks, his attention and emerging annoyance now settling fully on Jimmy.

Jimmy says nothing.

"I'm just trying to have a conversation with the pretty lady," the man says.

Like an old movie line, Jimmy thinks.

"Do you mind?" the man says. He gestures to the aisle in a very easy-to-interpret meaning.

Jimmy looks back at Cyn. "Do you mind?" he asks her.

"What I mind," Cyn says, looking only at Jimmy, in what amounts to a whisper, "Is that I don't know this guy and I don't want to talk to him."

"Jesus," the guy says.

"So, why?" he asks the man, keeping his attention on the man, although he has to fight the impulse to look at her. He wants to know, needs to know, that she's all right.

Jeezus! I want to be her hero, he realizes. Without realizing it, he's shaking his head.

"I have some questions, an offer, about the trouble the young lady is in," the man says to him, and then the man looks over at Cyn.

Jimmy darts a look and sees she has her eyes closed.

"You have a friend, a small kind of ratty looking friend, who likes to show us his gun," Jimmy says, feeling more and more like he's having an out-of-body experience, the situation so strange.

He adds, "Really, a pretty tiny guy."

The man stares at him.

"Rat Face, you know, the guy the police escorted off the train a few stops back," he adds, even while some part of him continues to wonder what he's doing and what he's gotten himself into and whether or not he's making any sense.

The man glances at Cyn, who's now looking down into her lap, and then he looks back at Jimmy.

"Yeah, I saw," the nicely dressed middle-aged man says. "He was talking to you, didn't seem happy."

Jimmy scoffs but stays silent, and then he flushes, it dawning on him this guy has been watching. The idea of it seems bizarre, unreal.

"Jesus, well, no, I don't know him," the man continues, "other than that the guy is an idiot, no question, if he flashed a gun."

To Jimmy, the man seems bemused.

The man turns back to Cynthia. "I just want to ask you some questions."

"Cool," says Jimmy, his back twisted farther, so he can lean against the window, both to give himself more legroom and to face the man better.

The man accommodates Jimmy's legs by placing one of his own in the aisle.

"I believe the *pretty lady* has made her point, and it's the polite thing to answer that first," says Jimmy.

"Jesus," the man says, surprisingly softly, looking upward. And then his eyes are back on Jimmy, and he leans slightly forward toward Jimmy, but then the guy leans back, back to looking at Cynthia.

"Why do you want to talk to me?" asks Cyn, another whisper, still looking at Jimmy rather than the guy.

"Jesus, all right," the guy says, tugging at his suit front. "Things got off to a bad start, I see that. Consider me apologetic, honest."

Cyn looks down, either at her lap or at her knees pressing into Jimmy's thigh, but he can't tell which with her head turned downward. She may be looking into some whole other place, some place where she seems to keep going.

"I can see you're upset, every right to be, but I'm here to help," the man says to her.

Jimmy is looking at the man, who he names, unbidden, *Mr. Coif.* He doesn't know what's going on, and Rat Face is somehow a disturbing part of it all, but he has a sense Mr. Coif may be something else.

No gun, no snarls anyway, he considers.

The man looks back and forth between Cyn and Jimmy with something close to a smile.

"I believe the *pretty lady*'s objection still has the floor," says Jimmy, and this time his use of the guy's earlier phrase puts a bit more of a smile on the man's face.

Cynthia actually is a lovely young lady, Jimmy is happy to stipulate.

"You two know each other?" the man asks.

Cyn glances up at Jimmy before scattering back to her long downward staring.

Jimmy keeps his face still even though the situation is strange and makes him feel like laughing, or maybe he's just nervous.

It's hysterical! pops into his thoughts.

He says nothing.

"Jesus," the man says with something like a laugh. "Something is screwy," he says, and then he reaches into his suit pocket, and Jimmy tenses, but he sees the man bring out a business card, which he hands to Jimmy.

"I'm Terry Bancroft. I'm chief investigator for AllServe CI, which means I'm the owner, ex-cop, now private investigator," he is saying to him since Cyn is still head down. "New small outfit out of Minneapolis, took this assignment from a law firm, new client, to find Cynthia here," nodding toward her, "and that shrimp asshole isn't on my staff, but a co-contractor, best I figure," he says.

Jimmy nods, looking back and forth from the card to the man.

"That guy's a PI," Jimmy says. "Huh."

Bancroft shrugs. "He actually flashed a gun?" he asks, shaking his head, but he may be talking to himself.

Jimmy wonders if what the man has just said is a question. It doesn't seem to be, but more of a statement.

"You know your girlfriend is being sought by the law as a person of interest in a shooting, in a death," Bancroft tells Jimmy.

Jimmy checks to see that his mouth remains closed, but he can't check his glance at Cynthia. She's still looking at no one.

"Look," Bancroft says, leaning back in the seat. "Best I can tell, the search is a nonexclusive bid-out, and I know of at least one other firm running with it, plus whoever that asshole might be, but maybe I'm hungrier, or better, or more used to the footwork." He stops and turns back toward Cyn, who now has her head back against the seat, her eyes closed as if asleep.

Bancroft shrugs, looking back at Jimmy. "Maybe just

luckier. Picked up the bus to Chicago from Vegas, the station agent was happy enough for the cash memory aid, and the choices out of Chicago at the moment are pretty slim and people, even ticket sellers, remember pretty girls." Bancroft checks to see if this elicits any reaction from Cyn, but it elicits no reaction whatsoever. Her eyes are still shut, her body holding still.

"I drove my car to the Bryan, Ohio station, got ahead of the train, boarded there."

Jimmy has nothing to say.

"A straight-forward locate-and-report, and thanks to that fucking idiot flashing a fucking gun, like you say, I have to assume—" Bancroft pauses, creasing his forehead and shaking his head, sharing with Jimmy, Jimmy thinks, the scope of Rat Face's idiocy.

"Sorry for the language," he then adds.

"Well," Bancroft continues, a modest grin again appearing, "I assume I get the bonus, and I thought at first it was thanks to his being an idiot, somehow, but it must have been that the processing took so long that my call came first."

"The processing?" Jimmy asks.

"Yeah, of course," says Bancroft.

Jimmy doesn't understand.

"I didn't know he was carrying, never mind flashing the gun, but even if you have a legal carry, it takes the officers involved time to confirm, that would be my guess anyway. That asshole may still be cooling his heels, although I'd guess he's out by now. If he was legal anyway."

"Okay," says Jimmy. Nothing seems okay.

He sees that even Mr. Coif—Bancroft—seems a bit unsettled.

"The call?" asks Jimmy. "You said your call came in first?"

"Locate, report, no law agencies, no contact with subject, but when I called this in, new instructions for contact direct," says Bancroft, looking at Jimmy, and now the conversation seems like they're just talking over beer. "No direct contact, then direct," Bancroft says.

"Okay," says Jimmy.

"And I drew a blank from my client contact about that guy I saw talking with you, the guy you said flashed a gun," Bancroft says, but then the man pauses, a look of puzzlement in his expression. "When I inquired, I mean, and I didn't know about any gun, but I did see what I saw."

But that doesn't clear up anything as far as Jimmy is concerned until he realizes Bancroft knew about the encounter and saw Rat Face removed from the train, and his mention of the gun had put it all together for Bancroft.

"That's what's weird," Bancroft continues after a moment. "I'd been thinking I lost the first-find bonus, the little asshole of yours getting it, although when I called in, I was told I was the first on the locate, they'd not received any call, so maybe the guy was late because of his getting caught up, put off the train, but I asked about him anyway and *nada*."

Jimmy is pretty sure this guy is talking to himself.

"I'd been reporting in progressively," Bancroft is saying.

"What does that even mean," Jimmy asks, still feeling entirely too confused.

"I mean, making progress in the assignment," Bancroft says as if it should be obvious. Jimmy must look confused because Bancroft adds, "My first call in was from Las Vegas, after confirming" — and here Bancroft vaguely waves toward her — "the bus to Chicago, and then I called in the train once I confirmed she had boarded."

Bancroft stops for another pause.

"Yeah," Bancroft says, glancing at her and then to Jimmy, "sorry, off the point."

"Okay," is what Jimmy replies.

"The point is that Cynthia is a person of interest, homicide, and the client is a law firm that has to know better, but no law involvement, and the message I'm now to deliver is that they just want to talk to, meet with Cynthia."

"Okay," says Jimmy. *Homicide?* he thinks.

"No, not okay, not really," Bancroft says.

Jimmy manages not to say *Okay* again.

"The money is good—surprising, between you and me—but the case instructions…"

Jimmy again kills the impulse to simply say *Okay* again. "What do you mean?" he instead manages to ask.

"And why the run-around on the client," Bancroft is saying, and it sounds to Jimmy like Bancroft is back to thinking aloud, but then Jimmy turns to look at Cyn, who remains still with her eyes still shut, which seems kind of weird to him, but he has no time to ponder this because Bancroft goes on. "I had assumed it was Cynthia's company," Bancroft continues, "but Carbon's End denied it—the guy there I talked to about Cynthia when I called trying to get some information, some background on her. We talked for a while, but he didn't know anything about the locate contract."

Jimmy manages not to say *Okay* again although what he really wants to do is to shout *What are you talking about?!*

"Okay, first," says Bancroft, turning to check on Cyn again, then back toward Jimmy. "I can arrange travel for Cynthia, go with her, or put her up and they'll come to her. I can't tell you why, don't know, has to be the law office with the lawyers apparently. I have no idea why, but that's the add-on case instructions."

"Why?" Jimmy asks, and he sees Cyn seems to be listening. At least he thinks so, although he doesn't know why he's so sure since she still has her eyes closed and remains stock still.

"I don't know, couldn't even say the exact expectations if I did. You know, NDAs, that kind of bullshit."

Jimmy does know what nondisclosure agreements are, but he continues to have a problem following what Bancroft is saying exactly.

"Part of what's off…" Bancroft says but trails off.

"Umm," Jimmy says.

Bancroft shrugs. "Well, whatever."

"So, umm, what? You're done?" Jimmy asks. "You reported?"

"About forty minutes ago, after reconfirming her

locate," Bancroft says, with a toss of his head toward Cyn.

"No, yes, I reported, but no, not done," he adds, "now there's this second part, the new instructions. I'm to offer Cynthia here $100,000 for the meeting, which sounds like a pretty good deal, but really, that's a bit off too. Well, a bit more than off."

Jimmy is completely confused. A rat-faced gun-toting asshole, and now a *private eye*.

"A hundred-thousand dollars," Jimmy says.

Bancroft ignores him and returns his attention to Cyn. "I'm talking a hundred thousand," he says. "It's your call."

Her eyes are open, but she seems unable to look at the guy. She does take a lightning glance toward Jimmy, and then her eyes are back to her lap, a flush creeping up her neck.

"Clearly they think the stuff in the news is bullshit," Bancroft says to her. "Whomever the client."

In the news, Jimmy repeats in his head a few times.

Bancroft seems happy enough just to sit there, but then a minute passes and he addresses Cynthia again. "You're just digging deeper," he says, but he gets nothing from her. "You're getting yourself in a mess for no reason."

"Please just leave me alone," she says, almost inaudibly. The train takes that moment to emit an ear-splitting screech in the lurch of a curve, which makes both Cyn and Jimmy jump, but when Jimmy looks over at the guy, he sees the guy's eyes are closed, the guy looks relaxed.

"I'm just here to arrange a meeting," he says, and then his eyes are back open but looking up at the ceiling and not at either of them.

There's only the sound of the train and the noise of people in their seats or standing, or talking, or walking about. The light is dimming, but there's still early evening light in the sky.

"Okie-dokie," the guy says, pushing off the armrest to raise himself up, his left knee clunking into Jimmy's as he stands. "It's your party."

He turns to Jimmy and with a nod asks for his name and contact information.

"Jimmy," Jimmy says.

"Jimmy what?" Bancroft says.

"Allbright."

Bancroft snorts. "That's funny," he says. "Allbright" — pointing to Jimmy — "AllServe," he says, indicating himself.

Jimmy hopes he's not blushing, but he wouldn't put a nickel on that being true.

"Your address?" asks Bancroft with a bit of a smile. He pulls out a small notebook and then a pen.

Of course he knows I'm lying, Jimmy tells himself.

"Fenway, you know Boston? Like the park, Red Sox," Jimmy says, but he can't help noticing he may be overselling it.

"Crandell Street, 02130, 15 Crandell," Jimmy says, even knowing he's likely blushing. He has just made up the zip code and the address.

Bancroft jots it down.

I'm not lying, I'm not lying, honest, Jimmy is making himself say to himself as he tries to keep a hint of a smile on his face, but his face begins to feel more like an obvious mask. He's sweating.

The man buttons his suit coat and then unbuttons it and reaches in. Jimmy sees the man has retrieved a billfold, the long narrow type his father uses, but wider, maybe taller. And then Jimmy corrects himself, marveling at how the mind works — it is a *wallet*. Jimmy's gaze is magnetized to the wallet, and he knows somehow he'll remember the details of this moment for a very long time, this wallet, the man's turning it open.

The man pulls something out of the wallet and writes something on it with the pen he has fished back out of his suit coat pocket.

Jimmy tries to keep his exhale from gusting and gasping through the train car.

The man doesn't seem to notice any of this, and Jimmy's breath is getting under control and the sweating is apparently done for the moment. A quick glance at Cyn sees her still looking straight ahead at him, her face numb.

The man reaches out to Cyn, who turns toward the movement. Perhaps simply automatically, she reaches up for what turns out to look like a business card.

"Change your mind about the offer," the man says, "call this office. It's the lawyers, for the client."

Cyn has the card but isn't looking at it, having dropped her arm, the hand holding the card falling like a stone down into her lap. When Jimmy looks over, the card is loosely held on her lap, the hand that holds the card looking just like how a stroke victim's hand might look, fingers loose, curled.

"Here," the guy says, bringing Jimmy's attention back to him. "Let me see my card for a sec."

Jimmy hands the business card back.

The man is writing something on the back of it and then stretches out his arm toward him, card held between the man's index and middle fingers. Jimmy takes it and glances at it and sees that on the back is the name of the law firm, or at least it looks like that, along with a telephone number. he looks back up at the man standing in the aisle.

"I like you, kid," the guy says, even smiling, looking right into Jimmy's eyes. "You are kind of a pain-in-the-ass wise-guy, but protective. I can see that, good for you."

Jimmy checks to see if his mouth is hanging open.

"She's just getting herself into trouble, running. You should help her out, not this way."

Jimmy doesn't know what to say.

"Either, both of you, just ask for extension 323," the man says, shrugging to settle his suit jacket on his shoulders. "It's written on the back."

Jimmy, of course, turns the card around again, and the firm's name, handwritten, and phone number and extension are still there.

The man salutes with two fingers, and Jimmy swears he can see a ghost of a fedora. He watches the man move toward the connecting door at their end of the rail car, and then Jimmy sees Cyn stretching upward in her seat, her neck and head twisting around to follow the sight of the disappearing man.

Cyn slumps back down, again looking forward, but probably not looking anywhere or at anything in particular, and certainly not looking at him. He can see how upset she is, and he feels bad for her. But he is also thinking back to what the man had meant, wondering at *person of interest in a shooting. A homicide.*

"Hey, big guy," the man says, a sudden reappearance, and Jimmy looks up, sees the man is back, his cell phone out, the digital sound of the shutter going off.

Jimmy is already starting to rise, although the cramped space makes it a clumsy move, especially since his right knee more or less bangs Cyn's own legs to one side, and even mid-rising, Jimmy opens his mouth to ask the man what he's doing, but before he can form the simple sentence the man is pointing at Jimmy's chest with a grin growing.

"It looks like Jesus," the man says so unexpectedly Jimmy decides to sit back down, his expression a look of complete confusion.

But he keeps his eyes on the man who is now chuckling, pointing at Jimmy's chest, more or less with his finger conscribing a small circle while pocketing the cell phone in his suit coat's side pocket.

"The sweat marks on the t-shirt," the man says, "they look like Jesus." The man turns, and with another casual small salute, he heads toward the automatic door at the back end of the car, stepping through it again.

The carriage door closes behind him.

Jimmy looks at Cyn.

"Jeeze, that's weird," he says, which gets Cyn looking at him.

She blinks.

Jimmy gestures with hand and face, a *What was that?* expression, and he releases a small grunt of wonder.

Cynthia is still looking at him, silent until she says, finally, "No. No, it doesn't," her hand now up toward Jimmy, her fingers also moving in a small tight circle toward his chest. And then she leans back, a slight slump toward the window, her eyes shut, face neutral.

Jimmy pulls the bottom of his t-shirt outward and a bit up, looking downward at it. "No. No, it doesn't," he says in a hint of a whisper, even still thinking it might be a matter of angle. He sees he'd dropped some ranch dressing that landed on the hem of his t-shirt. He's impressed by the amount of sweat stains and notices his now-exposed belly feels a tiny bit cooler and there's damp wet when he settles the t-shirt back in place.

"No. No it doesn't," he says, louder, but Cynthia remains still slumped, eyes now squeezing shut.

Chapter 25: The Updating Out of It All

L arsen is back in his Fairfax, Virginia, apartment, preferring to work from there and not his office, although there's a new client meeting scheduled this afternoon he will have to go in for. His weekly video call with Rocky is coming up, and the assignment is still in limbo with the slim possibility all will work out, but this view is battling with his near certainty it's already far beyond any and all likelihood of success.

Still, he seems unable to entirely shake his hope to pull this particular rabbit out of the hat. This is not the way he usually thinks, he knows, but then assignments don't tend to go so stupidly off the rails.

At least they've found Cynthia Wainwright, and she's on the train with Boston as the terminal destination. Locating her is one of the necessary steps toward even a slim possibility of solving this *shit show*, even if his run of bad luck still overwhelmingly offsets the positive.

Bad talent, not bad luck, he tells himself.

He's worried the guy out of the kill service who's been assigned seems like an idiot, somehow getting thrown off the train, and the service isn't one to provide detailed updates, but the information he's just pulled from the law firm back door from one of the legit private investigation services' report seems to suggest the freelance assassin was pulled for a gun license check.

How exactly this sort of development could possibly come about remains a mystery to him, and his query to the service has been entirely unsatisfied. Had the guy somehow fumbled it, dropped the gun by accident, or somehow, in some way, managed to get himself caught in a mag screen? As far as Larsen knows, metal detectors are still few and far between across the federal rail service, but in the end the how of it doesn't matter. And, he knows, he'll never get the details from the service.

What he has gotten from the service is that the freelancer is released, the alias background and gun carry holding up, and now Larsen has passed to the service the report of one of the private investigators made to the law firm, about possible destination, with Great Barrington likely, although the specific address hasn't been included. It also looks like the investigator is raising questions with Madaki about the assignment being odd, and he himself has contributed to the oddness by having instructed Madaki to expand the objectives of the investigator's assignment to include contact. It is his hope the new offer to the young woman could get her back within reach, but this change has triggered some suspicion from the Minnesota-based agency involved. He wonders for a moment if the Minnesota guy probably did witness the freelancer, but it seems highly unlikely it would ever be a problem.

Madaki doesn't know diddly about this part of the operation, and Larsen has kept the pertinent details from the clerk. That's why Larsen is using the law firm's email as the channel for the freelancer's reporting, which he accesses by running a background intercept, which also means he can email the freelancer through the firm and make it seem to be from Madaki. Still, it's just one more potential complication, which is exactly what he doesn't need, but the communications links are heavily protected and there's really nothing that can threaten him from the law firm clerk's end. Larsen would just as soon do this assignment himself at this point, but the boss man would be a lot unhappier about that, with its attendant increased risk of discovery. Even he knows his getting personally involved in the action would create a bigger threat than the assignment failure itself. He knows that it's getting to the point where the operation needs to be entirely aborted, but the girl is still running, and the only change point for the operation is if—*when,* he corrects himself— she goes to or falls into the hands of law enforcement.

There may still be time to get it done. The service has reported the freelancer is on his way to the Berkshires. Larsen will forward specific address information to the freelancer's service when he gets this via the back door email intercept, although the email and phone exchange Madaki is having with this Bancroft hire suggests that investigator might be getting coy about sharing information. Larsen hasn't released through the blind fund transit the bonus funds to Bancroft for the first part of the locate assignment, but he has already instructed Madaki to bump up the fees for the add-on objective in the hopes of getting more information about her destination.

Never fucking simple, he tells himself, not like the back door he put into the law firm's network that provides him with access to all the information he needs, and when the assignment is done, there's a disappear routine that removes all traces.

Elegant, he tells himself, but that's about the only elegant aspect of the whole mess.

He's less sure about the bank work he's put in earlier, placing untraceable funds into Wainwright's bank account, and then anonymously flagging the notion of embezzlement for *The Examiner* and San Jose's *Mercury News.* He's been careful about traces, but he may need to run a more robust trace hygiene analysis now that the situation seems more likely to raise flags. He may have to abort, or be ready to, at any moment, anyway, but he still hopes for some magic to happen. Maybe the embezzlement angle might keep her under the radar.

And maybe I'll pull a rabbit out of my ass, is the unhappy thought that comes to mind.

Chapter 26: Shut Up and Grow Some Trees

The selectboard meeting is running late, not that there's anything unusual about that, although tonight might be worse than usual given that there seems to be no end of the line of people who want to speak about the proposed town warrant for the new solar farm. The Town Meeting is still two months off, but nothing in Great Barrington ever happens fast when it comes to local politics.

Well, except the self-dealing, maybe, Davin considers.

He has other unkind thoughts aplenty tonight. One such disapprobation is for all the speakers who step up to the public comments podium and basically repeat what all too many others have already said, instead of simply saying they agree with earlier statements and let it go at that. He's especially ticked when a speaker starts with some statement or another about the evening getting late, or that the meeting has been going on and on, and then basically parrots at length, in not so different ways, points already made.

He steals a glance at his cell phone and sees he'll be driving to Pittsfield in four or five hours if the train's progress holds steady, and so far, Jimmy's texts still have this as likely.

He is in a crowded room on the second floor of the town hall on official business as reporter for *SCI*, and for the first time in such capacity, so he keeps fighting his impulse to stand up and scream, *That point has been made!* He's sure such behavior would be, as he likes to say, very much contraindicated. He's sitting toward the front and off to the side but in clear view of the board and crowd, and especially the plethora of podium-bound time-wasters. He's trying to be on best behavior because he believes in the power of good first impressions, and he's sitting next to the South County bureau chief for *The Berkshire Eagle*. This bureau chief is a surprisingly young pup who he is taking a shine to, mainly because the youngster has been muttering under his breath, "Eh, brother" or "Oh, brother," for each of the last seven commentators. He'll try to brace the fellow afterward — *If ever there is an after* — and see if he can't grab some local color from an *unnamed local media source*.

Oh fucking brother indeed, Davin thinks, still managing to stifle his groans as yet another member of the public reiterates points already well-reiterated, but then he is pleasantly surprised because the board votes to end public comments on the question at hand.

Unfortunately, relief is not to be since the board has taken this action merely to move on to the next agenda item, which is a vote for authorization of town general funds as requested by the town solicitor to deal with a pending lawsuit about the new solar farm. Everyone, despite the overabundance of comments, recognizes as a foregone conclusion that the town warrant for the solar farm will move forward, so the question at hand is potentially the most interesting one for the evening. Of course, this vote has to be open to public comment too.

Davin lets out a long sigh.

The youngster looks at him with a slight smile and shakes his head.

"A few more *oh brothers* coming our way, my guess," he says to the youngster in a whisper, and the young man shakes his head again and replies with more of a grin and less of a whisper, "*Oh, assholes*, is my guess," and Davin now knows he is a fellow traveler, not to mention a great quote, although he's pretty sure Alicia will disallow it on language grounds.

Still, the language seems on target to him, a matter proved right by the five second homeowners taking turns at the podium with near-identical comments about their houses being near the proposed solar farm site and how so very terrible that is. Each of these five speakers retells the same message one after another, which is basically that the town better not take the chance with a lawsuit threatening if the warrant passes, and one of the speakers even provides a short history of the town's poor track record with lawsuits.

Another speaker steps to the podium, but he doesn't have the same kind of dress as the first five, and Davin wonders if he's perhaps a local farmer.

His new friend leans over to tell him, "Guy owns High Ridge Farm."

The guy at the podium forgets to introduce himself, too busy twisting backward to pin the five earlier speakers with his glare. "So you don't like the view, huh, well I don't like too much CO2 fu—" He pauses slightly, trying to recalibrate his choice of words. "Too much greenhouse gases messing my goddamn planet, so shut the fuck up and grow some trees!" And the gavel is clanking and there's a rush of applause and a lot of the meeting attendees are talking at once, a crescendo of roars.

After the crowd settles down, the vote is motioned and seconded and the meeting is over.

Davin stands up and starts making his way to the hall as the chair gavels the adjournment.

He's got his headline and maybe time for an hour or two's nap before heading to pick up Jimmy.

Chapter 27: Between Syracuse and Saratoga Springs

C yn and Jimmy have been sitting across from each other for many miles, mostly in silence. The outside temperature has cooled significantly in the long movement eastward, and the train car is chilly now that they've traveled well beyond the heat wave inversion system. The air-conditioning has long since stopped struggling against the excessive heat but now instead is overcompensating.

In the coolness of the train car, Jimmy finds himself not entirely believing the heat wave that's been clobbering Chicago and much of the upper Midwest continues, despite his having lived through much of it. He once again checks on the weather in Chicago. According to a quick glance at the Google Thermostat app on his phone, where it's still set for his recently vacated apartment's Nest device, the interior temperature reads ninety-nine degrees with an outside temperature that has fallen cooler now the night is well underway—down to ninety-two degrees.

Jimmy considers rummaging for one of his hooded sweatshirts, but before he reaches for his backpack he realizes that he's done nothing about the ISP service, which means he's still getting billed. He decides to cancel the service when he gets back to Housatonic, but he concedes the very fast Wi-Fi router he and his two roommates recently bought has likely been irretrievably abandoned. Maybe his roommates can go by and pick up the router and a few other items he would have liked to keep, including his monitor. He recognizes too that the various other utility accounts need canceling, and this gets him wondering just how many other loose ends he's managed to leave behind in the heat wave. He'll text his roommates, but he doesn't want to do it now.

Jimmy is glad he'd at least turned off the air-conditioner, but even so he's impressed the temperature has stayed so high inside. Of course, it occurs to him, he'd taken down the old bed sheet he'd tacked over the big set of south-facing living room windows before setting out for the train station. He had left the sheet roughly folded on the futon couch and there it was no longer cutting back on the solar gain, and he guesses the apartment has simply absorbed too much heat through those huge windows.

He now starts inventorying all the items he's left behind and is surprised by the growing value of it all. Even though they'd bought the air-conditioner used, and well before the heat wave price hikes, the unit had been expensive. The router and the Nest Thermostat both had been purchased new. And then there's the desk lamp he really likes, and some clothes abandoned too, and the security deposit he has certainly lost, although the current month's rent hadn't been sent in, so that's a wash, Jimmy figures.

And now I'm heading home.

Jimmy decides this line of thinking isn't doing him much good, so he lets the sway and clacking of the train's movement eastward lull him into falling half asleep for brief periods, but even in those moments when both he and Cyn are awake, conversation limits itself to practical matters.

"Watch my stuff?" asked Cyn once after they'd left the Rochester station while she went off to the restroom.

It wasn't that Jimmy has nothing to say. He finds himself thinking about that guy, Bancroft, with his mentions of *homicide* and *person of interest* and the talk about one hundred grand and lawyers' offices and private detectives.

That had certainly caught his attention.

Post-Rochester, nearing the hour of nine o'clock, one of the more stimulating conversations involves him asking Cyn if he could grab her anything from the dining car. To his disappointment, this so-called dining car turned out to be more like convenience store food than the fancy linen tables of trains found in old movies.

"I should have ordered you a Gibson," he had said to Cynthia upon his return, but this was met with no reaction whatsoever, and Jimmy decided not to try to explain the allusion. Jimmy's father is a fan of Hitchcock, and Jimmy's childhood had included watching *North by Northwest* any number of times.

I gotta leave that shit to Daddo, is his exact thought.

He sees Cyn concentrating on dressing the one hot dog he had brought back for her to his three. He decides not to mention anything about her liking ketchup on her hot dog, and only ketchup, which is obviously a strike against her since he'd long ago adopted the Chicago approach to dressing dogs. Cyn seems to be glad for the cold can of Budweiser, which she polishes off quickly, even as he's still at work on the first of the two cans he brought back for himself. And while he drinks his beer down quickly enough, she's the first to burp, and the goofy face she makes of false shock makes him laugh.

She falls asleep quickly after her feast.

He keeps stealing glances at her and he loves what he sees, even with her hair mussed by being up against the train window and even with that dried drop of drool at the lower corner of her mouth.

Cyn wakes as they slow for Syracuse, and she busies herself with drinking from her water bottle and then inventorying and tidying her belongings and taking the remnants of their late supper to the trash receptacle embedded in the stainless steel wall next to the restroom at the end of the car. He can see the trash is overflowing, its spring lid refusing to shut, and he watches Cyn struggle to push their trash through the hatch, but he manages not to go rescue her effort. By the time the train comes to a stop she's back at her seat, and the train is a bit emptier as it leaves Syracuse Station, their car now less than half-full.

"You okay?" Jimmy asks in the dimmed lighting in the train car at this hour, and the sounds from fellow passengers is minimal too. While there are some other voices murmuring, only one voice is loud enough to make out, one half of a cell phone conversation halfway up the car.

Cyn nods toward the front of the car and touches her ear and nods again toward the cell phone talker. "Sounds like boyfriend trouble," she says.

She looks more relaxed, he thinks.

"Huh," she says. "Boyfriend trouble," in a near hush, and then she looks up at him. "Boyfriend trouble," she says, and she laughs, but it doesn't sound like a laugh, really.

He can't think of anything to say, but he's alert, thinking she wants to talk.

Indeed, she does.

"I was fucking my boss," is how she begins, keeping her eyes on Jimmy. "Plus, like he was a married man," she says with another of those non-laughs.

"The way I like them," she says, almost too low to hear, eyes looking out the window into the darkness beyond the moving train.

Jimmy is completely stunned. He keeps looking at her, so he sees when she turns back toward him, looking right at him, and then she shakes her head and tells Jimmy she would like to talk about "everything," which is how she puts it.

Jimmy nods.

"About Joe getting killed," she says, quiet, but clear.

Jimmy waits for her to continue, but she has again gone silent. He sees her jaw muscles clench, and he's looking at a different expression, something new, away from the fear and shock and shutting down, and he realizes she's angry.

Like, duh, he tells himself.

"Look," she says, "I don't need to involve you, you don't need the story if you don't want."

"No," Jimmy says, and he realizes he's being unclear. "I mean yes, I'd like to hear what happened, like, you know, if you want to, I mean. I know something is up, I mean, like, *person of interest...*" he just trails off, but he sees Cynthia understands what he means because she keeps talking.

The first thing she says is that she didn't kill anyone.

"Umm," he manages by way of reply.

"Joe Craigson was my boss, we were on a business trip, he got shot."

"Umm," Jimmy says again, his vocabulary shrunk down to this one sound.

She waves her hand as if clearing away smoke.

"My boss, and yes, lover, okay? Well, he got shot this past Thursday morning, and I saw it, a guy, a cop, a guy at least dressed like a cop, actually like a deputy, whatever, killed Joe, shot him, and I saw it."

Jimmy doesn't even manage an *umm*.

"Yeah, well," Cynthia says.

"Jesus," he finally says.

As silence stretches, he wonders if Cynthia is done, but finally she continues.

"I freaked out, got the hell out of there fast, and here I am."

Jimmy nods.

"With a gun-packing, rat-faced asshole and then this Dick Tracy guy, and that's part of it, don't know why I haven't been arrested if they know where I am, but the whole thing..." but she trails off again.

She lets her statement hang between them and he just waits.

"The whole thing," she finally resumes, "is too bizarre, with fake texts on my phone..." and she pauses again, back to looking into the passing darkness as the train speeds forward.

"I don't know who to trust," she says, looking back at him, and then her gaze shifts back through the train window, looking at nothing.

"Sorry," she says a few moments later. "This is a lot to put on you, and I'm not telling it right."

Well," Jimmy says.

They sit in silence for a bit.

"Well," he says, "we got hours on the train still, so...."

Cyn looks up at him and sees he has his hand pushing his right ear forward.

She smiles.

"Fuck," she says, and then she asks him to look something up, and when he pulls his laptop out of his backpack and opens it, she takes it, telling him she'll link to the newspaper, *The Examiner*, out of San Francisco, and when she's on *The Examiner*'s site, she hands the laptop back and gives him the name *Joe Craigson*.

As he types in the search term, she moves his backpack off his seat and sits next to him, looking at the screen.

"Start here," she tells him, pointing at the oldest story. "This is what is being said. Read it and then, whatever."

There are several stories in the search results, and he can't help glancing at the latest, titled, "Questions Pile Up on Climate Executive's Killing."

"I haven't seen that one," she tells him. "But I can guess since when I checked, well, the phone texts are raising doubts."

Jimmy looks at her, their heads close.

"Just remember I got my side of the story, and I was there, okay?"

"Okay," he manages to reply, even though in his mind various combinations of *holy shit* are competing for his interest as he continues to chase links and read the news items.

Cyn asks him to stop and go back, and she takes his laptop. She studies the screen intently and then hands the laptop back and shifts back to her seat across from him, her eyes once again looking into the dark.

"Yow," he finally says after a half hour of searches and chasing links. "It suggests that maybe you killed your, uh, Joe, because of something personal, a spat."

A spat, really? he chides himself. *Idiot.*

Cyn responds with a shrug. "There's that and the embezzlement inference, that's new, something Ell made sure to mention, another thing that I also did not do."

Jimmy leans back and looks at her.

She says, "Embezzlement, Jesus," shaking her head.

"It's like or, like, both or either/or," she continues. "It's like it's piling it on, like the texts, the ones I never sent and that Joe wouldn't have sent, the sensational stuff, but yeah, I know, no, not embezzlement, no *spat*, I didn't kill Joe, I didn't put the money in my account, but the stories...."

Jimmy leans forward again, back hunching over the screen, reordering the news queries hit results from *newest to oldest*.

After looking through a link he says, "Yeah, huh, there's one here, recent, this morning, suggests the deposit — money that's supposed to be embezzled — is questionable, uh, 'outside of the company's procedural framework,' whatever that means, and," Jimmy holds up a hand because he senses Cyn wants to grab his laptop, then continues, "...'an unnamed source suggests the phone texts are suspicious, there's something wrong with some of the metadata.'"

"So, some sort of hack, I guess," says Cyn. "I wouldn't know how that can happen."

Jimmy has some ideas about that. Hacking text messages had been a bit of a game his freshman year, but he only tells her that planting text messages is a real thing.

"And this last piece," he continues, sliding the laptop around to face her, "suggests ClimateProgress — that's like your parent company, right? — thinks something's wrong with the whole story, with what happened."

She shrugs, her lips pursed, looks back at him. "I know the whole story is shit, I was there," she says, staring off. "I should have already gone to the police, you know, a fucking *person of interest*, Jesus."

He wants to ask her why she hadn't done so, but he'll let her keep talking without him playing interrogator.

"The only thing they got right was that I was, you know, with Joe, but how would they even know that?" She stops for a moment, and then goes on. "Well, there's the itinerary, but we had separate rooms, it's not like we, well."

Jimmy tries to follow.

"There were a whole bunch of texts I didn't send, never wrote, and some from Joe that just wasn't him, couldn't be, but the idea that those are fake—"

"—inserted, you mean, the ones you two didn't send," he clarifies.

"Yeah, these were, I don't know, were making it seem like we were having a big blow up, even a mention of a gun."

"Shit," Jimmy says.

"Yeah, no kidding, shit," Cyn says.

"Joe is not the guy who would have a gun," she adds, "or would bring it on a business trip or could get it through the airport security."

She stops again.

After some silence, she starts in again. "The texts are bullshit, aren't by me or by Joe." She looks directly into Jimmy's eyes. "Well, at least one of the fucking texts came after..." and she pauses for a moment before going on, "were sent after I saw he was dead, so, yeah." She turns away, but not before Jimmy sees her eyes water, and for several minutes he simply sits across from her, silent.

The reading spots above Cynthia and Jimmy have been on the whole time, but as the train pulls into Schenectady, he reaches up and shuts one off and then the other.

"Thanks," Cyn says, but even before the train completely stops the main lights in the car come on. She pats his knee and shrugs with a bit of a smile. "Good idea anyway."

The car lights go back off once the train is out of the station and the conductor—a new one, a sallow tall man who whistles tunelessly—makes his pass through the car checking stubs.

No one new has boarded the car.

"Umm," says Jimmy after some more time passes in silence. The clack of the tracks and other peoples' voices offer a quiet background sound in the dimmed car. Others' reading spots are still on here and there. Jimmy's laptop, back on his lap with the screen open toward him, casts its bright glow until the laptop goes into sleep mode the screen going dark, but there's enough reflected light from the few spots still on in the car and occasional flashes of light through the windows — streetlights and headlights, mostly — sometimes have a strobing effect.

The dark surrounding them surrenders to his phone when he takes a quick look. He figures it must be two in the morning, and while it feels like he's been on the train for ages, when he wakes his phone he's surprised it's just past midnight. "The train is making better time than it used to," he tells her as he texts something on his phone. They sit in silence, both facing each other, giving themselves to the rhythm of the movement.

He's exhausted but imagines how much worse Cyn must be feeling, so he's surprised to see her reach up and turn on the reading spot above her.

She takes his laptop and seems to be looking up another site or two, but mostly she talks to him about the details of what happened in the desert, but haltingly, with pauses when she gets distressed or when she thinks to look up something new.

While Cyn takes a break from talking to drain her water bottle, a thought pops into Jimmy's mind.

He likes her even more, this side of her, her anger. He's amazed by this change in her affect. But he guesses it's more than just that. He and she are talking, really connecting. She seems stronger now.

Jimmy almost laughs at this.

No shit, Sherlock, he tells himself, as the train travels ever eastward into strange new territory.

Chapter 28: Welcome Home

The car ride back from the Pittsfield Amtrak station has been largely quiet after the first frantic burst of Davin's and Jimmy's greetings and hugs and various body thumpings, but that may have something to do with the hour, dawn not even hinted.

Daddo is not used to these hours, Jimmy is quite sure, but he's told him he's just glad to have him home, and there's no problem, hour-wise, really.

If it had been Gwen doing the pickup, it would be a very different scene during the ride home, Jimmy knows, but she's on call at the health service and so has to stay local to be available, just in case. He's relieved, since he knows his mother would be asking all sorts of questions to get all the latest news about his life. Or at least trying to anyway, it being her usual habit when seeing him after almost any length of absence to pump him for information — girlfriends, activities, work, work searches, to name some common lines of inquiry along the spectrum of persuasive questioning akin to old-time hot-lights interrogation. He would always try to hold that onslaught off, often escaping with a promise to talk later, which he almost always did, although his mom might dispute that.

And having Cyn in tow would really ratchet up his mom's questions.

Jimmy knows his dad is just as curious, but he also knows his dad long-ago developed the habit of holding off with questions of his own with Gwen not present, knowing she could not get over the idea of any sort of exclusive contact that could lead to missing any vital piece of information. Jimmy also had come to know, even before the divorce, that his dad was bad in relaying any and all sorts of information to Gwen, and Jimmy presumes that post-divorce any new and better habits haven't likely developed.

The last time he and Dad had had a substantive telephone call was a few weeks back, and Jimmy remembers something about the online newspaper thing Dad had done some consulting for last year, and him mentioning that some new work was coming his way.

Or so Jimmy thinks, although he wouldn't necessarily put a big bet down on it since he'd been kind of playing a game on his laptop while he was talking with him.

Of course, Dad had immediately noticed Jimmy wasn't alone as he pulled the car up toward the station's curb zone for pickup. Jimmy had provided the barest heads-up when texting him for pickup, including not mentioning the friend coming along with him was a young woman, and of course, Jimmy could see *The Question* flash across Dad's face as Cyn was introduced.

Thank god Dad hadn't outright asked whether or not she might be his girlfriend, but then Dad probably knew he most likely would just deflect the question on general principle, in keeping with the way he handles his folks when it comes to things he thinks of as personal matters. He would have simply refused to acknowledge the question, stating it was time to move on to another subject.

Moving on to other subjects wasn't hard, usually, with his dad. His dad, he'd noticed over the last few years, tends to talk about the things he's doing, which is fine by Jimmy, as that tendency keeps the degree of scrutiny much cooler than the interrogative onslaughts he would suffer with his mom.

"Daddo," Jimmy says from the back seat with Cyn. "Mom said in an email you guys were taking in a boarder." Jimmy stops, but Dad appears to be waiting for more.

"I mean, you are taking boarders," Jimmy corrects. The divorce had happened during Jimmy's sophomore year, a year or so past that Covid start time, and he had stayed at school and environs throughout the pandemic.

"Has that started?" he asks.

"Yes," Davin says. "About, almost eight weeks ago."

"How's it going?"

Davin pauses for a moment before launching into his reply. "Pretty good. There are two boarders, one's just started, just starting, helps defray costs for everyone," he answers.

"Cool," Jimmy says as a placeholder.

"Guy by the name of Chaplin, Chaplin Chalousky, was at Monument, says he was in your class."

Jimmy tries to remember something about Chaplin, but he's pretty sure they didn't know each other much, and he must be a local guy, he thinks. He's not really drawing a clear picture, and he's about to ask for more information from Davin to get a better bead, but before he forms the question, Davin is describing Chaplin as being about five-six, brown hair, works carpentry jobs.

Of course, Jimmy thinks, Chaplin, kind of a nice guy from what he can recall, at least not one of the asshole kids who think that somehow living out in the Berkshires all their lives means something special.

Jimmy asks if Chaplin has a tattoo on his wrist, underside, the left one. Jimmy's fairly sure it was a bird head or serpent, if he's thinking of the right person. He can half remember something happening in the halls, a group of kids looking at the new tat.

Davin answers, "Yeah, that's him. Nice fellow. Are you from around here?" he asks, addressing Cyn. "I assume Chicago, but then you know what *assume* means."

Jimmy knows what *assume* means, having heard this— *What? A joke? Folk wisdom?* – a hundred times, something his dad claimed he'd first seen on some work floor safety poster in one of those summer factory jobs he'd worked going through college.

But of course, that's not the issue. The point is Cynthia Wainwright is a *person of interest* in her boss's death.

Welcome home, Jimmy thinks.

Cyn seems surprisingly unaffected by her being in the

back seat of a car being driven by a guy she's just met, sitting next to another guy she'd only met on a train, more or less the day before. Jimmy doesn't think there's actual calm, *just some sort of zoning out.* But after all, she's just gone through a very long train ride, and if he has it right, a lot more before he met her on the train.

Person of interest.

On the train, she had kept going into what Jimmy thinks of as some kind of *suspended animation*, but now, his dad having asked a question, Cyn's body tension is palpably broadcasting high alert, and Jimmy sees her leaning forward, her body stiff with a tightness Jimmy can feel sitting next to her.

"I'm not Jimmy's girlfriend," she says, or blurts, and Jimmy feels a flush of embarrassment sweep his face. He notices that her voice is high and tight.

"Well," Davin says, but her tone is cluing him in to leave this alone, Jimmy's sure.

Jeepers, Jimmy thinks. This now feels weirder than those many strange moments on the train.

"I'm in a lot of trouble," Cyn says, trembling, whether from fear or rage, Jimmy can't tell, and then she's back against the seat, eyes closed, and Jimmy would swear she's just fallen asleep.

"Well," Davin says, looking at the road, left and right, as they stop at the crossing of Route 102 before rocketing across the intersection, now about ten minutes from home. And then a moment later, Jimmy thinks he hears his father say, "Ass You Me."

Chapter 29: Google Central Dispatch

Now home, and a guy who Jimmy really doesn't know from high school is now more or less a kind of roommate, and he has just been wakened by the guy, Chaplin, who has tried to be quiet, he supposes, but he knows the rooms on the third floor can be a bit sound transparent, especially the one across the narrow hall.

Movement in that other room has woken him.

Without doubt, this is a weird situation, he thinks.

He recognizes the sound that has fully awakened him is from the bathroom door across the hall, where the door can be noisy because it sticks against the frame. The door needs to be lifted upward and to the left to clear it free and it has to be closed just so too, or you can just slam it a bit, which he now believes is the noise that woke him. Chaplin as yet hasn't mastered the touch, is what Jimmy figures.

He thinks of getting up and saying hello, but he'll wait until later. Everything is too strange already, and he got to bed no more than two hours ago, after eating leftovers down in the kitchen, and he's not ready for any such meet-and-greet. He hears the person who must be Chaplin head down the creaky stairs, and that is more than enough to settle the matter of saying hello at this moment.

There hadn't been much talk with his dad when they got home. Davin had barely been able to keep his eyes open, and he begged off shortly after prepping food for Cyn and Jimmy.

And Cyn is no doubt asleep, he's thinking, as he sits up in bed and looks at the window fan drawing air from outside. The air is starting to get warm as the morning comes on full, so he gets up to turn off the window fan lodged in the window closest to the attic door stairway. She's up these narrow stairs, sleeping in a bed in the finished space, or maybe she's up, he considers, but Jimmy hears nothing, and it strikes him as unlikely she has gotten up and past him without his waking.

This is weird, he thinks again.

He wants to get back to bed, but he dresses instead, pulling some old clothes that have remained in the bureau of his bedroom untouched for quite a while.

The clothes seem okay, smell okay, if maybe a bit stale. The first t-shirt he pulls on is too tight, but the second one is okay. The bottom drawer has boxers and socks just where he'd left them, possibly years before.

Jimmy shakes his head, then quietly laughs.

He hasn't been back here since those two days last Christmas, and now here he is, just another adult child living at home. Not that this is unusual these days, and certainly during Covid that happened a lot, but even before, with the high cost of rents and everything else. Things are even worse now, with the on-off recessions and hit and run inflation that have followed the pandemic, so that adult children living at home has become practically common, normal.

He shouldn't complain, having held out so long, including riding out the disastrous pandemic in Chicago, at school, where he'd just gotten an off-campus apartment with a couple of other guys he knew from the dorms in his freshman year. The next two academic years had seen him stay in the city through the summers, more due to luck than anything else, that luck being a friend of a fellow computer science major whose father owned a distribution center, so he had spent those summers of junior and senior years doing warehouse work alongside his pal.

Jimmy misses the apartment, although not the last month, or the last dozen days anyway when temperatures rose ever higher and stayed too hot, the city fraying from the relentless onslaught. But he knows that he will miss his roommates and other Chicago friends. He's worried he'll find being back

home a step backward, and the addition of local roommates—
boarders—is another odd twist, but his dad is happy to have
him home, he's sure.

The more the merrier, Jimmy can't help wondering.

And there's the woman, Deidre, coming, from what his
dad mentioned during the car ride back from Pittsfield, and if
Jimmy's heard right, she's moving in today.

His dad had mentioned that Deidre is a bit younger, and
if Jimmy heard right too, her room is on the second floor on
the opposite end from his dad's office, the room that had long
been the old guest bedroom, back when he was younger.

Back when we were one big happy family.

That last summer he'd lived here before heading back to
college as a sophomore, his folks were already showing signs
of the upcoming split, even if they themselves hadn't had a
clue at the time, but he and Sis had talked about it.

As for this Deidre, she's completely unknown to him from
high school, or at least he thinks it likely he'd never run into
her. With her a couple of years younger, a freshman to his
senior, his never having met her wouldn't be surprising at any
rate.

This is weird, he tells himself again, the seeming mantra of
the day.

And then there's Cynthia, who seems to prefer Cyn, but
he's finding himself thinking of her as *mystery girl* as often as
not in his own head, along with *person of interest*, too.

Davin had suggested before he'd gone up to bed that
Cynthia could be put up in Chaplin's room across the hall,
maybe, or at least that was his father's proposal, with Chaplin
moving above him, up in the finished attic—*Well, kinda
finished, more like camping out* – going through Jimmy's room to
get there. Living up there means living with the really big
window fan in the attic's gable end window that blows out the
day's warm air overnight, so the door at the base of the attic
stairs is kept open to let cooler air get pulled in by the window
fan he's just turned off or through other open windows. If his
bedroom door is left open overnight, then it makes for more

cooling air pulled in for the whole house.

Jimmy doesn't keep his bedroom open unless the house gets hot, and then since Chicago, his standard for what's hot and what is not has shifted well upward.

Dad had told them he'd ask Chaplin if he wouldn't mind the temporary move, and Jimmy suspects, from an oblique comment or two from his dad, that Chaplin is light on rent this month, so it's probably a win-win thing. Jimmy had supposed Cynthia might stay in the Airbnb apartment, but when he'd asked, Davin simply looked annoyed before mentioning the state of disrepair of the apartment, which was something Jimmy had learned only in that moment.

The state of the Airbnb apartment is something that clearly upsets Daddo, and money concerns generally, he suspects. Some part of this could be Chaplin being short on rent, not that Jimmy feels critical or judgmental about Chaplin. After all, it isn't like he's in any better shape. There's no job income for him since there's no job at all, and there's nothing, really, in savings, and here he is back living with the folks.

Well, folk, singular, he clarifies to himself.

He figures job prospects look unlikely if he stays in the area. He knows well enough that his background in computer science and coding puts him in a much better position for employment than many of his contemporaries, despite the encroaching inroads of AI-assisted coding. But opportunities for any such work in the Berkshires are slim to none, although the telecommute option has to be considered too.

It could be worse, he knows. Several of his close Housatonic friends — two key ones anyway — are back in town living at home, in similar circumstances. He's kept in contact with these pals, though less by email and the rarer yet telephone conversations, but mostly by texting and in conversations held in between the trash talk that takes place during the online games the old gang still frequently play together.

Back at home, he tells himself again, a refrain.

For now, he reminds himself.

He actually likes his folks, which is apparently a somewhat rare thing as he discovered among his college peers. His folks are always ready to help, but they also give him space. Without them — and he wonders if he'll ever get over the persisting sense of guilt — he'd be in deep debt for his college degree, and even as it is, he's many tens of grand in.

The divorce feels odder now that he's back home, more real, harder to ignore, which is how he has mostly dealt with it up to now.

He also knows his dad is probably now hoping — *hope against hope*, Jimmy can imagine hearing his dad say — that he, *son and free labor*, will help out in the grand project, *the terraforming*, as Davin himself has quite often jokingly called the collected projects on the house, as Jimmy all too well knows

He feels bad about not wanting to help on the property.

Or being interested enough, he wonders if that may well be the real question.

He fishes his shoes from under his bed, puts them on, and stands up.

He picks up his phone and sees it's not quite seven o'clock in the morning, which means he's slept for only a couple of hours.

Seven in the morning, he thinks, tossing the phone back on his rumpled bed so he can rub his eyes. He's stayed up this late any number of times, especially after game jams, recovering from thirty-six-and forty-eight-hour sprees of game design competition, at least before he settled down to endure his work toward the computer science degree. He's pretty sure he hasn't gotten up before eight o'clock since he was laid off, old night habits growing worse and worse since then.

He just stands there, and he finds it interesting he feels a kind of loneliness, some longing, maybe, and part of it is leaving his life in Chicago, but there seems to be some pull toward *mystery girl*, just a stairway away and most likely in some deep crash of sleep. Maybe it's simply that he finds her attractive. It isn't that he hasn't had girlfriends out in

Chicago, and plenty of opportunities for sex too, although he is self-consciously proud that he has run Tinder-free the whole time. Still, he'd been generally disappointed with the women he'd dated, sensing there was something missing, not interesting enough.

That ain't the case here, he admits.

He knows his dad has some sense there's some sort of trouble dogging Cyn, considering she'd admitted as much in the car ride home, but there hadn't been an inclination on his dad's part to pursue it, or maybe his dad had simply been too tired, using that goofy expression he liked, *I hear my bed springs creaking*, to excuse himself from the kitchen while the two travelers settled down to their feast of leftovers.

Jimmy sneaks up the attic stairs, worried that Cyn, if awake, will think he's being creepy, but he just wants to shut off the big fan to keep the warming air of the day from undoing the night cooling.

He can't help but look over after the fan goes silent, and there she is, under blankets, dead to the world.

He edges back down and opens his bedroom door and steps into the hall, and he notes his dad's bedroom door is closed, which makes it likely his dad is still asleep. Jimmy starts to head down to the kitchen with his laptop in hand.

Up before Dad, Jimmy thinks. *Miracles happen.*

Jimmy pauses on the second-floor landing to look through the open door into his dad's office, and he sees the room is unoccupied, confirming his dad must still be sacked out upstairs. He tries as best he can to be quiet on the stairs down to the kitchen, but he's a big guy and it's an old house, and there's only so much quiet to be had that still leaves plenty of creaking treads and the occasional pop of the wood.

As he gets to the bottom, Jimmy witnesses a small pickup rolling down the driveway, just a glimpse through the dining room's glass door to a small deck, before the truck is out of sight. Has to be Chaplin, Jimmy surmises, and he's struck by the reappearance of the relief he'd felt just minutes earlier when he had put off the introductions.

His priority today is to get information about Cyn's situation together for his dad, knowing he'll will appreciate it, and besides, Jimmy figures this a good strategy for keeping Davin from freaking out, or freaking out more.

Hey Dad, Jimmy imagines, *this is Cynthia, who saw a murder and the police in California want to talk to her, she's a person of interest, and at first everyone figured she killed her boss who's this guy she was sleeping with.*

Yeah, no, he tells himself.

He places his laptop on the kitchen island, opening it to check if the Wi-Fi network is still the same, which, no surprise, it is. He keeps from rolling his eyes at the poor security hygiene, but then again, he knows a bit more than others about digital security.

He rummages around the kitchen and finds a half-full box of Hostess Cinnamon Donuts on top of the fridge. *Bad boy*, Jimmy thinks, silently reproving his dad, and then he has to wonder if these maybe are Chaplin's. He figures it's better to ask forgiveness than permission, and he puts four of them on a plate and tosses the box back up in place, then grabs a glass and fills it with cold milk after sniffing the carton and finding all is well. He pulls a stretch of paper towel off the roll near the sink, then half-way rerolls it when he spies a stack of folded cloth napkins and tosses one of them on the island next to the plate.

He sits.

The browser still has some open tabs he and Cyn had been looking at on the train.

He takes a donut and tears it in half with his teeth, but the half he's chewing needs milk to keep him from choking. Unfortunately, his fingers are now covered with a cinnamon coating sludge, and there's already something of a trail of cinnamon dust on his t-shirt.

He gets up, washes his hands at the sink, and brushes the front of his shirt. Then he pulls a butter knife from the utensil drawer and cuts the remaining three and a half donuts into quarter pieces. Next up he grabs a pickle fork from the drawer.

A dainty-assed donut-eating son of a gun, he says to himself, picking up a donut chunk with the small fork and popping it into his mouth, but he waits on another gulp of milk until after he's used the napkin to wipe donut schmutz from the glass of milk.

Laptop care is one of his few voluntary chores.

He opens a new Word document and goes back to the browser to start his search fresh, but not before setting up a Google Alert on Cynthia Wainwright, her company, her dead boss, and a few other terms he's gleaned from his earlier conversation with her.

The broad scope of her story becomes clear all within minutes of his starting in. He's getting the news hits right up top, but after these items fill the screen, the following search results for Cynthia Wainwright become the more normal sort, including a profile of her on the Carbon's End website and some links to her work at the Sierra Club. The search results fade into Facebook posts, and considering her most recent post's date, these look like she seems to have let Facebook go a couple years back. The second-to-last post is almost a whole year before that one, her Facebook run ending in a whimper.

It takes a while to realize he seems to be spending a lot of time looking at pictures of Cyn, including a lot that go back to her high school and early college days, candid snaps mostly, many posted by friends on her Timeline before her participation in Facebook had entirely faded.

He should be busy with the browser and his notetaking, but it's nice to see the photos. There are even some from what looks like summer camp and some with horses.

He renews his efforts on pulling together something for his dad.

Just the facts, ma'am. Another of his dad's sayings Jimmy has adopted, although he doesn't know the original source, only that it was from a movie or an old television show, he's pretty sure.

In a short time, he's piecing together *the whole murder thing.* He's saving links to the news stories, most of which are out of San Francisco, but also there are some from a climate change news site. The articles on the general news sites tend toward the sensational, some with salacious slants, but the climate change–focused news site has stories that look at what Carbon's End has been doing, including a piece containing some details of the divestment deal Cyn and her boss had been working on. Carbon's End's own web page is especially helpful in that way too, and the memorial content for Joe Craigson he finds there makes Jimmy feel something of the human tragedy of what's happened and a stronger appreciation too of the feelings Cyn must be going through.

Just a sex thing, right? Jimmy finds himself thinking, and he is bothered by it, but he thinks she'd been fond of the guy too. He understands the concept of women with married men, or at least as a trope in literature and movies, for sure, but he's never really thought about it himself before. He's feeling a bit young and naïve by it all.

Jimmy wipes his mouth and hands again and steps away from the island to stretch, palms flat against the ceiling, and in the morning light pouring through the south window and glass deck door near the stair landing, he can see on the ceiling of the kitchen a hundred handprint ghosts. Just traces, seen mostly in the right lighting conditions on the paint, but long an annoyance for his father, who for some time back had asked him not to do this touching, and later, a few times, to wash down the ceiling to rid the marks.

He shrugs his shoulders.

He knows that Dad had given up these requests some years earlier. The ceilings are not abnormally low, except, really, for him, and the ceiling press is a hard habit to curb.

He sits back down and continues his research. He's especially glad to read Carbon's End's press release countering a lot of the speculation and suspicion about Cynthia Wainwright. He notices this has been posted barely two hours back, which Jimmy calculates is three hours behind Eastern time and so in the wee hours Pacific time.

Someone is working hard on this mess.

He's also impressed the post even directly addresses Cynthia, urging her to contact them and the authorities.

Makes sense, he thinks. He wonders about her apparent resistance to doing so, although he doesn't have to look too hard to find any number of reasons for her to be nervous. There are continuing allegations in some of the current stories even, along with some common confusion that *person of interest* implies *murder suspect*. On the other hand, a quick tally reveals the majority of the most recent stories aren't alleging Cynthia Wainwright killed Joe Craigson, and even the allegations of embezzlement that had shown up in a few of the early articles and posts have been dismissed in most of current coverage.

He ends up going down the rabbit hole of searching for any coverage that might confirm the reporters are walking back their early speculations, and as best he can put together from the two instances he finds — one a letter to the editor — it's because there's been little to collaborate the embezzlement angle. The one follow-up news story he has found cites the outright denials of any such alleged financial wrongdoing from ClimateProgress.Org. ClimateProgress, Jimmy now knows, is the name of Carbon's End's parent organization.

Another thing that now strikes him as odd is how the story arc in so many of the very first articles and posts have so quickly subsided from the sensational coverage of a lovers' quarrel and its veiled murder story of the desperate young woman killing her boss. Like the embezzlement angle, this aspect of the story has largely faded. Even the indirect references of phone texts in a few of the early stories Cyn had mentioned have become rare, and he concludes a lot of what was first reported has turned out to be simply uncollaborated and speculative.

The *twitterverse*, when Jimmy dives in, is another matter altogether with some wild theories presented, including retweeting many of these early stories in a celebration of the sensational, including a hashtag *#savetheclimatekillyourlover* picked up and retweeted across many accounts. He guesses most of these are some sort of trolls, but he knows too that many people still fall for that sort of thing. Among some Facebook pages, Twitter feeds, and a couple of blogs on climate change activism, there are some conspiracy theories being floated that suggest organizations from the fossil fuel industry are involved, or in one instance that makes Jimmy laugh out loud, that England's royal family is behind a plot to discredit climate activism and is murdering them.

That one was most likely a joke, he concludes. Still, not a far stretch, he tells himself, since the Queen of England was behind the international drug trade, right? He's always surprised by what stupid things too many people believe, although considering the last few years and the 2024 election, he knows he should be inured to it.

He doesn't bother looking at Truth Social, but there's plenty of crass and hateful comments in other threads that he comes across, and that makes him feel that much more protective of Cyn. He thinks he's making a reasonable effort to look at the information online objectively.

On the other hand, the idea of Cyn sleeping with her boss, her married boss, produces some uneasy feelings.

None of my business, he tells himself, but he's bothered by how unconvincing this argument rings. He may just be experiencing a stupid crush, he supposes, hoping he can dismiss the upset he experiences every time he comes across another speculation about the relationship between Cyn and her boss.

Just trying to help, right?

And he does think he's just someone trying to help. Besides, he understands he has some responsibility to find things out, having brought Cyn to his home.

One of the more interesting things he finds after a while is a blog post about the Joe Craigson killing that focuses on the rapid dissemination of allegations against Cynthia Wainwright, with the author suggesting the timing is odd, exactly as he's already wondered.

The blogger is apparently well known, as best as Jimmy

bothers to determine, although he wonders if something published on *Medium* is still a blog or could ever possibly be considered as well-known. Still, he is interested to see that the blogger had taken the trouble to contact some of the reporters who had written the early stories to inquire into where and how they'd gotten such information, to ask why the early reports have been walked back, and two of the reporters quoted agreed the earliest leads were unusual, but they both are evasive about their early sources.

He's been at it for well over an hour, and he feels confident he's chased down as many of the few facts he can find and has already sent the one-page precis he's just finished off to Daddo's email and to the printer in his dad's office. But now, his task complete, a lot of what he finds himself doing online is looking for links about Cyn beyond those related to what has happened out near Barstow or the theories and speculations thereof. He knows he's spending too much time on her online presence, as sparse as it is, save the social media content around her work with the Sierra Club, which is mainly informational or logistical in nature, part of her organizing for the march. He knows his searching has nothing to do with her current situation.

I'm a cyber-stalker, he chides himself.

He also finds himself distracted by his last exposure to her in the real world, just a brief moment in the early hours before turning in. She'd come from showering, walking through his bedroom to get to the narrow stairs up to the attic space, looking great in the oversized t-shirt he'd given her.

Stay on target, stay on target, he tells himself, automatically adding, *Luke, your targeting computer's off!*

He shakes his head, but even as he is thinking of the old *Star Wars* line, his dad walks into the kitchen, a bit haggard looking from his odd night, but he's holding the printout and thanks Jimmy with a nod and without delay gets to work brewing coffee.

There's one quarter of one of the donuts left on Jimmy's plate, and he pushes it toward Davin, who looks at the piece and laughs.

"All gone?" Davin asks, but Jimmy nods toward the fridge and Davin sees the box and takes it down.

"Huh," Davin mutters, seeing there are two of the mini donuts left.

"Well," he continues, "Chaplin did tell me to help myself."

"I figured they were yours," Jimmy confesses, which makes Davin laugh. Jimmy knows they both know his dad has trouble resisting such things.

"Still don't drink coffee?" Davin asks and Jimmy shakes his head.

He tells Davin he's heading back upstairs but is happy to talk about the situation.

Davin tells his son he hasn't yet looked over the various links and asks him to sum up what sort of trouble Cynthia is in.

"Big time," Jimmy says, surprising his dad.

Davin's measuring spoon stops halfway toward the coffeemaker, but he says nothing and after a moment returns to spooning the ground coffee into the filter cone. "Hold on a sec," Davin says, his back still to Jimmy. "I don't want to lose count." When he's done and has started the coffee maker, Davin turns to face Jimmy. "What does that mean, 'big time'?" he asks.

"Wanted by the police for questioning, possibly as an embezzler, certainly as a potential witness or person with possible knowledge about the murder of her boss," he says, which not surprisingly stuns Daddo. Jimmy waits a beat or two and then lets his dad know most of these accusations are already being dismissed, including any likelihood of her being a murderer, or so it seems from what he's been able to pull together.

The conversation takes a few more minutes with Davin asking for clarifications.

"Well," Davin adds, "there's one thing I'm not getting."

Jimmy's pretty sure he knows what his father means. "Why hasn't she gone to the police?"

"Yeah."

"She says the guy who shot Joe Craigson" — and here Jimmy stops himself from saying *boss and lover* — "the guy who killed him was a cop." He adds, "Well, some sort of uniformed law enforcement sort anyway." He pauses, watching his dad's expression.

"Or at least was dressed up in uniform with what sounds like a law enforcement vehicle, flashing lights, the whole bit."

"Okay, fair enough," his dad answers, after mulling this latest item over. "But that was in Barstow, and Barstow is in California, and she's here in Housatonic?"

Jimmy just shrugs.

"I got to look up more stuff," Jimmy tells Davin. "I'm going up, work in the living room."

Davin tells Jimmy he's heading downtown, already pressed for time, and Jimmy feels bad about springing all this on him, and he's worried Daddo is running late exactly because he had to get up in the middle of the night to drive up to Pittsfield to pick up his son, or that his son happened to have brought along a woman who may or may not be wanted for murder, not that Jimmy believes Cyn has killed anyone, and from the most recent coverage he can see his view is the prevailing one.

Actually, he corrects himself, the emerging consensus is that Cynthia Wainwright is likely dead.

He looks back at his dad, who is silently looking at him.

"You okay?" Jimmy asks.

Davin waves the question away. "Just have to take this meeting, I'll be back soon enough, no problem," and then he is clanking his now empty mug into the sink and grabbing the car keys off the key posts by the door as he steps onto the porch. Before Jimmy is even halfway to the stairs, he sees through the glass door a car passing upward below the small deck, so that all Jimmy really sees is a red rumbling rush of something up the driveway, and his dad pops back in, asking if he'd mind going up to the parking area with him to meet Deidre and could he give her a hand with her things?

Chapter 30: Deidre Does Dizzy

Davin can't help but think Deidre seems a bit stunned, her move-in day finally here. This is what he sees after he's carried down a suitcase from her mother's borrowed car, having gone up to meet her up in the parking area.

It occurs to him that he might be projecting. This thing with that girl, and what Jimmy has told him seems stunning enough.

Still, he'll give her the tour. It isn't like Deidre hasn't seen the house, but the previous visit, admittedly, had been rushed. She'd gotten to all the questions he'd asked, and had a quick look at the bedroom, and had presented him the deposit check, but she hadn't really gotten a good sense of the place.

He hears Jimmy come in to drop off some boxes in the living room before heading back up toward her car.

Davin tries to look at the space from her perspective, and it is indeed a lovely room they are standing in, her new bedroom, lovely, albeit on the small side but with plenty of light. The room is looking even smaller, with the boxes and suitcase they'd dropped off yesterday, when he'd given her a hand. She's standing by the double bed that's part of the furnishings provided, but then she steps past him through the room's exterior entry door and onto a small deck that has a small patio table complete with table umbrella. She sits herself down in one of the two plastic chairs that go with the table.

Davin follows her but stops in the doorway.

"It really is a nice space, a nice house," she says. "The first time I saw it, I, I feel like I didn't really see it."

Her room is on the north side of the house, so the deck is

mostly in shade now, although there was still a bit of morning sunlight when she'd gotten here, he'd been glad to note. The ash tree close to the northwest corner of the deck helps keep the deck cool through the later part of the day, the shade of it blocking some of the afternoon slant of sun.

"With the sudden vacate notice and all, you know, I felt all in a hurry," she adds.

"So, an act of desperation," he quips, but he sees right away Deidre has taken this the wrong way.

He tells her he's just kidding, even as she says, "No no no."

Jimmy steps onto the small deck, a stack of boxes in his arms, and Davin steps back to give him passage, telling him he can drop her stuff in the library to give her some space for settling in. Davin pokes his head back through the outside door and tells Deidre he's happy to continue the tour, and she gets up to follow him through the bedroom and into the room with all the bookshelves.

"The library," he announces, rather needlessly, considering all the shelves packed with books, all except one shelf near his other office door, where many liquor bottles crowd together. He steps around the boxes Jimmy's just dropped in the middle of the floor and sees him head out the French doors in the living room to grab another load from the car up in the back.

"The layout of the house can be a bit confusing and takes some time to figure out," he says to Deidre, who can't help but look over the books on the shelves nearest her.

"Feel free to read what's here," he tells her, noting her apparent interest. "Just return them, please."

She is checking out some of the other shelves but shakes herself free.

"Great," she says.

"The house was originally a two-family, maybe 1890s, but when we bought it, much had already been opened up on this floor." He shows her the bathroom whose walls jut out in the middle of the library space and then he points to the door on the opposite end of the library and he tells her that door opens into his office, then walks her back around the bathroom toward her bedroom but jogs rightward through a sizable opening into the living room Jimmy had disappeared through a minute before, but Davin stops here to point out a large sliding door that can close the opening.

This sliding door, he tells her, he had built using the old windows that had been replaced by him with better insulated windows. "You'll find the house to be pretty tight, well-insulated, not much in the way of drafts."

He half-heartedly starts sliding the big unit along its barn door track and then reverses the motion to its fully open position.

"Slide this closed if people are using the living room, for quiet, and sometimes, if the fireplace in the living room is being used we'll close this anyway, so the living room warms up from the fire."

Deidre looks at the fireplace, nodding, and then she looks all around.

Watching her take in the living room, he smiles. It's a bit narrow in width, especially in the middle interior where bathroom walls also bump out a bit into the long room that runs the whole length of the house, with the fireplace tucked into the corner near the exterior French doors.

"Nice windows," she says, looking at the big span of windows at the southern end. Davin explains his thinking behind building what he likes to call the window wall, which is that these large windows are south facing so are good for solar gain. "Of course, when it's night and cold and winter, we pull down the insulated curtains." He steps toward these windows and demonstrates, partially releasing the cord that lets the thick roll of material unfurl, but he pulls the roll back up, tight.

"You can use the fireplace," he mentions, gesturing with his chin to the other end. "It really does a good job heating the space, has efficiency from ventilating fans, but wait until I give you a lesson on how to use it, okay?"

Deidre nods.

Davin points to the landing just past the interior door at the window wall end of the living room and at the stairs going down. "If you remember, these go to the dining room and kitchen, and there's a small deck on the south face too, but on the first floor, which is one of the ways people get confused about the layout as your deck and entrance are second floor, but at ground level because the house is built into the slope."

Deidre nods.

"Laundry is off the kitchen, in the big room I call the pantry because…" He hesitates, then adds, "Well, because it's also used as a pantry, and there's a half bath on the other side of the kitchen, the door near the stove and fridge."

He realizes he better get going since he is already late, even though he did text Alicia about being delayed. He cuts the tour short, but not before he mentions there's a second smaller fridge for the house sharers' use in the pantry.

He then again points to the door on the other side of the landing and tells her this is a second door to his office and then he gestures toward the stairs rising upward. "Third floor, three bedrooms, I have my bedroom up there with a bath, although the bathroom has a second door off the hall, and sometimes it makes sense for people with rooms up there to use that bathroom."

He wants to say he prefers the second-floor bathroom and the half-bath off the kitchen are what the house sharers use, but he can't quite get himself to say that.

Jimmy comes back through the French doors carrying a big plastic bag that probably has clothes in it, Davin guesses.

"Take a look around outside too," Davin suggests. "I have to get going to a meeting."

"Say hello to Alicia for me," Deidre says.

Davin is puzzled by this, since the two women had just met yesterday. Maybe Deidre is just the friendly sort, he figures.

But he doesn't rush out quite yet, instead taking a few more moments to tell her the landscaping is pretty, and makes a point to mention he hopes she'll like the small flowerbed at the front edge of the deck that gives entry to her room. He's proud of the plantings he's nurtured, including the large bed that runs along the other side of the bluestone and crushed-stone path ending at the start of the sloping lawn leading to the parking area where her mother's car is currently parked. The landscaping continues all along this rising strip of lawn, an extensive bed of hosta, vinca, and day lilies, and the day lilies are just starting to produce the stalks. Mixed in here and there are some tulips at the end of their bloom and some peonies beginning to leaf out. The north property line is about twenty-five feet from Deidre's deck, he mentions, and this runs parallel to the edge of her deck and the bluestone and crushed-stone pathway and the deeper bed there that holds a sea of vinca and several islands of irises now in bloom and a couple of clumps of baptisia, plus a bank of hydrangea that partly block the house next door.

He mentions that the pathway separating the small flower bed along the front of her deck and the deeper bed on the property line goes downward around past the ash tree, where steps of landscape ties and large bluestone slabs drop to the front of the house's first floor and porch. "In nice weather," he tells her, "you can even just pop out via the deck and head around down to the kitchen."

"The ties can get slippery when wet though, so..." he adds, but trails off.

Just get going, Davin tells himself. He's surprised by how much he wants to give Deidre a full tour, and then he realizes this is mostly pride. He wants to point out all the improvements he's made to the house and property.

Just get going, he tells himself again.

"Okay?" Davin asks her. "Gotta go."

She nods but asks him a question. "So, the deck off my bedroom, is that like my deck?"

Davin guesses she just wants clarity, but he figures it must seem obvious to her because who else would use the deck entrance since it only goes into her bedroom.

"You bet," Davin says, and he turns toward the landing,

and then pivots back again.

"Almost forgot," he says, "and we did talk about this a bit when you saw the space, but it's important."

When she had first come to see the space, he'd been sure to mention something about the small apartment making up one half of the first floor and that the main bedroom for the apartment is below her bedroom, and he'd been clear he needed a quiet house sharer in what will now be her room because he uses the apartment below for Airbnb, and that he had a Super Host ranking and wants to keep it that way.

"The Airbnb?" she asks him. She tells him she's quiet and she again assures him she's very responsible, and then he's repeating that he has to get going, but he hears Jimmy coming through the French doors, probably with another armful, and he hears Jimmy ask her if there's anything in the trunk, and that the trunk is locked, and as Davin heads down the stairs he hears Deidre say to Jimmy, "Davin never mentioned the room comes with a valet."

He finds this is said in just the right tone and so apparently does Jimmy since he barks out a laugh.

She'll fit in perfectly, Davin tells himself, starting down the stairs, but coming up the stairs is the young woman Cynthia, holding a mug of coffee, making her first appearance of the day as best he knows.

Davin tells her there's an introduction to be made, and he's telling her this as he walks up, taking backward steps. When he gets to the landing and is turning around, there's Jimmy with Deidre right behind him, and Davin asks Jimmy to handle the introductions.

"Gotta go," Davin says again, letting Cynthia pass by into the living room before scooting past her and down the stairs to get on with his day.

Chapter 31: The Virtue of Reality

Jimmy's been sitting in the big club chair near the fireplace, laptop open, and he's getting work done despite Deidre unpacking and moving about nearby, and he's focused enough to be surprised when she walks through the living room to head back outside through the French doors. He's not so focused on what he's doing that he fails to note she's nice to look at coming and going, but he doesn't think much more than that.

He's not sure where Cyn is, although he thinks she's still up in the back, likely on one of the Adirondack chairs on the lawn area south of the garden fence where's there's a pretty view out over meadows.

He's neck deep reality-testing a theory that's been forming as he checks out the law firm, Callow, Cullens, and McChusker, LLC, the law firm from the card the guy Bancroft had given him. He's seeing if he can access the firm's email logs.

He'ss already set a bit of Internet hygiene in place, including a bounce trace for his direct queries into the law office networks, and he thinks this has enough misdirection and stops and starts to discourage trace back. He's not entirely sure whether the re-direct server he still has access to remains robust, but he thinks it should work. One of Jimmy's college pals in the computer science and engineering department had been something of a hacker, and Jimmy spent some time helping out, learning a thing or two.

Worth the price of admission, Jimmy thinks.

His first pass is innocent enough, simply getting the big picture of the firm by cloning the law firm's public-facing site, so he can take apart its structure offline to pull the internal links to the protected parts of the site and analyze the server architecture.

The server platform is one of the standard server platforms he knows quite well. He's lost in his exploding, his poking and prodding, and is surprised when, an hour or so later, Chaplin is back from whatever job he has, and Jimmy takes a few minutes saying hello, even though he feels awkward.

He feels self-conscious,. He can't help wondering if Chaplin thinks he's just playing video games or otherwise just screwing around, and this sense grows stronger when Chaplin tells him he'll be back down to work outside. This makes Jimmy feel even worse, and he's sure whatever Chaplin's off to do when he's back down and out the door undoubtedly will make Davin happy.

Before Chaplin can leave, though, Deidre and Cyn come through the doors, chatting, and there are now introductions all around. Chaplin says he'll move his stuff out of his room and into the attic area, and though Cyn suggests she's fine where she is, he tells her it's all settled with Davin and he wants to, really, and then Deidre is off to her room and Cyn to the attic and Chaplin is back upstairs, too, packing up his room.

Jimmy remains at work in front of his laptop. He's already done a site search for every specific thing he can pull off the card from the law firm's name down to the extension number Mr. Coif, as he continues to think of Bancroft, had told him to call. Gratifyingly, this effort has resulted in some further clues about the secure parts of the firm's server, the *https://* side, which he has used to guess-hack his way in just moments before Chaplin showed up. The hack is hardly impressive since he'd simply used the default admin login, something that's hard for him to believe still happens, default logins not changed, but he knows this remains far too common an occurrence.

As stupid or lazy as the system administrator might be, he still assumes this approach will be noted in the *sys admin logs,* and the admin could even have an active report script in place. But he assures himself that it being a Sunday, and with such reports pretty routine, it's unlikely there will be a big alarm.

And the sys admin seems pretty damn lazy, he reminds himself every time he gets anxious. Even if there's an active report script in place, the server bounces Jimmy has set up should keep any trace-back efforts stalled, and he has his own script in place to alert him of any such attempts. There must be smarter ways to do this, he assumes, but he doesn't know those ways.

Except work from an IP address that isn't your home network, of course, he thinks, but he's pretty sure this is a level of paranoia not needed under the circumstances.

He then works the hack with some small victories that mainly consist of seeing route strings of three email log databases he knows places like Callow, Cullens, and McChusker, LLC need to maintain in compliance with the Sarbanes–Oxley Act of 2002, a federal law that spelled out expanded requirements for all US public company boards, management, and public accounting firms. God bless SOX, as one of his teachers used to say. SOX, the bringer of much work for the coding community in its time. This federal law requires record transparency for many types of companies, and he's sure any law firm worth its salt would be in compliance since any law firm of any worth was likely to be working with accounting services or securities companies or some other of the many types of fiduciary activities that fall within the law's purview.

And hence, email SOX archive storage, and hence — Jimmy has been hoping anyway — a potential attack for email retrieval. He sends a quick email to his old college pal with some questions, and his pal replies gratifyingly quickly. This reply contains this friend's most up-to-date torrent site recommendations and suggestions about decrypts best suited to the server architecture Jimmy mentioned.

But Jimmy feels like dope slapping himself as soon as he

reads *You're using a VPN, right?* Immediately he sets up an effective virtual private network. All in all, he feels pretty surreal, foggy in the way only sitting in front of a computer for six hours can produce.

After barely sleeping, he realizes.

He keeps going though, and soon enough his brute force program beeps and he's in. He sets up a script to clone the email database and sits back to wait, closing his burning eyes or a moment.

Or maybe it's that I haven't eaten anything, he tells himself, that knowledge coming to him because his stomach is growling, and his stomach is growling probably because he smells cooking.

Jimmy puts the laptop aside, stands and stretches, and heads down the stairs to the kitchen.

Deidre is finishing up at the stove. Both she and Cyn turn to watch Jimmy lumber through the dining room.

He just stands there looking at them until Cyn laughs. He notices three plates are already set on the island.

"You two are having lunch?" he says.

Brilliant, he chides himself.

"Deidre and I are putting together a grocery list," Cyn says, nodding at Deidre.

Deidre smiles. "You were so engrossed with what you were doing," she tells him. "We figured you hadn't eaten."

"Uh, yeah," he manages to reply.

"Deidre and I were outside, walking around," Cyn tells him. He knows he can get absorbed working on problems, but this thought and pretty much any other thought trails off when he sees tht Cynthia is still in his borrowed t-shirt.

Back in it, he corrects himself. Earlier, she'd been dressed back in her other clothes.

"Um," he says, "you going back to bed?"

"No," says Cyn, puzzled by the question, but then she gets it.

"Oh," she says, lightly plucking at his loaned t-shirt that's like a dress on her, albeit something of a mini dress, in Jimmy's view. "I just took a shower and came down with Deidre because she said she'd cook something up."

He doesn't say anything. He's looking at the two of them, not sure what to think, but aware he's finding himself feeling embarrassed.

"Another shower, I should say," Cyn says. "The last couple of days, the travel, that griminess, I feel like I'm still working on washing it all off."

Deidre's at the stove on the other side of the island, her back to him, doing something that seems to demand her attention.

"Um," Jimmy says, and then he's convinced he's sounding like an idiot.

I am an idiot, he tells himself, but he can't stop himself from saying what comes next.

"Um, you know," he says to Cyn. "Uh, maybe you should, right? Get dressed?"

His face feels like the skin is on fire.

She laughs, which helps a bit for some reason. Jimmy tries smiling but doubts his success.

Deidre, watching this transpire, stands back and looks at Cyn and tells him the t-shirt is like a dress on her, that she thinks Cynthia looks very cute.

Deidre calls her by her full first name, *Cynthia.*

Cyn is simply looking at Jimmy, and he hopes it's a smile on her face, a slight smile anyway.

And then she grins.

"Sorry," she says, gently tugging the hem, which pulls the hem almost as low as mid-thigh, but her pull tightens the fabric against her breasts, and Jimmy closes his eyes.

"You're killing me," he says although it's more a croak than speech. He opens his eyes to see the two young women grinning. Cyn walks past him and pats his arm lightly, telling him she'll be right down and then stops at the foot of the stairs.

"We don't want you dead before you try Deidre's omelets," she says and disappears up the stairs.

When Jimmy turns back around, there's Deidre,

grinning, shaking her head.

Chapter 32: Corn as High as an Elephant's Eye

avin has pulled up into the parking area just in time to say hello/goodbye to Deidre, who's on her way to Price Chopper, she tells him, and then off to return her mom's car. He waits in his car, pulling onto the grass to be out of the way as Deidre backs out and heads down the driveway. Only then does he pull himself up and out of the car.

There's only Chaplin's truck and his Hyundai up top now, but it occurs to him it might start getting crowded for parking if Jimmy gets a car, especially once the Airbnb gets going again, although he often parks in a small space he can squeeze into out front of the studio entrance. Even then, it seems only a matter of time before parking gets problematic since Deidre's waiting on repairs on a car she's apparently purchased, according to what she'd told him.

The meeting at *SCI* had taken far longer than he'd anticipated, although there was a lot accomplished, and he's still logy from his odd late-night pickup in Pittsfield. His plan to spend a good part of the day out in the garden is already history.

When he looks over to the garden he finds Chaplin there. He's surprised by seeing Chaplin doing garden work, considering Chaplin is now back on a job, although he's grateful for any help he can get. It looks like Chaplin's been at work on the weeds threatening the rows of still tiny vegetable plants. Davin's had the garden long enough to know keeping weeds under control at this stage is critical for success.

What exactly isn't critical for success with this goddamn garden? he asks himself.

He simply waves and doesn't bother asking Chaplin

anything but turns back toward the house, knowing his day is yet, unfortunately, far from over.

He also knows the garden is ever demanding a lot of work, something he had been long and frequently warned about, especially after Gwen first heard his plans for such a big garden. But he had figured that while he was using a backhoe to dig the perimeter trench, down into which the animal fencing bottom edge would be sunk, it made sense to go big, and he could always just use only what he wished of the area. Of course, once the fencing was complete — deer-proof anyway, but doing little to stop crows, squirrels, and chipmunks — Davin could see no good reason why he shouldn't plant the entire space. Even in the garden's fifth year, when he has every reason to know it's indeed a very large and therefore very labor-intensive garden, he just won't let himself say no to planting it all.

There have been some steady successes in the garden's short history, including the ever-expanding potato patch, especially after the first year's harvest had kept him, and Gwen, until she moved out, in potatoes of several varieties well into January. Tomatoes were pretty good too, including the many Roma plants he'd discovered have a tendency to self-seed and volunteer in the next growing season, and which made for quarts and gallons of sauce at a time, most to put up. Cucumbers, depending on factors not yet well understood by him, could be gangbusters or anemic, and so pickle levels varied year to year while even just a couple of squash plants provided, at their height, too many zucchinis and summer squash to keep up with. Strawberries, in their nicely arranged three-tier beds and netting against the birds, were plentiful as long as there was so much fruit the damn chipmunks could eat their fill and still leave plenty for the humans, not that humans getting any of these strawberries had yet happened. And now in year five, the strawberry plants are reaching the end of the line, and he is far from certain he'll bother to replant this next year.

Turnips, parsnips, carrots, and a range of winter squashes all kept well and harvested late. Peas and beans had a mixed record, while spinach had failed completely, going 0-and-4 so far with only minimal planting planned for this season. A nice long asparagus bed was finally coming into its own, and next year's May should see a good yield until July when the plants would be allowed to recover for the next season.

There are the basic herbs plus a wide range of greens from mustard and collards to various kales and several types of Swiss chard, and all these planted tended to grow well and supply fresh greens for cooking down through the entire season. Davin has hope that with some experimentation he'll successfully freeze bags and tubs of the cooked greens for a winter's day.

Lettuce works well, and radishes are usually a good early yield, although the hot start of the season this year will most likely see the radishes mostly flower out. Broccoli and cauliflower and eggplant and cabbage are still something of a gamble, and the results so far aren't always pretty. The cabbage moths that made a light appearance last year are likely to be a much bigger problem this year, although signs of that are not yet being seen.

The biggest challenge for him, all four years running, has been the sweet corn. With each new season, yet more rows were planted in the hopes the various enemies attacking the stalks— a ground hog that had found its way through the fence, the first year—crows picking at the seed corn, and squirrels or whatever was chewing at the stalk bases like lumberjacks felling trees— has meant his best season so far yielded two ears not otherwise already sampled by some goddamn creature, and even the only slightly nibbled ears that could be trimmed into edible items were themselves disappointing in number.

The more corn, the better the chances of a harvest Davin might enjoy is the still-unsuccessful theory. But as he'd heard from somewhere, there is no better fool than a farming fool.

Last year the corn was looking good, but then the several absolutely devastating rainstorms put that down, along with the rest of the garden, pretty much.

He's prone to curse his luck, he knows, and he's had his share of it with that summer's destructive rains wrecking the garden. His spending on food had gone much higher that particular summer with the whole region's farms having suffered crop damage. Not that Davin thinks of himself as a farmer exactly, but not a dilettante either. A victory gardener of sorts perhaps. *Or a defeat gardener*, depending on results, he thinks, not for the first time.

And then, of course, there was that November storm damaging the Airbnb apartment with some flooding when the rain that fell couldn't run off fast enough, despite the series of drains and berms and swales and redirects Davin had landscaped in. Locally there was a lot worse damage to lower-lying properties and to the recently rebuilt Division Street bridge, which had its two new abutments undercut to the point of collapse by the suddenly raging Housatonic River.

But he understands perspective. Last summer's local rains had been overshadowed by the Texas floods with hundreds dead, and worse yet, the South Asia floods, the second time terrible climate change–charged monsoon floods had occurred there in the past four years. The death toll was in the many thousands and the economic damage, compounded by the failed restoration work still underway from the previous disaster in 2022, had again put Pakistan on the brink of being a failed state.

Davin is thinking about all this as he heads toward the house, and he's thinking about this summer and musing that there will be a few old challenges, like the thieving chipmunks and squirrels. He'd been seriously considering buying an air gun, going so far as to research the basic categories for air rifles, from break barrels to PCP, or precharged pneumatic. The PCP air rifles fascinate him, and he'd been surprised to learn this type of air rifle could run up as high as .50 caliber. He'd been amazed to learn people went big game hunting with such machines. A .22- caliber air gun would be about right for his needs, although a .25 would make dispatching groundhogs more likely.

The problem with PCP air guns, he knows, isn't so much they're more expensive, which they are, but that they require high-pressure air pumps to fill the long pressure reservoir cylinders on the rifle itself. That means pumps such as those used for scuba equipment, and he's pretty sure there aren't too many dive shops in the Berkshires. Another option for charging the PCP types of air rifles is a manual pump that looks a lot like a bicycle pump to Davin's neophyte's eye, but according to the online reviews, these are far harder to pump, which he finds not at all surprising considering air pressure can be well over 3,000 psi, higher by orders of magnitude than the requirements of bike tires.

He's finally pulled the trigger, after all his research, having just ordered a Gamo Whisper G2 air rifle, especially since he'd come across an online sale at well under $200. The package could arrive sometime tomorrow if Amazon delivery times hold. The Gamo is a spring piston break barrel and comes with a scope. It's the .22 model and has high marks all around in the reviews. He'd really wanted a .25 PCP, but that sort of thing is three or four times the price, never mind the pump requirements and cost. But he's reasonably certain the groundhog fence leak of the first summer has been permanently plugged, and his need to go after groundhogs seems unlikely now.

Davin knows quite well this purchase would have been dead- on-arrival if Gwen was still around since Gwen had made it plenty clear she would have no guns in the house.

Well, she has her own house now, is what Davin is thinking, stepping through the French doors, even while admitting he shared some of her sentiment. He's a bit embarrassed by his fascination with guns and a whole lot more embarrassed for the raging madness guns represent in the country at large.

Gun porn galore, he tells himself.

But this isn't a gun, not really, but a tool, and no license required, and a whole lot less expensive than electrifying a band of the fence, which would mean running a line up and installing hardware cloth around the perimeter. Besides, he thinks, the garden with its tall framed-out deer fences already looks like some GITMO surplus, as if he's planning on leasing out the enclosure as private prison space. Electrifying a band around the garden would be too much even for him.

But goddamn, he tells himself, thinking of the lost strawberries, *I want to shoot some chipmunks, array their tiny heads on kabob stakes around the garden walls.*

In the living room Davin sees crumpled napkins and an abandoned glass on the rug next to the big, upholstered club chair, but no Jimmy.

He let's that curiosity go. He is already having some difficulty shifting focus, but he's got to punch out a story on the solar farm brouhaha, and Alicia wants it today. Somehow these days all feel busier than ever, and the long and short of it is he needs help in the garden and not simply in the form of rodent assassination accessories and tactics.

Fortunately, there is Chaplin, who so far is not providing anywhere close to the cash for rent they'd agreed on, but has been more than making up for it with working at the house. Davin sees the results—good weed control, the mulching system getting in place—and there's even the restacking of a small hill of cut wood now made ready for splitting, and the grass—and there's a lot of grass—is being kept mowed and trimmed. Davin appreciates Chaplin's contributions, and he actually likes the kid, which is a mild surprise. Davin's work with *South County Interactive* has been growing, and without Chaplin helping out, the property would be much more of a mess.

Or I'd have to pay someone, he suddenly realizes, none too happily.

As he sits at his desk and fires up the laptop, he thinks, of course, Jimmy is now home, a welcome if somewhat unexpected development, and in tow—and completely unexpected— Cynthia, the very nice-looking young woman who's in some sort of mess of her own, it seems, and was, or maybe is, *a person of interest.*

Jesus, Davin thinks. *Who knew taking on boarders was going to be so dramatic?*

There's still the meeting about Cynthia's situation, and as tired as he is, it needs to happen ASAP, which means as soon as he can get all parties on the same schedule.

He pulls up his latest draft of the solar farm story and gets back to work. He'll let Jimmy and Cynthia know they need to talk, but ASAP will have to wait until he's sent the article to Alicia.

Chapter 33: Angry on Arrival

Dennis Jymsom already knows more about this train than he'd ever want to know, and that's from what he's learned from one particularly chatty couple one row up, across the aisle.

A *couple of faggots*, is his assessment.

One thing he's learned is that the crowding on the train may well just be more New Yorkers responding to the early hot weather in the city, not that he cares. The client has sent Dennis information that the target is likely in Great Barrington or environs, so whether or not he likes the train is immaterial.

But now, like it or not, he also knows, for instance, the passenger rail service is up and running, but the track upgrades are taking what seem like forever to complete and the service is now in its second year, and that the passenger rail service from Grand Central Station to southern Berkshires has experienced a surprisingly large increase in ridership for this point in the season.

And all this to the apparent dismay of said same couple of *queers*.

Dennis isn't interested in any of this, but the train, he'll admit, is uncomfortably crowded and worse yet everyone seems to be talking, while he'd rather they shut the fuck up. He knows he can't simply kill everyone, as much as he plays with that thought in the hope of offsetting his growing annoyance with the noise of far too many people far too close.

Yakkity-fucking-yakkity.

He'd rather not be stuck with all these people, but the benefit of trains is there's no weapon screening to pass through.

Blah blah fucking blah.

He also now knows the Midwest heat wave is still happening, including that the Illinois National Guard is patrolling certain sections of Chicago, but *queens* behind him seem intent on talking about everything in the world.

Shut the fuck up! bursts into mind yet again, a reaction to all the talking, which is interrupting his thinking.

He's overhearing others, too, including some asshole who thinks the weather is quite pleasant in the Berkshires as the summer starts, if more like July, and the vegetable gardens and fields have gotten off to an early start, with the mix of rain and warmer-than-usual weather falling just about perfectly, according to this person sitting right behind him.

Mr. Fucking Green Jeans. Shut the fuck up!

The train tickets are hardly cheap, but the trip up from Grand Central has comfortable enough seats, at least, if not fast, and hardly restful and quiet. He doesn't care about the expense anyway since Carl will reimburse that sort of thing. He does care that there are annoyingly frequent delays once they hit the Housatonic Line as the passenger train dances into and out of sidings to let other trains by. And the earlier transfer wait where the Housatonic line meets up at Southeast Junction had seemed downright stupid to him, including requiring all the passengers to debark the Metro North MTA train and walk across the other side of the platform to get on the Housatonic train.

At least the bar car was open in the Housatonic train, which picked up his mood, but only for a moment. In line for tomato juice and vodka, he had to hear that the person in front of him commutes to New York some days, and don't you know, according to this guy, there are pluses and minuses this commuter guy feels compelled to tell the woman with him. Or maybe the guy was trying to chat her up, but that idea seemed crazy because Dennis had trouble imagining trying to fuck a woman like that, going through the bother—too old and too ugly.

And then it occurred to him, standing there, listening to that guy blathering on and on, that maybe the woman would hire Dennis to shoot the guy for being boring, and the thought made him laugh, which caused a couple of glances toward him, and that made Dennis think he might do it all for free as long as everyone on *this fucking train* was included in the deal.

And now, finally, after sitting through a couple of station stops, he's standing in a line to exit *this fucking train*. He has glimpses of the outside as those waiting to disembark in front of him move and shift.

He's waiting.

The client didn't have a specific address for the target, but when Dennis looked up Great Barrington, he figured it was small enough to make discovery of the target's location easily.

The exit line has stalled.

Get the fuck out of my way, Dennis Jymsom is now screaming inside his head, in the place where he has most of his conversations, his angriest ones anyway. He's trying to get off this *fucking Podunk train* and instead, he's standing behind an older black man who looks like a *goddamn professor cunt*.

The tall black man turns around, looking downward a bit to smile at him, and that just makes Dennis feel how small he is, and that just makes him want to pull out his gun and start shooting *everyone aboard this fucking train*, which makes him feel better, thinking on it, even smiling a bit, and then he realize *the jigaboo thinks I'm fucking smiling back,* which makes Dennis smile even more because it's so not that, and then, finally, he's out onto the platform and pushing past the crowd.

Dennis stands just off the platform for a moment, noting this it is in fact a pretty nice day *here out in the middle of bumfuck country*, and pretty warm too, not unlike what passes for a cool day in New Orleans where he rents that little place out toward Ninth, but it's one of the houses that's never been a victim— *Well, fuck, not yet anyway*, he thinks—of the storm surges and flooding.

He'd wear his windbreaker there on a day like this, but

he's looking around and people are wearing shorts, summer dresses, short-sleeves, t-shirts, sandals, and god help him, those *fucking stupid straw fedora shit hats*.

Dennis could ditch the windbreaker, but it doesn't bother him, and he needs something anyway to cover the holster and gun tucked into his belt. Unlike Ohio, when he'd got taken off that train, Massachusetts doesn't have concealed carry and he is pretty much the worst state for guns. He'll have to be careful.

Like not shooting every asshole on that fucking train.

But really, for all the hassles, he loves his job. He loves he gets to go all over, not taking shit from anybody.

He finishes looking around and realizes most people have moved off the platform.

What a fucking job, he says to himself, hardly for the first time. Behind him, the train starts to move again. Everyone is heading toward what turns out to be a little pedestrian underpass that lets out on what looks like the *fucking ass-end of this fucking Podunk*.

He hitches his bag up on his shoulder and moves toward the main street, wondering where the motels are. He's a big adherent of the travel advice he'd heard when he was a kid, some family joke from his Aunt Paulie, he's pretty sure— *Pack half as much and carry twice the cash*. His hand gently swipes his zipped windbreaker pocket holding his billfold, and then he touches his pant left front pocket where another fold of dollars resides. He gets mad at himself for these tells, long having tried to break himself of this habit. *The fuck?* he mentally yells at himself.

In his head he yells at himself as much as he yells at other people.

And then he calms a bit once he's on Main Street, seeing that a bar is open, which is a whole lot better than on the train where the dining car was serving booze one drink at a time and then it was back to the end of the line, but the fear of having to listen to more yakking had driven him back to his seat sober.

The bar he descends into has food and whiskey and beer, and he likes that the bar is down some steps, below the sidewalk. He feels all set for the moment, and he's mapping out what's next, and that includes eating and drinking, and asking about places to stay, and overall getting the feel of the place.

If he needs a car, he'll steal one. Right now, he's happy to be on foot, but he does wonder if this *Bumfucksville* town even has buses or taxis.

He gives his order to the waitress, a young woman who's on the heavy side and who he thinks takes up a lot of room in what he can see is pretty cramped quarters. But he's fine where he's at, a two-top up against the glass, looking out at the concrete steps that lead up to the sidewalk.

He takes out his latest Carl-supplied smartphone — *hate these fucking things* — and starts texting his client contact. He's annoyed about the coded language Carl insists on, and this now carries over with this irregular job, and it seems to him he has to keep checking in with this new client. This job is a pain in the ass, but he's keeping his focus on the payday.

But hey, I love my fucking job.

Chapter 34: Cry Baby, Cry

Jimmy hears his dad declare that a highball may be in order for the meeting about, as his dad has taken to calling it, the *Cynthia Situation*.

The declaration is annoying, though, but only because his dad finds him up in his bedroom napping when he makes this announcement. It's early evening and Jimmy's been at it all day. He'd just wanted to close his eyes for a minute, but the lack of sleep and the work he's been focused on all day had him drift off, and now here's his dad wanting to talk about Cyn, and this after his dad had already put it off and instead did some business, or whatever Daddo is doing with that online thing.

Whatever exactly his dad does had kept him busy in his office after he'd gotten back from *SCI*, with the two of them barely grunting hello until now when his dad pokes his head into his bedroom.

And wakes me, Jimmy admits, feeling caught out.

Why he feels guilty is a good question, considering he's been full out, on the case as it were, excepting when he was introduced to Deidre and had helped her with her things in the morning, and he'd gotten right back to the server hack and checking out what he might learn from it, and that hadn't been easy. More than once what he'd found himself doing had made him think of the system architecture class he'd struggled with back in his last year in the program. His email exchanges today with his classmate discussing his attack options on the server structure felt like something of a flashback since it was this very same friend who had helped him pull his grade up in that very same class.

His friend's email had been biting with some comments on his proposed attempts, and he could have done without that, but it all proved helpful, even with the barbs. After all. he has gotten into the secure email logs and he's found plenty to think about.

This work had carried through much of the afternoon with frequent trips to his dad's office to grab printouts, his last trip finding his dad annoyed with the interruptions, trying to focus on his own work.

Some sort of writing, Jimmy had assumed, but he'd been too caught up in his own efforts and hadn't asked. The work Jimmy had been doing is fascinating in many ways, he has no doubt, but it's been plenty demanding too. And it really hadn't helped his concentration, his replaying that moment of embarrassment down in the kitchen.

He feels a ghost of his blushing, but a smile too as he pictures yet again Cyn in his t-shirt in front of the sink, and that smile of hers kept repeating in his mind afterward even as he tried to concentrate on the server work. He knows what had amused her was that comment he'd blurted out that made him sound like an idiot.

You're killing me.

Still, he welcomed some distraction, all things considered, since the work of combing the cloned email database had proved deadly boring in its content, only briefly relieved now and then when he came across the content instances and IP log entries he'd been hunting.

And then after that he had found himself digging deeper into Cyn's presence online, and he was good at digging.

It had been fun until it wasn't.

She had mentioned her twin brothers on the train and the town where the three had grown up, and Jimmy had looked for information about her family. Almost immediately he'd found, he was sure, the most recent address, telephone, and emails for her folks.

Facebook is for old people these days, is what he'd thought, not that this opinion is original to him, as he well knows. His surmise about Cyn's mom's Facebook had been easy to confirm, and he found that the mother had only joined about a decade back, which is how Jimmy got to see pictures of Cynthia and her younger brothers in their tween and teenage years. Were Cyn to tease him any further about what happened down in the kitchen, he realizes he can threaten her with numerous awkward pictures of her teenage self, the sort of snapshot only a mother might post.

You're killing me.

Each time he thought of this, it made him smile. But such pleasant distractions had ended abruptly the moment his broader Internet Archives search hit on newspaper articles from many more years before, and his reaction to the old news piece was to take the stairs up toward his bedroom, seeking Cyn out to talk, but she was napping in her new room.

He is still feeling confused about what he'd found, and even heartsick, but he hadn't wanted to wake her, so he had gone into his own bedroom and stretched out on his bed to wait. He had closed his burning eyes, and then there's Daddo standing at his door, now telling him there's something about cocktails, in his opinion, that demand being clean and well-dressed in order to really enjoy them. At least that's what Jimmy thinks is being said, but he's still struggling to breach into fully awake.

And then Davin is saying they'll meet downstairs but only after he showers and dresses in clean clothes, so just come down, ask Cynthia down, and then his dad disappears into his own bedroom and Jimmy is still swimming back to the land of the living.

He sits up.

"Did I hear the word 'cocktails'?" comes the query of a rather croaky-voiced Cyn, herself newly awakened, and even as Jimmy starts for the hall, there is Cyn stepping through his bedroom door, her hair a mess. She's dressed in her clothes, now a bit rumpled from her nap perhaps.

Jimmy's heart feels aflutter, scrambled with what he's learned.

But Jimmy simply smiles at her, slips on his shoes, and tells her Davin wants to talk about what's going on. She's nodding, and he can't think of what else to say. He doesn't know how to talk about what he's discovered, so he tells her he'll see her downstairs.

He's not there long before she's down and then practically on her heels is Davin, all showered and dressed and carrying a gin bottle from the small bar shelf in the living room. Davin places the bottle on the island as he opens the door of the freezer and pulls out an ice cube tray. He roots around the fridge and adds the tonic mixer to the growing collection that includes three highball glasses taken down from the glass-faced cabinet before him.

"Gin and tonic good?" Davin asks, now busy with grabbing limes from the bottom of the fridge.

"Yes, please," Cyn answers, and Jimmy's about to tell him lemonade is good for him, but she continues.

"Short, if you will, just a splash or two of tonic, two or three wedges of lime," she says.

And there is Davin nodding approvingly if Jimmy is reading him right.

"GT, English style," is what Davin says, swapping one highball for a rocks glass. "Very good."

Jimmy suddenly feels like a kid. He doesn't drink much, or much in the way of cocktails anyway, but still, it's like Davin and Cyn are speaking another language, some adult *patois* about which Jimmy has no clue.

"Lemonade, American style," he says, but then he's off up the stairs because he's left his laptop in the bedroom, and by the time he's thundering back down and swings into view with his laptop balanced in one broad hand, the two are on their second or third sips. Jimmy's lemonade sits on the island, and he drops into the empty chair near it, placing the laptop gently down, then opening it.

No one says anything.

He has assumed his dad would take the reins, but it now occurs to him his dad might expect Cyn to start in first.

"The law firm," Jimmy says, then stops.

He knows Cyn knows he knows what happened in Barstow, and on the train, and the business card from the guy Bancroft, and he can guess she therefore thinks Davin knows, which thanks to his morning's precis, is an assumption that is on the money. But still, he tells himself, talking about your boss getting shot can't be easy under the best of circumstances.

His heart has that sinking sensation he's been fighting since finding the old news reports.

Cyn and his dad are looking at him.

Jimmy opens. "So, we know this guy Bancroft, the second guy on the train, gave Cyn contact information, to Callow, Cullens, and McChusker, LLC, and talked about, well anyway, we both have his card.

"I hacked their servers," Jimmy continues, now holding up his hand, preemptively expecting all sorts of reactions, although, looking right at Cyn, there's not much reaction to see, but Jimmy barely has a moment to experience his disappointment at failing to impress her because Davin asks what he was thinking and starts right in about how Jimmy could be in real trouble and is otherwise making the sort of worried sounds any parent of a would-be criminal is liable to make.

"I used a re-direct service, so even if they notice someone's been poking around — which is unlikely — they would be hard- pressed to track back here," says Jimmy.

"I hope you're sure about that," Davin says rather anxiously.

Jimmy nods.

I hope so too, he tells himself.

"Did you find anything?" asks Cyn, her eyes now bearing on Jimmy, and he's feeling even more self- conscious.

"Well, I don't know how much useful I found, just one

specific name associated with the extension, a clerk, not a lawyer, not a partner," he says, and he sees Cyn's eyes flick and a frown appears.

Davin, when Jimmy looks, presents as simply confused. *And impatient?* he wonders.

Jimmy grins at his dad. It is just like him wanting things cut to the chase.

Except when Dad's telling a story, it occurs to him.

"The name is Jabutu Madaki," Jimmy answers, "which I think is Nigerian, and I'll get to more on him.

"I got into their email archive," he continues, deciding not to bore them with the various details, but indeed cut to the chase. "Using the name—Madaki—that I found associated with the extension, I used the name as a filter, which led me to a lot of really boring stuff but also I'm pretty sure emails from each of the two train guys, one certainly Bancroft, and says so, those are straightforward, but there're some double-talk emails too, and times and places make me guess these must be Rat Face."

"Times and places?" Davin asks.

Jimmy clarifies. "Well, times and IP addresses," he says, waiting for nods, which he gets.

"There are emails from another couple of other security firms, although those are mainly queries or business stuff, anyway, and it looks like only this Bancroft guy's company did much of anything beyond getting a retainer."

Jimmy shrugs. "The emails I think are most interesting are those ones using no names, although there's something like a codename?"

Jimmy pauses, then continues.

"Birddog," is what he says.

He pauses for another moment before going on. "There's just this, I don't know, a distinct style, vague, but some things that kind of match up with what Cyn and I went through." And here he stops and looks back at Cyn.

"Remember that second guy, Bancroft, what he said about

Rat Face?" Jimmy asks her, and while Cynthia is nodding, Davin is asking who the hell or what the hell is *ratface*, so Jimmy sketches out a barebones account, but he sees he's just further confusing Davin, so he stops himself to start again.

"Right," he says. "I mentioned in my note that two guys had approached Cyn on the train, but I didn't bother with details. Rat Face, this guy that looks like a rat, we both thought it fit," he tells Davin and then explains this is the first guy to hassle Cyn on the train.

"About this stuff, about Barlow," Davin says, getting it.

"Barstow, yeah," says Jimmy. "That was Cyn's impression—" Jimmy hears her scoff at his word choice, then continues, "But there's a reference in the emails to another participant by Bancroft, this Madaki, likes he's the client, or, like, the guy actions get reported to, but Bancroft emails"—Jimmy looks at his laptop screen—"'high exposure liability' and 'unprofessional behavior,' along with what I'm pretty sure is a recommendation to recall the guy, to fire the guy basically, especially since—" He pauses again, looking through scrolling screens, angling the screen so Davin can see from his side vantage email bitmap-capture images. "Yeah, here it is, 'suggest said participant have his contract terminated for cause.'"

His dad remains in listening mode, which is a bit of a surprise to Jimmy, so he continues. "I'm pretty sure he's talking about Birddog, although he hasn't any idea that is the name, but the sequences are right."

He hears his dad grunt.

"There are a couple of other, what, you know, companies, private investigation outfits, like I said, some email back and forth, like I said, business details," Jimmy continues. "But our Mr. Bancroft was apparently telling us the truth about being first in on calling in with the locating of..." Jimmy looks over at Cyn again, nods. "You know, you."

Jimmy pauses again.

"Uh," he says, still looking at her, "what's weird is these

efforts are all, uh" — he looks again at Cyn, then over to Davin, then back to Cyn—"no connections, no communications with law enforcement, and I looked it up, like only Barstow County Sheriff Department has a BOLO on you, as POI."

"Person of Interest," Davin says.

"Yeah," Jimmy says. "Well, as far as I could find, anyway, but I didn't spend that much time looking, or how, exactly, to be honest."

He pauses, and then says, "It sort of seems like what Bancroft was suggesting."

Jimmy now looks at his dad, but then turns back to her. "Of course, I don't have access to law enforcement service, so I can't tell you really."

Cyn just looks at him.

"Like Bancroft was talking about, right?" he asks her, but he doesn't wait for an answer. "Like I said, it seems like there are two other participating investigative services that took the contract to find you, two others that are clear in the emails back and forth, like Bancroft, but the guy who, you know, Rat Face, or Birddog, with the gun — "

" — What gun?" Davin asks, but Jimmy holds up a finger, a *just hold the questions* sort of gesture, which he's pretty sure is going to drive his dad into a frenzy, but he continues. "Not from Bancroft but from the Madaki guy to someone I haven't identified with emails back and forth from Madaki, with the actual client, not the law firm, I think, but also from Birddog, and well, those are like trying to read pig Latin, everything couched in a way that could mean almost anything, no specifics."

Cyn is telling him she'll keep calling Rat Face Rat Face, although she's open to renaming him Ratdog too, which makes Jimmy smile.

"Ah," Davin says. "What?"

Jimmy is sure Davin's again lost.

"A big question is who," Jimmy tells him. "There are a few emails to Madaki, emails from the would-be client, but I can't find anything about who has this, who uses this email. There's an anonymizer email address involved, I'm pretty sure anyway, since the reverse email lookup is a dead end."

No one says anything, although Jimmy can feel Davin's question about a gun, the question beaming intensely at him like a physical object, but Davin holds himself quiet.

"The pig-Latin stuff is weird," Jimmy says.

Davin asks him what he means.

"Well," he says, then pauses to look at his screen. "Like here," he continues, although he's not offering the screen to the other two to look. "'Project parameters still positive' and 'Essential subject gets credit,' and if you want to tell me what that means, I'm all ears, like he was the first to find you?" Jimmy says. "That stuff, the substance of those emails, it's nothing like the emails out to security firms and back, like from Bancroft's, those, they're just basically businesslike."

Jimmy takes a long pull of the lemonade before going on. "Just weird," he says. "It's like some of Madaki's email to Birddog-slash-Rat Face is normal, and it's like some of Madaki's emails are written by someone else, someone with coded language, right?" he says, but he shakes his head.

"In any case, how come the security agencies went out when they did, like?" He stops to scroll through the bitmaps. "Yeah," he says. "The first submission to the thing, the service RFP or whatever, goes out from Madaki less than two hours after" — he looks toward Cyn—"ah, you know, Joe, from the time you told me, when he was…"

"Killed," Cyn says. Jimmy just nods.

"What's the point here?" Davin asks.

"I've grouped the selected email into categories," he continues after another pull of lemonade, "one for each of the two train guys—best guesses anyway—and replies to them, plus the back and forth between Madaki and in some cases, presumably, the client is contributing direction to Madaki, right?"

The two look at Jimmy, apparently expecting him to

continue.

"Still," he says, "the funny thing is then there's no sign of those client emails showing up, it's like whoever Madaki is working for doesn't have emails, no replies direct to Madaki, nothing in the logs, although some of the responses from Madaki show he is responding to something, but those client emails I'm presuming are not getting logged, not retrievable."

"What does that mean?" asks Davin. "Maybe the guy is just updating his boss, verbally, I mean."

Jimmy shrugs. "Could be, but if there was verbal reporting, you think there would be at least some email at some point. "And who is the client?" Jimmy then asks, looking back to Cyn. "Your folks wouldn't know to look for you, not that early on, no way, right?"

Cyn nods agreement.

"Maybe your company, right?" he says to her but then turns to Davin and says, "But where are the emails, from her company? Instead, early on, there's something missing, like emails to Madaki, but nothing leads anywhere, the email has no information, not afterwards, either, not the later ones."

He pauses, feeling a bit flustered. "So, like what I said."

He's finding even he is confused in trying to explain things. *Should'a written this out,* he realizes.

"So the clerk, whatever, Madaki?" Davin asks. "Not the guy looking for Cynthia?"

"No," he replies. "I don't think so. This Madaki guy, he's just the contact point, some kind of a message conduit."

Neither Davin nor Cyn seem to follow.

"Just my hunch based on how he's replying, the time response gaps," Jimmy adds. "Not the decision maker."

"So, we don't know who's looking for her," says Davin.

Jimmy's thinking. "Yeah, probably won't, to be honest. Any effort to discover the instigating email, the who or an affiliation requires a lot more information than I'm ever going to have, even if a trace-back might be a start, or why the earliest emails from this client are logged but later ones aren't.

It's weird there were emails to start with, anyway."

No one seems to dispute any part of Jimmy's statement, which leaves him feeling a bit disappointed.

"Just a gmail account," and he glances back to his screen. "*smith128456*," and there's nothing, no lookup directory entries, *nada*."

"How unusual is that?" Cyn asks.

He shrugs. "Well, I know the basics for look up."

He sees Davin look confused by her question, but Jimmy has a good idea what she means.

"Like the text insertions," she says, maybe a question.

"Yeah, different, but could be, could be some server-based program, a file extraction or deletion routine."

He shrugs again. "After the RFP request from that email, plus a follow-up, two, it is as if that email disappears, no logging."

Davin grunts, clearly lost.

"Um," his dad says, but then asks Cyn to explain the gun thing to him, which she manages to do, impressing Jimmy with her terse matter-of-factness style.

"Yeah," Jimmy adds. "Bancroft seemed to think the guy was an idiot and anyway seemed glad for it since it meant he — Bancroft — got the find bonus."

"Apparently," Cyn adds.

Davin gets up to get himself another G&T and looks at Cyn's glass. She nods and passes him her empty glass. Jimmy pushes his lemonade glass toward Davin.

Davin fusses for a minute, and then is back with his and her second G&Ts, sliding the refreshed glass of lemonade back toward Jimmy.

"I don't see how this gets us anywhere," Davin says. "We can't even say for sure what emails may be from whom, or even if some of those emails are from that weird guy — "

" — Rat Face," both Cyn and Jimmy say.

" — and it doesn't seem like we can figure out for sure, right?"

Jimmy grins.

"Jesus! Come on," Davin says, rather sharply, but Jimmy's too pleased with himself to take offense.

"Two things," Jimmy begins. "First, all the metadata in the email headers give IP addresses of origin, well, except that weird gmail address, but some of those I figure for Rat Face match to the Amtrak wireless on the North Shore Limited at the right times, so confidence is high about who sent what when in these cases."

Davin simply nods. Cyn, Jimmy sees, is also nodding.

"It's just a matter of cross-referencing with DNS and do the look-ups," adds Jimmy, but he's pretty sure neither Davin nor Cynthia follow. "Except for the would-be client, the real client, I'd say, who definitely is using an anonymizer, and something else to delete some email, maybe.

"Second," Jimmy continues, "a *whois* search on the IP of a recent stream of emails I believe are from Mr. Coif" — Jimmy ignores Davin's puzzlement — "who's exactly who Bancroft indeed claims to be, not that he wouldn't be." Jimmy stops again, feeling like he's just confusing everyone. "What I mean is his emails are coming in from the same IP the last day or so, and that IP and MAC belongs to a server at a small private investigation services company."

"Did you…" Cyn begins to ask as Jimmy swings his laptop around, showing the *About Us* page for AllServe CI, 1440 North Street, Suite 22, Minneapolis, MN, 55401, complete with telephone numbers and email addresses and headshots of the principals, including their Mr. Coif, a.k.a. Terry Bancroft, Chief Investigator.

"Jesus, Guy Noir," says Davin when Jimmy swings the screen toward him.

"The guy is legit," says Jimmy, stating what's obvious to all assembled.

"They were the private contract that found you," Jimmy says to her. "What Bancroft said is supported by the emails."

She nods and then takes a big pull on her drink.

"And what he said about the strange situation with law enforcement, or rather, lack of involvement. Except for the Barstow County BOLO thing, and the few other alerts, maybe, I haven't figured out how to learn that" — he looks over at Cyn again—"well, you know, the POI thing." He pauses, a bit flustered. "From, in, other law enforcement agencies."

Jimmy stays quiet for a moment, and then says with his eyes fixed on his glass, "I mean, I don't know how these things work, but, like, with the shooting, within a day or so after, it's like law enforcement isn't doing much to locate you. Your boss gets shot, killed, you are nowhere to be found, right? And it's only these guys through those lawyers, the contracts with them, all private…"

Jimmy turns away from her, flustered, and feigns deep interest in his lemonade glass, which he's now turning with his hand. And the he adds, "Looks like, even early on, the cops, law enforcement, don't think you were, uh, had anything to do with it."

"This is four days ago," Davin says or asks.

"Or maybe they, the state stuff, or even federal, I'm not connecting, not seeing those efforts?" Jimmy ventures. "I guess that's possible, equally possible."

"I'm lost," Davin says.

"Yeah, sorry," says Jimmy. "What I'm seeing is that law enforcement seems to have dropped the idea, or not much active, anyway, on the idea that Cyn had anything to do with Joe being, you know, at least after a day anyway."

"Huh," Davin says.

"Not that the POI notice got taken down," Jimmy clarifies. "It wouldn't though, right? They still would want to talk with you."

All eyes turn to her.

"The latest news reports are more often speculating those texts, in more of the news stories, show up as fake, well, insertions. This is getting more attention, it looks like."

She nods but remains quiet.

Davin speaks up, asking what they are talking about. "What texts?' he asked.

She nods but says nothing for several moments before taking a deep breath and retells the two others her story, this time starting with what her job entailed, and about her boss, the organization, the timelines of the trip, the texts, Mile Marker 27. It takes quite a while to tell this all to Davin, mainly because Davin often seems confused, even though he'd gotten a rough sketch of much of this from what Jimmy had sent him earlier, but he keeps interrupting with questions.

Davin holds up a finger. "Hold on a sec," he says, and it's clear to Jimmy he's trying to understand the timelines, but mostly he's trying to understand why Cynthia hadn't gone to the authorities.

"I mean, after you got out of Dodge," Davin adds.

Jimmy can see Cyn is growing tense. It seems like Davin's last comment, and his probing, is distressing.

Jimmy breaks the silence.

"I got that answer, Daddo," he says. He says this softly, and he pulls another document up on screen and turns it toward Davin.

Jimmy is looking at Cyn, seeing her distress, and then he's glancing back down at his glass and again starts fiddling with it, turning the glass in the growing condensation ring.

Davin looks at what Jimmy has put in front of him, his face changing as he reads.

"I'm sorry, Cynthia," Davin says quietly after he's read and reread the article about the domestic dispute incident and her father being killed.

Jimmy knows the exact number of years and months and weeks ago this had all taken place, back to today, but he can't think of any good reason for him to have done the math.

Seventeen years, eight months, and three days.

He keeps his eyes on Cyn and sees the shadow pass over her, the one he'd seen several times on the train with her, and he reaches out across the island top, his big hand light on her forearm, but then he withdraws his hand.

Cyn looks up at him. Her face breaks, and she says in a hoarse whisper, "My father was killed by a cop," and the strain and anguish in her voice stills the others.

Jimmy sees his father glance at her, and then away. Jimmy picks up his pencil and puts it down again.

The silence is interrupted only by the sound of Davin's ice sliding down, clacking together as he tips the glass up to drink.

Then Davin asks, "Do you think a real cop, or, you know, I mean, a real deputy?"

For Jimmy, there's nothing surprising about Davin's confusion because it's confusing, her boss getting shot by a man in uniform out in the middle of nowhere, for what, a divestiture deal, maybe?

"We don't know yet, Pop," Jimmy says quietly. "One of the things we need to find out. A uniform, that would be easy to fake, but the police vehicle, that's hard, I'd think. If it was really a cop, or you know, then that would be in the stories, right? Part of the story."

His dad considers this further. "Well, not necessarily, if Cyn is the only witness, of course. Who would know if it was a cop, or anything, really," and he shrugs, "what had happened, how."

There is another uncomfortable stretch of silence.

Jimmy tells him he agrees. "The only way cops—well, it is the San Bernardino County Sheriff's Department that gets mentioned about the discovery of the car with, uh, and the time of all that, and that first got called in more than an hour, way more, later, when Cyn was well on her way already, already on the bus to Vegas as best I figure."

"The rental car with Joe dead," she says, low.

"Yeah," he answers. "Some of the news articles cite the reports." Jimmy looks at her, and he figures that this talk has gotten her thinking again about her dead boss, her friend, out there, dead, in the car.

He reaches across the island again with another squeeze of her forearm, and then he's up and holding Cynthia Wainwright in his arms, loose, warm, and she's weeping.

Chapter 35: Rat Face Is as Rat Face Does

D ennis can't believe his luck.

He'd been on his way back from Bradley — *Bradley International Airport*, he snorts with amusement about the grand pretentions of the place — where he'd driven to exchange cars, a little over an hour and some away from what he now thinks of as his *Area of Operation*, since it was only pushing for trouble to use the same stolen vehicle for too long, especially if it was local, swapped plates or not. Besides, there was a nice back way through a lot of forest, some small towns, and best yet, *no fucking E-ZPass camera shit.* Dennis has started to think of this car run like the vacation part of his assignment, although he would also admit his efforts to find the bitch were getting kind of old.

Just how hard should it fucking be in a small town? he's been increasingly asking himself, and then he started to wonder if maybe she was holed up in some house in the woods.

We'd need fucking NSA shit.

Still, his client is happy to pay to keep him on the hunt, and this town really isn't so bad, and there's good food, especially if you avoid the weird stuff, like he'd never seen kale so much. *What is it with these queernuts?* he's asked himself more than once when looking at menus.

And fuck, the price for a drink in this fucking place.

And then at the stoplight in front of this burg's town hall, while sitting behind the wheel of a very nice stolen Avalon, *good room, good engine, sort of like the Buick of Toyotas,* who does he see but the target her very self with that big asshole kid, the kid on the train who he would be happy enough to shoot *for fucking free.* There is also an older guy. *Maybe big asshole's old man*, he immediately wonders. The guy is middle-aged or a bit older with gray hair, thin on top. Dennis takes a closer look and feels that the big kid and the other man look related.

Maybe. Or maybe a cop.

Dennis had been thinking about that, wondering if they'd gone to the cops, and he wonders too if when he sends out something about locating the girl he might also include that maybe they've gone to the law. It's a good question, after all, but after thinking on it for a bit, he figures he would've been alerted by the client if this had happened and suggesting the possibility might kill the assignment.

Kill the assignment.

He thinks that's funny enough. What he doesn't find at all amusing is when, sometimes, a target is no longer a target and the payout changes.

Fuck that.

He knows the law firm isn't the client, as much as they pretend to be. *Thinking I'm an idiot, assholes.* Still, whomever the real client, they've kept themselves insulated, which is exactly how he likes to play it himself. They, whomever, are smart, and connected most probably, and he figures he would have been told if something was out on the wire.

He decides to play this break of finding the girl by driving past to find a parking spot higher up on Main St. He keeps them in view using the rearview mirror, and he sees they've gotten into a car four or five parking places behind him. He slouches as the other car passes the Avalon, all three in some white piece of shit car with the old guy driving, and then Dennis pulls out, exactly one car in between him and the car with the old guy, the big asshole, and the target.

Straighten that the fuck out, yessiree.

A few miles later, he sees the white car take a left off Route 7 onto Route 183, which means Housatonic probably, from his earlier exploring, getting the lay of the land. Both cars pass Taft Farms, and Dennis has to fight the urge to pull in for some of their cider sugar donuts again, which are *really good,* but then he laughs out loud thinking about telling the client like how he had the target but lost her because he had to get some donuts.

And then they're coming into the village, and he takes the right they take, a road that climbs steep, but he sees the *Dead End* sign, so he peels off at the first left, turns around, and heads back out slowly. He spots the old Kia going up a driveway that looks kind of like an extension of the road but even steeper.

Why the fuck would someone live there? he wonders while also noting the house number and the street name, and then he heads down over the bridge with some old mill buildings to his right. He pulls over across from a corner market and parks. He grabs his binoculars and starts his stroll.

Just a bird guy, nothing strange here, ma'am.

He likes what he sees, figuring the rooftop out back of one of the old mills is the place to recon after dark. It looks like it should have a good view of the house on the hill.

Last email check-in, the project is still a go, which is a good thing, although Dennis hates the jobs that are supposed to be done so they look like suicide because that sort of thing always ends up being a pain in the ass. And the client contact he works through, checks in with, that guy has to be some kind of a dope, an amateur. Dennis keeps thinking over the most recent reply from the guy at the law office, who seems completely unaware of the special instructions he gets through the server, or even, maybe, probably, the moron doesn't even know what Dennis is here to do.

And then he walks back over the bridge, casual as he pleases.

Chapter 36: Security Audits and Paychecks

Larsen doesn't much care for assignments that don't go well, especially if such assignments are fast approaching the state of *fucked beyond repair*. But while he waits, he's keeping himself busy at his home office working his legitimate side, and at this moment he's analyzing the performance of a new firewall structure by running simulated attacks. He's pleased with the robustness of this aspect of the corporate site he's working on.

He's used the same service that has supplied him with the attack routines for most of the intrusion tests he uses. That service is more expensive, but the intrusion test packages are easy to use, and the cyber security service provides effective and actionable defense instructions and patches. More important to Larsen is that the protective patch and software packages are solutions for the ever-evolving up-to-date exploits and brute-force breach tools that make up the intrusion tests. He's usually able to use the intrusion programs for a while before patches and fixes get disseminated and active.

His email alert sounds, and he sees it's an update from the very same service provider, which seems eerie timing considering what he's in the middle of doing. This makes for something of a pain in the ass because he knows he'll have to add the new patch and start the analysis all over again, but then, it has to work that way.

The legitimate uses of the intrusion test packages are good, but Larsen wonders how many other people use this service as a way to identify and procure the most up-to-date hack programs, which is certainly the other and more essential way he uses the service, to reverse engineer updates and patches, and he'll dig into this newest patch later because this offers clues about how to alter the particular specific intrusion software to render new patches ineffective.

He's gotten some of his best intrusion programs this way. Even if a patch rectifies the vulnerability and he can't figure out a workaround, that doesn't mean the vulnerability is no longer useful. He knows perfectly well there will be many networks that won't update quickly and therefore have computer networks that remain at risk for some time.

More than many, he considers, still surprised this is so common despite his years in the business. He's been able to use such tools to good effect quite frequently, and he's never been seriously threatened with exposure, but then again, he's usually going in for proprietary information and not resource transfer in systems handling money. Those systems tend to be better hardened and maintained more robustly.

He runs the new patch and restarts the analysis. The runtime will be close to three hours, so he turns to his other laptop, the one he uses for his unofficial field work. He boots this up and connects it to his virtual private network and its metadata stripping routine. He sees there's an alert from his sneakware he's installed on the law firm's network and pulls up an email the clerk sent out to a dead address with no traceable ownership to him, but his sneakware lets him pull these emails' content from the Sent folder and no one's the wiser since such email records will disappear each midnight.

No muss, no fuss.

The email address Larsen uses to send Madaki instructions is a complete fiction, as is the persona, although the money Madaki receives is real enough, with cash drops through well executed spycraft. The clerk seems happy enough with the arrangements made through the persona email and it doesn't seem that the clerk has bothered looking for the daily disappearing emails Larsen causes by the email server hack he'd installed. Just in case, of course, he uses coded content when he sends email direct to Birddog via a hijack of Madaki's email. Even if the clerk noses around in that twenty-four-hour window and reads the Sent copy, and even if the clerk correctly guesses what the terms and phrases really mean in the hidden email by Larsen's persona, it's all another layer of deniability.

If things go sideways, Larsen can flush the email threads for a full delete, and not just locally but across the various backup servers, but such a scorched-earth approach inevitably makes network security take notice. If any hypothetical people looking into such a wipe knew the art he's put into this other side of his work, they'd be impressed, but then, of course, he knows that would defeat the whole purpose.

He reads the emails from his freelancer to Madaki.

Finally, he says to himself. Cynthia Wainwright has been run to ground. Some small village he's never heard of in some part of Massachusetts he's got no sense of.

There's been nothing on the law enforcement front, no alerts tripped, which itself is somewhat mystifying to him, but he'll take the win, although his overall outcome assessment for this assignment remains pessimistic. But success remains possible if Birddog can act quickly enough to tie this all up nice and pretty.

He fears there's potentially a serious issue with the texts he'd planted on the two telephones in their metadata irregularities, because there is already some mention of this among several news stories, but he doubts that this, or the embezzlement evidence plant for that matter, will be looked at carefully if the distraught lover kills herself. Any such oddities are likely to be moot. No one will have sufficient motivation to do the heavy lifting it'll take to make the case about the inserted texts or the fund transfers into the girl's account that he can admit was clumsily done. And if so? There's no way any of this can be tied to him.

Case closed, all done, over and out, thank you very much.

He'll have to do a discovery on the modem at the location

where she is now that he finally has the address. He'll keep finessing the suicide note for intrusion into her laptop, given the opportunity, although he knows he'll have to be that much more careful with the metadata. An alternative he's considering is to have the text ready to insert in one of the national suicide chats, but he'll wait on this decision until he determines the Housatonic location's network vulnerability, and whether the girl's laptop is on the network and vulnerable too.

He's not happy that the plan keeps growing more complicated. Deep down, he doesn't see this resolving the way he wants it to, but while there's any chance, there's hope.

Rocky has been upping the pressure on this, and Larsen can't really fault him since the operation keeps going sideways. The emails he gets from Rocky are ostensibly concerning the legitimate side of his business, but the last email, escalates Rocky's pressing on the security job estimate figures, and they both know this refers to the current operation, not the legit services. The line that made the point especially clear: *Estimated time for estimate delivery: ASAP.*

So, he'll play it out until the job's done or until it makes no sense to continue, which means he'll send the go-confirmation to the Birddog's handler service.

Chapter 37: The War Council

The war council is being convened in the living room. *The War Council* is how Davin thinks of it following the surprising revelations two days before, and he'd wasted no time the following morning getting some legal advice.

He's no longer confused about the situation, at least about Cynthia's need for help, although he knows there are many questions still to be addressed and any number of ways the situation might play out. He gets quite anxious at various points when he imagines worst-case possibilities.

Definitely need to come up with a guest policy, he says to himself, and that comes close to making him laugh. Today, he'd been up at his desk from early morning on, mostly working on an *SCI* assignment but also emailing back and forth with the lawyer he'd used in the divorce about remaining points of confusion related to what he'd discussed the day before. He had gone down to the law office to gain some clarity on potential legal liabilities he might face — *Or Jimmy*, he thinks yet again, worried about his son's online actions, and yet again his anxiety spikes.

Joey Palamo, of Palamo & Associates, is the only lawyer in the Berkshires Davin has had any experience with, and yesterday the lawyer was happy enough to talk at the office with him, although this first involved renewing a legal services agreement with a new check as retainer.

The retainer is modest, and Davin has previously gotten good value from Palamo, although there hadn't been all that much for Palamo to do around the divorce because neither Gwen nor he had disputed much of anything, although the transfer of property and the wording of the various agreements had benefitted from the attention to detail.

Law practices in the Berkshires, he'd discovered when first exploring services, tend to span several areas of law. His choice of divorce attorney had settled on family law, of course, but he'd noted at the time the firm covered criminal cases too. Quite a few lawyers in the county seemed focused on personal liability law, and *ambulance chasers* is how Davin sees such practices. He was determined that the lawyer he chose would not be a member of that clan, but it hadn't taken him long to understand criminal law out here in Western Massachusetts was mostly a matter of addressing DUI arrests. Now, it seems good enough that the law firm had a criminal law practice and that would likely mean Palamo knows the DA, and knows the law enforcement agencies, and would more likely know or get the answers to the questions bothering Davin.

Harboring a criminal was one such point of query.

Initially Davin was going to have Cynthia and Jimmy sit in on the meeting at the lawyer's office, but as he drove the three of them downtown yesterday morning he'd reconsidered. Best first that he got some basic questions answered.

Like, will I have to pay for three retainers?

The meeting had gone well and had gone quickly enough, at least after he managed to empty himself of all the facts and fears he could think of, which, mainly, remain that there is a young woman currently at his house who is a person of interest in a murder and that there is or was a *Be On the Look Out* on her, at least in California.

Palamo made some calls, although to whom stays unclear to Davin.

"Yes," Palamo had said into the receiver, after citing the pertinent name and dates, "the BOLO is local, not national, but I want to know if there's a warrant—" and some comment from the other end of the conversation had interrupted.

"No." Palamo continued. "My client read about her in

the papers, he knows her, is just concerned," and the lawyer was listening again.

"I don't know," he'd then replied and had looked up at Davin, his hand over the mouthpiece. "Which paper, wants to know."

Davin looked at the printout Jimmy had given him.

"*San Francisco Examiner* is one," he had told Palamo, which the lawyer then repeated into the phone.

Another pause for Palamo, and then he said, "All this stuff is online these days, that's how, or maybe my client's got a subscription, who cares—" and he was listening again and shaking his head.

"Al, Al, Al, doesn't matter, remember *immaterial* from law school?" But Palamo was laughing. "Maybe he left his heart in San Francisco—"

"Yeah," he then said after listening briefly to the person on the other end of the line. "Okay, great, sure, Tanglewood, sounds good," and he had hung up and told Davin there had been no warrant issued. He had been clear this didn't mean it couldn't happen and then made clear that presently there was no problem with the young woman staying at his house.

Most of what Palamo had talked about did help him feel easier until, that is, Palamo had suggested to him that the young woman get in touch with the DA's office.

In for a penny, Davin thinks, sitting at his desk this morning, recollecting yesterday's conversation. He has a note pad and pushes himself away from his desk when he hears Jimmy and Cynthia settling in the living room across the landing.

Deidre is still at work, but this isn't a house meeting anyway, and Deidre's been keeping to herself.

A sign of inherent intelligence, is what Davin thinks of that.

The only conversation he's had with Deidre in the last day or so was her asking who that person was whom she'd met in the *SCI* office when she'd been waiting for Davin. Deidre knew that she was the publisher of the online service he works for, but she'd asked some questions of Alicia's personal life, and that had struck him as bit curious. He had been unable to answer most of the questions.

Chaplin is home, back from his work that is back to full-time, or he claims, but for however long may be the more pertinent question. Currently, Chaplin is out in the garden, putting in a bit more time. He's pretty sure Chaplin knows something is up but he hasn't asked about anything, even giving up his room to Cynthia and decamping to the attic without asking why.

This line of thought has Davin figuring he'll have to give up Chaplin's full rent for this month, and then he corrects himself, realizing he'll actually forgive the rent since Chaplin has not yet paid it.

If I don't end up actually paying him something if he keeps up with so much garden work, he then thinks, frowning at his conflicting ends, which gets him thinking that he needs to look at his budget again. The quarterly property tax bill had arrived at the start of the week, and as usual, it's gone up, and the latest power bill is higher than ever. Adding green electricity capacity apparently doesn't do much to lower bills if the demand keeps building faster, and there are sizable numbers of electric cars these days, and a lot of charging, and more and more houses heating with mini-splits, and the news keeps squawking about data centers and AI.

Davin has barely sat down in the corner recliner when Jimmy jumps up off the couch and runs upstairs. He takes the moment to put his purple Chenier recliner back a bit but then brings it fully upright again. The recliner remains his favorite piece of replacement furniture after Gwen took the antiques that had populated their living room, but this meeting demands no lying down.

And then Jimmy is thundering down the stairs and he, Jimmy, and Cynthia get settled in.

Jimmy sits down on one arm of the old, slipcovered couch with Cynthia sitting at the other end, but then he slides down with some speed to sit squarely on the seat cushion. Davin flinches as he watches Jimmy drop onto the old couch and experiences a flash of worry about that piece of furniture, the only one not to make Gwen's list. He also sees that when Jimmy lands, Cynthia gets a bit of a bounce. Both ignore this, and instead Jimmy and Cynthia are each looking at him.

"Well," Davin begins, deciding the two others are waiting on him to start things off.

"I, uh, well, as best I figure it, there's a couple of steps we should be considering taking, which, first, is for Cynthia to get in touch with ClimateProgress, and I think that you...." Davin, talking while looking up toward the ceiling, trails off and re-directs his gaze at Cynthia.

She nods.

"I want to do that," she says. "The post on Carbon's End's website by George Morales makes me think I might as well go direct."

Davin knows nothing of any particular post nor does the name mean anything to him until she explains Morales is the founder of the organization. He asks her how she'd contact him, and she tells him that email would be the first thing, then telephone or Zoom.

"It's time to do this," she adds.

Jimmy nods.

Davin nods, too. "And then see if their legal wants to help, but either way, I should have Palamo explore the meet with the DA."

"The DA" Jimmy asks, making Davin realize he hadn't mentioned Palamo's suggestion to them yet.

"We should wait to see what Cyn's company's reaction is, what they offer," Jimmy suggests, and Davin sees him look at her, perhaps gauging her reaction. "I thought we were going to be talking about what to do, but —"

Davin interrupts him. "Hold that a sec. I want to be clear about something." Davin turns to Cynthia and says, "This is really your call, it seems to me. That's why we're having this conversation."

Both Cynthia and Jimmy nod.

"So, tomorrow," he continues, "let's get you on retainer with Palamo. I don't know if he's going to be that much help, but I agree with him, you should be repped."

"Represented by a lawyer," Davin adds, annoyed by how inarticulate he sounds.

Cynthia nods, visibly relaxing.

"Or if you prefer someone else, whomever," Davin adds.

"Thank you," Cynthia says. She sits up straighter.

"Good," Davin says.

"We should do it," says Cynthia. "For one thing, I want this cleared up."

"Also, there's some other stuff we need to talk about," Jimmy adds.

Davin holds up his hand, not wanting Jimmy to talk over her.

"I'm about as angry as I've ever been," she adds, "and Joe...."

He and Jimmy keep quiet as Cynthia falls silent for a beat or two, before she adds, "I'd like to know what's going on, to get, to find, to fucking arrest that guy, the guy I saw shoot Joe, sorry about my language."

Jimmy says to her, "Don't fret, he doesn't *fucking* care about that language. Right, Daddo?"

Davin just shakes his head and sighs.

"That's number one," she continues. "No way this shouldn't be the priority, and I'm thinking I've been screwing this up, being screwed up, and it has got to be messing up investigating, and...."

She's goes quiet again and the three of them sit with her silence until after another moment passes, when she adds, "I am really angry." But it comes out soft and hard for Davin to catch.

Cynthia clears her throat. "Number two, I'd really like to see my brothers, which isn't going to happen until this is cleared up."

This is the first Davin has heard her mention anything about brothers, but Jimmy seems to know something because he nods.

"I was so freaked out, so out of it, so—" Cynthia stops herself. "Well, whatever. That shit is over. I'm more than ready."

She looks at Davin, then Jimmy, and then back to Davin.

"Thanks, by the way," she adds. "I don't think I've said that to you guys."

Davin just shrugs, while Jimmy is nodding.

"Really," Cynthia says.

He's uncomfortable about the gratitude, but he's saved by what Cynthia says next.

"And," she says with a small hint of a smile, "they owe me some backpay, I figure," and the three laugh, the mood lightening.

Davin clears his throat, picking up his notepad, ready to get to the to-do list, but Jimmy interrupts him.

"There's some other stuff," Jimmy repeats, and now he has everyone's attention.

"I went back to the Callow's email-archive servers after we talked in the kitchen the day before yesterday," Jimmy tells them.

This annoys Davin. In fact, it is downright maddening since he's still worried Jimmy doing this kind of thing can become a problem for his son. "Jesus, James," he says, and he starts mentioning all over again the recently passed cybersecurity laws again and all the potential trouble that could visit his son.

Jimmy looks at Davin. "I was careful, Dad," he says. "First, the whole thing took just a couple of minutes since I know how now. Second, my friend from school pointed me at a new re- director, one of the best at the moment, he claims."

Davin tries to keep his worry at bay.

"Three things," Jimmy says, but then corrects himself

immediately. "Really four things."

Nobody Expects the Spanish Inquisition, pops into Davin's mind, but he shakes free of it. It occurs to him that three days ago he was simply excited about Jimmy coming home, but now here is this person who saw her boss killed in front of her and has been on the run, and some rodently-visaged man flashed a gun, and then a private eye, and now there's going to be a meeting with a DA, or his office anyway. Palamo wouldn't hazard a guess who was likely to take the meeting.

"First," Jimmy continues, "there were two new emails from Terry Bancroft, which according to my interpretation, in the first one, is more or less a repeat about another operative — a.k.a. Rat Face, has to be — needing to be fired. I think I mentioned the first one yesterday."

Jimmy stops, furrowing his brow. "The day before yesterday," he corrects. "The last one, the last email, from Bancroft, well this email is a resignation containing a request for final invoice."

Jimmy sees the confused looks, so he hurries on.

"The resignation email followed on the heels of the reply to his first email, and that response was basically a rejection, basically told Bancroft to M.Y.O.B., in effect, that there was no such person."

"We know better though," Cynthia says.

Jimmy nods. "We," he says as he nods his head toward her, "certainly know there is a Rat Face, otherwise called Birddog in Madaki's emails, and we can safely assume he's in contact with this Madaki guy."

"IP metadata, etc., right?" asks Davin.

"Bancroft," Jimmy tries to continue, but Davin interrupts him again, "so the law firm" — and here Davin preempts a counter-interruption holding up a hand toward Jimmy — "this guy Madaki, we know definitely is lying about this other guy, the rat guy as you call him."

Jimmy nods. "Which is weird."

"Which is weird," he agrees.

"The second reply is, basically, ok, farewell from Bancroft, along with reference to some contract and payments schedule but without any specifics. Already on file, my guess," Jimmy says.

"So you believe this Bancroft is off the case?" asks Davin.

"Yes," Jimmy simply says. "What is more interesting is I did some more looking around the client list of the law firm, which I got both from their public website, which is of stuff they are happy to have everyone know, plus from what I could pull out of headers of emails going back a ways.

"The law firm has some oil and coal clients but not a big number," he continues. "Madaki seems to work for, report to, one of the firm's partners, and from what I can see from the internal email, that guy has the fossil fuels clients, so I concentrated my search on the archives of those clients. I'm proud of myself for the effort, because these emails are massively, like black hole–level, boring," he says, which gets no response, which makes him look around.

"Okay, well," he says, "tough crowd," which does get a laugh.

"Okay. Well, there's an oil service company by the name of Northstar Producers on the firm's accounts with the firm taking the lead on doing due diligence — don't ask me — on the acquisition of another oil services company, and that company's name cross-references to Joe and Cynthia's trip, which I got from the trades."

"Trades?" asks Cynthia.

"Yeah, you know, the industry publications. There's *The Oil & Gas Journal*, *OILMAN*, *Energy Intelligence Group*, there's like a million of them," Jimmy says. "There's a lot of news about it, it's a big project, but a lot of rumors, well, questions, about trouble clearing the financials."

"Yes," says Cynthia. "That's right. Northstar is major top-tier,
one of the bigger ones."

"Top ten in its sector, from what I read," adds Jimmy.

"We weren't sure how real the pipeline project was, there had been a lot of hype," Cynthia adds.

"And Carbon's End set up to meet the investment group that was considering investing big in the proposed oil pipeline project in Southern California, right? That is what the trip was about," Jimmy adds.

Cynthia nods.

"Huh, yeah," says Jimmy. "It seems the investment thing, group, whatever, had some worries about buying into the acquisition, well, the project, on the fence anyway, best I can figure, about the investment because of divestment" — Jimmy looks over at Cynthia, who is looking at him. "Sorry, my brain is fried from so much looking over this shit," he adds, and then pauses.

"The name of the investment group is AJB Funds," Cynthia says.

Jimmy nods. "Right. AJB Funds. They were considering investing in the pipeline project being managed, run, whatever they call that, by Tally Oil Services Inc."

Jimmy looks back at Cynthia, who shrugs and tells him she hadn't known that level of detail, didn't need to, their focus being on AJB Funds overall. The pipeline deal had just been the occasion for the approach.

"Anyway," he goes on, "Thing Number Three — Northstar Producers is the company acquiring Tally Oil."

Jimmy rises slightly and tips his head in a bow.

"Yeah, wow," says Davin. "Huh. That's interesting. Top marks. Top marks." Davin sees Jimmy is blushing and Cynthia notes this too, and Davin watches her smile, and then Jimmy sees that smile and nods to her, his grin breaking out like crazy.

"I mean, it's interesting, those companies," Davin says. "But." He shrugs.

"Um," says Cynthia. "You said four things," she reminds Jimmy.

"Shit, yeah," he says.

"Fourth, there are new emails from Rat Face, as I said, best guess, all brief, and they mostly don't say anything much, well, not making sense to me anyway. His most recent one is from last night."

"Don't say much understandable, except our street address is in the text."

Davin and Cynthia are still.

"The fourth thing is that I traced the IP Rat Face has been emailing from the last couple of days." He stops, seeming unsure suddenly. "Maybe I should have led with this," he says, still looking like he's thinking. "The IP is from the Wi-Fi network at the Lantern House Motel. The one on Route 7 after Price Chopper, near, across from the bowling alley."

The group is silent.

"Less than four miles from here," Jimmy adds.

"You should have led with that," Davin says, finally.

Chapter 38: Hello Mr. Bancroft, Should You Accept This Assignment

At the conclusion of their meeting, both Cyn and Davin agreed Jimmy should contact Terry Bancroft, PI and ask his advice about Rat Face being close by, and that they'll mention this at tomorrow's meetings. Jimmy is happy to let Bancroft know Rat Face is in town, and he would especially love to hear that there is nothing to worry about, but he still can't get that guy's feral look out of his mind.

Not to mention the gun, he reminds himself.

Another thing they'd agreed upon is that his dad will call Palamo in the morning with pretty much the same request about what, if anything, should be done, and who, exactly, this information should be reported to.

In some ways, the thing that bothers him the most is the guy at the law firm, Madaki, shutting down any acknowledgment to Bancroft's email queries. This Madaki guy had been open enough with Bancroft about two other firms that had also signed on to the search contract but has denied Rat Face even existed.

Birddog, he reminds himself.

Cyn sticks her head past his open bedroom door to let him know her call into ClimateProgress has gone well. She'd called right after their meeting earlier, and with the time difference, it had still been business hours there.

Her transformation is obvious, showing a palpable relief, he sees. *Exuberant* is the word that comes to mind.

She is even more excited when she speaks in a nonstop rush about her call to her brothers, and in the next breath she asks if he wants to go out for a drink or two with Deidre and Chaplin and her, telling him with a grin the tab is on her.

"Hey, the credit card is open!" she says, before remembering to return his phone, having previously deciding to not use her phone as yet. He's glad she's keeping her phone off as he's advised, suggesting it might help with any investigation. Her laptop, on the other hand, has been active since the day after they'd gotten here, *but then no weird texts*, he knows.

As much as going out for drinks sounds like a very excellent idea, he reluctantly begs off. She seems disappointed that he's declining, but her new relaxation is the overall impression he has of her, and he's glad to see it.

He looks at her retreat from his doorway, back to her room.

He will stay in because he wants to get the Bancroft email out, the very email he's in the middle of typing, sitting on his bed, his back increasingly protesting his posture slumping over his laptop.

The Rat Face situation could be nothing, he reminds himself, or simply the guy is still on the clock keeping track of Cyn's location, although she has already been in touch with ClimateProgress, and Jimmy knows they know where she is now, and her family knows. Just about anyone with the right access, such as law enforcement, would, he imagines, getting a ping when she buys the first round.

But if Rat Face knows where she is, then why no contact? he mulls. If there's an offer from the law firm, and they now know where she is, he finds himself thinking, why nothing now? Of course, Bancroft had all but concluded when speaking to them on the train that the offer he relayed didn't seem to make much sense.

Why is Rat Face here? he ponders. *Who is the client?*

Although maybe Rat Face isn't here any longer. He hasn't gone back to the law firm network for hours and he is not inclined to call the motel to inquire. He's worried about Cyn going out, but he tells himself he's just being stupid, and besides, she'll be in public and with the other two.

The two others, that is, sharing his house, and this is just another piece of his odd feelings, on top of everything else.

He gets himself back on track.

He's trying to accomplish another thing with this email, which is to update Bancroft about what they've found about Northstar's plans to acquire Tally Oil, but he doesn't know for sure if he should, with it being too much speculation perhaps.

On the other hand, a lot of what he's found is a matter of public knowledge, including Northstar's acquisition interest. He can show Tally Oil and its connection to the law firm, and there's also the divestment connection with Tally Oil and AJB Funds and Carbon's End, but that all adds up to a lot of conjecture.

He's feeling completely and utterly out of his depth.

He has no definitive knowledge of any direct connection between the law firm and Northstar, not related to Cyn, anyway, and he can't really see how he'd be likely to find out. He wants to ask for Bancroft's advice, even hoping Bancroft might know how to find out who Rat Face is and whether there's actually anything to be nervous about. And maybe, even, Bancroft might know who the actual client is, and that would be helpful.

Confidential is part of the name, he considers, his own confidence plummeting further.

Still, he's hoping that Bancroft might be sufficiently curious and actually reply instead of telling him to bug off. He's read Bancroft's emails to the law firm and subsequent withdrawal from the assignment, which makes him think Bancroft might be interested, could be curious.

For a while Jimmy keeps going back and forth about whether there's any real reason to send this email, especially since there's some danger in mentioning he knows what he knows, because this implicitly confesses the *how* of what he knows, and the only self-protective approach he can think of is to put it all *hypothetically*. He might, *hypothetically*, have copies of the emails from Callow, Cullens, and McChusker,

LLC, and specifically— *hypothetically, of course*—between the law firm and Rat Face.

He types this out, but looks it over and deletes the *hypothetically*, realizing this makes no sense, not if he's reporting content on the emails he clearly has not *hypothetically* read but actually read. The devils are in the details, and the details are right there in black and white from his email archive hacks.

It comes down to trusting his own intuition about Bancroft, which is nervous-making enough, but maybe less nervous-making than not having a name for Rat Face, or a good sense of what Rat Face is doing here in town.

On the other hand, his mom's always talking about him needing to trust his instincts.

Go with the gut, he tells himself.

The problem is his gut once again feels something akin to nausea.

And then, of course, he's most likely to simply get ghosted by Bancroft, which helps a bit with his upset.

Still, he thinks there's something about the guy that seems reliable, so he's still confused about what to do.

What he isn't mentioning in this email is that Cyn has already had two telephone calls today with ClimateProgress, the first going to HR where she said she got confirmation an internal audit of the putative embezzled Carbon's End accounts showed no actual missing money. If he understands her right, a forensic accounting trace shows that the money that had appeared in her bank account did come through the direct deposit mechanism ClimateProgress.Org uses for their paychecks, but not drawn from their payroll account.

She had told him this conversation was odd enough, but the instructions to call Morales's direct line had been entirely unexpected. She described this second telephone conversation as *surreal*, reinforced by her confession that she had no clear sense of all the conference call participants, although legal was one, and of course, Morales, and the president of Carbon's End, the fellow who'd hired her. According to what Cyn also told him, the organization's investigation is already well underway.

And now she's off having a beer and I'm sitting here trying to game this through, Jimmy thinks.

And pretty much failing.

He makes another effort to get back to his current task. He's basing the email on his hunch that Bancroft might be helpful because Bancroft might want to get out in front of his own involvement.

But before he can think further upon the matter of the email he's struggling to finish, Gmail pings a notification of an email. The email is from Terry Bancroft, AllServe CI.

"Wow," Jimmy says out loud.

Chapter 39: Code Eight-Six

Larsen means to keep checking for alerts from his sneakware lurking in the law firm's networks, but he's presently caught up in laying the groundwork of a different assignment, which means he's reviewing head and body shots of good-looking middle-aged women in an online catalog of actresses.

"*Actresses*," complete with quotation marks, is how he thinks of them.

Unfortunately, this directory, called *Extra Help*, doesn't have too many to select from for the type he seeks. Fortunately, any of them in this category will likely do.

He's used this service once or twice before, and is fascinated by its very existence, but then his military training, as much as he'd enjoyed it, didn't cover all that much about show business and such odd corners of civilian life. The service is indeed for actors, but exactly of the not-famous type, and used for commercial work, and as extras, and a big line that had surprised him is the business side, whether moderators for focus groups or exhibition booth staffers. He, of course, knows about those types from his various conferences and exhibitions attendance, including the one in Anaheim, although he'd been too busy there to spend much time on the show floor to appreciate that show's crop of *booth babes*. But reading between the lines, the service also has a lot of business of another application, although mainly for divorces and mainly by private investigators in that same line of business. But the only real interest in this site at the moment is that he has is to find the right woman for the assignment.

Classic Honey Trap.

Rocky is excited about this assignment, the conversation over the encrypted video chat had been quite energetic on his part, and he had hardly remonstrated Larsen about the hang-fire nature of the Mojave assignment, but even there, surprisingly, Rocky's complaining was restrained, more disappointment than anything else. Of course, that assignment hasn't been a wash for the overall goal since it looks likely the pipeline project is moving forward, so for Rocky's bosses, not a total wash, really.

But in Larsen's mind that assignment is a failure and needs termination. The locate on Cynthia Wainwright is no longer useful, not with the changes in the BOLO status on the networks he has access to. The status change tells him her location is known, and it would be a bona fide miracle for his freelancer to work fast enough to get the job done before she's too public, and he has stopped believing in miracles. He does not like messy, but at least the potential for blowback seems minimal. With a tiny possibility of completion entirely discountable, he is declaring the assignment finished. The timing tells the true tale, and even if the guy from the kill service is skilled or lucky enough to pull it off, Larsen is going to go simplicity rather than luck.

So, it's done. He's pulled the plug.

He turns back to what he's been doing, trying to finish the selection for this current assignment. He knows the woman he's looking for has to be good-looking but not so good-looking the senator might sense the trap. The key is to offer up a woman who seems just slightly out of the man's league, but nonthreatening. She's got to come across like a real conquest prospect. Getting the senator in a compromising situation isn't likely to be much of a challenge, given his reputation for womanizing, but then again it isn't rumor that provides leverage but fact, and the fact of his fucking another woman will likely prove an effective threat. The thinking is, as the prepped backgrounder argues, the leverage is provable fact, since the man's upcoming campaign is the family-values sort and his wife is a popular campaign surrogate.

There are a total of three opportunities coming up for this assignment, and the best option will likely be the fundraising event in D.C., but there are two other scheduled events that may offer good operational environments too.

Whether such threat as compromising evidence, either video or photos, proves effective or not is above his paygrade, he reminds himself. The target is a Republican, and he would have thought the senator is one of the choir from what he knows of the guy's politics, but Rocky had mentioned something about a key committee vote and alluded to this senator's resistance to a particular deregulation provision. That tells Larsen there's a lot of money riding on getting this right. It's a ballsy move, acting on a senator, and that will require the best operational hygiene.

Not that any of this matters to him. His job is to implement the right set of conditions and document the results. He has to choreograph the ways the encounter will work out, and that may depend on what the woman is willing to do, but he'll think through other alternative plays too.

As part of the hygiene, the woman will be approached for hire and briefing by someone double removed from him, just the way he likes it.

He's already started in on scenario notes.

A notification tone he's been waiting for from the law office's server sounds, and he switches over to access his secret mirror cache within the law firm's network so that he can review the latest email purportedly for the law firm's clerk, Madaki, even if Madaki will never be able to produce the email once the daily cache is cleared.

Larsen has already learned, not more than two hours back, that Cynthia Wainwright has finally surfaced with ClimateProgress, and he has sent out the shutdown order.

He skims Birddog's reply.

Fuck!

The asshole, whoever he is, has not clearly acknowledged the shutdown. The language, as unclear as it would read to others, seems clear enough to Larsen. The freelancer appears to be haggling. He'll have to contact the kill service direct. He can't chance being clearer even if the pass along is through the false cache mechanism, since, as improbable it may be, Madaki could still see the email with the coded talk being sent in his name. All that has to happen is for the clerk to go through his Sent messages before the daily disappear routine cycles. Larsen wants to exercise care to minimize such discovery, and the last thing he needs is for Madaki to realize there is something not kosher with the email server, but even more threatening is the clerk realizing what the message is actually relaying with the freelancer: *Too late. Don't kill her.*

And there is a definite need to get the message to the freelancer, considering that guy's confusing response so far.

Larsen sighs. He'll have to contact the kill service directly.

Chapter 40: Bumfuckville

*T*he *fucking client is always the worst part*, Dennis thinks. He knows this is pretty much always the case, but this job is turning out to be a lot more complicated than he likes, more complicated than what he signed up for as far as he's concerned.

He hates working through intermediaries, even if this is the best for all parties concerned. Still, the *fucking double-talk* is getting on his nerves. The most recent email reply he'd received was especially fuzzy and could mean any number of things.

Including stop, he grudgingly considers. But he's read it over and over, and the main conclusion is maybe the guy on the other end can't speak English.

Well, fuck that. Dennis doesn't like quitting. Dennis doesn't like complicated. As far as he's concerned, if this is unclear then it's still a go, and they better honor the second fee, the completion payout.

Getting up on the roof of the mill building wasn't complicated. For one thing, the mill buildings are largely empty, although not as abandoned as Dennis had first thought. *But that's why you look, not just fucking guess*, he thinks. He had spent part of the day going back and forth, walking around the collection of different mill buildings that had no doubt once been part of one big complex.

Big for Bumfuckville, Dennis snorts.

He can't believe he's been out here in *Nowheresville* for these many days.

There's a dance studio in one of the mill buildings, some sort of school, lots of young schoolkids come by, off the school bus, mostly young kids, but there are a few high school girls.

Hey little schoolgirl, Dennis thinks, but then adds, *Fuck that*. He knows this kind of thinking will lead nowhere good. He's not here for sightseeing, he tells himself.

Which makes him laugh because here he is lying on the flat roof on the mill building closest toward that big house on *that fucking hill, who builds a fucking house on a slope?* Where the target is with that *fucking ape of a kid*, and what seems to be that kid's family, if he's figured it right, getting the name from the phone book at the library in town, not the one several blocks away in the village, but the other one that's bigger, on Main Street, where he's less likely to get noticed.

The one close by, up on some street he hadn't bothered to learn, is a much smaller building.

Ramsdell, Housatonic Village, fucking puking quaint.

If he wants, he can see a lot of the village from his current vantage.

The dance studio is in the better-maintained attached mill building on the south side of his eyrie. That building has a new metal gable roof, and he's seen that the two other floors don't seem active, only the top floor with the dance school. There are no windows on the back gable end, fortunately, because that would make his lookout useless to him.

There is a smaller building attached to the corner at the gable-roofed building's opposite end that faces the street, and this attached building seems to be used in some way, but the only clear indication of how some part of it is being used is a window sign for a massage place he'd seen from the street. Not the sort of massage place he goes to when he can since this one seems serious about physical therapy. *Integrated Wellness*, the sign in the second-story window reads.

Integrate my dick is the thought that had popped into his head, knowing there would be no *happy ending* at such a place

All in all, the traffic at these buildings is light. He hasn't seen anyone walking around out back of these mills where there's a big open area along the river that probably used to have other buildings because it looks like there might have been some structures razed at some point in the past—a bit of rubble still scattered about with a piece of what must have been foundation stone visible here and there among sparse weeds and small saplings. The back of his building is mostly blank brick with only two doors along the back, and part of the back section seems to once have had another structure attached to it, the ghost of mortar outlining where the connecting walls used to be. In fact, the mill building he's atop is also otherwise ramshackle, with different-level roofs like it was put together from several separate buildings at some point. The front section of this amalgamated building faces the street but still set back from the small bridge that spans the river. The front of this building is as far from his look out as possible, and has plywood over its windows, but there's a big garage door and a regular entrance that remain active. He knows this because in his first *flyby recon* he'd seen a rental truck at the open garage door with some men unloading boxes.

That's been the extent of any activity, and he has to wonder if the place is only used for storage. He's seen no other activity after that truck, but that suits him just fine.

He is really b e g i n n i n g t o hate this assignment, but he keeps reminding himself that the money he's due is substantial.

One challenge is that it's not easy running silent in a place like this.

Everybody knows everybody.

He's sure of this, and that makes him careful.

More careful.

He is always careful, but this assignment is turning out to be a giant pain in the ass and taking more and more care. He can't wait to forget what he's had to learn about the place.

Monument Asshole Mills.

He can't wait to be out of here.

There is one good thing to the whole town being small. Using the phone book didn't take that long, especially since he was only scanning for the street name, *easy-peasy.*

From his surveillance of the house, he would guess there seems to be a number of siblings also at home, all close in age, unless they're something else. *Maybe a goddamn hippy habitat,* he thinks, quite pleased by the turn of phrase. He is less pleased, though, by the number of people coming and going because he has to wait and see if there's a schedule he can rely on in order to go do the deed.

He does think it could be kind of pleasant where he has set up his watch nest with the river that runs nearby bubbling and gurgling down below, and that's kind of nice, really. But it can get pretty hot up on the old flat tar roof, which is shitty, but that's why he gets paid the big bucks.

Never fucking big enough, he can't help thinking.

But the day is getting long in the tooth with the sun slanting and the heat finally dropping beneath the pulled-back tarp he'd brought for his nest, his *Forward Operating Position,* and no one would think twice about a tarp up on a shitty roof. He has his F.O.P. at one end of the roof on the side toward the houses up the hill, and when the sun was at its highest, he'd pulled the tarp up over an old pallet he'd hauled up in the predawn hours, using a rope for that purpose. He then had broken a couple of loose slats from the pallet to form legs for a lean-to, using a couple of spring clamps he'd bought at the hardware store downtown when he'd gotten the tarp and rope.

He's pretty pleased with the setup, but he's not pleased he's been up here sweating like a pig under the tarp, keeping his eyes on the house, jotting down the comings and goings in his notebook. The job is made difficult with the number of people in the house, and the different schedules, but it looks like a couple of the people are out in the mornings, early, regular. He worries that can leave as many as three still in, and the big ape kid seems to have no schedule from what he can see. The older guy comes and goes, but he's back again, having returned a little after lunchtime.

Dennis is pouring himself another cup from the thermos when he sees the pickup truck coast down the long steep driveway from the parking area that must be up top on the other side. The pickup truck is the other young guy, already leaving again, not long after coming back after being gone all day. As he watches the truck descend, Dennis glimpses the target, she's in the pickup truck, passenger side, and he sees that the young *whoever the fuck he is* is driving, not *the big asshole kid*.

7:14, Dennis jots down in his scratchy handwriting in his little spiral notebook.

He hasn't a clue about where they're going, but he knows *this Podunk town turns in early*. He expects that when he's back tomorrow morning he'll find everyone is in.

He's about through for the day, and he'll want to get some rest since he'll be back in the early morning checking out other approaches. Google Satellite shows a lot of woods in back of the target property, so he'll set an approach and spend the morning checking on movement from there. He's guessing the best time to get to the target will be after the young guy and the other young woman leave in the morning, the only ones with regular schedules, is his guess. And the parking has to be out back, so he figures he'll have a good check on the remaining occupants.

He hears a screeching sound again, and by now he knows it's from some kind of hawk. It's one of those big ones that makes that sound, and he's been enjoying looking at them throughout the day. He likes to look at them flying and catching thermals.

The best part, though, is when the big bastards get chased and harassed by little birds. Crows usually, but sometimes even smaller birds. That surprised and amused him, and he's again tracking the hawk, finally having spotted it.

Then he scolds himself for his distraction.

Pay attention, he intones, a regular exercise he finds helpful.

Pay attention.

Although he knows that observation comes before planning, he can't help thinking about how the job will go down, his waiting until the house is clear of at least some of the residents, and then going in and taking care of business, putting down anyone still in, *easy-peasy*.

Not a hard target. Chances of there even being a gun is low.

Massatwoshits, good citizens, fuck 'em.

He certainly wouldn't mind having some fun with the target, she's a good-looking bitch, but he's a pro.

Too bad, he thinks. *The fucking rude way she treated me.*

He will check out the parking area tomorrow, that should tell him a lot.

Tomorrow or day after next is when Dennis thinks he'll finish up.

Easy-peasy.

Chapter 41: The Midnight Bell

And, of course, Davin is supposed to be finishing up the latest article for *SCI* about the big solar farm, but he's feeling overwhelmed and unsettled and behind the eight ball. His job description seems to have expanded with this Cynthia business, landing somewhere along the lines of camp counsellor and amateur criminal defense attorney.

Hard thinking is always exhausting, he considers, and he's decided he'll start back up with the *SCI* work in the morning, although he suspects that tomorrow will likely be filled with cops and lawyers and who knows what else. Cynthia has gotten in touch with ClimateProgress and apparently help is on the way, whatever that will turn out to be.

"Whatever, whatever," he says out loud.

It's closing on midnight, and he pushes away from his desk, intending to get himself to bed.

But the doorbell rings and startles him.

What the hell?

In three quick steps he's through the landing and dropping down the stairs and swinging through the bottom landing and past the dining area into the kitchen. At the kitchen-entry doorway, he flips on the porchlight.

There's a guy out there. He sees him through the doorway pane, a white guy, middle-age, wearing a good summer-weight suit, squinting and batting away the moths and other flying insects drawn to the sudden light of the carriage lantern by the outside porch door. The man looks a bit bored or tired despite all the aerial action circling about, diving and swerving and engaging in strafing runs.

Some big drops of rain start, falling through the porchlight, adding to the movement around the man standing on the steps.

Davin realizes it's that guy Bancroft from the website photo Jimmy had shown him.

What the hell?

He opens the kitchen door, stepping through to the porch door.

He swings that door open.

"Come on in," Davin says, easy as you please, and Bancroft step into the glass-paned porch.

"Thanks," says Bancroft, with one more bat, a tiny one of his hand making a casual movement in the air above his brow.

"I'm Davin Caine," he says, letting Bancroft step past him as he closes the door just as the rain suddenly lets loose. "Wow," he says, looking back out at the sudden downpour.

He turns back toward Bancroft. "You are Terry Bancroft, a private investigator," he says before Bancroft can introduce himself. Davin thinks he's being cool as a cucumber, or so it would seem to any observer, unless the observer has ears to hear the beating, booming heart pushing blood past his ears or eyes to see what probably looks like a textbook high-blood-pressure stroke warning sign. A moment ago, he was about to head up to bed, and now he has a genuine PI standing in his kitchen.

There's some rumbling of thunder way off.

Bancroft smiles and holds out his hand, which he takes, shakes, and the he says, more than asks, that Davin must be Jimmy's dad.

"Yup," Davin says, and then he's suddenly out of words, questions, or any sort of suggestion of what should come next, so he surprises himself when he blurts out, "You look like a cop," which immediately strikes him as a stupid thing to say, but he's rescued by Bancroft's big laugh.

"That's what your neighbor said too," Bancroft tells him, and then he recounts stopping at the wrong house, the one on the other side.

"But no one's in the Airbnb apartment," a confused Davin tells Bancroft even as he scrambles to figure out what Bancroft might be talking about.

"Yeah, well," Bancroft says, his face puzzled. "Uh, it got weird for a moment, I must have startled him, it being night and late and all."

Davin nods, now realizing what house Bancroft means. "That house?" he asks, pointing in the right direction down the hill.

Bancroft nods. "The guy sort of jumps and I'm flashing back to my old police days, the reflex about he's going for a weapon," Bancroft tells him with something like a smile. "Because, well, that sort of thing is always there, even retired, and then the guy asks me if I'm a cop."

Davin nods.

"Is that a New England thing?" Bancroft asks, but Davin sees that the guy is just joking.

"It's a late-hour New England thing," he replies, and Bancroft is suddenly off-kilter, apologizing. Of course it's late, he admits, and he wants to explain why he's in such a hurry to get here. Bancroft tells him he's got a room at the Holiday Inn, and then mentions a series of names Davin doesn't follow until he realizes he must be talking about Rat Face.

"Rat Face," he says, which makes Bancroft smile, but then it turns into something less like a smile.

Davin gestures him through the main door, ushering Bancroft off the porch and into the kitchen, and Bancroft drops a portfolio briefcase with a shoulder strap on the kitchen island. "Yeah," Bancroft says. "Your boy coined him that back on the train."

Davin is still trying to settle himself.

"Well, yeah," Bancroft says, his smile dropping entirely as he repeats one of the names from moments before. "That's a worrisome guy."

Davin lets out a laugh, or something close to it at any rate. "Buddy," he says, "believe me, I'm worried enough."

Bancroft smiles and settles back to his easy-going way,

just nodding.

He steps behind Bancroft to close the kitchen front door, remaining at the door for a moment to look back out at the sudden downpour curtaining through the porchlight, and then he turns back to look at Bancroft, who's looking around the kitchen.

Davin is looking around too, feeling at sea.

I'm not a late-night guy, he's thinking.

He's thinking he was on his way to bed, but instead is now standing in his kitchen, trying to figure out just exactly what's going on.

"Your kid is a sharp fellow, has some balls too," Bancroft says, and then there's Jimmy, at that moment, his heavy steps cantering down the stairs, then ducking his head through the doorway at the foot of the stairs.

"Hey, Mr. Coif!" Jimmy says, far too loud for the hour, stepping into the dining area, and Bancroft has something of a grin in answer, and then Bancroft turns back to Davin and says, "And a wiseass too."

Part of him hears Bancroft talking, but Davin is mostly focused on trying to figure out how Bancroft is here standing in his kitchen. He knows Jimmy's been trading emails with Terry Bancroft, Chief Investigator, AllServe CI, but that was only after the talk he and Jimmy and Cynthia had. *Umm, was that earlier today?* he considers, and then he glances at the kitchen clock and sees the hour has slipped midnight.

Technically yesterday, I guess, he answers himself.

Another late night seems in the cards because now here is Bancroft, but that confuses Davin since Bancroft only could have gotten Jimmy's email or emails the day before.

The day before, only technically though, he tells himself. *But really just hours before, so what is he doing here already? What's he doing here at all?*

Jimmy, on the other hand, seems just fine with Bancroft's presence, stepping forward to shake Bancroft's outstretched hand, and it occurs to Davin maybe he's the only one not in the know, but he drops that line of thinking for the time being and suggests they go upstairs. As he is marching them all up to the living room Davin listens to Jimmy ask Bancroft how he got here so fast, so it seems that maybe Jimmy is confused about it too.

Davin's reflex as a host kicks in, so he is off downstairs again to pull some drinks together, and then he's on his way back up, tray in hand, which gets put down on the coffee table in front of the couch in the living room, then he ducks into the library room, coming back with a bottle of bourbon and hears Jimmy ask what Bancroft is doing here.

"What are you doing here?" Davin repeats, setting the bottle down on the coffee table next to the tray with glasses and ice and a pitcher of water. He gestures for Bancroft to sit.

Bancroft takes the stuffed armchair across the couch and near Davin's purple recliner.

"Call me Terry, please," Bancroft says, looking over to Jimmy who's in the process of taking up the couch.

Davin sits by Jimmy, who shifts over to surrender a bit more space.

Terry smiles, a fraction away from a grin.

"What?" asks Jimmy.

"I had your address, name, ten minutes after I took your leave on the train out of Chicago," he tells Jimmy.

Terry waits for Jimmy to catch up.

"The photo you took," Jimmy says finally and Terry's nodding.

Davin's head swings back and forth between them.

"Your college ID, your driver's license, both worse pictures than the one I snapped," Terry says.

Terry reaches into the portfolio-bag he's pulled back up onto his lap. He takes out a folder and fishes out a cover page. Davin glances at it as Terry sets it down on the coffee table. On the sheet of paper are some black-and-white images of Jimmy and what look like addresses, telephone numbers, and quite likely Jimmy's Social Security number.

"Well," Jimmy says, but he seems impressed, and among the several images, one that Davin recognizes is Jimmy's driver's license photo, while another looks like it's indeed been pulled from his son's college ID, and there are some other pictures that make Davin wonder if they might well be from one or another of the social media services.

"So, you figured I was with her?" Jimmy asks Bancroft.

"That it was possible anyway," Bancroft tells him. "What it looked like anyway, so I kept an eye on you too, and when you both got off in Pittsfield, yeah, that's what I figured."

"You were on the train all that time?" Jimmy asks. "Jeeze, that's weird."

"Hey," Bancroft says with a grin. "I've had a lot of practice."

"These people, organizations, they just give you this information?" Jimmy asks, nodding at the folder in front of him, although the answer is obvious with Terry's non-reply.

"Shit," is Jimmy's follow-up, interrupted by Davin handing out the glasses of bourbon, along with glasses of water too.

Bancroft drains his water glass.

"By the time I met Cynthia, accompanied by you," Bancroft continues, a vague wag toward Jimmy before looking at Davin with another economical wave of his hand. "Your son, on the train."

Davin finds himself trying to deal with the general scale of disorientation he's experiencing.

"Anyway," Bancroft continues, "you telling me about the guy you called Rat Face, that troubled me, something sounded off about it. I saw him taken off the train, although I didn't know about him hassling you at that point, but that's not professional, and the way you described him, his actions, it was questionable, both morally and legally." He pauses.

Davin pours himself some bourbon.

"Well, not enough concern to stop me from reporting in on having found Cynthia Wainwright, which I'll admit was nice for the bonus," he adds, maybe to no one in particular, and Bancroft grunts, looking at his glass of bourbon in his hand.

But something hadn't felt right, he tells Davin and Jimmy,

and he tells them how the story about the guy with the gun had him following up with queries to the law firm about that guy, and things went downhill from there.

"If the client had just kept denying that the guy," Bancroft says, "your Rat Face wasn't theirs, or say, asked me to look into having some unknown element, a potentially dangerous person poking around, that would have been okay, but I was told to not bother, forget it, rather plainly and several times underscored at that."

"You resigned," Jimmy tells him, then he gets up from the couch and smashes up the stairs.

Davin winces.

And then Jimmy is back down, carrying his laptop and handing one sheet of paper to Bancroft.

Bancroft takes a minute to look it over.

"Well, back at you," Bancroft says, looking up at Jimmy, who's settled back on the couch, now slurping bourbon, grinning.

Davin is drawing a blank.

"You cover your tracks?" Bancroft asks, and Jimmy's grin fades, but he's telling Bancroft he thinks so.

Davin gets it. The email printouts.

Jimmy starts talking about the email logs, and Bancroft asks him questions, including some that don't occur to Jimmy to wonder about, if Davin is following the conversation right, and then Bancroft tells Jimmy he'd love to see them, maybe fill in some blanks, but there are other, more pressing issues.

"Rat Face," says Jimmy.

Bancroft nods.

"My new client has brought me up to speed on Cynthia's communication with them," Bancroft says, and Davin sits up, and sees Jimmy sit up and both start asking questions, but he holds his hand up, asking them to wait.

"Wait, wait," says Davin, "What do you mean new client? Who the hell is the old client?"

Bancroft sighs.

"I'd worked through the CC&M lawyers, or their clerk,

anyway," he's telling them, "which isn't such an unusual arrangement, but when I decided it was best to cut my company loose from the stinkpot the whole thing was becoming, I had my guy dig deeper, and our best guess is that it could be McMurty Alliance, a new boutique lobbying firm recently spun out of the main lobbyist operation of the American Petroleum Alliance."

Bancroft then stops. "Maybe," he adds.

"Maybe?" asks Davin.

"According to OpenSecrets anyway, which tries to follow dark money, but their efforts are limited to date and the McMurty entity is pretty much newly minted, but there's a likely connection."

Davin doesn't know what to say. He isn't even sure what to ask now.

Bancroft adds, "Tentative links, like I said, but digging should show whether there's the connection, a business affiliation, between this McMurty Alliance and Callow, Cullens, and McChusker, LLC."

Davin is stunned. *What the fuck* is about the only thought he can form at the moment.

"You said new client," Jimmy says.

"Actually, really, Cynthia is my new client, *de jure*, and you guys, by extension, *de facto*." he says.

The room is silent, the way it can sometimes happen, as if the sound has been turned off.

"Through ClimateProgress.Org," Bancroft adds finally.

He coughs. "Okay," he says, continuing with a hint of a smile. "That might be confusing to hear."

"Um, yeah," says Jimmy who has put his empty glass on the coffee table and then sitting back, waiting on Bancroft.

"You should receive an email tomorrow"—Bancroft glances at his watch—"well, later today," he adds with a laugh. "Things are moving fast.

"I was following up on the Carbon's End angle after withdrawing," he tells them, but Davin's still not following and can see that Jimmy might be confused too.

Bancroft adds, "From that angle, Cynthia's company, first early, when I'd signed on to the locate case, trying to check what I'd been briefed on against what little I'd gotten from the law firm, and trying to get more info that could help. My follow-up queries at Carbon's End after I resigned, well, that call got booted right up to the top."

Davin feels like he has early onset dementia. It's like Bancroft is speaking in tongues.

"Yeah," says Jimmy. "Your assignment came through the law office with Madaki."

Bancroft waves his hand again, and Davin thinks of the porchlight bug swarm.

I'm hallucinating, he tells himself. He can't help but look at his watch.

"No, no," Bancroft says. "I mean, yes, Madaki for the purported missing person job, but I mean the new job from ClimateProgress, that's what I'm telling you about.

"After," Bancroft adds. "After the locate for Callow, Cullens, and McChusker, LLC. That's the old assignment."

"Morales," Davin says, halfway a question.

Bancroft turns toward Davin, nodding his head. He tells Davin and Jimmy about why he withdrew from the locate case. "Yeah, right, of course," he says, "the $100,000 meeting incentive itself was just such an outlier, and the lack of interest about Dennis Jymsom, your Rat Face."

"Dennis Jymsom?" asks Jimmy. "You have his name?"

"Yeah, I'll get to that but let me finish."

Bancroft explains he'd talked to Carbon's End after resigning the assignment with the law firm, just as a courtesy follow-up, and he found himself talking directly to Morales and the parent organization's house counsel, both keen to put forward their own questions about the Joe Craigson killing and their suspicions about the initial claims of Cynthia's involvement with the murder.

"And the embezzlement thing had too many anomalies when ClimateProgress.Org did their own investigating," he adds, and then he talks about his own interactions with

ClimateProgress, and tells Davin and Jimmy how the organization's lawyer, a guy named Giacometti, presented a job to him, and here he is.

"Where's Cynthia, by the way?" Bancroft asks. "She should be hearing this."

"Out," Jimmy tells him and adds she'd been feeling cooped up after today's meetings and had gone with two of the people who board here.

"Two, both, of the house sharers," Davin adds.

Bancroft nods and continues. "ClimateProgress.Org dug up some interesting connections that Callow, Cullens, and McChusker, LLC has with a number of fossil fuel clients."

"Tally Oil Services, right?" mentions Jimmy.

Bancroft seems a bit stunned.

"All right," Bancroft finally says, looking over to Davin, then fixing his eyes back on Jimmy. "Looks like you know some things too."

Jimmy tells Bancroft he'd put together an email for him that included this, but after hearing from Bancroft first, had decided not to send it, just the abbreviated one to mention Rat Face was local.

"Send it now?" Bancroft asks, and Jimmy nods and flips open his laptop.

"You two can compare notes," says Davin, "but you still need to explain what you mean about us being your client."

"*De facto*, he said," Jimmy corrects, but Davin ignores him, keeping his eyes on Bancroft.

"Okay," says Davin, growing annoyed. "You're here, and that's great, I'm sure, but why exactly are you here, and how exactly are we your *de facto* clients, and what the fuck does that mean?"

Jimmy looks over at his dad and mugs a look of shock at Bancroft.

Bancroft suppresses a smile, shifting his focus back to Davin.

"Right, yes, sorry," he says. He again fishes into his bag he'd put back down on the floor, pulls out a big manila interoffice envelope, and starts unwinding the ties and then pulls out a sheaf of papers from it.

Davin watches, feeling as if he's a bit stoned. *I am definitely up past my bedtime*, he tells himself.

"This should help," Bancroft says, handing over the sheaf to Davin. "Basically, I'm working for ClimateProgress, in support of the resolution of Ms. Wainwright's situation."

Davin barely hears Bancroft, because he's already thumbing through the papers he's just been handed. He sees they're broken out into sections, and he skips over Bancroft's multi-page contract but stops on a colored sheet titled *Memo of Understanding*, which has a list of *Whereas*es and *Therefore*s and *Stipulated*s, which Davin finds to be in some strange way quite compelling reading.

Bancroft is saying something, but Davin holds up his hand and keeps reading.

Davin hands the sheaf of paper to Jimmy who seems to make faster work of the documents, but then he knows Jimmy's regular hours aren't his, and he finds himself wondering, yet again, just when Jimmy tends to go to bed.

I'm not going to be sleeping anytime soon, he realizes.

Bancroft is talking to Jimmy about the CC&M emails Jimmy had copied, and Davin listens in on Jimmy's replies.

"I'm not sure how helpful this might be, other than what I've confirmed through the metadata," Jimmy says to Bancroft. Then Jimmy talks about the last indication Rat Face is still in the area, and that was a day back, before he'd replied to Bancroft's email. The law firm email intercepts came to an abrupt end with a URL 405 message, so he's got no current information.

"So, like the firm's server was changed," he adds, "likely to address the security problem I figure I triggered."

A day ago? Davin asks himself, realizing he's having a problem keeping track. He's leaning back on the couch, eyes closed, trying to listen to Jimmy and Bancroft talk, but he keeps losing the thread. He thinks he should read through the stack of papers Bancroft handed him, and then wonders if he should really hire a lawyer for Jimmy, which Palamo had strongly suggested, and then he hears Jimmy say, "Yeah, that's him, that's Rat Face," and Davin is back upright, eyes open, looking at Jimmy leaning over looking at an open folder Bancroft must have had in his bag.

Bancroft looks over to Davin.

"Name is Dennis Jymsom," he says, his eyes still on Davin. "At least, I'm pretty sure. There still isn't confirmation and there's a long list of aliases. Jymsom may be just another, but the guy, his aliases, shows up in a lot of files."

"Jeeze," Jimmy says. He's looking at one of the sheets he's pulled from the folder. "Eight suspected assaults, two failed indictments, one of which involved, what's that, *actio personalis moritur cum persona?*"

"Someone's rights die with the person," Bancroft tells Jimmy, but Jimmy's clearly not listening as he talks over Bancroft.

"The guy has a string of POIs related to homicides," Jimmy says.

Davin is not any less confused, even though he now realizes they seem to have information on this rat-faced guy, the one who is or was apparently staying about four miles down the road at a motel. "Huh, person of interest," Jimmy says. "Just like Cyn, I guess, person of interest."

"Nothing like Cynthia," Bancroft says. "We're worried about Jymsom. Nobody is worried about Cynthia as a murderer, not since early on anyway because the stink of a setup itself, it's far too much. As best we can figure, the idea must have been to kill both Craigson and Cynthia, and it looks like they hoped to put it up as a murder-suicide. There are phone texts, and then the money in an account, but somehow Cynthia screwed up their plans."

Bancroft pauses.

"The texts were for shit when looked at closely, any solid investigation would have seen that," he adds.

"You're talking about phone texts?" Jimmy asks.

"Yeah," says Bancroft. "Probably wouldn't have been

looked so closely if the two were dead." Then he goes on to explain the texts had been found on Craigson's phone, in the car with him, a back and forth with Cynthia that pointed to an affair and some sort of crisis, the sort of thing that fit the murder-suicide theory.

"But she wasn't with Joe," Jimmy says.

"Right," says Bancroft.

"The texts that get mentioned, referred to, in some of the early stories?" adds Jimmy.

"Right," says Bancroft. "Some of the news pieces. The ClimateProgress guys checked with the phone company—with company phones, you can do that—and they learned the texts, some of the texts, were off, not right, not"—Bancroft is waving one of his hands—"not, whatever, not kosher."

"Metadata was off, probably," Jimmy suggests, but Bancroft looks puzzled. "HTTP, the protocol, it's designed for redundancy, so data packets get broken up, routed every which way, but the stream has to reassemble, so, metadata."

"Ok," says Bancroft.

"Well," Jimmy adds, "we're talking texting, not the Web, but there's a similar functionality."

"Yeah, whatever," Bancroft says. "Not really important at the moment."

"She said she didn't want to get tracked by the phone," Jimmy tells Bancroft. "I'd been assuming she just dumped it, the phone, but we were talking yesterday and she still has it, battery out."

"Doesn't matter," Bancroft replies. "The phone company has it all."

Davin is stunned. "Affair?" he asks, looking to Jimmy, but Bancroft is already speaking.

"Right, whatever," says Bancroft. "That could be just another part of the setup."

Affair? What fucking affair? Davin asks himself. He looks at his son, but Jimmy seems intent on keeping his eyes on Bancroft.

Bancroft then shrugs and continues. "What matters is that

the whole thing went sideways and that likely sent whoever is behind the murder into a bit of a panic, at least that's what I now figure was why the locate job got posted quickly."

"How fast?" Jimmy asks.

Davin wants to catch Jimmy's eye, but Jimmy's attention remains on Bancroft.

"Well, that's part of it," Bancroft responds. "Because Cynthia must have been running already, her phone goes offline, but the local cops didn't find Craigson for nearly two hours after the last text.

"I'd read just over an hour," Jimmy says, but Bancroft tells him some of the news reports had gotten that wrong.

"Lonely out there in big sky country, I guess," Bancroft adds, but then he's asking why she ran, why she just didn't go to the police.

"She says it was some sort of cop," Jimmy tells Bancroft, "or at least someone who was in uniform with an official-looking vehicle. She thinks Joe was pulled over."

"No shit," Bancroft says quietly. "She saw it, jesus. Okay, that's interesting."

No one says anything else for a moment or two.

"I'll be right back," Jimmy says, and he goes back up to his bedroom and comes down holding a printout Davin recognizes from what he'd seen only on Jimmy's screen before. *The newspaper article*, Davin thinks, *about Cynthia's father.*

"No shit," Bancroft says quietly after taking his time reading it through. "Okay, that's interesting."

Davin notices the rain has stopped.

"Okay," Bancroft says, and then falls silent. "All right," he begins again. "The way the locate bid went out—"

"—Sorry," says Davin, lost again. "What are you talking about?"

"Sorry," Bancroft says. "From the clearinghouse listing." Davin is sure that his own expression clues Bancroft because Bancroft sighs before adding, "Okay, most private investigation companies, it isn't like in the old movies, you know, some dame walks in from the street. There are services that connect potential clients looking for confidential investigation services, and things like summons servers, bond-skip tracers, background checks, a lot of corporate work, missing persons, whatever.

"Well, if you build the timeline," he continues, "the posting for a locate job for Ms. Cynthia Wainwright went out over the service less than two hours after Joe Craigson's time of death, as best I figure, which is weird in and of itself since the first police report on Craigson being dead in the car hadn't yet hit the system."

Davin figures out Bancroft probably means the murder getting logged, or some sort of reporting mechanism anyway, but he's already too confused to ask for clarification.

"But, you know, we didn't know any of that then, and the rate was premium, actually the bonus was, with bonus builds..." Bancroft stops himself.

"Sorry," he says. "The important thing is there was a full-court press to find her—"

"—Cynthia," says Davin, catching a look of annoyance from Jimmy.

"Yes, yes," says Bancroft, "and I took a contract, nonexclusive, but you know, I'm a new company, attractive terms, and I set to work."

He pauses for a moment.

"Yeah, the clearinghouse, on nonexclusives, lists all under contract," Bancroft says to himself, it seems to Davin, but Bancroft then starts up again.

"Names meant nothing to me. There were two other outfits in all, I only knew, heard of one of them, so I didn't think much of it, but after I located Cynthia on the North Shore Limited and called it in to the client, well, their law firm contact, I'm waiting for confirmation on the bonus and to see if there are further instructions—"

"—Instructions?" interrupts Davin. He's feeling stupid.

"—Yeah, although I didn't see what else, except keep the track on—"

" —Track?" asks Davin.

"Yeah, keep tracking the missing person. A train isn't typically the final destination."

Jesus, thinks Davin. *I just can't stay up late these days.*

"But I'm also inquiring about what the two kids told me about the other person, Jymson, not that we knew the name then, but I'd seen him get walked off the train, the gun-flashing incident, and worried too about an asshole getting the bonus if I'm honest, but I get nothing, complete denial, none of the investigation firms, nothing," Bancroft says and pauses.

"Well, he," Bancroft tries to explain, "this guy the kids called Rat Face, the guy Jymsom, he made contact with Cynthia first, but I reported my contact first, maybe mainly because I'm not a stupid asshole who gets pulled for a firearm check, and you know, whatever, but it puts the guy on my radar of course."

Bancroft picks up the whiskey glass and takes a sip. "Not that it mattered if the client says I'm first in and get the bonus. Of course, I had picked up her trail in Las Vegas, my first report, just not a confirm."

Bancroft takes another sip. "But anyway, I ask my partner back at the office to check this out. He picks up on the guy getting taken off the train, and my guy talks to the station security, on Amtrak it's Amtrack police, but we're ex-cops, so the guys at that station, at Elyria, they were helpful."

"Helpful to this Jymsom guy?" Davin asks but then tells Bancroft to never mind because he's just figured out that Bancroft was talking about his partner finding the Amtrak people helpful.

"You were on the train the whole time too?" Jimmy asks.

Bancroft shakes his head and laughs. "No, actually got on at Cleveland, taking a regional hop out of Gary/Chicago, I hate those little turboprops."

"You were in Chicago?" Jimmy asks.

Bancroft laughs again. "Yeah, for about two hours, just long enough to show Ms. Wainwright's picture around, got lucky in that the train station there—"

" — Union Station," Jimmy says.

"Yeah, right, that was the second place I canvassed after the bus station."

"Um, okay," says Davin.

Bancroft says to him, "Sorry, I know it's late."

"Yes, okay," Davin says.

Bancroft takes another moment before he continues. "You know, just basically the guy's a moron, Jymsom I mean, although he had an alias when he talked to the Elyria station cops, and I was already thinking the whole assignment was starting to smell, and there's no cross-reference to any of the other agencies contracted in, so Ju-Ju — "

" — Ju-Ju?" asks Davin.

"Yeah, sorry," says Bancroft to Davin. "Nickname for my partner."

"Okay," says Davin.

"We didn't have Jymsom's name yet, but my partner knows guys on the Fed side, and he does some cross-referencing with them on the alias from the Amtrak police query on the firearm permit."

Bancroft pauses.

"Don't ask because I'm basically clueless about half the stuff Ju-Ju can do, but long and short the alias your rat-faced guy used for the relevant permit flagged an a.k.a. for Dennis Jymsom, among other names, but also the associated files for the guy too."

Bancroft is silent for a moment, until he says, "I closed my involvement then and there."

"Did you end up getting the location bonus?" Jimmy asks.

Bancroft laughs, or something like a laugh anyway, Davin thinks. *Sardonic* is the word that comes to mind.

"Well, we'll see. I hope so, but it isn't in my direct deposit yet, that's for sure, but that's not the main point here. The main point is I'm not happy Jymsom is here. Feels bad."

What the fuck? is what Davin is now thinking.

"And when I say *here*, I'm not one hundred percent sure since I don't know where Jymsom is exactly since he's no longer at the Lantern House Motel, at least not since yesterday sometime, I checked this after I got here."

Davin's hands have gotten sweaty, and he pulls out his handkerchief and quietly mops his palms. He steals a glance at Jimmy and Jimmy's looking a little pale.

"Sorry to say," Bancroft says, looking at Jimmy, "but your little stunt going back, the 405 response, probably tipped them."

"Well…" says Jimmy, but he doesn't have anything to add.

But Bancroft's not done.

"The fact they bothered to tell him, that someone at the law firm, or from McMurty could be, or maybe a handler, that anyone would care, worries me, and the more I've learned about Jymsom, the more worried I get."

"How bad is this?" asks Davin, but he starts when the terrace French doors toward the other end of the living room open and in walks Cynthia with Chaplin and Deidre.

A wave of alcohol builds in the air as the three walk toward where Davin, Jimmy, and Bancroft are sitting.

Davin remembers then that Jimmy said Cynthia had gone with Chaplin to grab a drink, picking up Deidre because her car—the one she was supposedly buying, at least at some point—was still getting work.

Cynthia stops stock still when she sees Bancroft, then she looks at Jimmy, who shrugs, and then at Davin, who feels red in the face.

Bancroft cranes around in his armchair, smiling at her. "Hey, my client is home," he says.

Davin hears Cynthia make some sort of sound, but it isn't quite any real word.

"Let's get some sleep," says Bancroft, smiling. "Tomorrow we have an appointment with the district attorney, and we'll start straightening all this out."

Davin hears Cynthia make some other sort of sound, but again he's pretty sure it isn't a real word.

Chapter 42: Dawn's Marbled Head

Davin had gotten into a bit of an argument with Bancroft about getting their own legal help, and Bancroft allowed, after a few minutes, there would be no harm, and after showing him out, he takes a few moments to collect himself. He is standing on the front porch steps, thinking about the day ahead, watching Bancroft's taillights roll down the street and take a left onto Park Street, heading back toward the Holiday Inn.

Up in his office, Davin considers putting on some coffee, but he figures the caffeine would ruin him for the next day.

Which is already here, he realizes.

The predawn light will glow soon enough. He has long known he'd never been particularly good at all-nighters, even back in his school days, and he's certainly not a schoolboy anymore.

The first thing he needs is to figure out the legal help. Details and retainers for Jimmy shouldn't wait, and Davin will ask Cynthia about what she thinks she needs, although Bancroft said that counsel would be made available to her courtesy of ClimateProgress.

He'll have to remember to talk to her about the need to make sure the lawyer represents her and not the organization.

Before he left, Bancroft had given Cynthia a brief explanation about the meetings lined up for the coming day, and he'd suggested they try writing up the facts and timelines as best they could recall. Davin's pretty sure Jimmy and Cynthia are up in her room, Jimmy with his laptop and Cynthia with hers.

The two seem destined to share an all-nighter with him,

and Davin can hear Jimmy's rumble and the drifting hints of replies floating down the stairs past the open office door. Jimmy, at Bancroft's request, is supposed to be pulling together the various email copies and writing up that part of the recent events. Cynthia has the harder assignment, it seems to Davin. He can't really imagine what it must have been like for her, seeing her boss get shot, or, he wonders, maybe he simply chooses not to try to imagine it.

He gets back to the task before him, which is lining up options for Jimmy — and maybe Cynthia — for legal representation, and he tries not to dwell on just how much this is going to end up costing.

The lord giveth and the lord taketh away, is what he thinks.

He knows they'll have to tread carefully to protect Jimmy against charges related to his hacking. Maybe, he wonders, ClimateProgress.Org might pick up the tab, but he considers that unlikely.

The main thing will be to keep the lawyer's involvement short, and basically to use him to broker their — *What? Surrender? Submission?* — interaction with the DA, or whoever it will be. It could be a federal matter, he considers, just one more question along with many others he wishes he had thought to ask already.

It takes some time, but he gets his list of questions and concerns down on paper, including, of course, the issue of immunity for Jimmy, not to mention, despite Palamo's assurances, the possibility the household itself may be prosecutable for knowing Cynthia was wanted for questioning. Davin thinks there likely will be no problem since this should be an issue only for the State of California.

We all here in Massachusetts are probably all la-de-da, he assumes.

He sits back in his office chair, stretching, arms up, groaning mightily.

He pulls himself back to his desk.

His head is spinning. He feels Cynthia being here is taking on the tenor of *a goddamn full-time job.* He still needs to finish the notes and probably do quite a bit of phone follow-up early, assuming his lawyer can even make the time. That could well be a problem.

But Mommy, he says to himself, trying to relax, *I don't wanna go to school tomorrow*.

He's dreading problems with Jimmy's email archive hack. He gets up from his desk with another groan and plops himself down in the old, well-worn recliner he keeps in a corner of his office. He's thinking that tomorrow, *no, actually later this morning*, he'll be meeting with *the district attorney*, and he keeps thinking about the bottle of bourbon across the landing in the living room still right where he left it, but his body feels too heavy to move, and he leans back and closes his eyes, *just for a minute*, and then he's almost asleep when he hears loud shouting from upstairs.

"It doesn't matter!" Cynthia shouts. "Fucking my boss is irrelevant! Getting the people who killed him," she says, not shouting, but loudly still, and Davin sits upright and leans forward. He barely hears her add, "Joe shouldn't have been killed, that's what's wrong, that's what's awful, and I could have been killed, and these assholes, we have to find out, we have to get them, that's what's important!"

There's a rumble, some comment by Jimmy, but unintelligible.

Cynthia's reply is clear enough. "I don't fucking care."

There's another rumbled response.

"It's going to come out," she replies, voice still raised, but things are becoming calmer upstairs, and each of their voices become indiscernible again. Davin leans back into the recliner and after a while entirely gives up trying to make out what the two are saying, and then without meaning to he falls asleep.

And then he's scrambling forward, nearly toppling himself from his recliner. His cell phone is screaming on his desk, and there's light in the early morning sky in the windows beyond.

Chapter 43: The Right Side of Furious

I don't fucking care," Cyn says loudly, angrily.

Jimmy is taken aback, she can see that, and she is herself surprised by the sudden veeri n g anger about her phone texts.

"I don't see why your, the affair, has any relevance to the investigation," he says softly.

"It doesn't matter!" Cynthia shouts. "Fucking my boss is irrelevant! Getting the people who killed him," she says, not quite shouting, and then more softly she adds, "Joe shouldn't have been killed, that's what's wrong, that's what's awful, and I could have been killed, and these assholes, we have to find out, we have to get them, that's what's important!"

Jimmy says something, but her ears are hissing with her anger and what he says is almost unintelligible.

Cynthia's reply is clear enough. "I don't fucking care."

"It doesn't necessarily need to come out," is his next comment, at half volume.

"It's going to come out!" she snaps, and then, in a more normal tone, "It's going to come out."

She feels bad about shouting. It probably doesn't help she's fighting the drinks she's had earlier.

She feels bad about shouting and about the anger erupting because she knows Jimmy is just trying to help her out with her timeline, and the hour already late.

As if on cue, Jimmy picks up his phone to check the time, and it occurs to Cyn his action may have more to do with giving him something to do that involves not looking at her, whether in an attempt to hide embarrassment about his question, or his reaction to her dramatically intense responses, or both.

Jimmy glances up from his phone, then eyes back down, and then he tells her they have an appointment at the Berkshire District Attorney's office in less than five hours, and they are supposed to be meeting with ClimateProgress lawyers and some local guy beforehand.

Jimm has already told her has finished his notes about the emails from the law firm's email archive server, and now he's trying to assist her with her notes, which makes Cyn all the angrier at herself for her reaction. She's having a lot of reactions, and one is that she feels like she could be working on these notes for hours upon hours, and as such, she finds it annoying to hear from Jimmy his task has been readily completed. It makes sense, of course, since the hacked emails were already organized by him and printed out during his review in the days before, but she still begrudges his comment that it hadn't taken him much time to generate an index referencing the key exchanges.

She feels hopelessly behind in her effort to get done what at the moment is feeling like a homework assignment from hell. She knows being a bit buzzed from the drinks with Chaplin and then another one with Deidre and another with one of the other servers joining in at the end of their shifts isn't helping her focus, but she suspects the bigger issue is she's been looking over her actual phone texts with Joe, since there aren't all that many false texts, and they're conscribed within a short period of time. She's had to check to see if other texts could have been planted, although there doesn't appear to be any others.

Still, getting to that point of confidence has proved unsettling. There were more texts between her and Joe than she would have guessed and looking over these make her not like the picture that emerges about how she'd treated the whole relationship, and even its very existence.

What the fuck was I thinking? Cyn asks herself for what seems like the hundredth time.

She's worried about tomorrow and whatever other

number of days that likely lie ahead, and she experiences a specific prick of anxiety when she thinks about everyone looking at the false texts between her and Joe.

And by extension, the real texts too, she tells herself again and again.

The idea that the dick pic is in there is humiliating, but unfortunately, she also sees plenty of other text exchanges that are quite embarrassing in the bright light of a murder investigation.

Fuck!

It's good of Jimmy to help, although she'd first thought to decline his offer, but the going has barely started and she keeps bogging down reliving the history of the affair as documented by texts. It all makes for an archly upsetting moment-by-moment replay.

Dick pic dick pic dick pic, a line that keeps repeating.

The things they had texted to each other.

Cyn shakes her head.

When Jimmy offered his help, he told her he hadn't bothered describing in any detail how exactly he'd come to access the archives, and he's anxious about who might end up looking at the hacking. He also hopes, it seems to her, that some sort of immunity will be one of the pre-meeting issues for the lawyer his dad is bringing in to help. There could be help too, he has several times intimated, from one or another ClimateProgress lawyer, based on comments Bancroft had made. Cyn hopes for Jimmy's sake this holds true.

Despite his own worries, she knows Jimmy is being a big help to her, and they have already marked the false phone texts, along with the time marks, and transcribed them in a Word document. To this document she's tried to add how these texts correlate as best she can reconstruct with what actually happened, and they've largely put together the *when* and *what* of her activity and the *when* and *where* she saw which texts and her reactions to these texts.

And then Jimmy had simply asked her if she was worried about her relationship with Joe coming out.

And she snaps at him.

Fuck.

She repeats her answer, but in a quiet voice, and when he looks toward her, she looks at him.

"I don't care," is what she repeats. "I can't care."

But she can see Jimmy is uncomfortable, and she feels for him. She has a good idea he's interested in her and some part of her still likes that comfort of being wanted, but mainly she's angry with herself for even thinking about such things and angry at the multitude of her other mixed feelings about what will become known. But there's one feeling that trumps all others. She's furious about Joe having been murdered — *shot, put down like an animal!* is how she now frames this in her mind — and somewhere there's the man who did it and somewhere out there the people who put this in motion.

For some stupid pipeline?

"I want these assholes, these fucking assholes caught," she tells Jimmy in almost a whisper. "And my thing with Joe, yeah, I'm not happy about everyone knowing, but…" Cyn trails off, eyes still looking right at Jimmy, who nods.

"But that's not important," he says.

She nods.

They sit in silence for a while, Cyn on Chaplin's once and future bed and Jimmy still in the rocking chair he'd dragged into the room from his own bedroom across the hall.

Cyn closes her laptop and tells Jimmy she's done for the night. She tells him the lawyers will get the information, this is no doubt part of their job, especially if an investigation is really what ClimateProgress wants, and that she believes Morales.

She sighs again, and it's like she can do nothing but sigh. She feels like she'll never breathe normally again.

Jimmy puts down the notepad and pen he's been using along with his laptop that's been serving as a desk.

He looks back at her after he stands and straightens up. "Yeah," he says, low-voiced. "Still, the whole thing, this has to be hard." Cyn doesn't respond for a moment but instead takes in another long breath, keeping her eyes on Jimmy. She nearly smiles when she sees his effort to return her gaze, battling his discomfort.

"Yes," Cyn says. "And that makes me mad because it's a distraction. I'm not excusing what we did, what I did, but there are people…" And she trails off.

A moment later she scoffs. "But hey, at least that call got me moving faster to the right side of furious."

And then she tells him about her first effort to reach out for help, when she was in Chicago, and the telephone call with her colleague, a woman her age she works with, who Cyn had thought to be a friend, a woman named Ell. Cyn finds herself telling Jimmy about the other woman's reaction and the pain and confusion it had caused, and then without transition Cyn talks about her tendency to be with older men and that she's been thinking a lot more about it.

She goes silent.

Jimmy nods.

"I do actually," she adds in another near whisper. "I know it's fucked up and I want to fix it, but this, tomorrow, catching the assholes who think they can kill someone, *that*'s the important thing."

And then she adds, in what may be a whisper, and to herself, "Right now."

Jimmy nods and turns toward the door, stepping through it, but then turns back to look at Cyn.

"Thanks for talking about this with me," he tells her, and then he steps toward his bedroom door but stops and turns again and says something about them both trying for a nap considering the day coming up, and he turns toward his bedroom again, but yet again stops and turns back.

"And they were out to get you too," Jimmy reminds her.

She nods. "Huh, yeah."

She's quiet for a moment and then says, "That sure doesn't make me like them more," but there's the hint of a smile too, although tears in her eyes linger. "Well, thanks for the reminder," she adds. "There goes my good night's sleep."

Jimmy smiles, walks into his bedroom, and shuts his door.

Chapter 44: Rat Face in Nature

Back on the mill's roof, Dennis Jymsom observed a lot of comings and goings at the house earlier in the day, including the presence of another older guy showing up midmorning and coming back out not long after.

This man is not as old as the guy he figures for the big ape's father, and something in the way the guy carries himself made Dennis wonder if he might be a cop. Watching the guy climb the steps to the front porch, it had struck him the guy seemed known to the older guy who let him in.

Had he missed an earlier visit, somehow? It isn't like he could watch the place 24/7.

He puzzled over this for a while. He doesn't like complications, and this might be another complication but probably not since the guy had come back out not long afterward, walking down the driveway to climb into what Dennis is pretty sure was a rental car parked on the street where the slope leading down from the house stops right at the edge of the pavement, and he hadn't seen him the rest of the day.

Of course, Dennis hadn't seen much of the target either, or the big kid, or the guy he thinks more and more must be the big kid's father, must be Davin Caine, the guy who lives there, from the phone book and recently confirmed by Dennis as the owner through a quick visit online to the property tax lists.

The three of them had left not long after the guy who might be a cop had come and gone, about midmorning, and have only returned late afternoon, and there wasn't much that happened beyond the return of the small pickup later, before the growing dark had him surrender the day.

A fucking waste of time is what Dennis thinks when he's finally back at his new motel as he sets out what he'll bring with him the next morning.

The Day, he thinks of tomorrow, when he hopes to make his move.

Fucking well better be.

He is sick of this job, its special instructions. The whole thing is fussy.

Fuck it.

He has considered earlier simply going into the house and waiting for their return, but with the other two people staying there, the young kid with the old pickup and some young dark- haired cunt, things would be too likely to get too messy, be too unpredictable. And he had to account for the fact that the guy he thought might be a cop might come back with them.

The light was already fading by the time he'd stopped at the Taft Farms store for a sandwich for supper and donuts for the morning, and two coffees, white and sweet since he knew he would want to be on a buzz later, needing to rise early.

Back at his motel, Dennis makes quick work of the sandwich, which he thinks is good.

It better be at that fucking price.

The two coffees he would reheat in the room's microwave when he is up and on the move, but he knows he needs to nap before heading back out early. He's able to fall asleep anywhere, anytime opportunity presents itself, and this is one of his skills as he thinks of it.

It is still dark when he rouses.

Right on time, he tells himself. *Rise and shine, motherfuckers.*

It had been a good nap, and the reheated coffee is good, especially for washing down a couple of donuts, and then he's heading out, reaching into a small knapsack hanging off his shoulder to reassure himself the rest of the donuts in their greasy brown bag are there, although he knows they are.

They ain't going to evaporate.

He has already put his larger carryall into the current car, a silver Chrysler LHS, an old model that's probably not the best choice, but he likes his cars big, and he likes the model, but the ride on this one is showing its age, shocks bouncy, and the tires maybe have too little left in the treads.

Enough to get me to Hudson, he tells himself, hoping to get the job done today, and then he will be driving directly to Hudson where he'll catch an Amtrak, *adios*.

If today doesn't work, he knows he should get a different car as he's pushing it with this one, already a day over when he likes to switch, but he'd just as soon not have to hot-foot it over to Bradley again.

It's the last fucking time I take a job in Massatwoshits, he tells himself. The state's strict gun laws make it too hard to get any gun, including a long gun, and he'd be done if he could set a shot from a distance, but that makes him think of *Lee Harvey Oswald* who some bitch had once told him he looked like.

Fuck her. He'd been furious when he'd looked the name up and would have hurt that bitch if he'd been able to find her on the street again.

Jesus, give it up, he tells himself. *That was, what, twenty years ago?*

He knows he needs to focus on the job at hand. A long gun would be *easy-peasy*, but that isn't what the client wants since it's impossible to suggest suicide with a shot from 200 meters away, *so, fuck that*.

It had again rained heavily sometime in the night and the road is still wet, now steaming a bit off the asphalt, but the pre-dawn sun is brightening the morning sky, still early, but now more than just a hint of the glow. Dennis figures out where best to park, deciding against parking up near the small library. Even though he sees no one up and out, he is worried he would be exposed in his long stroll across the bridge, past the mills, and up Grove Street, the first left that curved around and dead- ended in the woods behind the target house property with a couple hundred yards of trees between.

He drives up Grove Street and parks, and then he slips into the woods without notice.

The light is still brightening but full daylight hasn't yet hit by the time he's trudging toward the edge of the woods at the back of the target's house. The lack of direct rising sun might be because of the mountain behind him. *Mountain, big hill, whatever*, he tells himself, but nonetheless aware of the shadow it casts.

The trees are thick where they abut the back border of the property, a border that is marked by a crude stone wall beyond which there's a mix of lawn and a sizable fenced garden. A few small trees are scattered about, and the small pickup and the old guy's white car are parked toward the back of the house that is beyond and lower than the parking area, about 200 feet farther, if he had to guess.

By the time he gets into position behind the stone wall he's soaked, first from all the underbrush he's swept rain drops from as he walked through the woods, and even now as he settles down, he's surprised to find the leaf litter is sopping under a drying top layer.

Oh fuck this, he says resignedly, but this is balanced by his excitement about getting to the job.

He looks at the vegetable garden, the closest part of the fence about forty feet from and parallel to the property edge and a bit to his left.

He's got good sightlines on the house's back door, or the top half of the double door arrangement, anyway, and while he knows there is a specific name for that kind of door, he can't think of the word. His view of the parking area is perfect, and he's confident in his inventory of the vehicles and the people in the house. Time to settle in and get to the business at hand, said business at the moment, he knows, is to watch and wait. He'll find the chance, he's sure.

Patience, said the fucking spider, he tells himself. He repeats this every now and again as the minutes pass.

His gun is laid out near him, and the donut bag too, and the coffee thermos, which has managed not to leak much in his knapsack. He now places it on a flattish rock he figures had at some point tumbled from the wall. He uses one of the few napkins he'd grabbed at Taft's to wipe some smeared drops of coffee from the barrel of the binoculars he has also pulled from the knapsack, cleaning up before placing the binoculars on the rock next to the coffee thermos.

The modest bath towel from the motel laid down beneath him isn't doing much to keep him dry, and he shifts the now empty knapsack under his torso.

At least my nuts can stay dry.

There's a tick crawling on his hand.

Fuck! he screams mentally, and he has to exert great effort not to jump up, not to scream out his rage at this offense visited upon him.

Dennis pinches up the tick and then he awkwardly positions it between his two thumbnails, intent on crushing it, annihilating it, and his rage drives his two thumbnails together, twisting. When he inspects the tick, it's torn and spread out, fragments, a smear with legs.

Fuck you, he tells the fragments, but now he's feeling itchy all over — the idea of ticks crawling all over him something he can't suppress.

Jesus fucking Christ, he says and tries to ignore the feeling of ticks all over him.

Should have brought bug shit, he thinks and turns to pull up a pant cuff, but sees nothing.

The humidity of the day is already rising, the sun now bright in tiny glimpses through the leaves overhead, the barest of breezes swaying them into peeks of lighter and darker leaf shadows, and then he catches movement in the corner of his eye. He sees the young guy, the kid who has the small beat pickup. The kid is opening the garden fence gate on the opposite end facing the house.

Dennis, peering over the top of the stone wall along the property's edge, keeps watch on the young man. He sees him bending over the various low plants, and he concludes the young man must be weeding, although he has never weeded, would never do that.

The kid is a fucking chump, he thinks.

The mosquitos have found Dennis, but he keeps his movements still, and then he slowly sinks down behind the wall to take a swipe, knowing he'll be feeding *these assholes* all day, maybe, nothing to be done.

Patience, said the fucking spider, he tells himself, trying to relax his jaw. He knows he's got to keep cool, not let himself get angry.

Dennis resumes his observation, eyes just above the stones at the top of the wall.

The young man straightens up and seems to be staring right at Dennis, but Dennis knows the kid can't be seeing anything, not in the deep shadow of the trees, the stone wall his blind.

Spooky though, he tells himself, fighting the urge to jump up, to yell out.

The kid stretches, bends over, and stretches up again, slow, and does this a couple more times before stopping that motion, only to now swing his arms, and then his right elbow is captured in his left hand, his arm bent into a shoulder pull Dennis recognizes from the PT he once had after *that asshole Curruthers* jumped him and gave him a pretty good going-over before he'd managed to get a brick to the side of *that asshole's head.* This memory from his young Cleveland days brings a smile to his thin lips.

After a short time passes, Dennis sees the kid climb into the *shitbox* pickup, back up, and then disappear down the steep driveway.

One down, he thinks.

Dennis takes the opportunity to pull his pant cuffs up again, one and then the other, looking closely for more ticks. He finds one on his white cotton athletic sock.

"Fuck you," he says to this tick before crushing it the same way as the one before.

He turns back to the house, which remains quiet for a while until the curly black-haired girl makes an appearance at the back door.

French doors, Dennis is pretty sure that kind of door is

called. She walks up the slope and then seems to be just standing there, face up to the sun, and then Dennis can see, using the binoculars, she has a mug in her hand.

He sees her take a sip.

Dennis has a few lewd thoughts as he glasses her, and he's disappointed when she turns and heads back in. His eyes follow her ass toward the door until his view is blocked by the slight rise between them, and the door closing ends any show.

He looks at his watch and figures she's off to work. He's seen her walk down to the bus around this time before.

Two down, he thinks.

His plan is simple. Observe, wait for the older guy to leave, and then walk in and shoot the girl.

And the big guy, he tells himself, feeling his anger rise. *How do you like that, asshole*, he says, picturing the look on the big kid's face, and that makes Dennis excited and impatient.

He had been upset enough on the train when he'd found the girl, the way she'd reacted, her superior attitude, but to have *that fucking asshole* looming over him, so he wasn't thinking — flashing the gun was a simple response, *not thinking, fucking up.*

He knows he has this tendency, with his anger.

I'll throw the big kid in for free, he thinks, calming himself.

A day later, after the train problem, Carl had had a town destination for him, and there were instructions too, a reminder anyway, *make it look like suicide*, but using the code words. He had been surprised to hear from Carl at all since he was supposed to go through the client.

So much for protocol, Dennis thinks, letting his thoughts wander. But his thoughts keep coming back to imagining various acts of violence he might visit upon the big young man. And then he's thinking of the *gobble-de-gook* from the client, and then the even more confusing message Dennis had replied to. A bit unwisely, maybe.

Yeah, well fuck you, he muses in anticipation.

He thinks about how many *fucking tick bites* he's probably gotten, but he's quieting himself down, knowing that letting his feelings run free makes it more likely to *fuck up the job*.

Like on the train with the girl. He had gotten shit for that from Carl.

He knows he can get carried away, thinking like this. He had thought for a moment that Carl was going to cancel the job on him.

Patience, said the fucking spider, he tells himself.

He is hot, wet, and uncomfortable, and he wants to get this thing done, head back to the new motel instead of driving right to Hudson. He wants to take a long hot shower, get rid of the ticks, and whatever else this *Godforsaken piece of shit Podunk country* has landed on him, *crawling up my ass*.

He slaps his forehead, seeing the blood pulp of a mosquito that'd been feeding on him, *fuck you!*

And then he's trying to settle himself, going over the plan again, again feeling the comfort of the exercise, seeing himself steal into the house, shooting anyone there, *old guy too*, he thinks, if it comes to that because he isn't going to wait much longer, his hate rising toward anyone and everyone in that *fucking house* as if they had all personally arranged for his ass to be lying in *sopping piles of leaf shit* soaking through his jeans, seeping under his windbreaker, making his belly wet, *swatting at flies and fleas and ticks and whatever else this fucking place is trying to shove up my ass!*

He walks through the steps, which helps calm him. Inside, a quick survey of the second floor, clear anyone, down to the first, clearing anyone, and then back up to the third floor where he figures the bedrooms likely are. *Boom, bing, bam*, he imagines.

So fuck you!

Make it look like the target goes crazy, kills the old guy, the *big asshole*, the *cunt* then killing herself.

The client wants it to look like the target killed herself, so he'll have to remove the silencer after he shoots her nice and up close, rub the end of the barrel on her shooting hand for the nitrates trace, leave the gun.

Shit, I like this gun, he tells himself.

He starts to pick himself up, gathering the items he's brought, stuffing all but the gun and its accessories into his knapsack. *Shit, I must have smushed the donuts*, he tells himself, angry with himself as he thinks this, but it's too late now, *whatever*, he can always get some donuts, and then he checks his gun again, the clip, the extra clip in his pocket, old habits, and he stands up, screws on the silencer. He's half onto the stone wall when he freezes.

A window is going up, the second one from the left, top floor, and he wonders if he's been seen. He ducks back down, panic flushing through him, hot mixed with cold, his entire body like a blazing point of heat on the cool wet leaf litter, but then he figures he's not been seen, so he peeks up.

And immediately ducks back.

There's a rifle sticking through the window.

Fuck!

Chapter 45: Crackpot Shot

Davin is still wound up from the night-into-day hours, and it feels like there will be no letting up.

For a moment he stands there, in the kitchen, not knowing why he's there.

Ah, yes, coffee.

The time at the district attorney office yesterday while one or another of the kids were in one room or another, talking to one group of people or another, had been nerve-wracking, and he repeatedly checked on what was going on, getting next to nothing from Palamo other than introductions that were as numerous across the hours as they were too easily confusing to keep straight, despite his efforts to take notes.

He'd been unable to get any work done, even, really, when he'd driven back home toward noon, before giving up and driving back, hanging around more, waiting to fetch the kids.

But despite the exhaustion and tension of yesterday, he's awake, and he knows there's no point trying to sleep in, that talent long past.

Unlike those two up here, he thinks. Jimmy and Cynthia are sound asleep after their second late night, wound up from the day with the DA.

He envies their ability to sleep this morning, but a day of depositions can do that to anyone, he supposes.

Not me, he can't help thinking. His feeling that the world has been turned upside down is still nagging him, and that certainly makes for bad sleeping, although he suspects this is mostly the consequence of all his worrying from yesterday with the lawyer and his own late-night work two days ago with the Bancroft visit.

After retrieving Cynthia and Jimmy, he had tried to get to his *SCI* work, which is still behind deadline, so he'd worked yet again late into the night and finally gotten the story about the solar farm battle in, but Alicia is pushing him for a second part on developments expected at the state's advisory board meeting taking place later today.

He makes his coffee in the kitchen but brings the mug up to his office and sips at it while trying to read the news online, but it is the same old shit about one or another of Trump's cabinet going off the rails and more stupid hateful shit-talking by Trump himself. He tries to ignore these sorts of articles and now never reads related opinion pieces, but today's paper seems to cover nothing but.

He wants more coffee, but he doesn't want to overdo it, knowing it'll just jazz him further and kill any chance for his getting, finally, a good night's sleep if or when circumstances might allow.

He would love to take a toke or two of the pot he has on hand, from the black market, not the local legal, mainly because he bought it from an old housepainter he knows, years back, just before the legal sales law went active, now that he thinks of it. The guy had known the guy who grew it, and it was far cheaper than the store-bought sort looked to be, and just as good, or better. The dope has kept well, tightly sealed in a small mason jar. He tokes infrequently and still has half of it left. He figures the potency has got to be going, but that's okay.

Too busy to get high, anyway, he tells himself.

He always has too much to do. Today they're meeting with the county district attorney again in the afternoon. Another reason getting stoned doesn't seem like the best play.

More chauffeur duty but no meetings for him. *Fine by me*, he tells himself, relieved not to have much of anything to contribute. He's still wooly-headed and plenty talked out from the day before.

So, he settles into his desk chair, sifts through some notes for yet other *SCI* work running the ad/lead/sale numbers for the past month.

He puts the printouts down and slowly revolves in his office chair. He just can't do that work now.

His eyes light upon the cardboard box for the Gamo Whisper G2 air rifle that's been sitting there untouched since delivery. He picks it up, dropping the box onto Gwen's desk — *former desk* — and retrieves an X-Acto knife from a glass jar otherwise filled with pens and pencils and a Sharpie or two. He unpacks the box carefully, in stages, until the air rifle is laid out, the user manual next to it, and a plastic oiler and the pellets in a sampler set next to that.

Davin picks up the manual and reads, picking up the rifle now and again, cross-referencing diagrams with the actual object.

He reads through the safety instructions, half of which strike him as overkill.

You're going to put out your eye with that, he thinks, recalling that movie, the one with the stockinged leg lamp, *A Christmas Story*, but he gets back to the work at hand, oiling the seals and pumping the air rifle to full power.

Chaplin is already out, his truck gone from the upper parking area, but Davin hears someone coming up from the kitchen. He guesses it is Deidre since she's probably off to the shop, and she keeps to a good schedule.

Well, has to, to catch the bus.

He hadn't heard her earlier, but then she might well have used her bedroom's outside entrance to walk around the side of the house, down to the kitchen.

One of the living room French doors opens and shuts, the sound clear through the length of the living room on the other side of the landing. Even though he'd closed his office door before picking up the Gamo box, he knows well the sound of the French doors being opened and closed, faint as it is in his office.

Davin continues his study of the manual and then loads some pellets.

His hands are sweating, which he knows is normal enough for him when doing close work, especially if the work is nervous-making, and setting up the pellet gun is apparently making him nervous.

Jesus lord, he says to himself, putting the air rifle down and taking up his coffee mug, draining the last and now entirely cold swallow.

He pulls his handkerchief from his pocket and wipes the gun down where he can see sweat traces.

Sweet Jesus lord, he tells himself. *Such a sensitive flower.*

But he is excited, he'll admit that. He also realizes he feels like he's doing something wrong and won't confess, but then again, *Gwen ain't here, is she?*

From behind his closed office door, Davin can hear Deidre is back in, and a few moments later he hears her going down the stairs again and out to catch the bus.

He opens his office door, climbs the third-floor stairs, and heads into his bathroom. He places the rifle flat on the floor before climbing into the clawfoot tub and pulling the shower curtain back so he can raise the window behind it.

When he'd imagined sniping the chipmunks, he had imagined using the window in the room that's now Chaplin's room, but that's where Cynthia is now, asleep, and he doesn't think his argument that one or another of those east-facing windows in her room offers the better vantage is quite good enough for the intrusion.

And here's a gun, it occurs to him, what her reaction might be, considering what she has gone through.

But the third-floor bathroom is all his, so it will do, and the door is closed, and it's an air gun. *How much noise does it make, right?* he tells himself.

He's got an hour or two to kill before he needs to see Jimmy and Cynthia are up and ready to go, and he's no good for getting any real work done before they head off to Pittsfield to talk again, and this is exactly the sort of distraction he can use.

He sets himself up kneeling in the tub and this seems

pretty good, except the range of fire is a bit more constricted than it would be from Cynthia's room, but he really just wants to get a feel for the gun, check its simple scope, see how accurate it is. He rolls up a bath towel to put under his knees, and with the rifle using the windowsill as a rest he's scanning the rocks of the retaining walls by the edge of the studio. He sights a chipmunk almost immediately, although it takes him some practice to keep the scope on the tiny scurrying *strawberry-eater motherfucker*, and he squeezes the trigger. The resulting pop is surprisingly loud, but he actually seems to have killed the chipmunk since it hops in the air as it's hit and then falls back, still.

He's having mixed feelings, with some distant chant along the lines of *chipmunk murderer* hinting in the back of his mind, but he remains excited, too. Using the break barrel pump, he draws up on another shot, and there is a hop and fall again. It occurs to him that *beginner's luck* could be at play, which has him miss the next one, and a fourth one is a miss too, but the pellet hits so close that chipmunk is down and still after a short scurry.

I think I gave it a heart attack.

He raises the gun barrel and pushes the safety on. In the distance he sees something, he thinks, out in the woods. Maybe it's a deer, or a dog. He has the scope up, but that far away it's hard to get a visual bearing, and it isn't a great scope. He figures it's nothing, and then Jimmy is banging on the door, asking if he can take a shower since according to him, Cynthia is using the second-floor bathroom.

"What the heck are you doing in there anyway?" Jimmy asks through the door.

He doesn't answer immediately but sets the window down, the curtains back, and hangs the towel back on its bar.

Air rifle resting casually over his shoulder, Davin opens the door.

"Oh, I don't know," he says to Jimmy.

Jimmy is surprised to see the air rifle.

"Just shooting the shit," he says, stepping past Jimmy,

thinking some preemptive groaning might be in order.

Chapter 46: Rat Face Head-Over Heels

uck! Dennis shouts inside his head, scrambling for an explanation for *why is there a fucking rifle?!* and how they know, a n d how he has fucked up, and he is trying to think through whether he can crawl out, back to the car, and if they have a shot.

What the fuck? he asks himself again.

It's a long way for a shot, he realizes, but the image of the opening window, the rifle moving past the frame is crystal clear, even if he isn't looking now.

Instead, he's frozen flat on his back, on the soaking towel.

He hears something, and then again, but what he hears doesn't sound like a shot, shots, and there are no rounds landing anywhere near. He ventures another peek.

The old guy is leaning partway out the window with what looks like shower curtains surrounding him.

The old guy fires, but Dennis doesn't duck.

The guy is not shooting at him.

It's not a real gun.

Wow, he thinks. *A fucking plinker.*

The old guy is shooting at squirrels, he is pretty sure. *Maybe the neighbor's cat.*

Dennis feels a laugh rising, a strong bubble of a shout, a hoot, but he keeps it down, keeps it in, even as he shakes his head, and then, *fuck*, because he knows now he can't walk in, the simple plan is fucked, *not with Davy Fucking Crocket a'hunting we will go.*

Dennis is unhappy. He really wants this job over, and here is another fuckup.

Fuck!

It's now far less about getting it done and far more about *how fucked this is!*

Dennis wants to be out of the woods, away from these fucking bugs! *Jesus!* Away from this *fucking Bumsville asshole goddamn bumfuck of a town!*

He tries to calm himself.

He'll have to shower when he gets back, get his clothes washed, dried, and he's already thinking if it will be too big of a hassle to do this all by hand, picturing the small sink in the bathroom while he's swishing through the underbrush heading back to the car parked on Grove Street.

The leaves still hold a surprising amount of water although Dennis thinks he can't get any wetter. But what he is mainly thinking about is what he's going to do to the big guy, that kid, although he knows that *asshole big asshole* isn't actually the target, the job is the target, but he figures he can work these two targets, *two for the fucking price of one*, and he's thinking he'll knock *the fucker out, the bigger they are*, and take his time, figure out how to put it on the target. He's thinking a lot stabbing will be part of it—fingerprints easy enough to set for that, after the fact.

I'll have to ask the girl if she is right-handed or not, he realizes, but as he mulls this over, he sees something through the shrubs and understory growth, something on the street and he stops short about one hundred feet from Grove Street and the latest of his stolen cars.

Fucking fucking fuck! He mentally screams because the police are there, a police car, and he sneaks a bit closer to get a better look, wondering how they could be on to him. Although then he thinks maybe they're not, and when he observes the cop, he sees he's interested in the car, the radio squawk not clear, but he can see the cop standing next to the cruiser, mic in hand. It looks like the cop is reading off the car's license plate.

Oh fuck, Dennis tells himself, but he's already calming down. Police do stolen cars all the time, almost routine, there's nothing in the car that will be a problem, they won't run prints for larceny grand auto.

My shit's in there, he then thinks, a coldness growing in his gut, but then he runs through what's in his travel bag stuffed behind the driver's seat. He does a mental inventory and it's okay, he assures himself, sure it doesn't matter. Just clothes, toiletries, some rank socks.

But fuck me, Dennis tells himself as he tries to figure out his next steps that obviously will involve some walking.

He pictures the Google Satellite image of the area and the map he'd studied closely on his phone, small but it doesn't matter, and he plots a path that will cut back through these woods, into the backyard of the target house's neighbor, the second-to-last of the four houses on the dead-end street. He figures the exposure will be minimal with the only danger in crossing Grove Street down lower on his way to the mills through the woods.

He starts off, angling obliquely through the trees and undergrowth, moving away from the end of Grove and the cop car there, but staying shy of the big house, that place he's still sure he'll get to, do the target, but now it's time to regroup.

He stops behind a wobbly stockade fence at the back of the yard he'll cut through on his way back to the mills, to his aerie up on that roof for more observation and to figure out next steps.

The neighbor's house appears empty, and Dennis looks for a way around the fence but decides to simply push the rotting post over to create enough of an opening he can step through. He then walks swiftly around to the right of the house and sees there's a car in the driveway, so he continues on, wasting no time crossing the road and traversing a brief slope down to the edge of Grove and pausing for a moment before he scurries across. He throws his leg over the galvanized guardrail.

Fuck.

The long, steep drop toward the mills and the river is going to require care. He steps into the woods of small brush under canopy trees. There are some scattered daylily shoots near the guardrail.

He's in a half crouch and looks down at his feet.

Poison ivy! Shit!

The day can't get any worse, he thinks, but he hears a car coming down Grove, so he steps lower down the slope, intending to crouch there and plan his route down, but his foot catches on a clump of daylilies and he pitches forward, the sloping drop speeding him forward. He tries to halt his fall by grabbing at a sapling and manages to swing himself around with his half catch, but the balance is off and he's stumbling backward, thrashing madly in his efforts to catch himself. He's low enough to not see the passing car, happy enough with that break even as he's wildly wondering how his back has gotten turned toward the drop. With what should be his arresting step, his heel catches on something else, and he continues falling, the slope sliding him down. His head whacks against a sapling — shooting stars.

He has come to a stop, spread-eagle, now thirty feet below the road edge and the steel guardrail.

Fuck, fuck, fuck! he tells himself, trying to listen to how much noise he's made, whether anyone might have heard him, although he's pretty sure he hasn't yelled, but the saplings he banged into on the way down still move, still sway, from his grabbing at them.

Fuck!

He feels off-balance and the steepness of the slope keeps him from feeling he's on solid ground. He twists around, places his feet against a large trunk of a nearby tree to steady his position, trying to get a grip.

He feels the bump and sting where his head cracked against the sapling. He sees he has a scrape above the wrist. His knapsack is twisted around his torso.

One of his ankles feels pretty bad.

Fuck!

Take a fucking minute, he tells himself.

He looks around. He seems out of sight of anyone, everyone, the underbrush thick around him, although he can glimpse the mills and the river below.

He feels dizzy, but is pretty sure it's not a bad concussion, if at all. He knows what those are like.

Fuck, he tells himself, and he slowly starts moving back down the slope, staying low, more or less dragging his ass over the ground, sliding on the damp leaf litter, trying to keep an eye on fallen branches and other potential snags. He's crabbing down, making progress, but stopping now and again, checking his progress, until he tentatively stands and starts down again, using tree trucks and saplings as hand holds, trying to keep some of the weight off his ankle until he hits an access path leading down, big enough for vehicles, made for vehicles, but long disused, and this makes for faster progress, until he's waded across the shallow swift water and stands at the edge of the large clearing behind the mills.

And then he's standing on the backside of the mill building, looking over the iron rod that goes from ground to roof edge with spaced cleats or clamps, *whatever the fuck this was for*, but he has been using this to climb up, and it works well enough for that purpose.

He'll get to his pallet, the one up on the roof, and the tarp, and then figure what comes next.

He sticks the wet toe of his shoe between the rod and the first clamp against the brick, almost having to wedge it there, and then he's moving up, a ladder just for him, although his toes are getting kind of sore with the tight wedging fit, and he's worried about the ankle, but then he's on the roof, and sure enough, he's back to the good view toward the house except for some few tree branches in the way. He sits, crosses his legs, *Mr. Buddha*, slowing his breath and listening.

All is quiet.

He pulls the donut bag back out from his knapsack and takes a big bite out of the largest piece of the crumbled-apart donut, putting the remaining piece down on top of the flattened bag. After he finishes up the coffee in his thermos, he takes up his binoculars and starts scanning the house.

Fucking all right, he says silently, the donut bite still being worked on, somewhat gluey in texture. He stops chewing to steady the image of Cynthia and Jimmy and the old guy coming out on the front porch. He loses sight of them as they step down the big front stairs to the driveway, but then he catches the flash of the old guy's car exiting the driveway and going off until the mill buildings block the view of the road. He thinks of getting up and moving to the other side of the roof but stays put, figuring it doesn't matter if he knows which way they turn, left toward Great Barrington, or right, which heads north.

Fuck.

He's soaked, bitten, has a bad ankle, is banged and scratched up, and is a *fucking failure, a fucking loser, a fucking asshole. Goddamnit!*

He's feeling consumed by rage, but he tries to quiet himself. He's got to figure this shit out.

Fuck.

But he's not going to do it now.

It's hot up on the roof but he's glad for it. He figures he'll lie down, dry off, take a nap, get back to the motel, although that means he'll have to steal another car, local, but *what the hell*, or maybe he'll just hoof it, bum ankle and all, down the tracks, since the same tracks, some miles down go behind the motel, *good cover.*

It's late when he wakes, twilight coming on.

Fuck, he tells himself, surprised by the time. But he's dry enough. His need to take a piss, this is what has awakened him. He wonders if his head blow is worse than he'd thought—a headache still there, a light pounding.

He looks over at the house, the many lights on, a charming enough glow.

You fucking idiot, you asshole, he thinks, pissed off about his sleeping so long.

At least the dark will make it easier to get down to the tracks, back to the motel. He picks up the binoculars and lenses around the house and the short dead-end street. The streetlight has just come on. It all looks quiet with the occasional shadow past a window.

He puts his glasses down.

Why not just walk up, shoot them all, walk down, grab keys, get in the old man's car, drive away? He's trying to think of a plan, which way to go, or whether he needs to check in, or should he just finish *this fucking job?*

He decides that acting now would be unwise.

He'll collect himself, get a new car, get cleaned up, something to eat, which makes him look around for his knapsack. Finding the donut bag, he reaches in but there's nothing left but some fragments of pieces of donut. He shakes the bag empty into his mouth, although his mouth is dry and he's got nothing left to drink.

He is chewing but stops because he's heard something, and he chokes down his mouthful as quickly as he can, but otherwise remains stock still, and sure enough he hears what he'd thought he'd heard before, the unmistakable sound of someone talking and then a laugh.

Dennis crabs over to the roof edge and takes a quick peek.

It's a couple of kids, teenagers, and the smell of cigarette drifts up along with another laugh.

He sits back, trying to figure out what he should do. He can try to wait them out, or just climb down and be on his way.

He looks over the edge again. This time he catches the scent of marijuana and can see in the fading light part of a six-pack at their feet.

Partying.

That's good enough for him.

He stands up and packs the knapsack. He leaves the tarp and still damp towel where they are, and then he's going back to the iron rod he uses to climb.

"Hey!" he calls down, and the two boys start, which makes Dennis laugh.

What the fuck, man?" the one with his cap on backward says, but he's got something like a smile on his face, his neck craned tight to look at Dennis at the edge of the roof. The two boys watch him swing down, slowly getting his left foot wedged between the rod and the second-to-top clamp.

Over his own grunting, he thinks he hears the boy say *What the fuck?* again.

Dennis is doing something like slow-walk rappelling, and then he drops the last couple of feet, landing a bit hard, at least for his ankle, and he grimaces, but he's turned away from the boys.

Fuck! he says to himself, wishing he'd remembered about the ankle.

He turns around, not more than six feet from the two kids.

He can really use a beer.

"Give me one of those beers," he says to the backward-capped kid.

The kid looks at him like he must be speaking a foreign language, but the other kid bends down and gently tosses a can.

Dennis pops the tab and there's a lot of foam, but he's drinking that as fast as he can, his thirst driving him.

"What the—" But the backward-capped kid decides speaking tough isn't called for under the circumstances. "I mean, what were you doing up there?" he asks.

Dennis still has his head tilting back, draining the can.

He tosses the empty toward the other kid, the one who'd given it to him, and lets out a long belch.

The two kids find that funny.

"All right," the other kid says, nodding his head.

"Give me another beer and I'll tell you what I was doing up there," Dennis says, and the back-cap kid seems affronted by his request, but the other kid bends down and gets another can. Dennis closes the distance and takes the beer from him so it won't get shaken so much.

Dennis adjusts his knapsack and pulls the tab and takes a short sip.

"I was taking a nap," he says, walking past them, and he keeps going, disappearing around the building, heading for the tracks.

Chapter 47: The Troubled Sleep of Relief

Cynthia wishes she'd gone to bed early because the coming day promises to be yet another big day, finishing with the depositions they'd talked about at the first meeting with the district attorney, but the day is supposed to start e v e n earlier with Bancroft, according to Jimmy.

Not that she can for the life of her remember the names of the others who are supposed to be there too.

Did I even get the names? she asks herself. *Is that lawyer for me or for Davin?*

It's dark outside. It's late—*early already, really* — she thinks, squinting at the clock radio next to the bed. It reads a little after 12:00 a.m. All she can think of is why she hadn't gone to bed early, and that now she'll just have to push through the coming day. She knows a part of her is feeling something like relief about moving into some sort of resolution, but mainly she's still feeling anxious.

And when am I going to get my phone back?

She'd been told there would be some people sent by the state attorney general, and the ClimateProgress.Org national office is sending another person or two too, she's pretty sure, from something Bancroft mentioned yesterday.

Well, the day before yesterday actually.

Yesterday had been anticlimactic, a lot of waiting around for the county DA, and then handing over her phone for cloning, then someone from the state police had come by with a picture of the guy she still thinks of as Rat Face, which Bancroft had showed her the first night before being sent along her way, somewhat intoxicated, to write up the timeline of events.

Of Joe getting killed.

This is the essential part of the timeline, and she still can't think of it without feeling something like the out-of-body sensation that had overwhelmed her for many hours, and even periodically, later, although she's figured out this is, or something like anyway, the dissociative state that had followed her father's death.

She scoffs. *Like a hangover, worse.*

She'd been a bit hungover yesterday and that hadn't been fun, although nothing about yesterday had been much fun.

She looks at the clock again and sighs.

Seeing the photo of Rat Face again yesterday was triggering. She knows his real name now. *Or what they think is his real name*, she tells herself, since there seems to be some question of aliases.

A.k.a. Fuck You Rat Face, she repeats in her thoughts.

Bancroft had told her not to worry about—*Jypson? Jymsom?*—saying there wouldn't be any point for him to keep after her now that the whole matter of Joe's death, the facts, are becoming public record.

She had appreciated that Bancroft used Joe Craigson's name.

Poor Joe, she thinks.

She feels bad about what his wife must be going through, and the kids and the new child of theirs on the way, and it doesn't help that she feels like a complete shit for sleeping with Joe. She's hoping this won't come out, n o t t o h i s w i f e, o r f r i e n d s, but she's unconvinced, and that despite the district attorney's explanation that it doesn't necessarily have relevance with the pertinent text exchanges already shown to be false plants.

Just me and my guilt.

She's been thinking a lot about her choices, the ones she's made in her life, the choices about the relationships she has found herself repeatedly drawn to, and those thoughts aren't helping her feel better.

Time for more therapy, she finds herself wondering, even though another part of her thinks she's had more than enough to date. Whether all the therapy has actually helped is a another question she keeps asking herself.

Apparently not, that's her repeated reply, but she sometimes adds, *Fourth time's the charm.*

She does her deep-breathing exercise, and after a while she thinks it helps. She keeps her eyes closed, slowing her breathing, and then she's slipping off but starts with a gasp when the image bursts forth, the back window of Joe's car, and her heart is pounding and she bolts upright, sitting up in the bed, a body sweat starting, and she flings the blanket off across her.

No no no, she says to herself.

Her body feels full of ashes.

She does her controlled breathing again, and it helps, but she still feels shaky and desperate, afraid to try to sleep again. She hears through the wall Jimmy is still up, which surprises her. He'd been by her side much of the day, often just being there, enduring the waiting too with a quiet comforting presence, but then she realizes she's not entirely surprised he's awake. He keeps odds hours.

She hears his laugh and listens more closely. She thinks he's watching a video, the patterns of television dialogue subliminal through the common wall but enough for her to know he's up, awake.

She can't help herself. She just can't be alone, and maybe he'll talk or just let her hang out. She swings her bare legs to stand, tugs the t-shirt down, and then she's across the narrow hall, knocking lightly on his door.

She hears him move off his bed, and then the door opens halfway so he can see who's there. His hand flicks a wall switch, and the bright ceiling fixture makes them both squint. He says, "Oh, hi," and steps back to fully open the door. And there she is in his t-shirt and just her panties, and she can see it makes him uncomfortable that he is wearing only boxer shorts.

"Um," he says while looking around for something. "Come in, what's up," he says, turning away, pulling his robe on.

He's been watching something on his laptop, but she doesn't recognize the program's shifting images on the screen, although she thinks it might be a comedy.

"Thanks," she says quietly.

When she turns back, Jimmy is standing in his thick terrycloth robe more suited for cold nights, not this summer night. He has the small window fan running, the air coming in a bit cooler, but it's not much better than what her open windows have provided.

"Don't wear the robe on my account," she says. "It's too hot."

She thinks he's blushing.

"I just, it was so nice of you to hang out with me today," she tells him.

There's a silence in the room interrupted only by the tiny speakers of the laptop and the small window fan.

"It was comforting," she adds.

"Sure," he says, watching her move onto his bed, over to the other side, taking a pillow, putting it behind her back, pulling her attention to the small screen halfway down on the middle of the bed.

He is still standing.

"I can't sleep, all these thoughts," she tells him, looking as if she's watching the movie. She is doing this with a fierce determination.

"Sure, yeah," Jimmy replies. "It's all pretty weird. I mean, the DA, how weird is that?"

She nods and has to fight a sudden wave of feeling.

She doesn't want to cry.

I'm not a crier, she tells herself. It passes.

Jimmy takes off his robe, sits down on the bed. The robe in his hand ends up draped over his midsection, she sees with a side-eye glance.

It makes her want to smile.

"I'm not going to bite," she says, turning to look at him, but then what she's just said strikes her as a strange thing to say, and she adds, "The last thing I need is sex, just company," but of course saying this just renews Jimmy's blushing, but she sees something of a grin too in his profile, sweet, and he keeps his own eyes on the screen, adjusting his own pillows, settling back into his bed.

"Well, that's good," he says, a quick glance at her, then he makes a face before his gaze returns to the screen.

That makes her smile again. She turns her eyes back to the screen, but she asks no questions about what he's watching. It doesn't matter to her.

Jimmy reaches over to slap off the overhead light switch, and the only illumination now is the laptop screen.

Cynthia is sliding down the pillow, slowly slipping flat.

Her eyes are closed. She tucks the t-shirt down—a prim gesture. Her right hand rests on her stomach, her left hand, toward Jimmy, is stretched out along her torso.

She's already asleep, and so she doesn't know Jimmy has taken her hand to hold, gently, softly.

Chapter 48: Don't Worry About It

*F*uck you, fuck you, fuck you," Dennis has been saying, almost a whisper, but a whisper with a snarl in it, and his incantation, his phrase, repeats with every step he takes that brings his weight down on his left ankle.

He's almost entirely hopping one-footed when he moves from the bathtub to an ad hoc clothesline he rigged up out of curtain cord, slinging some of his wet clothes over the cord and limp-hopping back for the rest.

This situation is enraging to him and not because he's been hopping around buck naked but because he's back in his motel room after a long and painful hike along the rail tracks and he's been washing up, not just himself but the clothes he'd been wearing.

He had rather obsessively searched for ticks while sitting in the tub, clothes soaped up and floating around him. The final count was only three of the *fuckers*, although he'd spent quite a bit of time to make sure.

He'd found the first of them on his shirtsleeve, an easy find.

The third and last tick had actually attached, but only partially so, he was pretty sure. It was the last of the three he had found, but that tick had been in his groin, trying to settle itself between his inner thigh and the start of his scrotum.

Fortunately, that tick had offered barely any resistance to its removal.

The second tick he had felt moving across the fine hairs at the base of his neck, and he had jumped up, the soapy water sheathing off him, almost slipping in the tub he'd been soaking in. In front of the vanity mirror, dripping, he had twisted his neck as far around as he could and *there, you little fucker*, but his attempts to pinch it were frustrating since his view was from the mirror, and his searching hand was hard put to match up with the mirror's reversed eye. He had to really make an effort, but finally, he had pinched up the moving tick.

And then he'd sat in the tub for quite a while more, soaping himself heavily, especially his hair, hoping any undiscovered ticks would be rid by the soap, but thick glaciers of suds kept sliding into his eyes as he worked the clothes in the bathwater surrounding him, he trying to squeeze the dirt and insects he imagined had infiltrated every fiber. His twisting and pummeling and plunging of the clothes had caused a lot of the bath water to slop over the sides.

It had taken him a long time to rinse the soap from everything.

Every fucking thing is taking a lot of time, he thinks.

It had taken a lot of time to walk alongside the tracks on his way back to the motel because early on he'd realized that stepping from tie to tie was worse for his ankle, even with the stick he'd found in the woods he'd passed through to get to the tracks. He'd used the stick to lean on, to take at least some weight for much of the distance but not all the distance because the stick was more hindrance than help on the two bridges. The hike had started off in failing light, but the growing darkness had made it more difficult for him to watch his footing on the trackside ballast, and by the time he'd come to the first of two rail bridges over the Housatonic the night had gone completely dark with an overcast sky negating the small amount of moonlight that might have helped.

Those crossings had made his ankle throb even more, with the pain growing, and by the time he got to the second bridge his knee didn't feel all that great either.

Every time he stumbled on the bridge's rail ties, he would flash with worry about falling off the bridge or through the ties, his fear competing with washes of anger. After a particularly violent stumble and very sharp pain in his ankle, he had settled on advancing on his hands and knees to finish crossing the second bridge.

But now, finally, back in his motel room, he is clean, his clothes are on their way to being wearable again. He is naked on his bed, ankle raised on a pillow getting soaked by the bath towel he'd wet with cold water to drape over his swollen ankle. He can't even go get ice out of the machine halfway down the stretch of motel rooms because his only clothes are still dripping. He pictures himself hopping past other rooms, wrapped in a towel.

Fuck that, no.

He could really use a bottle, but he's without a car, *which is why I'm without other clothes, you asshole,* he tells himself, but the more he thinks about his situation, the more he sees a lot has just been bad luck.

Or holding on to that car a day or two too long, asshole, he then tells himself.

But everything he really needs he'd packed in the knapsack. The knapsack, now emptied, is another dripping item hanging from the improvised clothesline.

Some of the contents of the knapsack are scattered on the small nightstand and some he has already put into the stand's drawer. His wallet and phone are resting on the bed cover next to his naked torso.

His Smith and Wesson is tucked under his pillow at the head of the bed. The extra clip, unattached silencer, and the box of cartridges are in the bedside drawer.

He's been checking his phone, looking for some food delivery since he hasn't really eaten for quite a while. There's a Chinese restaurant down the road, but he sees they don't do delivery, and there is only one other place open this late, so it's going to be pizza for him—*Again!*—but he's too hungry to care, and so he phones in an order with two of the big Coke bottles added to the order at the last minute.

If only he could have them add a bottle of whiskey or rum, this is what he'd been wishing after he'd hung up.

The fucking car, he's again thinking. He figures he'll just have to boost another, but he'll give it the night.

He hasn't felt this beat for ages, and he's hoping that a welt on the side of his face, right above the sideburn, might not bruise too badly, but he's guessing it will. There's a thin scratch along the jawline on that side of his face too, but he hadn't even been aware of it until he'd given himself a good once-over in the motel room's bathroom mirror. Plenty of small scratches, some shin bruises, and a heavy scratch — *not quite a gash* — on his lower back above his right kidney. He's pretty sure that's from when a broken branch caught him under the knapsack early on, in his first tumbling.

I fucking hate this place.

He'd like to close his eyes, but the food's on its way, and he needs to be ready for that, ready to get up and wrap a still-wet towel around his waist so he can go to the door and pay.

He knows he has to check back in with the client, but he's reluctant to since the last email might have been saying the hit was canceled.

But the fucking code-talk, assholes, who knows, really?

It did mention *holding*, but it hadn't said anything about how that could affect his fee, and he isn't going to let the assignment go unfulfilled until he's sure the full payment is coming through anyway.

I fucking hate clients.

He picks up his phone and then lets it fall back on the bed. He considers closing his eyes for just a minute.

The knock on the door happens as soon as he's drifting off, *of course.*

He gets up, picks up the wet towel from the carpet, wraps it around him, and gets some cash out of his wallet. He tries to hop-walk to the door, yelling out he's coming, and there it is, a big box of pie and the two liters of soda hanging from the kid's wrist, the plastic bag encasing them pulling tight.

"Put it there," he tells the kid, a tall kid, but skinny, *looks twelve*, and he nods his head toward the small round table near the front of the motel room. The kid has to duck under the assortment of clothes hanging from the cord, but he catches the sleeve of the shirt and with a startled look watches the shirt slide off and drop to the floor.

The kid is standing stock still.

"Just put the fucking box the shit down and take your money," he tells the kid, who nods and drops the pizza and the bag with the soda on the table, and then he turns to retrieve the shirt, and the liter bottles topple on the table, but they don't roll off, stopped by the bag. The thump of the tipped over bottles has the kid turning back, and he goes to put the bag back upright.

Dennis feels that he's about to scream.

"Hey!" he shouts. The kid turns back to look at him, and he can't read the expression. The kid might be scared, *or maybe he's pissed off,* he wonders. *Well, fuck him,* is his main thought, and then he's waving the money, stepping toward the kid. "Git!" he says, half a growl, and the kid tentatively slips the bills from his hand.

This kid's a moron, he thinks.

"What the fuck," he says to the kid, who seems *absolutely clueless.*

"Go, go, go," he shouts as he points at the door.

The kid pushes the door fully open on his way out and leaves the door that way, making him step-hop toward the door to push it closed.

Dennis just stands there for a moment at a loss what to think until he thinks, *This fucking town.*

He hops back to retrieve the shirt from the carpet, noting it still seems very wet. He hopes it'll be dry by morning.

Dry enough anyway. Shit.

At the table he sits, and it isn't long before half the pizza is gone and one of the big Coke bottles is largely empty.

Then he's back on his bed, the towel dropped on the carpet, and he tries to compose a reply to the client.

What he wants to email isn't going to be what he will email, he knows that. You don't threaten to crush your client's head *like a goddamn fucking grapefruit,* and he knows it's an empty threat since *this goddamn fucking email thing means I don't actually know who, or where.*

He misses the old days when he knew who he worked for, back when he worked for Diego, back when he still lived in Cleveland, before he'd had to leave.

Mr. Diego, Dennis corrects himself. Dennis had been good at finding people. And doing other things to people too.

That gets him thinking he's still good at that sort of thing, but a long time has passed since any of this has been simple.

Fuck!

He doesn't like being on a leash. And that's exactly what all this checking-in is, and with the language this sort of process always insists on, it's like reading *tea fucking leaves.*

Dennis is rereading the second-latest email from the client's contact from the day before and his own reply requesting clarification.

As he looks over his own email reply, he finds himself wondering if he'd been unwise to add anything about expecting full payment if there was a change in the *project's* status. *Terms of current project apply until the new project terms determined,* he'd emailed.

The client's reply had come in this morning, Dennis is surprised to realize. *Jesus, fucking feels like days ago, not this morning*, he thinks, after noting his phone shows the current time is not even 11:00 p.m. It feels like he's been up for days, despite his rooftop nap.

But he is just seeing the latest email now. He typically doesn't check emails until he's out from the area of operation, and after this *morning's inglorious fuckup*, and his subsequent state of alarm and discomfort, he's only now looking at the new email.

This email still doesn't say anything about full payout.

Fuck you! Dennis imagines saying to the client, *whoever the fuck*, they can't just change the deal, the assignment, in the middle like this, and not make it clear he, the guy out in the field, the guy whose ass is on the line, isn't going to take a loss on it just because they changed *their fucking minds!*

He thumbs in the same reply he'd sent in earlier and

presses *Send* and then he decides to forget all about it, and after a while he finds he's enjoying lying there, naked, the room's air-conditioner on low, but comfortable this way.

A good time to get my dick sucked, he can't help thinking, but then he finds himself getting angry again.

This fucking place!

He takes a deep breath, then another.

He shuts his eyes then catches the pizza smell, but his only thought is that he'll have that for breakfast, and tomorrow he'll probably take it easy and rest the *fucking ankle.* But Dennis isn't that good at taking things easy, and he finds himself getting worked up again and he finds himself imagining the target, what he would do to her, *Cynthia,* and he is thinking about making her strip. He is seeing her breasts, *maybe fuck her from the back, the cunt,* and his hand has drifted to his penis as it slowly swells. *She's holding back her cries because I told her I'd kill her if she makes a noise, but you can moan, whore, you like that?* His hand is holding his half-erect penis, lightly stroking, and then he imagines the other one, the big guy, looming behind him, and he decides sleep makes more sense than jerking off, but he can't not imagine what he would do to the big guy, *that big fucking ape,* but he's already half-asleep, and his hand on his penis slides back to his side.

Dennis awakes in the morning, and the first thing he does is look at his phone and see he's been asleep nine hours. He's naked, but that's not unusual, and he rolls off the bed, remembering just in time to check on the ankle. When he puts some weight on it, the pain seems to be less than the day before.

He figures he'll get some ice after he's dressed, and that makes him gingerly approach the hanging clothes, which he strips from the cord, noting there's only some mild dampness, mainly in the seams.

He drops them by the table and lets himself fall into the chair, reaching for the leftover pizza. He stuffs a big piece into his mouth and puts the rest of the slice back into the box, wiping his hand with the least-crumpled paper napkin from the night before.

As he chews, he picks up one item of clothing after another, inspecting each of them, looking for signs of ticks, getting angrier with each new inspection but glad he finds nothing after each thorough search, but his anger mostly stems from his review of the fiasco of yesterday and in remembering he's still in *Bumfuckville.*

He figures he better get some other clothes, maybe from the Goodwill across the highway, and that he'll have to boost another ride.

He methodically works his way through the pizza while slowly dressing, flinching once when a still-damp area of his briefs makes itself known on his balls.

He washes the pizza down with the last of the Coke liter and opens the other, which sputters, but he has held himself far enough away from the spray.

Fuck you, he thinks.

He flicks his hand free from the Coke that's sprayed, and he hobbles over to the bed. He sits and pulls his Nike knockoffs onto his feet, not thrilled by the squelch of the water in his shoes soaking his socks that had been mostly dry.

"Fuck," he says.

He stands and now the socks aren't at all dry anymore. "Fuck me," he says. He sits back down, noticing his left toes feel sore, but he figures this is probably from climbing up and down the *fucking roof.*

He pats the pillow for the gun, to check it's there.

Fuck you, he tells himself after this reflexive confirmation.

He stands and stuffs his wallet into his pants, the multi-tool in another pocket, and some cash from the side-table drawer into his front left pocket, like always.

He'll put the *Do Not Disturb* card on the knob, go to Goodwill, pick up some clothes — *shoes too* — and a windbreaker or light jacket because his is not to be found, and he reckons it could be up on the mill roof.

He figures he'll grab a car locally, drive it to Bradley, get set up with another good one from long-term parking. *The place is like Christmas*, he tells himself, still amazed by the lack of security in those satellite lots.

He looks at his phone and sees there's a text from Carl, not that it has the name, but he recognizes the burner number in use for the assignment. He figures he'll look the text over in a minute and puts the phone into his still damp back pocket.

What he doesn't figure on is that there's a knock on the door.

He thinks it must be the motel desk, looking for more cash since he'd paid only through today.

But at the door are a couple of guys, both dressed in dark suits. They are both tall, the slightly shorter one is also slimmer than the other, Dennis notes. The taller one looks like a linebacker.

They are smiling, easy.

Dennis sees the slightly shorter one is wearing running shoes with his suit, except it isn't a suit, but a dark sports jacket, lightweight with black chinos.

"Ya?" Dennis says, the door stopped at half-open.

"You going to let us in?" the bigger of the two asks.

Dennis is confused.

"Uh, not interested," he says, but he doesn't think to shut the door.

"Hey, Jymsom, right? That's what you call yourself," says the taller one.

Cops? Dennis wonders, but there isn't the cop vibe.

"He's not being hospitable, is he?" the shorter tall guy says, the one with the running shoes, from behind the bigger one.

The taller guy keeps his eye on Dennis and says, "Hey, thanks" as he pushes into the room with Dennis giving way.

A linebacker, it again occurs to him.

And somehow, he is backing away, trying not to limp-hop, but the ankle is complaining. Then he's somehow sitting on the bed, the mattress edge finding the back of his thighs, sitting him down on the bed.

"So, what, you hurt your leg?" the taller guy asks. "What's with the limp?"

"No mention he's a gimp," Running Shoes says from near the now shut door, but he's looking at the cord Dennis used for a clothesline but hasn't yet taken down.

Running Shoes gets an end loose from the light fixture near the door and tosses the cord toward the other still-tied end where the curtain pull pools on the floor against the wall.

"This automatic garrote setup, not so good," Running Shoes says to the other guy, who laughs, at least Dennis thinks it's a laugh, but a quiet one, just air through the nose.

"From the client?" asks Dennis. *What the fuck?* he thinks.

"The penny drops," says the bigger guy. He still seems like he's smiling, friendly, but Dennis catches his tone.

And then there's silence, and Dennis is the first to break it. "What is this," he says, waving at the two of them. "Why the fuck are you here?"

"That's a great question," the taller guy says, looking at Dennis. Running Shoes is still hanging back a bit, leaning against the wall near the door.

The taller guy is maybe six feet from Dennis, and Dennis feels like it can't be that far, really, because it feels like the guy is standing on him.

Dennis takes a deep breath, then laughs. "Well, when you can answer that, let me know. Otherwise, I think I'll just nap while you figure it out."

Assholes, he wants to add.

Taller Guy does that strange nose-laugh, again, like a snort or a sniff. "That's okay, stay awake," he says. "Stay up."

These guys are vibrating, wired, hyper, it occurs to Dennis, and this makes him that way too.

Taller Guy starts talking about the client, the client's change of mind on the assignment, and how nobody is liking Jymsom's reaction to it.

"Seems obstinate," Taller Guy says.

"Does that mean *pain in the ass?*" Running Shoes asks from behind, but he's just making a joke, Dennis is pretty sure.

"Hey," says Dennis. "I'm just waiting for confirmation

about the original terms."

"Yay," says Taller Guy. "Seems more *mad dog* to me."

What the fuck? These two are starting to seriously piss him off.

"Look," he says, trying to control the unpleasant mix of feelings he's experiencing, but he wants to sound calm. "You report in, to the client, the service, him, her, whoever the fuck, the system they use? I understand OpSec, but this is just double-talk, right? Nothing's clear with these guys."

"Huh. So you're just confused, you saying?"

"You mean about the hold," Dennis says to the linebacker.

"The man knows about the hold," Running Shoes says.

Dennis looks at him.

"I got it, I get it," Dennis allows. "I was just trying to get clarity on the payout, it isn't my fault the project gets changed. I wanted to be sure I wasn't shorted—"

"—Too late for that," Running Shoe interrupts. "You're already short."

The taller guy, still looking at Dennis, laughs through his nose.

Fuck you, Dennis thinks. He's really hating these guys. He wants to say something about he's not being a big asshole like them, but he keeps his counsel.

"You get it," Running Shoes says to him. "You know, like you're a shrimp."

Dennis just has to bide his time.

I'm going to kill these assholes, he thinks. *Free of fucking charge.*

"Yah, very good, you should fucking do stand up," Dennis says.

Running Shoes seems to like the suggestion.

Dennis turns his attention to the taller man, but they are both plenty big and they are making the room seem tiny, too intimate. "I just wanted confirmation about payout with the change," Dennis tells the bigger guy. "I just got a text from my handler."

He leans so he can pull the phone out of his back pocket.

"Let me check in, see what he says."

He is pulling the phone out, having to tug a bit, the pocket still damp, and his posture isn't a help.

"Fuck it," the taller one says, and he brushes back his suit coat and produces an automatic.

Oh fuck you, Dennis says to himself, thinking about his own gun, knowing it's too far from him, under his pillow.

Dennis is looking at the man's gun, pretty sure the gun is a Browning Hi-Power. He tries to see if the safety is set, but he can't.

Round in the chamber?

"Hey guys, like, okay, okay," Dennis says.

The taller one is reaching into a side pocket and pulls out what Dennis realizes is a silencer.

"Come on," Dennis says, a look of exasperation on his face. *These fuckers think they can scare me,* he is telling himself, feeling his anger rise. *Fuckers are playing around, making their fucking point.*

He looks over at the other guy, the one with the runner's shoes that don't look so great with the jacket. That guy is looking over at the taller guy, watching him screw on the silencer, and then he looks at Dennis, his eyebrows up a bit, like he's making some sort of comment on the whole proceedings, but Dennis can't really read it. His best guess is these assholes are trying to bust his chops.

"All right, so, I get it," Dennis says. "All right, got it."

The two men just look at him, both faces still, at rest.

"The messages, they were not clear, believe me, you know that sort of shit," Dennis says and he realizes he seems to be talking a lot.

He keeps talking. "Fuck, guy, all right, message received, I'll email the confirmation, like, fuck, *roger,* right, *ten-four,* whatever, I got it."

He glances down at his phone and then at the night table, being careful not to look at the pillow but trying to inch closer. He half stands for a stretch, rolling his shoulders, setting down a little closer to the head of the bed, *easy-peasy,* holding up the phone, showing the taller man the screen.

"Let's take a look," Dennis suggests, holding the phone out farther, now leaning toward the man who remains still by the door.

"You think he needs to worry about that, L.J.?" the guy with the gun asks the man near the door, but his eyes haven't moved off Dennis.

The guy named L.J. doesn't say anything, which makes Dennis think they're just fucking with him.

That makes him mad.

Fuck you, he says, but only thinks it. He's concentrating on trying to keep his face from showing how pissed off he is, but these guys, they are dicking him around, and he's raising the phone higher back toward the man closest to him, turning his body slightly more, his right arm behind him, closer to the pillow, his eyebrows up, part of his play. "Okay, I'll call it in right now, no problem."

The taller guy lets his pistol drift a bit, looking in a quick glance at Running Shoes.

Yeah, fuck you, cunts, Dennis thinks and fumbles the phone so it drops toward the floor, he dropping after it, his right arm stretching back to support his stooping for the phone, stretching for the pillow, his gun.

The last thing he hears is the taller man telling Running Shoes, "No, I don't think he has to worry about that," and from the corner of his eye Dennis sees the pistol rise up.

Something kicks him back onto the bed, the flash and the noise and the kick a sharp hot knife that cuts into silence.

Chapter 49: A Concentration of News

*N*ews, *news, news,* thinks Davin.

He knows Alicia is rather curious about how exactly he would be in the know, but he has told her she'll have to wait. *South County Interactive* has gone all out with the Dennis Jymsom killing, including the rather sensational headline *Gangland Killing!*

Not that online newspapers really get to express headlines like the olden days, of course, but he knows Alicia is going all out and had been moving full on the story even before he got this helpful tidbit of Jymson's name to her.

He wants to roll his eyes at the headline. But being able to add in the name of the victim of the shooting at one of the old-style local motels is not exactly immaterial to the story, and Alicia is over the moon *SCI* has scooped all the other outlets carrying the story, including the big papers out of New York, Albany, Boston.

Davin has lived in Housatonic for years, and he can recall only one other murder in the area over this period.

Well, South County, anyway, he realizes.

The real number is likely higher and guaranteed higher if Pittsfield is included in the counts. Whatever the count, adding in a sidebar of such crimes over the years may be a good way to expand the coverage and keep people reading.

And keep people seeing the ads, he can't help thinking.

He'll suggest this to her. He'll have to have something to placate her curiosity because he can't divulge more information about the who and why Jymsom was here, although now that she has the name, the who and all the unsettling details of the asshole's life can be found with a bit of legwork.

She's going to ask me to do that, Davin realizes. *Probably better if I do.*

It isn't that he doesn't have interest in writing about Jymsom, but he's been asked by the investigators to keep the Craigson connection out of any story. There's more at stake in keeping the Carbon's End angle from the press, since this way the investigators hold better odds in getting to the bottom of the whole story.

The Cynthia Affair, he can help thinking.

Alicia is glad for the name he's given her, but she strongly suspects he's standing on more, and he knows he'll have to read her in on what's going on and what he wants to do. This will involve her signing her own NDA, and she'll have to agree to the story embargo too, and he's a bit worried this agreement will be much harder for her than it was for him. She's got ink running through her veins, he understands, but then he takes a moment to try to think what the right metaphor is, now that actual print is rare and electrons is the common medium.

Whatever, he tells himself.

A sidebar on past Berkshire County murders should keep her from throttling him for the bigger story and give him more time to speak with the investigators to get her read in.

Homicide, Berkshire County Massachusetts will be the search terms, he figures. There might be a dozen such out of Pittsfield alone, but maybe only the one other in Great Barrington.

He has no problem understanding the story is an opportunity for *South County Interactive*. That is obvious enough since one can safely assume a local-interest story that involves a killing that looks a hell of a lot like some organized-crime murder is going to pique peoples' interest and therefore sell newspapers.

Click bait, he silently tells himself.

But he also understands the larger story will be an even bigger opportunity, and it isn't like she doesn't owe him. Right from hearing the news of the shooting at Mountain Rise Motel the day before, Alicia understood what she was calling "The Hit" would be a challenge in getting the story since the town's police department was playing things close to the vest.

The problem for Alicia earlier is that this morning's statement by the police department had been pro forma and not something that made for good copy. On the other hand, he knows the picture she'd run with the otherwise light copy made the copy compelling. *SCI* has run an image taken by the chambermaid doing a room-check, and that has more than made up for lack of factual details. And cheap, considering, he knows, still shocked by the $200 price the young woman had insisted on, as Alicia told him the story. She'd expressed to him the hope the young woman wouldn't get into trouble for taking the picture of the dead man in the motel, but in the next breath she told him that she suspects the young woman who brought her the photograph is undocumented, and the young woman had insisted she be anonymous, so this had been an attribution-free cash deal.

It won't take a genius to figure out the likely source, he figured, listening.

And then, to his amazement, in the very next breath Alicia had mentioned this particular motel had been consistently resistant to her advertising queries.

Mountain Rise Motel, We're a Hit! Is the faux headline she had related to him, and the idea of making this a new pitch made her laugh.

The digital-image acquisition had been a very good deal for *SCI*, he doesn't doubt, although he had given Alicia his opinion that the same picture or others taken at the same time would probably find its way into other publications. But for the moment *SCI* running the image means more visitors to the site, hence driving more ad revenue.

He still doesn't know if *SCI* will succeed, but now just about everyone has smartphones, if not several digital devices, and almost everyone has decent broadband, so he's confident the opportunity is strong. Add to that, the classified ad engine is fully ramped up for *SCI*, and that part of the business will likely increasingly undercut the classified ad side of the *Shopper's Guide* because with *SCI*'s template-driven submission and classification interface, the only human input on the part of *SCI* is a quick review of the self-submitted classifieds for obscenity, illegality, and in a few instances to date, simple poor taste.

As happy as she is for this news turn, he knows she's also annoyed with him. He's been hard to get hold of the last several days, and his latest piece on the new solar project has gone significantly over deadline, although with an online publication, deadlines mean something different from deadlines for the traditional rolling presses. Alicia had been surprised by him going AWOL, as she has made clear to him, but that simply helps confirm how much she's been relying on him.

He had phoned her this morning with the victim's name, adding this helpful piece of information to the first anemic police report-based story, and now that story is updated with Jymsom's name. He takes a moment to look up the most current police department press statement, which he sees is now two hours past updating, but it still remains name-free. He does notice though, in this latest statement, there's now mention that several other law enforcement agencies are involved in the investigation, including the FBI.

He is already well acquainted with the widening investigation. He is a good full day ahead of the police's second public statement when it comes to investigation organizations involved.

While *The Hit* incident has certainly caught fire, Alicia still has other demands on her time, as curious as she is about where he's getting his information. One of the pressing matters is meetings with two potentially big advertisers, and she had wanted him to go with her. But despite his weakness for flattery, he's managed to beg off, even while she's several times repeated he has a knack for explaining the benefits of their ad-lead-sale mechanisms.

Well, he considers, he should be good at describing the ease and flexibility a business has for both controlling and measuring the results of the ad because the performance of that mechanism is key to part of his own remuneration. He's also getting more writing fees now, as she was happy to remind him, but that is currently her problem because he's busy with something else, and that something else is competing with his *SCI* pieces. He can't explain this to her until he sets a meeting about embargos, and he's far from sure just who the meeting is with, but he'll ask the people who set up the NDA he has signed.

The best he can do is tell her he has another story altogether, one that ties into *The Hit*, and that she'll just have to wait because some part of the story involves someone living in his house, something to do with a murder of a climate activist out west, and he's sent her a couple of links, as he'd promised to do, and he has shared that a young woman, Cynthia Wainwright, is involved, but he had mainly emphasized that the story may be big.

"Really big," is what he'd said to her.

In return for her patience, he's promised her *SCI* would have an exclusive, but that some parts of the story would have to wait.

"We have to tread carefully with the Cynthia story," he'd told her on the phone. "There's a much bigger story here but still very much in play."

Alicia, Davin could tell as he ended the call, very much liked the last thing he'd told her, which was, "Get up to speed on syndication deals."

Chapter 50: Cynthia Back on the Horse

Cyn keeps thinking it's been quite the few days, even as she wonders when things will get back to normal, but then things have hardly been normal for what now seems like a long, long time. Her sense of time remains warped, and she again takes measure, and again reaches the same conclusion, which is that it's only been a couple of weeks since she left Jimmy's home.

She's been in her rental car already for a while today, on a drive forecast to take a little over one and a half hours.

If she counts out the weeks from when she said her original goodbye to South County after her Climate March work, and add in the job offer at Carbon's End and her moving to California and starting that new job, the period mounts up to about a half a year. The last four weeks, starting from Joe's death, itself feels like a year.

No wonder I always want to take a nap, she tells herself.

But she's done with the napping since there hasn't been any time really, not since she started at a new ClimateProgress.Org project that, if things go well, could be another of the organization's spin-offs like Carbon's End. It's early days yet, which is one of the exciting things about the project. There's not even a name for it, not a final name anyway, just a working name.

MEAT.

Cyn loves this. It carries enough weirdness and she secretly hopes the project's working name will somehow survive to become the actual name of a funded real entity.

She loves the work itself, or at least she thinks she does, but she knows she's hardly come close to settling in yet. Some

of the work she does is like what she'd done at Carbon's End —
some research, some administrative organizing. But what
she's really excited about is the potential to have a significant
role in shaping the program.

If the project moves forward, she reminds herself.

The goal of the project is to design a public outreach
program to support meat-alternatives with the goal of
reducing greenhouse gas emissions levels of CO_2, and even
more so, the methane that gets produced by industrial
livestock agribusiness. She had known livestock production
was a contributor, but as she sank her teeth into the subject,
she'd found herself shocked by the actual numbers.

Or as her colleague Ethan likes to say, perhaps a bit too
often, *Ronald Reagan was right.*

Ethan Buckner, Lead for Agribusiness Outreach, grew up
in a ranching family, cowboy boots and all. She finds him
funny, in a good way, although his *Cow Burps!* greeting could
well get tiresome in the long term, but then she doesn't work
in the same office he does. His effort is located in Manhattan,
Kansas, and she's pretty sure he has a PhD from Kansas State
University. The full team mostly assembles by teleconference,
so her exposure to the barnyard humor will likely be minimal.

She's still unclear about how many people there are
within MEAT, with all the interviews and hires that make up
some of her admin work, and she knows all this is likely to
remain fluid until the project matures. Her department is
working out of a Middlebury College office. It's early days yet,
but she's glad to be involved, even if the learning curve is
exhausting, especially with her still sometimes meeting with
the ClimateProject.Org team liaising with law enforcement
and a seemingly ever-changing assortment of investigators
and lawyers. She'd heard just recently that there's someone
representing Trump's Attorney General now involved, but it
looks likely to be bit of political play acting, considering the
upcoming midterms.

*Or a way to check in on how much trouble their friends could
be in,* she can't help suspect.

Of course, she's to remain silent when it comes to anyone not part of the investigation, which means she still has to remind the twins not to talk about any of it. She has visited them, of course, and she'd talked to them about what happened but stopped after a pressing series of questions had her telling her brothers she'd been interrogated enough already.

But otherwise, in the two weeks since her new job began, she's hardly had the time to breathe, never mind visit family or friends.

Except now her presence has requested by the Berkshire District Attorney's office as they wrap up their part of the investigation into Rat Face's death.

She still refuses to use his real name.

She doesn't know exactly why they want her down there, but then she's discovered that the whole thing is nothing like detective shows on television because such shows are not devastatingly boring. The reality is there's so much repetition and the questions to answer and the documents to sign and affidavits to declare drag on and on and on.

But today feels special. Jimmy is also going to be at home, coming back from Boston where he's been interviewing for a couple of jobs. She is driving to Davin's house where she'll stay before tomorrow's meeting.

Well, at least I can pay room and board, she tells herself, knowing full well that none will be asked for, but for her, this reinforces her change in status. This attempt at light-heartedness is tempered by the thought that no longer living there is in some way kind of sad. Davin's place was a place of safety, and it could even be, well, nice.

Well, except for a killer stalking me, she thinks.

She and Jimmy mostly text but talk by phone sometimes, and in their latest conversation, Jimmy has mentioned that if he gets one or another of the Boston jobs, he'll stay with old Cambridge neighbors, the parents of his best friend from childhood. Apparently housing costs in the Boston area are as bad as San Francisco.

She still needs to find an apartment. ClimateProgress.Org has been putting her up at The Middlebury Inn for the last two weeks, but she knows that's pricey. The students are back and so apartment availability is a problem, and so far she's looked at only a couple of possibilities. There is that garage conversion on Lower Foote Street that's surprisingly nice but a bit of a hike from the office. Not as nice, but just over a half a mile from the college and the project's office, there's a house share opportunity, and that house is set back a little from Court Street, otherwise known as Route 7, the old route that reaches through Vermont and Massachusetts, all the way to Long Island Sound. This is the very same old double-lane Interstate she's been driving down.

Everything she's going through, all the changes, feels exciting, but also really complicated, and she has no reason to think it'll be any different anytime soon.

And Jimmy, she thinks.

She's not an idiot, she knows Jimmy likes her, more than that, really, and she likes that, but why start something if she's gone again in a day or two. She knows it's likely Jimmy will be hurt, she knows he's already confused about the limbo state of their potential romantic relationship, not that this has ever been said out loud by either one of them.

As she drives, she spends some time pondering their just being friends.

She feels bad, she really likes Jimmy, sees his confusion.

Best that it's over before it starts, she tells herself, although another voice tells her she's playing it wrong. For one thing, she finds Jimmy is interested in a lot of things, and she likes that. She likes that a lot. It isn't just college, his having gone, anyway, but rather it's that he's excited about life. She loves the kind of conversations he has with Davin. She's met his mother, too, accompanying Jimmy in his dad's car, driving down from Pittsfield to Lenox on one of the rare afternoon breaks in that week of interviews and depositions and question-and-answer sessions with so many different individuals from such a bewildering variety of agencies. Gwen is sweet and clearly thinks the world of her son. It's clear to her Jimmy has a loving heart, learned from his family, and she thinks she'd really like to meet his sister. According to Jimmy, his sister really wants to meet her, and Cyn would love to have Jimmy get to know the twins, *the bros*. Her folks—her mom, her stepfather—maybe not so much.

She knows she's feeling a lot of things and a big share of these feelings are strong, maybe too strong, and Joe is in her thoughts a lot

All the recounting, I guess, she assumes.

She can talk about him now. Gone is the frozen state she'd kept sliding into those first few days.

What she most fiercely wants to know is if Rat Face had anything to do with Joe's murder, but no one seems to know. She's certain Rat Face wasn't the deputy-whatever in the desert, the man who turned out not to be a real cop but someone in a uniform, using a stolen police vehicle.

Bigger. Taller. Short dark hair, no facial hair. Her too-sparse description now become rote.

That had been about all she could give them during those two sessions with a younger man and an older woman from whatever agency or office. She'd been repeatedly interviewed by them and pushed for details about the man she saw kill Joe, and that had been the toughest thing she'd had to do. And despite all their tricks and techniques and tenacity, there wasn't much she could give them. Taller than Rat Face, bigger than Rat Face. And dark hair, cut short, like most cops, and maybe close to six feet in height, but even that was without much confidence.

The investigators know the man wasn't a real cop from the area, but not because they've caught the killer. No one local from the different law-enforcement forces matched for time and place or was otherwise unaccounted. The vehicle, an SUV, had gone missing from the San Bernardino County Sheriff Department's lot, and was found later, but wiped clean and of no help.

The vehicle had never been logged missing or stolen,

probably out of embarrassment, according to what Jimmy tells her Terry had heard from the investigators.

Wiped, they'd told Terry. Terry, as he likes her to call him these days, is still in touch with Jimmy and from the sound of it, still actively in contact with some of the investigators. Jimmy talks with her about what Terry tells him, the latest bit about how the phones were hijacked and the text messages inserted, which, according to Jimmy, turns out to be an interesting gimmick Terry wants to know for his own work. Jimmy has, he's told her, repeatedly asked Terry for details, but Terry, apparently, had each time just rolled his eyes.

She had pointed out which text messages were hers for the investigators, and did her best too with Joe's, indicating which were the real ones and which were not, so they could concentrate on the intrusions. She still thinks of the real ones with Joe, and from Joe, talking about sex and clearly showing they'd had a thing going on. She'd had to acknowledge the dick pic.

Fuck, Cyn tells herself, still feeling the embarrassment, but also with the distance of some weeks, she has to admit there's also something stupidly funny about this in a way.

Fortunately, the issue of the actual affair still isn't being raised as an essential aspect of the ongoing investigations, at least as far as she knows. But Jimmy knows the story, her having an affair with a married man.

Fucking my boss.

He knows about it because they'd talked about it, but light on details, and she remains troubled by the possibility of his finding out more.

Of course, he's going to know, she tells herself, *sooner or later. The truth will out*, she tells herself. It's all part of the bigger picture, all part of the details getting established, confirmed, pinned down. At least this is what her new therapist suggests is likely. Cyn has had only the first session to date, but she thinks it might work out.

One of the things the therapist has asked of her is to consider talking to Jimmy about her relationship with Joe and about her relationship history overall and to write down as much as she can about her reactions and her feelings as she does this. *Maybe*, is all she will commit to at the moment. She doesn't see this as likely to happen today and tomorrow.

She is through Pittsfield and on a field-lined stretch she thinks might be Lenox, and she takes a moment to enjoy the scenery, but she finds herself thinking of the way Terry is being toward them — it's funny and kind of cute really. Terry seems to have a soft spot for Jimmy and likes him and gets a kick out of him, but Terry has been protective with them both.

He had accompanied Jimmy to the meeting with the investigation team about Jimmy's hacks, and Jimmy told her Terry was watching his back and more so than the local lawyer Davin had arranged. On the other hand, the lawyer provided through ClimateProgress had impressed Jimmy, and while he has told her on several occasions he's still keeping his fingers crossed, it looks like no one seems to care about Jimmy's activities those first few days in Housatonic. The real issue is that because the emails he had retrieved are now an important part of the investigation record, he technically remains open to charges because somehow it may be relevant to something called chain of custody. They are still looking at a *pro forma* grant of immunity.

In their most recent phone call, Jimmy mentioned how pissed off his dad seems to be about the bills he's gotten from the local lawyer, feeling, as he apparently does, that the guy did nothing for them, not even getting an immunity deal. "Dad's been quoting that lawyer line from Shakespeare," he'd told her.

She had looked it up afterward. "The first thing we do, let's kill all the lawyers," was from *Henry VI*, part II, act IV, scene II, line 73. The line, she was surprised to see, was uttered by a character named Dick the Butcher. She still doesn't quite know what to make of that particular detail.

Dick the Butcher, Jesus.

She sighs.

The investigations aren't looking so great. At least that's

her takeaway from what Terry's been telling Jimmy. He thinks there may be some real problems moving the investigations forward. According to Terry, the investigators have definitively established a connection between the law firm and that new lobbying firm with the name she doesn't remember, but that in and of itself is nothing, and there's nothing solid connecting Northstar to any direct evidence of criminal involvement. *No smoking gun* is how Jimmy put it the most recent time the two of them talked about this at any length, and she'd had a strange reaction to the phrase, but in the end laughed in response to Jimmy's mortification at having used the phrase. She also found his fumbling effort to apologize amusing.

Sweet guy, she thinks.

No one is happy with not finding clear and actionable ties to any of the big fossil fuel service companies, or the industry 501(c)/4 organizations, or any of the oil billionaires who back that new lobbying group, and there's nothing so far that directly connects to Tally Oil Services either. Nothing, either, identifying or linking to the person who killed Joe or the person or persons behind that person, or any clue as to whoever hired Rat Face.

She knows Jimmy's disappointed his hack hurts the case because his intrusion throws into play the validity'of the emails retrieved from the law firm, but Terry believes that the law firm has been doing a solid job covering their collective legal asses regardless. If she follows correctly, from what Jimmy's told her, some of the law firm's positions include that the most relevant emails are seen as being so unspecific in language they can easily be read in different ways, including as a missing person assignment instead of a murder contract. At least this is what the guy at the law firm, Madaki, continues to maintain.

The clerk's position is that he was serving a valid client, who he has claimed was a lawyer representing her family, at least within his reasonable belief. Unfortunately for Madaki, concerning that client, no trace exists, including the emails he'd allegedly received. The biggest problem for the clerk is that the law firm fiercely and continuously denies the firm was engaged by such a client, effectively hanging Madaki out to dry on possible obstruction charges.

And shitcanning him, she knows, but she finds far too little satisfaction in that.

According to Terry, Madaki is likely to face other charges in addition to obstruction, since a cache of cash was uncovered in his apartment and the various explanations for the cash are, as Terry had put it, *all a variety of crap,* and if the money was from the client, as Madaki had most recently claimed, the money should have been in the firm's funds and not, as Terry reported, in a clumsily resealed cereal box.

And, of course, her family hadn't engaged any lawyer. They hadn't even known anything was wrong until her mom found herself fielding telephone calls from two of the contracted private investigation companies, which meant Madaki's claim of parents-as-clients is provably false, and the existence — or more accurately, nonexistence — of the would-be family lawyer or of any hint of communication from the client looks bad for the clerk.

Boo-fucking-hoo, Cyn thinks about Madaki. *Too bad, so sad.*

She hopes the obstruction charge will go forward, but she has lingering doubts.

The takeaway is that tracing the money paid out to Madaki is a ghost trail, and it's increasingly unlikely Madaki knows much of anything that might help reveal who is behind it all. There seems no legally valid tie-in with any and all of the various fund transfers connected to the PACs or other entities.

It is called Dark Money for a reason, Terry had remarked.

Terry, of course, never got the bonus, although all three investigation services had got the sign-on fees, but the money trail is another problem, and she now knows more about offshore havens and the mechanisms for money transfers and the nature of numbered accounts and cryptocurrency than she could have ever imagined.

Nonetheless, she knows there's a strong theory as to the

why of the killing, but no one so far sees much of anything to point to a *who*, not in an evidentiary way.

As for the guy who killed Joe, Jimmy has told her Terry thinks he's probably buried someplace in the desert, especially considering Rat Face getting shot to death. *A classic pattern of coverup.* She thinks that was the phrase Terry used, at least according to Jimmy. Jimmy had also told her Terry said that something is likely to emerge if the investigation keeps slogging through. Those involved are more likely at risk because efforts to cover traces often end up showing the connections.

Jimmy had then said, "Hopefully Terry's right, so who knows?"

Not me, she thinks.

She's been thinking about all this while driving, and she's surprised when she realizes she's at the intersection of Route 183 where the Glendale Middle Road shortcut out of Stockbridge that Jimmy had shown her — *how many weeks ago?* — winds through a golf course and shaves off a couple of miles.

Somehow, she's made all the right turns, but she can't for the life of her recall where she's just been, as if someone else has been driving.

Driving on automatic. She doesn't like it when that happens.

She makes the turn onto Route 183, heading south. In a few minutes, she'll be in Housatonic.

Jimmy is supposed to get there sometime late afternoon.

It's clear to her Jimmy is finding what he calls *forensic computing* fascinating, and she gets it but doesn't have the same feeling. What she wants, what she's interested in, is for the people who Joe shot to be exposed, crucified, lose everything, *eat shit and die.*

People want a lot of stuff, she knows.

She wants to do something important to keep oil in the ground.

To fight climate change.

She wants to get back to that work.

She wants heads on stakes. She wants to see her brothers.

She wants Jimmy.

At least if I can do that without fucking it up, she adds to her list.

She also wants to put all this shit behind her.

People want a lot of stuff, she tells herself.

Chapter 51: Let the Presses Roll!

I t's not even Thanksgiving, but for the second year in a row, the Northeast has been hit with a massive snowstorm, and this time the Berkshires are dead center.

Davin hates snow, even if he hates it a bit less than heavy rain, especially if that kind of house-damaging rainstorm comes less than two weeks before a major snowstorm as had happened the previous year.

He stops shoveling for a moment.

It occurs to him that he hates big rain more than big snow only because of what that huge rainstorm had done to the apartment the previous November. He has lost almost the entire rental season and ended up doing the repair work with Chaplin's help during yet another slow period for the carpentry laborer. At least Chaplin showed up and did the work with him, unlike the contractor Davin had signed up, but who had never, in the end, showed up.

He knows another project he'll have to plan for when the warm weather returns is building up the swales and expand the rain and gutter redirects. He recently received a letter from his house insurer announcing inspections of select properties that match particular profiles, and he can guess his sloped property is one such match. He wonders if this means big data has come to small insurance offices.

There's nothing like the mindless work of shoveling to let all kinds of thoughts run free, he muses.

He periodically thinks about heart attacks, too, now that he's back out yet again hand shoveling the long driveway, having done the clearing in stages over the last two days to keep the narrowest passable way open to the top of the driveway.

Chaplin has helped. He had recently outfitted his small pickup with a plow, but that only helped on the first pass, going down the driveway. The truck can't make it up the driveway plowing, so hand shoveling it is since that first pass.

He has to keep reminding himself to take it easy, to pace himself, but he gets sweaty regardless of his intentions. He stops again, bracing his boots aggressively because he's on a particularly steep part of the driveway, up toward the top before it levels out into the parking area. He pulls a glove off his hand with his teeth and rummages around his parka's pocket for a bandanna, and then he's pulling off his fake fur trapper hat to wipe his forehead.

The sweated headband is icy when he puts the hat back on.

He hates snow mostly because it's a big pain in the ass to keep his driveway clear enough, but he also hates whenever there's a cold snap or snow, that some idiot or another is guaranteed to say something about how there's no global warming. After so many years of explanations, there should be no one now thinking that, *but there you go.*

He knows the basics. Warmer ocean, warmer atmosphere, more moisture, more instability in the jet stream and gulf stream, big drops in temperature, huge rains or snowstorms, and welcome to New England.

He manages another weak throw over the ever-higher banks of shoveled snow threatening the cleared parts of the driveway. If the cleared center gets any narrower, the driveway will be completely useless.

Davin thinks again how he should have been clearing even more frequently, but the amount of snow that's fallen and still falls has proved too hard to plan for. He thinks this just about every time he lifts the snow shovel high enough to get the snow far enough away from the cleared edges so that half of it doesn't shift and slide back down into the shoveled part of the driveway.

Davin sniffs, amused by the thought he's never

missed Chaplin more. But Chaplin is making good money with the plowing, as inadequate as his rig may be. Plenty of small parking lots and level driveways to clear.

Davin looks down his driveway, close to giving up the current effort to clear the latest layer of snow. Chaplin and Deidre can always park down near the mills and walk up, he's now thinking, and he sure doesn't need to try to get his car out anytime soon.

Except for the one or two massive storms that have become part of the new normal, the winters otherwise typically have less snow than years past, and if it's a light snowfall, mostly the snow melts off before Davin has to shovel. He also uses a lot of salt, mainly because the melt-off often freezes at night and the icy driveway, given its length and pitch, makes for a far too dangerous driveway when icy, so he uses dozens and dozens of big bags of salt over a typical winter.

I'm the Romans salting the fields of Carthage.

But other than his growing despair with the snow shoveling challenge, Davin's mood lately has been good.

For one thing, the hoped for mid-terms have broken for Democrats in both the House and the Senate, so maybe the worst of Trump and his band of fools, fanatics, and asshole billionaires can be kept in check.

From my lips to god's ears, he mentally prays, although, unfortunately, his faith in the Democrats is weak.

The best thing he's excited about is that the go-ahead to publish his story in *SCI* had finally come, albeit much later than either he or Alicia had anticipated. The article release had to wait on investigators' summons and warrants and subpoenas going out, which finally happened the day before yesterday, as per the press conference regarding the investigation given by the Massachusetts Attorney General.

Within moments of the email receipt lifting their press embargo, and not without some trepidation, his long article appeared online on *South County Interactive*, and at pretty much the same time the Attorney General's Office's press release was issued containing a link to the *SCI* article.

Trepidation and excitement, Davin mulls. *Not one of my favorite combos.*

The article, nearly 11,000 words long, starts with a summary of Joe Craigson's murder, derived almost entirely from the deposition by Cynthia Wainwright, although the San Bernardino law enforcement reports provided some local color. He thinks he's done a passable job balancing the emotional stress of what Cynthia witnessed, providing a sense of what happened but not letting his personal sympathy for her get out of hand.

Just the facts, ma'am.

Davin stops mid-shovel push and stands up straight, but he's unsure whether the groan he experiences is physical or mental.

He stretches experimentally.

Okay, physical, he thinks, identifying the dull pain in his protesting lower back muscles.

Rereading his piece before its online release had brought the stress and tension of those several days back to him, and last night's sleep was fretful for it.

Well, that and getting up several times to see how much snow was falling, he reminds himself. He had been up early, still dark enough to need the floodlights to start in on the first pass of shoveling of the day.

The article also describes Carbon's End's efforts to get organizations to divest from fossil fuels investments and the roles Craigson and Cynthia played. The most controversial part of the article, addressing the alleged conspiracy to keep Tally Oil Services' pipeline in play, had been written with care by Davin with one hell of a lot of consultation with lawyers, but even then, the description of the various entities with alleged or possible involvement was carefully reported from the angle of the investigation efforts, and that itself had taken up what he'd worried was too much of the article. There had been a lot of subpoenaed companies to mention, starting with McMurty Alliance, the small, brand- spanking-new lobbying firm with its connection to Jabutu Madaki, of extension 323 at the law firm Callow, Cullens, and McChusker, LLC, as well as the PAC, America for Energy Sense, which proved to be the main client of the lobbying firm and which also happened to use Callow, Cullens, and McChusker, LLC.

Alicia had brought in *SCI*'s own lawyer, and he had been quite clear Davin should always use the modifier *alleged* in reference to the PAC tied to McMurty and in regard to the connection between McMurty and the law firm.

Alleged, my ass, Davin says to himself. *The guilty parties are somewhere in the mess.*

He looks around at the thin layer of the newest snow covering the just cleared part of the driveway.

Clear the fucking stairs, he says to himself. He figures at a minimum he needs to clear the snow off the wide front steps that lead from the lower driveway up to the front porch of the house, through which one gains entrance to both the main part of the house and the small first floor apartment used for Airbnb. Not that the Airbnb apartment is an issue at the moment, not during the winter season.

Thank god, he thinks, another small prayer of gratitude because the driveway problem would certainly mess with his Airbnb ratings.

He manages to clear the bottom step, and then another.

That's a fuck of a lot of snow, he admits.

Every shovelful of snow thrown past the sides of the stairs as far as he can manage finds half of each throw cascading down to partly refill the cleared steps below.

He laughs. It had been like that trying to work with the investigators from the several agencies. Every time he had asked for access to a document or deposition, he'd be surprised if he got half of what he'd requested.

Even Bancroft had gotten tired of his calls.

He'd kept chipping away, trying to flesh out the story. The number of potential unindicted coconspirators had impressed him, and he still thinks this pseudo-identification of those people and organizations is a ballsy move on the part of the prosecution team.

He pauses again and decides to switch snow shovels. He carefully crab-walks his way down the driveway to where he'd left the other shovel speared into the snow bank, and then he baby-foots it back toward the wide steps, taking great care to keep from taking a spill. He wants to get inside, shed the monstrously puffy shell of winter coat and all the other cold weather accoutrements. He wants to head up to his office to check back in on the syndication effort.

But the snow still falls.

In the end he and Alicia had decided to keep the story more focused on the local angle, trying to squeeze it for all the sensational slant possible, including the discovery by him of a windbreaker behind the back property that could have been Dennis Jymsom's, not that any forensics was done, but the argument was easy enough to make, and Jimmy and Cynthia both had been sure.

Well, pretty sure, anyway, he reluctantly admits to himself.

Davin scrapes clear another small part of one of the stairway's stone treads.

Killer stakes out house in Housatonic!

Davin softly laughs, sending out a puff of breath cloud. He hadn't gone so far as to stoop to tabloid writing, or at least he's pretty sure he had shown stylistic restraint.

Two teenagers had come forward to report on the guy who had been up on the roof of a mill building near Davin's house, and there was plenty on that roof to show Dennis Jymsom had been up there, including a greasy bag with some donut crumbs, and playing a hunch, Davin had stopped by Taft Farms with a copy of file photographs of Jymsom, and sure enough, Jymsom had been in for donuts and coffee several times, according to two of the Taft Farms people.

Maybe Alicia should try that angle to see if Taft Farms wants an ad. *Taft Farms cider donut – so good, you'll kill for them!*

Davin decides he'd better pay attention to his task at hand, but now he's having trouble not thinking of the Taft Farms donuts.

Well, they are good, he admits.

No one could actually ever know what Jymsom had intended to do. Perhaps he was here to simply report Cynthia's location or perhaps something more nefarious up to and including murder, but it had been easy enough to suggest the danger, and he had pushed the part of the story of the discovery of Dennis Jymsom's presence in Great Barrington, certain it made for great copy.

He grunts as he tries to throw another shovelful of snow as far away from the piles of snow already narrowing the steps' half-cleared pathway, and he succeeds to spare the stairs, but the snow he has tossed creates a bit of an avalanche down into the cleared path of the driveway.

Fuck you, he thinks resignedly.

The prosecution team felt it didn't have enough to pursue criminal charges for the PAC staffers, never mind any PAC board members, although that poor clerk had everything possible thrown at him, and Davin will be checking on his sentencing hearing coming up in a few weeks. That guy deserved some punishment, but after reading and rereading the court transcripts, he has to conclude this Madaki was guilty of venality and stupidity, but malicious intent strikes him as unlikely.

The investigators were confident on circumstantial evidence linking the pipeline project and associated companies, but there was no sufficient basis for indictments. It's an ongoing relief for him and Alicia that the lawyers feel strongly there would no threat of civil suit against him or *SCI* from those named alleges or hypothesized upon, since in civil suits evidentiary requirements were far more flexible than for criminal cases, and the roles of the lobbyist firm and PAC, in any discovery phase, would add sufficiently unwelcomed lines of inquiry not in their interest. As one of the lawyers had put it to him, *Dark money wants to stay dark*.

Unfortunately, dark money had also meant that no one was able to prove crime or conspiracy. He's made reluctant peace with the main outcome of the investigation not being criminal prosecutions and convictions, at least so far, but rather in the sending of a political message that vast wealth is not an unfailing shield from accountability. More subtly—although hardly all that subtle—is the message that the political influence of the fossil fuel industry is now not to be tolerated.

The recent midterms seem a good sign.

These are public interest forces in play pushing for climate mitigation and against fossil fuel interests and not just in coming months but probably for years to come. Whether there is to be enough consequence in the next national elections remains to be seen.

Who knows? he finds himself wondering.

He knows ClimateProgress.Org is playing a long game, and there are political alliances being strengthened and new ones formed, and the prospect for more effective carbon-tax legislation in Congress is being revived along with a new push to highlight fossil fuel subsidies and make a play for shifts of budget priorities toward this year's version of the Green New Deal.

Well, I'll believe that one when I see it, he can't help thinking.

He looks down at the narrow driveway path again.

I'm either freezing my nuts off out here or sweating like a pig, he is now considering, feeling the chill seep in because he's been standing still, lost in his thoughts.

He has another thought. *I hate winter!*

The weather forecasts are calling for a polar express, and the present storm is the precursor to this, and he can already feel the drop in temperature. Even salting the driveway will be pointless if the temperature drops as low as forecasted, as he knows well from past experience. He decides it's okay for him to give up the current effort to empty the sea of snow with a sieve. But he knows too he would much rather be inside so he can check—yet again—on the reception his article is enjoying.

He shakes his head, keeping himself from flinging the shovel out into the yard, but he he'd just have to wade through the banks of snow to retrieve it. He's at the top stair, working to clear the last hour's snow fall from the short bluestone path to the front porch. The snow is still coming down, but he thinks it might be slowing, finally.

The article has enough direct quoting and local color, and he hopes the ties to the breaking national story hinting at conspiracy — *alleged!* — will be enough to drive links to *SCI*. Neither he nor Alicia have any clear projection for the potential syndication fees. It also remains to be seen whether other publications will pay to reprint the entire article or at least significant segments of his story, but Alicia had already pinged him a text that seemed to indicate this is going quite well, if he's correctly interpreting the rather cryptic — or perhaps merely overexcited — message.

He certainly hopes so.

He could use some extra cash, that's for sure, but more importantly, he's been promising himself he'd get back to several projects in his studio left in suspension for months because of his *SCI* workload and the work on the article. He understands some wishful thinking may be taking place in that regard, but he's trying to think positively.

On the other hand, Alicia is fired up about the syndication model and wants some proposals from him to build other opportunities.

There's a writer and analyst of climate policy who lives in town who's focused on the national and international scale of the crisis, at least as best Davin can tell based on some skimming of her blog and a look at some past consultation clients of hers. He intends to suggest to Alicia they see if this person may be interested in expanding her practice to address local climate issues, or *hyper-local*, as he wants to call it.

Except he's not calling anything that, and he's not yet pushed Alicia at all about it. He knows Alicia is the one who would have to reel this Jeannie Louise Smith — *or maybe its Smythe?* — into the fold, and Alicia seems unlikely to act on this anytime soon.

But if she did, she'd no doubt want him involved.

Hence my hesitancy, he reminds himself.

He makes it into the front porch and spends a minute knocking snow from his hat and coat and boots. He tries rolling his shoulders to ease a burning sensation that's been building for the last half hour of his snow clearing work.

"Fuck," he says, the expletive smoking out past his lips into the frigid atmosphere of the enclosed but unheated porch.

He steps into the warmth of the kitchen. He struggles to strip off the cold-weather clothing, worrying again, after feeling a twinge, about his back stiffening up.

And then he's up the stairs and into his office. He flops down into his office chair, grimacing as he does as the cold damp of his pants, which are soaked at the knees, settles an unpleasant new chill on his legs. The damp sweat of his shirt and undershirt is uncomfortable, and he knows he should change his clothes, but he can't help himself. He has to check his email.

He wakes his laptop, and there is his Google News feed up on the big monitor, and a headline catches his eye.

DRC On Fire. The article from *The Wall Street Journal*, carrying the deck "UN-Done, the United Nations Reforestation project in the Democratic Republic of Congo goes up in flames."

That's too bad. He had been a fan of the United Nation effort to promote reforestation in large-scale projects, and the DRC was the first truly huge effort, albeit still a pilot. Poor weather conditions in the form of an extended dry season had been showing up in the news, but this, he can't help feeling as he reads through the news report, is *a goddamn kick in the balls.*

Always bad news, is what he's thinking.

There's nothing new from Alicia in email, and he has got to get out of his sweat- and snow-wet clothes. He pushes his office chair back, but his phone chirps its text notification tone, and he stands to wrestle the phone from his pants front pocket.

There is a text message from Alicia with preliminary figures about syndication requests so far.

The numbers are more than enough to make Davin grin.

Chapter 52: Only the Shadow Knows

All the important precautions are holding, Rockland DeFries is happy to see.

Not that they wouldn't, he reminds himself, but a lot had gone wrong.

The man is standing in front of the big plate window, a wide span of glass that looks out over the Cape Hatteras dunes and offers a panoramic view of the Atlantic. He's in what he now thinks of as his *throwaway house,* although he does love the place. He knows the next big storm can take this all away, even with all the overbuilding he'd commissioned.

There's no house insurance for the property but only because it's now illegal for insurers to provide such insurance for structures within certain designated areas, and those designations determined by the North Carolina Department of Insurance are slated to expand each year, but where he has this beach house is in the first Exclusionary Insure Zone of the original legislation. The cost of insurance, even if he were allowed to buy a policy, would be close enough to replacement costs to make it an unattractive option anyway. He knows the day is coming when the house will be lost to the ocean, but he's a man unafraid of risk.

That thought makes him laugh. His main work is avoiding risk, and certainly for himself, but that's really just part of mitigating risk for his clients.

When he was young, he'd been a McKinsey & Company man, but he's run his own consultancy for years. His company ostensibly focuses on business management and process efficiency improvements, and his days at McKinsey had shown him the way.

At this point, after some years tinkering with the process software he'd managed to take away from McKinsey, he is able to produce reports that look good but are nearly automatic in their generation, taking the McKinsey half-bullshit products further toward complete bullshit, and thus creating an excellent billing front end for his clients to pay for his real work for them.

He even has some regular employees to do the bullshit work, and he pays them well enough to keep them convinced the consulting the company provides is valuable. The main value of the company, however, is a very different service that comes with effective and confident layers of protective insulation for those clients.

He picks up his crystal rocks glass and takes another long pull of eighteen-year-old single malt, holding the glass in his hand as he looks at the ocean.

The man loves his life.

The ocean is frisky with the effects of an oncoming polar vortex that will reach, quite likely, as far down the eastern seaboard as North Carolina, and there's a massive snowstorm underway up north. But he's confident in his house. It's well made and weathertight, and he has an oversized generator to feed the heat pumps and other essential systems should the power fail.

The main room, where he stands admiring the tossing ocean, is tastefully decorated, except for an ornately framed and expensively lit poster of Rocky Balboa, from *Rocky IV*.

Rocky is what Rockland DeFries calls himself. He is a fifth generation Philadelphia scion of bank and coal and oil money, but the main value his lineage offers is connections. The family money, distributed ever more widely across the last two generations, and in ever more incrementally small amounts, had been such to educate and socialize him among the still truly wealthy but not much else.

He works for his money.

Rocky knows he's good at what he does, brokering services for clients who need to never be associated with such services. There have been some problems, and he's honest about these. The first big failure of his most recent contract, for instance. He's still plenty annoyed about it since his operator's hire should have been smarter and should have simply walked away when the expected conditions had gone sideways.

Larsen knows this, and Rocky is confident Larsen has been properly chastised.

Rocky shakes his head thinking about it.

The service had been beautifully designed, of that he's sure, but the key is always in the execution, and that had been botched.

FUBAR, indeed.

He, of course, had had to keep himself insulated, which means he has to rely on his man getting the right freelancers, and both of the freelancers who were commissioned turned out to not be so good.

Well, the pipeline contract did go forward, didn't it? He reminds himself.

That was the only thing the client might be happy about— certainly not about the investigations that have been poking around the edges of their businesses, but they remain sufficiently insulated from any real danger.

He would have loved to use the ABJ Funds triumph as a portfolio item, but instead he's taking a hit and expects some business will be paused for a while. *The clients will be back,* he tells himself. The dead ends of the investigations are good calling cards too, in their way.

But that doesn't mean he's not disappointed with the failure of the murder/suicide gambit for those two anti-oil activists. The fuckup out near Barstow had metastasized into a much bigger problem. Larsen had really scrambled to try to salvage the operation, and he appreciates the effort, but he prefers to pay for results, not effort, especially when the effort fails. Even the subsequent activities Larsen pursued to find the young woman hadn't produced results.

A good lesson, he hopes.

He'd poached Larsen from an acquaintance who had tried to involve him in what he'd immediately seen was a needlessly stupid fraud, and that man's operative had thought that too. He'd seized the moment to hire him away.

Not that Larsen is an official employee in this capacity, and Rocky is momentarily amused by the idea of the stupidity of allowing any connection back to him for the off-book work. Instead, he works with Larsen through offshore money accounts and the occasional cash transfer, and communication is only through highly encrypted channels. He and Larsen had only ever met once in the real world, beyond, that is, that meeting with his acquaintance whose scheme had radiated danger signs for anyone smart enough to see them.

He knows Larsen is smart and that he possesses expert tech skills. Larsen's front with Rocky is as a network security consultant. Rocky's company uses him that way sometimes, as a subcontractor, with the legitimate subcontract side of things typically handled by other staff.

Still, Rocky always weighs the potential for connection back to him on any of the special operations, unlikely as it may be, which is why he keeps screen shots of the text exchanges coupled with enough potential evidence incriminating his operator. The most recent example of that is his requiring Larsen to provide confirmation photos when he disposed of the freelancer who fucked up the beautiful plan by precipitously killing the Carbon's End fellow.

The photos sent in would contain sufficient geo-location metadata such as cell-tower pings.

Cover your ass. This is Rocky's mantra.

Larsen is a whiz with that sort of thing himself, Rocky has no doubt. Larsen had been the one to propose the idea about text plants, although it hadn't been done as elegantly as originally described, but it doesn't matter. The connections and communications between his operative and the freelancers are virtual, and he requires Larsen to monitor their exchanges and report through another encrypted service so he can track what's going on, and this is mainly to confirm the participants remain ignorant of any identifying information that could come back to him.

The payments Rocky receives for such operations are not refundable, regardless of operational failure, and that's because the payments are in the form of consulting fees for management assessment and recommendations, and no one can show his McKinsey-lite work isn't valuable since the value is in the eye of the client.

That's what he'd learned at McKinsey.

Even with the problems in this latest operation for the PAC, any such paying back of the big fees could create other risk exposure instances, and the clients know this.

Rocky takes another pull of his whisky, watching the breaking waves.

It's all just the price of doing business.

Acknowledgements

It takes a village, or so they say, but any and all errors and shortcomings in this book are entirely the responsibility of the author and not the virtual village I am lucky enough to be a part. There are many people for me to thank, starting first and foremost with my partner MAP and my daughter Isabel and son William. My friend and colleague Larry Gussin has been a huge help over the years of this work, and his expertise and commitment to climate change education and mitigation efforts have been essential to my efforts with The Steep Climes Quartet. Other friends and family are due a tip 'o the hat, too, with their encouragement and patience as I blathered on about the project over too many years, and for their early reading of manuscripts and suggestions and their impressive control of their exasperation. A particular thanks is due to my brother Michael whose close reading and feedback was very helpful across the writing this book. There were many beta readers involved in not one but two major drafts and each and every one of these have left positive traces in the work. My editor Judy Roth deserves special attention for her hard work and patience as she improved the book and then improved it more, and for her good cheer and encouragement throughout the editing process.

About the Author

David R. Guenette has been writing for a long time, both as a trade journalist and as author of critical essays, fiction, and poetry. He is the author of the climate fiction series, The Steep Climes Quartet, a series with the first title, *Kill Well*, published in September 2023. He worked in book publishing as a developmental and acquisitions editor before shifting his focus to digital publishing, long serving as a journalist and editor for electronic publishing trade periodicals, and as a consultant and electronic publishing business and technology markets analyst, including working with Tony Fadell's Fuse and Intertrust Technologies and NetMarquee start-ups.

While undertaking a deep energy retrofit of his house in Berkshire County, Guenette combined his background in digital technologies and his growing understanding of building science, house renovation, and deep energy retrofitting to found Retrosheath, a start-up that aimed to reduce costs for energy efficiency improvements in the built environment. He still lives in the Berkshires, writing, making assemblage sculptures and cocktails and bar programs, and working with Averosa Records as digital marketing consultant.

He is active in Citizens' Climate Lobby and 350Mass.org and is a frequent blogger at www.davidguenette.com.

The Steep Climes Quartet Series

The Steep Climes Quartet examines the near- and mid-future consequences of climate change through the lens of Berkshire County, Massachusetts, where subtle and not-so-subtle consequences reveal the future world of global warming is already here.

The Steep Climes Quartet, Book One: *Kill Well*

In *Kill Well* (The Steep Climes Quartet, Book One), the second Trump administration is underway. Cynthia is a young woman and a fossil fuel divestiture activist, and on a trip with her boss, a VP at Carbon's End, a ClimateProgress.Org spin-off, Cynthia witnesses his murder on the way to a meeting with an investment group near Mojave. Panicked and terrified, she's on the run, moving in and out of disassociated states caused by a childhood trauma re-triggered by what she's seen. She is obsessing to find a place she might be safe, and Great Barrington, in the Berkshires, has good memories for her. Meeting sixty-one-year-old Davin Caine's son, Jimmy, who is homeward bound on the North Shore Limited, she ends up at Davin's Housatonic house, and a great news story for the interactive newspaper he has helped start lands in his lap. On the other hand, a contract killer comes to the Berkshires, looking to finish the job of making it look like Cynthia is simply a suicide post-murder of her putative lover and boss.

The Steep Climes Quartet, Book Two: *Dear Josephine*

Dear Josephine (The Steep Climes Quartet, Book Two) finds

Davin Caine, now sixty-four years old in 2029, frustrated by the constant game of financial catch-up he's forced to play in order to keep his Berkshire County, Massachusetts, house. High energy prices and jumps in costs for insurance policies are just the latest challenges, and he must take on more paying work at the online newspaper service he helped design, but that means spending less time in his art studio. Food prices too keep increasing because of adverse climate trends in some of the biggest food production sectors across the country, and his vegetable garden is more important than ever, as are the people who now share his house. As the national elections approach, there's confidence that some of the victories with climate change legislation might be saved and built upon, but not so welcome are the costs that come with the budding number of such legislative initiatives.

And then Hurricane Josephine, the earliest and strongest on record, hits Florida's Gold Coast, and the devastation of South Beach and the Miami Metro area and the count of the dead and displaced staggers the nation.

In other national news there is the story of a series of murders and a possible terrorist organization calling itself *Kill the Rich*, but it just may be that fossil fuel-funded operatives are using this as cover in the latest behind-the-scenes effort to influence and control of the nascent Sea Wall Act. Jeannie Louise Smith, a national climate change politics expert who lives in Great Barrington, and her research collective, The Library, are applying AI to uncover sources of dark money, triggering a level of pushback that isn't academic.

The Steep Climes Quartet, Book Three: *Over Brooklyn Hills*

In Book Three of The Steep Climes Quartet, *Over Brooklyn Hills*, six years have passed since The Sea Wall Act was enacted, thanks in part to the exposure of The Kehoe Institute's criminal efforts to push the goals of an informal group of the extreme wealthy who hold vast fossil fuel interests.

For Davin Caine, now seventy years old, the economy finally has some bright spots, including ongoing renewable energy infrastructure programs that are relieving unemployment and chipping away at the country's carbon footprint. But these efforts are expensive, and for many, including Davin, the cost of living remains expensive too. The rich still aren't paying their fair share and monopolies and industry trusts still hold record profit-takings, while the energy transition remains slowed by fossil fuel industry's headwinds. It doesn't help that China has grown belligerent as it tries to recover domestically from its ferocious recession, and a big point of contention is China's hundreds of additional domestic and exported coal plants.

The resulting economic sanctions against China are making that nation desperate to expand spheres of influence by any means necessary, and US defense spending and debt are spiking yet again. Mass climate migration is adding fuel to the fire with border wars raging.

Even the Berkshires is having its own migration challenge with increasingly shocking numbers of young and economically marginal New York metro residents trekking to the relatively cool hills of the Berkshires to escape a brutal summer in the city and the power cost demands for vital air-conditioning. Great Barrington's attempts to deal with an out-of-control housing crises and spikes in crime results in an "us versus them" reactionary response, and civility and basic rights hang in the balance.

The Steep Climes Quartet, Book Four: *Farm to Me*

Twelve years after the events of the previous book, *Farm to Me*, The Steep Climes Quartet, Book Four, sees eighty-two-year-old Davin Caine losing sight of his dreams, literally, as his worsening macular degeneration is making it difficult for him to continue his art. Climbing all those stairs in his house in Housatonic is getting hard, too, and he's having trouble believing he shouldn't sell the house and studio and move somewhere more sensible. Costs are still high, but electricity costs are moderating as the clean energy infrastructure drives down energy costs. Food costs—beyond what he needs out of his garden—are moderating too, at least locally, with more and more local farms expanding regenerative agricultural production as the concentration toward local economy heats up.

But where there is business opportunity there is conflict, and *Tri-Interactive*, the expanded online news and information service Davin still occasionally consults for, has been hearing rumors about a play for consolidating the local food distribution business, and it's looking more and more like extortion is becoming part of that play.

Davin's been mentoring some of the newly expanded *Tri-Interactive* staff of writers, and when the young reporter chasing a story about shifting affiliations among small food distribution companies dies in an unlikely accident, he finds himself caught up in a hometown conspiracy. It's complicated for Davin because he's long known Marion Fletcher-Gray from covering town politics over the years she's been the Great Barrington town manager, but it looks like the town may be choosing the wrong side.

DEAR JOSEPHINE

Chapter 1: Hear Noothink, See Nootink

He doesn't mind waiting in the dark.

In fact, I like it, William McPherson tells himself, although his telling himself this yet again, in what is likely the fifth or sixth time by his count since getting into position nearly thirteen hours before, suggests otherwise.

It is late March, 2029, and that it is 2029 seems barely possible, as if the turn of this century couldn't be more than just a few years old, but his sense of time has altered radically since he decided on his mission.

He's sorry that he hadn't been ready for the Ides of March. He likes the idea of the date for killing this first target, but he likes even more getting all the preparation done, and he simply hadn't felt ready, and this has him now thinking of his new life.

His old dread is gone, the dread of heading into work, the dread of all those endless conversations with his wife, some complaint or other he'd never understood, some formless criticism. But now he mainly feels excitement, although there is dread, sure, but it is an excited form of dread, a worry about getting caught, but that's why he spends so much time reducing that likelihood. It is a puzzle, exciting like a good puzzle, the sort of feeling that reminds him of how he had felt in his early career when he was doing interesting things and figuring out solutions, finding the best processes, but that had all disappeared over the years, substituted by his sense of simply grinding things out, like what the marriage had come to, too, a seemingly endless grind, day after day of growing dread, any hour, any week like any other, a deadening blur.

He's pushed back into the foliage near the front entrance, behind a cascade of what he is pretty sure is wisteria, pressed back into the boxwood, or whatever exactly the evergreen that forms the long hedge. Tight up against the hedge is a high iron fence. Behind the fence is a stone terrace right off the side the house, and a tennis court is somewhere a good hundred feet or more from the side of the house.

House, he snorts, thinking about how big the place is, *a goddamn mansion, a goddamn palace.*

He's been snuggled into the boxwood since before dawn.

The urine bladder strapped to his left leg feels dangerously full. The Texas catheter feels loose.

He resists the urge to move to look at his phone, but he knows quite well the movement would be a waste of effort since his phone is turned off and in a foil sleeve.

Not to mention stupid, he tells himself. He's been ping free for two days.

Keeping the private residence's motion detectors and the video cameras off the whole time, he knows, is not a good plan, with resets being one thing and a full-on and long-running shutdown quite another. He'd done his homework, spending many hours combing corners of the dark web for schematics and tutorials, and the reboot signal device is one of the results.

Thinking about this, he reaches down, knees slowly bending, so his gloved hand can brush the top of the knapsack that sits at his feet, pushed into the boxwood. He's tested out the blind spot for this front corner area's motion detector, but limiting his movement is still a sensible precaution.

He's wearing a dark green coverall, plus cheap synthetic work gloves, mechanic gloves that anyone can buy anywhere, not that he'll leave anything behind. The coverall is loose fitting, does a good job reading as shadow, and with the cap, the gloves, the tucked and black duct-taped cuffs, there is little chance leaving much in the way of forensic traces of himself.

He knows he's got to be good at this.

Goddamn right, he tells himself as he moves slowly back to lean fully up against the crinkled branches and tiny dark green leaves, his weight now largely resting again against the dark foliage compressed against the iron fence. The dense branches of the hedge feel like a spring, and he feels ready to shift fully forward at a moment's notice, ready to step through past the wisteria toward the top of the driveway circle.

The hardest part is the waiting.

But he remains excited. His new life is a mission, and he can sometimes wonder how long it has been since he'd felt alive, not feeling kicked, stepped on, suffocated.

He takes a deep breath.

He is standing, pushed back into the deep and ancient boxwood hedge, the trailing big vines of wisteria providing more coverage, and the gloom of the darkling evening coming on in this late-March day adds to his sense he is invisible. From behind the thick bare wisteria vines he can partly see the front of the driveway circle where he is sure the target will park. He's sure the target will go up the stone steps, pause to dig out his keys, and work the lock open.

He's managed to nap in short stretches, leaning this way into the hedge, knowing his driveway-approach telltale will vibrate and sound if anyone turns off the country road to drive up the long driveway toward the house. He knows the fastest the target has ever gone from car and through the front door is eleven seconds, and the target seemed in a hurry that one time. Most of the recordings capturing the target getting out of his car are more like half a minute or a bit more if the target reaches back in for a briefcase or small travel bag. In one of his surveillance videos, the target retrieved a takeaway bag from the Chinese restaurant the target passes when staying out in his country place.

He waits. He knows there's a small shed behind the hedge and the iron fence that is tucked behind where he waits at the front corner of the main house structure. He feels like he knows so many things about this property, about the target's habits, about the net worth and assets of this target he's researched so deeply.

He still too often disbelieves that there are people like the target, that there are so many of them, *goddamn world-eaters*, and he starts to see he's letting himself get upset, so he does his breathing exercises.

He doesn't want to get caught, of course, but he has done so much so that he won't, not with all the work, all the time and attention he's expended thinking through how to do it, how to start on his list pulled from the Fortune 400, the list of targets that he aims to kill.

He waits in the gathering dark.

He'd like to know how the shed gets used, what the purpose is of this small structure behind the hedge, but it doesn't really matter.

Probably tennis stuff, he guesses.

It doesn't matter. He has thoroughly surveyed the property, using a stealthy drone preprogrammed and operating without a radio or Wi-Fi signal, grid-programmed and running dark at night when the house is unoccupied.

He's previously retrieved the video camera he placed in a tree branch of one of the trees that form the wood's edge on the other side of the road opposite the long driveway's start. The camera's placement provided clear line of sight to the front of the house, and even though the camera was a far way off, the lens and resolution were still good enough for his surveillance needs, and the many days of video have been streamed and carefully reviewed.

All without any trace or anyone's notice of anything, he is confident. He is pleased with this system he's been developing and refining.

Earlier thermal scans showed him the house remains at heating and lighting levels that should only happen when someone is home, although even then, this itself would be a huge energy expense.

Got it, flaunt it, is what he thinks. *Assholes.*

The full structure amounts to nearly 11,000 square feet, he's figured, and that isn't counting the several outbuildings. He knows the target comes here infrequently, but more this time of year when the target's in the city for the annual meetings, a busy time with many other meetings scheduled.

The house gets used by the target during this time, and the target almost never brings anyone back, as best as he has determined. There are no full-time servants and no active security staff, but everything is digital with on-call drive-by security checks a person could set his watch to.

He now knows this schedule well. He's seen the checks come by twice today, with one more to go, but he'll be long gone by then.

Idiot, the waiting man thinks, judging the target. *The arrogance, the presumption*. The waiting man snorts in the dark, then starts, seeing a brief glint of headlights through distant trees further down the small country road.

It's him, the waiting man tells himself. He has to fight against his excitement and struggles to keep his breathing even.

The telltale vibrates as the car turns into the driveway, heading toward the house.

In the hedge by the corner of the house where the ancient wisteria vines run up naked onto the stone façade front portico, the man slowly moves his hand to the black knapsack, draws it up slow-motion and painstakingly slowly, slings one shoulder strap over his head, settling the knapsack, its top open, so it's midway down his chest, the contents easily available.

He reaches in and locates the reset switch box by feel, hand grasping it, thumb over the button.

The car pulling up is a Tesla, the newest luxury model, as he learned when doing background on the target, a small complication in that it uses a biometric locking system.

I got to hand it to myself, the man says, somewhat embarrassed by the joke, but also liking it. Still holding the switch box, the man shifts slightly and gently touches the back of his hand against the top of the bolt cutter, which was vertically placed with care on one side of the knapsack so it can be easily drawn when needed. Then the man is back to concentrating on the car's approach.

The target always swings leftward into the circle and is doing this once again.

The man lowers his face and the dark cap visor and the dark overalls create a blending shadow as the car's headlights sweep over the boxwood hedge and wisteria vines for the briefest of moments, and then the car stops, shuts down.

Showtime.

The man presses the switch that triggers a reboot and system check of the house security systems, taking the security system and the cameras offline for almost a minute.

The man lets go of the switch box and shifts his hand inside the knapsack to wrap around the pistol grip. The Tesla's driver door whines open and the target is climbing out, so the man steps out from the hedge and gently and carefully teases the pistol from the knapsack and raises it, walking closer to the target. The target is turning back to get something from the car, and as the target straightens back up, the dark-covered man sees the Chinese takeaway bag, and then the target is reaching into his suit coat pocket for *the keys*. The man steps toward the target and squeezes the trigger, the first-round dead center in the target's forehead.

The man fires two more rounds into the target's center mass.

The target is still falling as the man's strides bring him close up.

He lowers the knapsack, dumps the gun in, and grabs the bolt cutter. It takes a moment to pull the target's right arm clear and another brief moment to finger the man's semi-clenched hand and placing the bolt cutter carefully at the base of the target's thumb, cutting between the thumb joint, through the tendon and skin. He picks up the thumb, then picks up the keys with the car dongle. He grabs his knapsack and steps over the body to the Tesla's still-up door, which is a timing bonus, he realizes.

Perfect, didn't think that through.

He rummages for the signal block and flips it on and tosses it onto the passenger seat. There will be no outgoing signals, no wi-fi, or cellular, or satellite as long as the signal blocker is on. The car is effectively air-gapped.

He settles himself in the Tesla, presses the door close paddle, and places the thumb to the ignition. The panel blazes with LEDs and a gentle voice chimes, "Welcome, Mycroft," which confuses the man for a moment since this is not the target's name, but he mostly concentrates on ensuring the car is set for manual control before he eases down the driveway, glancing only once in the rearview mirror.

The dead body is still slumped on the gravel drive, and the man figures he still has about a quarter of a minute to spare.

Mycroft?

Now on the road heading toward the covered place where he left the old gas car he stole earlier, the man finds himself puzzling about the use of that name by the car's system.

And then it clicks, Mycroft, Sherlock Holmes's older, smarter brother, the man behind His Majesty's Secret Service.

The man snorts, almost a laugh.

"And that's why we kill the rich," he says, not caring if the car hears him. He'll digitally wipe the car when he gets to the other one. He knows where the CPU and memory is, and he has a brick-maker in the other car, the first of two switch vehicles he's using. The degausser is too heavy to have brought with him.

He pats the rosewood trim embedded in the safety foam plastic dash surround.

"*I hear noothink, I see nootink,*" he says, his effort at the fake German accent of a long-ago television series Sergeant Schultz giving way to the adrenaline shaking and giggling that is coming on as he drives away.

Visit Amazon or https://davidguenette.com/ for information on where to buy this book, including other places where you may purchase buy *Dear Josephine*.

DavidGuenette.com

My website, davidguenette.com, has information about The Steep Climes Quartet and where the books in this series can be purchased, and there's my "About" information, a link to CMTI Publishing website, and contact form.

There is a sign-up form on the site if you'd like to receive notification of new posts.

There are three categories of posts:

1. **The Steep Climes Quartet**, which presents posts about the ongoing work on and aim of the series;
2. **Snips of Passing Interest**, where I note and react to content on climate change that catches my eye;
3. **Other Writing**, where I talk about climate fiction generally, and where I offer other of my own writing work.

www.ingramcontent.com/pod-product-compliance
Lightning Source LLC
Chambersburg PA
CBHW021129260626
47169CB00005B/1519